CHANAKYA RETURNS

Also by Timeri N. Murari

FICTION

The Taliban Cricket Club
The Small House
The Arrangements of Love
Four Steps from Paradise
Enduring Affairs
The Last Victory
The Imperial Agent
Taj: A Story of Mughal India
Field of Honour
The Shooter
Lovers Are Not People
The Oblivion Tapes
The Marriage

NON-FICTION

Limping to the Centre of the World: A Journey to Mount Kailas
My Temporary Son: An Orphan's Journey
Goin' Home: A Black Family Returns South
The New Savages: Children of the Liverpool Streets

FOR CHILDREN

Children of the Enchanted Jungle

CHANAKYA RETURNS

TIMERI N. MURARI

ALEPH BOOK COMPANY
An independent publishing firm
promoted by *Rupa Publications India*

Published in India in 2014 by
Aleph Book Company
7/16 Ansari Road, Daryaganj
New Delhi 110 002

Copyright © Timeri N. Murari 2014

All rights reserved.

This is a work of fiction. Names, characters, places and incidents are either the product of the author's imagination or are used fictitiously and any resemblance to any actual persons, living or dead, events or locales is entirely coincidental.

No part of this publication may be reproduced, transmitted, or stored in a retrieval system, in any form or by any means, without permission in writing from Aleph Book Company.

ISBN: 978-93-83064-02-1

1 3 5 7 9 10 8 6 4 2

Printed and bound in India by Replika Press Pvt. Ltd.

This book is sold subject to the condition that it shall not, by way of trade or otherwise, be lent, resold, hired out, or otherwise circulated without the publisher's prior consent in any form of binding or cover other than that in which it is published.

*For Marjorie, and Alain in memory, who befriended a stranger.
And for Maureen, with love.*

(i who have died am alive again today,
and this is the sun's day; this is the
birth
day of life and love and wings; and of
the gay
great happening illimitably earth)
—e. e. cummings

I have ever hated all nations, professions and communities,
and all my love is towards individuals.
—Jonathan Swift

ONE

LOVE, I ADVISE, and I speak from experience, is fragile as rotting silks and will disintegrate when infidelities, jealousies, betrayals, impotence infect it. The heart is not to be trusted as it is brainless and mistakes lust for love while the loins mistake love for lust. Love is a watery foundation on which to build one's life. Love is violent too, be warned of its treachery. Men and women murder for love; the clash of bodies, hearts and souls only leaves behind the ashes of defeat when one is vanquished and abandoned on the battlefield of the bed. Believe me, love has sent more men and women to the gallows of tears, despair, grief and suicide than a thousand tyrants his enemies to an executioner. No, love will prove to be unfulfilling and transitory, but power (and I shiver at the word)—on the other hand—is to be pursued. It is an aphrodisiac, it is unending hot sex of 1001 positions, it is magical, it is miraculous. Your followers will worship you like an idol that can confer riches and miracles, more than any god, on those fortunate to worship you, and you will feel their outpouring of love in gratitude. Your subjects cannot take it from you, unless you give it away through foolishness, and you can keep hold of that lightning rod until you are buried in a grand tomb, accompanied by great pomp and ceremony and outpourings of grief.

My prince(ss) listened carefully to what I had to say. I wondered which would triumph—the power of love or the love of power. It is a crossroad—right or left—there is no middle way.

■

On this day, it is hot and humid, the sky overcast with clouds. The monsoon is very near, the still air perfumed with the promised rain. The light is luminous as beaten silver. But the city is always oppressive, monsoon or not. Only in winter does the cold lighten the weight of the city. High walls surround the large garden, with an extensive lawn, and mango, peepul, neem and tamarind trees stand as sentinels along the borders.

I follow discreetly as Avanti slips through the shadows to the arbour at the far end of the garden and see him pacing, waiting for her, dressed in his best—a cream silk shirt, jeans, polished black shoes, his long hair tied in a fashionable pony tail. She is in his arms. Smothering him with her silks and perfume, hot skin and the sweet taste of her mouth. They are breathless with laughter in the heat and the wanting. His hand slides up her waist to her breasts and I know the sensation of the first touch of those wondrous orbs on a woman's body that drive men insane and befuddle their brains. He bends his head to grasp the erect nipple in his mouth, knowing this is the pathway back into the womb that ejected him into the world and where both pain and pleasure lie hidden between those legs. The heat of a woman's loins melts men's minds. She allows him a moment of drunken sensation, also arousing the erection that is hard as a cane between his legs, and then pulls up his worshipping head. He tries to resist, he is determined to seduce her, in the arbour, on the hard earth.

-No, not yet.

-Give yourself a present you'll remember all your life.

He tries to gently, tenderly wrestle her down. His voice is husky with longing.

-And get my new clothes dirty, she laughs. We have the whole night. You said you'd reserved a room in the hotel.

-I can't wait that long. We can fuck again there.

Ahh, the beauty of the language. That word, which I savour, even though I was ignorant of its meaning at first, just the sound of those four letters conjures up the collision of bodies, the pelvic thrust of sexual pleasures in countless variations, an orgasmic heaven. It didn't exist in my time. I wish it had, for it encapsulates our basest desires and greatest pleasures, pithily.

-You're always so impetuous.

-And you're conservative. Let yourself go. Celebrate with sex and sensuality. Experience becoming a woman.

-You make it sound like a disease. Am I really conservative?

-Yes. And spoilt.

-I know that. You do love me?

-Since I was knee high. It was instant, a lightning bolt. I'm crazily, madly in love with you.

-I'm never sure whether to believe you or not. You're so crazy.

-I know. And you?
-I think so.
-Love isn't a think; it's a feel, a fire, a volcano, an insanity. Give into passion, not thoughts.
-Then yes, I do love you.

But she remains stubbornly resistant, teasing him, yet always with kindness. A wraith, just always out of reach, yet warm in his arms. I feel no envy, no jealousy, my only concern is that love will warp my plans. As I wrote so long ago: *The world's biggest power is the youth and beauty of a woman.* My wisdom still awes me.

His name is Aditya, a nobody, and love will only lead her to the role of a housewife, serving one man and not a nation. She has known him since childhood when he had looked over their compound wall in the old neighbourhood and saw, what he always told her, 'an angel haloed in sunlight'. They couldn't have been more than ten years old. They were together in school too. When she was sent to board at the convent school in the hills, Aditya had followed to a boys' one nearby. And she had followed him to the States, though not to the same university. He went to the New York University Film School; she went to New York Art School to fulfil her longing to become a painter. She is moderately talented, applying herself diligently to her art daily. She calls it abstract; I consider it indescribable. It was as if they were destined for each other.

-Wait, he says.

I know he loves her truly and I grow wary when he offers up his heart with the engagement ring in the small, velvet-lined box. I can barely see the diamond, the size of star dust.

-Happy Birthday, my love.
-Is this a proposal?
-What else?
-I must ask my parents.
-You're of age. Let's run away and marry.
-I can't do that. I'll wear it on my right hand until we're officially engaged.
-There's an inscription on it.
She peers. It's too dark to read it.
-Tell me what it says.
-We'll read it in bed together tonight.

She admires it, kissing him, and I pray she won't slip it on. An heir to power cannot nurture a vulnerable heart. Power and love are incompatible, for power cannot trust the love offered up to it on a gold platter. Men and women are devious as serpents in a pit, coiling and uncoiling their calculations to win the love of power. He is not a serpent, yet. I break the spell with a low cough, breaking the enchantment of suppressed passion. She has to heed my whisper 'your mother calls', a necessary lie. She pecks him. They aren't to know then it is a farewell kiss. I meet his malevolent stare with my bland dismissive glance as I follow her back to the house.

She hurries out of the arbour, pausing a moment to remove the engagement ring and knot it in the pallu of her saree. Her mother's sharp eyes will spot it. I follow at a stately pace, having placed her mother at the entrance. An advisor must justify the lie. He follows slowly, disconsolate. He had expected her to throw her arms around him and shriek 'yes, Aditya, yes.' That's the way he'd planned it in his script. I rewrote it. I have no shame, no remorse at breaking a young man's heart, knowing it will self-repair. My ambitions are more important than paltry love.

The bungalow has two floors and sprawls in many directions as rooms were added as afterthoughts. Its entrance is through a pillared verandah that circles it and is the ancestral home of this family. Armed guards at either end block the road leading to it and the quiet is an escape from the din of the city. The garden is strung with coloured bulbs, as if this is a festival, Diwali, Pongal, Christmas. A long table is set on the front lawn, covered with a white tablecloth, laid with expensive crockery and polished silver. There are twenty places, though Aditya is the only guest. A military band stands to attention beyond the table. In the periphery are shadowy men, clutching machine pistols, as ineffectual as men with swords and shields to stop a determined assassin. Her mother waits under the porch, a lonely silhouette. Now, she is looking around as if unsure whether she should be where I had placed her. Behind her are a dozen bearers, carrying a cake, checked for poisonous substances. The ritualized twenty-five candles rising above it like deodars on a plain.

-Oh, Mother, Avanti says crossly. I'm not a child anymore to have birthday cakes and candles.

I move into the shadows, always the observer unless needed to participate to guide the events.

–Birthdays have cakes, and cakes always have candles, her mother says placatingly, softening Avanti's petulance. Isn't that right, Aditya? She has an enchanting voice, soft and husky, and almost sings her words.

–Yes ma'am, he says, standing beside Avanti, admiring the splendid cake, large and flat as a cartwheel, enough to feed a hundred. It's a very beautiful cake.

Avanti leans across to him and whispers. You're always sucking up to her.

–When are your friends arriving? You did tell them the time, didn't you? her mother says in a calm yet stubborn voice that she knows will wear down Avanti. Avanti frowns and at the same time manages to wink at Aditya. She always disagreed with or teased her mother. I thought they were mismatched, two people trapped in a wrong relationship. They look somewhat alike.

–The same straight nose, the high cheekbones. Except her mother's mouth is sensual, compliant, loose enough to capitulate quickly. No doubt, marriage shaped it that way. Avanti's is a firm line, inherited from her father.

–I can't remember, Avanti says. What did I tell you?

–Seven, Aditya says. It was for high tea. He checks his watch. It's seven thirty now.

Avanti shrugs. Maybe they're not coming. Maybe I didn't invite anyone else. She links her arm with Aditya's. Maybe I only invited him.

–I'm sure they'll come soon, her mother says complacently. You're a very popular girl and besides, they wouldn't dream of refusing.

–Who says I am popular?

–I did, she says and tells the bearers to take the cake to the table.

Avanti is popular, she is the sun to a small group of privileged young women and men her age. They are a secret society, and take no other members, unless they can prove their privilege is equal to theirs. They party in exclusive clubs, they dance together, lunch and dine together, text each other constantly. They live within an enchanted square mile, guarded from the city not by walls, but by the ring of security police that protect her residence, and theirs, from interlopers, assassins, the poor and the envious. They are her courtiers, her favourite being Monika, an astounding beauty who is in love with herself, mostly. They were in the convent together, then at a Swiss finishing school and continued on to New York for their higher studies. But on this evening, she hasn't invited even Monika to witness the celebration; it is private.

When her mother follows the cake to the table, the band strikes up the first bars of 'Happy Birthday'. The bandmaster is taking his cue from her mother. But then a swift finger across her throat from Avanti silences him, and the tune dies apologetically, leaving a haunting sadness in the air.

-If your guests are not coming, we may as well go ahead. Light the candles, she tells the bearers.

-You can't, not until Father comes. The bearers don't need any further instruction. They put away the matchbox, knowing whom to obey. He's the most important guest.

-He's not coming, her mother says in triumph. The weather's so bad that his plane can't take off. Then with satisfaction. Even he can't command the weather.

-He'll come, Avanti says stubbornly. He always comes for my birthday. Always.

She sits with an immovable weight. Her mother too; they will wait each other out. Beyond her, I see her mother shyly take a box from the folds of her sari. It looks larger than the one in Aditya's pocket.

-Happy birthday, my dearest Avanti, her mother sings out and gives her the present.

-Oh my god, I'm blinded, Aditya says, when Avanti opens the box. He shields his eyes from the diamond earrings. The stones are large as peanuts, winking with an internal light.

-They're beautiful, Avanti says and kisses her mother. It is a delicate brush of the cheek.

-Put them on.

She shifts in her chair, lifting her hair to expose her ears. They are bare. Avanti seldom wears jewellery, rebelling against the custom. Her mother fixes one, then the other. They weigh the lobes down. Then her mother pinches her cheek and brings her fingertips to kiss them.

Avanti turns to Aditya, hair tucked behind her ears.

-They're stunning, he says.

–They were my mother's, her mother explains. When Avanti gets married, she'll get all the jewellery.

–And is that going to be soon? Aditya says, trying to tease Avanti into committing herself.

She smiles and shrugs.

He looks down at her right hand, pointing to it to show her mother his gift which had one tiny diamond. But it isn't there. He notices the knotted shape in the corner of her pallu where she's hidden it.

It makes him feel discarded and angry. We'll be late for the movie. Come on.

–There's always a later show, she says sweetly and pats the chair.

–Which picture… her mother says.

Avanti's shriek cuts her off. That was the shriek Aditya had wanted to hear when he had proposed. A shriek of joy, excitement, happiness. Except this is caused by the headlights of a dozen cars racing up the curve of the drive. The lead car is a SUV, a red lamp spinning above the driver. Guns stick out from the side and back. It drives under the porch and through to stop. Commandos jump out, taking up positions. Two other cars pull aside to let the third glide through and stop under the porch.

TWO

–I TOLD YOU... I told you...Avanti jumps up and down like a child.

She runs to the car under the porch and flings herself into her father's arms even before he's managed to step out. They embrace tightly, laughing and chattering incomprehensibly. She drags him by the hand over to the table.

Her father has an imperial look, his skin slightly pale brown, almost cream or off-white. He is an immaculate man. Despite the journey, he looks as fresh as if he's stepped out of the dressing room. His kurta neat, stiffly ironed, not a wrinkle. The advantages of power—out of the air-conditioned jet into the air-conditioned car waiting on the tarmac, only a moment or two of discomfort in the heat.

They come towards us, his arm around her shoulder, hers around his waist, whispering and smiling. They exclude everyone. His entourage trails them, black uniformed commandos with stens across their chests, fingers in trigger guards, plain-clothes men, looking unarmed except for the automatics bulging at their waistlines and secretaries, peons, party workers, chamchas. Power is also the clutter of people.

–Are you staying? she asks.

–Not long. I came only for your birthday, as I'd promised. There are piles of files and queues of people waiting.

–I never get time to spend with you and I miss you so much.

–So do I.

–You look weary. She examines the lines on his face, each day they grow deeper, age carving out its territory in his soft flesh.

–I could sleep for a week. What are you planning for tonight?

–Aditya's taking me out to a movie.

This makes him pause, check his step. I know his thoughts too well.

–Do you have to see him?

–He's fun and intelligent and talented.

–Should I touch his feet? He mocks.

—Never. No one will ever be as handsome and clever as you.

—Thank you. And he plants a kiss on her cheek where Aditya's lips once rested.

She drags him forward and announces: I told you he'd come, she says defiantly to her mother. And do you know what? He commanded the fog to lift and it rose just for five minutes for his plane to take off.

—I told the fog to clear off, as I had to be home for my daughter's twenty-fifth birthday and off it went. He has a good voice, firm, some depth to it, tinged with humour. In full flow, he is mesmeric, quoting poetry, statistics and of course promising unimaginable bounty to the impoverished electorate. But look into his eyes, shadowed with distrust.

—You remember, Aditya. Avanti drags her father over.

Aditya has the advantage of height over her father, it gives him a little confidence in facing him.

—No.

—How are you, sir? Aditya says, hiding his irritation. Each time they meet, he gets the same response. He knows it is deliberate, intended to diminish him in front of Avanti.

—Fine, her father says and turns to his daughter. Happy birthday, Princess.

Another box, drawn not from his person but passed to him by his secretary. Avanti takes it as her father's arm draws her away. She looks back to Aditya, an apology in her eyes. He returns to his seat by her mother who has not risen. In the commotion, like me, she is aware her husband hasn't even acknowledged her. He continues to talk to Avanti, his alter ego, his cherished child. She has his features, her mother's eyes and an awkward grace. In her eyes lies adoration for her father, shining like starlight. She knows that, like her, he loves fawning and flattery, he has trained her well, although she nurtures ambitions of her own. Apart from Avanti, he trusts no one, including himself and, while he sleeps, he records his snores and snorts, and, when he wakes, replays the tapes to discover whether he has spoken any secrets aloud or revealed his innermost thoughts in his sleep. I had also advised my Emperor: Never share your secrets with anyone, as they will destroy you. Avanti is his progeny, his only seed to create his dynasty that will rule the state for a hundred years. We are a democratic country and we need dynasties. Only democracies can be so manipulated to create them, for which we must thank god. We have had many examples in our past and we must forge the future one to rule this state.

–Thank you, Father, she says. Avanti has a honeyed voice, on occasion. She uses this voice for her father. She has a coarser tone for those who are beneath her dignity, including her mother for whom she has no patience at all. Apart from their biological connection, they have little else in common.

–The more expensive the present, the smaller the box, Aditya says.

Avanti is looking at the contents and throwing her arms around her father, strangling him in her delight.

–Which film are you going to see? her mother asks.

Again, in my day there was no such means of communication as films, only words written on palm leaves which would disintegrate in time. I too now watched them, amazed by the stories they told. I absorbed them through all my senses, and my favourite actress was Siggy Chopra. I saw her films many times, sitting in the front row, staring up at that astounding beauty. What chance would I ever have of touching her feet, let alone caressing those rounded breasts? I wished there were movies in my day, I could have recorded the life of my emperor, digitized it for posterity and also protected the intellectual property rights of my work against that plagiarist Machiavelli. Palm leaves are no longer proof in the halls of justice.

–There's a retrospective of Godard films, he says. Tonight they're showing *Breathless*, a classic.

–I've never seen a French film. Is it good?

–Brilliant, Aditya says with passion. Jean-Paul Belmondo is a small time crook who kills a cop, falls in love with this American girl and runs around Paris looking for someone who owes him money.

–It sounds like our masala films, she says dismissively.

Silently, I demur as I am an ardent admirer of Bollywood, a geographical place that does not exist when I search for it but stands for a certain kind of right-to-copy of films made in Hollywood, a name board on a hillside. At one time oral storytelling, and later the written word, shaped the minds of men, now it is film that is the university of learning for the young, as they share their common experiences and interpretations in the dark. How can one discourse in the darkness with images that mesmerize one as they flow so swiftly, deafening us at the same time? Thought needs silence, only the sounds of nature, the sigh of the wind, the call of a bird, the rustle of leaves, truly inspired me when I wrote my immortal work.

-No. It's the style of the film that is exciting. He was a part of the New Wave in cinema back then.

-I prefer Indian films, she says firmly. I watch a lot of them on television now. They're all there, all the old ones, and they were so good. You love film, don't you? I hear it in your voice.

-Yes. I'm going to make them.

-She smiles. Like your father.

-He makes rubbish, Aditya says cruelly. Songs, dances, fights and no plots.

-But they're successful.

The son rebels against his father, even as princes do against kings. I want to encourage him to pursue his dream and in that pursuit leave this kingdom in search of his glory elsewhere so he will forget Avanti and she in turn will forget him.

-You will make great films, I tell him, stepping out of the shadows, leaning to whisper, as I know you have the talent. I saw your short film, *Let's Do It*, and I thought it was brilliant. You should remake it at greater length.

It is, as I've mentioned, necessary to lie in order to encourage ambitions. He studies me warily, suspicious of my flattery.

I am not a pleasant sight to behold, although always immaculate in a black bush shirt and trousers that are in stark contrast to the full head of white hair that I was born with, I am ageless. My complexity lies in my face. On my left side, I have the proud profile of a god stamped on a Greek coin, minus the laurel crown and when women see it, they swoon for seduction; the right side is truly hideous—blotchy pink, puckered, skewered from childhood, the right eye weeping, the half lip a gash of raw flesh. If the left side is the gold sovereign of good fortune in life, the right side is the cheap coin of the true brutality in the same life that affects us all. I am just the visual reminder of this constant conflict. Others, who speculate on my appearance, believe that the left is the good in me; the right the evil. I am what people wish to believe, capable of both as we all are, despite our belief that we are more good than evil—a self-delusion. Evil is our true nature—examine yourself—and see the greed, envy, jealousy, gluttony always present—and the capacity for murder that simmers among the juices of our true nature. It's only fear that keeps our evil in check, fear of retribution by an unjust society, and a belief that a god watches us, ready to strike if we commit any of our evil acts. God does not exist, nor does Satan, both powerless to punish or reward, to praise or condemn, not even as silent spectators of our follies. I speak from experience, having wandered the infinite for millennia. I can affirm there is nothing up there or out there but infinity—vast, interminable, boring, dull, eternity. Apart from my appearance, I am also a man of limited height but none dare look down on me.

I am Chanakya. Chan-ak-yha. Kautilya. Cow-til-yha. I respond to either name and they possess the same meaning—falsehood. Remember that, even as I speak. I lived around 2,300 years ago, from 350 to 283. In your Gregorian calendar, Before Christ, whoever he was, centuries away in that future. Due to confusions in the universe that I cannot explain, I have returned to inhabit the body of a stranger. Reincarnated, though not entirely intact, with a fractured memory and morality. These new religions believe in heaven and hell, even in a Paradise, but mine recycles us continuously, as if there is a shortage of souls, until we attain moksa, if ever. It wasn't instant, as you see. It's a slow process, a few patient souls queuing to return, taking a break from eternity and the collisions and catastrophes, of which there are countless, in our universe. I wondered whether I was waking from a dream or awakening into one. It's a puzzle I need to solve, eventually. I have not revealed my true identity to anyone as I know, from my previous existence, that when you are among strangers, you need to keep your true self a secret. You never know who is the friend and who is the enemy. If a few with a knowledge of history remark on my name, I feign ignorance of its origins and insist this name was given to me at birth. Besides, who would believe that Chanakya has travelled through time, and yet here I am—blood coursing through this body, a beating heart, skin perspiring in the heat, eyes watching, ears perking, nose twitching to earthly odours. No one remembers me. In my distant past I had guided the prince Chandragupta to appoint him Emperor of Maurya, and met Alexander. Which Alexander you may ask, as if there are many? *The* Alexander, King of Macedonia who crossed the Sindu River to sit at the feet of my Emperor. Alexander had read the works of Herodotus, who wrote an imagined account of our 'Hindu land' a hundred years previously, and was inspired to visit us. You call him 'The Great' but in my day he was a nuisance man, young and arrogant, with his greedy ambitions of conquest. I told him that for all the lands he had conquered he would end up possessing only enough for his grave, and to return home.

But in this present world, worse horrors awaited. My life's work, my treatise on statecraft, *Arthashastra*, was stolen by that Italian plagiarist, Niccolò de Bernardo dei Machiavelli. I skimmed *The Prince* (*Il Principe*), a trifling work, a child's primer to power, a bagatelle of thoughts and, if the Prince should follow such advice, he'll surely end up in his own tower. However, no one is Chanakyan or Kautilyan; they are Machiavellian. That is the problem with death—one thousand seven hundred and fifty-two years later your work appears under another man's name, granting him the immortality that is rightly yours. And you are a helpless spirit, unable to scream 'plagiarist' and assert your copyright. Such is the fate of great minds. There is no shame in this world. I am comforted that as a plagiarist he remained true to the theme of my great work *Arthashastra*—Chanakyan and Machiavellian describe one who deceives and manipulates others for gain; whether the gain is personal or not is of no relevance, only that any actions taken are important insofar as they affect the results.

Already, I have uttered falsehoods. My given name is Mohanlal, son of Vishnu—not the god, the *farmer*—a humble baby in a humble family. I was an only child, as my parents, despite many efforts, could not bear another, causing bitterness in my father. I came into the world in our hut, four mud walls supporting a thatch roof of fronds. My village is 150 kilometres due south of the capital and my father cultivated less than a quarter acre of land. There were forty-five families in our village, a little kingdom, half were relatives, the others friends, even familiar enemies. We eked out a living. When it rained we survived, when it didn't we died. I was learning to walk when I stumbled and fell onto the wood fire where my loving mother cooked our meals of lentils and rice. Half my face was burnt, and the scars healed, leaving me as you see me now. There was not a doctor within ten kilometres of my home to correct this disfigurement, not that we had the money for him to perform such a miracle. I have learned to live with it, mocked and humiliated by those more physically perfect than me. Through such a shock, my mind awoke and I discovered I could memorize a page of my school book in a second, the whole one in a minute. The only school was three kilometres away and I walked with the other children there and back daily. They knew of my brilliance and for a fee, one rupee a week, I did their homework. Those who bullied me, I refused to help so they were punished, and soon understood they needed me. There I learned the art of manipulation using my intellect. During those years, something mysterious was growing in my mind, knowledge that surely I could not have gained from the one-room school. Mohanlal was receding; Chanakya was growing more powerful, claiming my thoughts and heart. Like Mohanlal, Chanakya too was born in a village, though near the ancient city of Takshashila. He was an ugly child, mocked and bullied too. His home of wood, Mohanlal's mud and thatch, he is of a high caste, I of a low one, and there must have been a mistake in this transmigration of his soul to find me. Nothing is perfect. His memory of his past, he admits, is defective in this descent back into a human form. He studied at Takshashila University and became an acharya, a teacher. He moved to the capital, Pataliputra, and entered the service of the King, Dhana Nanda, whom he learned to dislike intensely for his misdeeds in ruling the Nanda Kingdom. He openly criticized the king who, finally expelled him from the court, and the state, even while he sat with others at a feast. Humiliated, and alone, he vowed to return and overthrow the king. He wandered the country until he saw a village boy enacting the role of a king among his playmates. The boy, Chandragupta, so impressed Chanakya with his wisdom, that he trained him in statecraft, and, together they recruited an army to attack and finally conquer the Nanda Kingdom. He remained by Chandragupta's side as his chancellor, guiding his wise rule, until court intrigues drove him once more into exile. There is no doubt that such a great mind existed and he wished to experience life once more and descended on me in his new avatar. In the *Gita*, it is said: *worn-out garments are shed by the body; worn-out bodies are shed by the dweller within the body. New bodies are donned by the dweller, like garments.* As you see, I am a fine new suit of clothes for Chanakya. Was it the convenience of location, the exact second of conception for him to slip through into my mother's womb? I wondered why he chose me as the doorway into this modern world. Why not blight another's life, why mine? I try to think of an answer, it has haunted me all these years and I've never found it. I have accepted him, yet he disturbed the destiny of that boy. As if life isn't hard enough without harbouring an ancient spirit.

When I moved to the city, I searched for and found my prince. Avanti. She is not the President (an elevated title he bestowed upon himself, preferring it to mere 'minister', though a chief among them) of this state but the man's daughter, an only child. She is the heir, young and malleable. Power awaits her. I had written that it is easier to inherit a throne than to win one by an outsider. Avanti is shy, unsure but aware of her strengths. And her favoured position in life. She is lonely, and accustomed to it, a good trait for a ruler. Chandragupta, the emperor I advised, knew power isolated and imprisoned. A ruler should be mentally and emotionally self-sufficient as he cannot trust those nourishments offered by others. I began service as a humble clerk though not humble myself. I live a simple life, despite my years in such close proximity to power. Other men would have accumulated mansions and palaces, held bank accounts with millions in Switzerland or Luxembourg. My needs are few, even as they were when I served the emperor, and, as I have no intention of marrying, will never bear the burden of disobedient, rebellious children. I wear no gold chain, dangling the image of a god for good luck, nor do rings adorn my fingers. I ensured I was loyal to Avanti alone and to none other. She noted this loyalty and confided her thoughts and emotions in me.

–You really think so? The child disappointed in love breaks the long silence.

–Yes and I will do all I can to help you be a great film director.

We can't continue our discussion on film. Avanti is coming towards us, her father, with the mobile to his ear, is going into the house. His hotline is red. Even I possess such an instrument. We have a thousand ways to communicate in this day, but mostly with nothing wise to say, only the babble of disjointed thoughts.

–Let's see what your father gave you, her mother says, as Avanti, breathless as in a film, sits between them.

–No, you can't. It's our secret.

–Oh, come on, Aditya says, to save her mother embarrassment

at Avanti's tone. Let's see it.

–No one will ever see it. She clutches at her throat. The locket is heart shaped, gold with an emerald the size of his fingernail.

–Oh, for god's sake, what can a father give his daughter that a mother can't see? Her mother snaps.

–Something very special, Avanti surprisingly doesn't snap back and instead answers flirtatiously.

–He always gives her jewellery.

–Your husband will see it one day, Aditya teases her, still plying his troth like a salesman an expensive motor car. Or will you go to bed fully clothed so he can't pry open the secret.

–Not even him. I'll ...hide it.

He goes down on one knee, laughing. Come on, let's see it.

–One day. And get off your knee, it's embarrassing me.

–Why? They're only security guys and chamchas. They've seen everything but don't see anything.

–Even as a child they kept their secrets, her mother says to me, not distracted by his clowning. I had hoped you'd change your habits, as you grew older.

–Why should I? There are things I don't know about you and father and there are things you don't know about father and me. He's a wonderful man and...'

–I thought so too, once, her mother says. And I was very special too. We had our secrets but I've forgotten what they are now. She turns to Aditya and in a warning voice says. They will never allow you into the select circle of two.

You now understand what I meant earlier when I said love is a watery foundation and she has drowned and beaten her way to the shore of disillusion to haul herself out of it.

–Of course I will, Avanti says.

–Will you? Then do it now.

An aide hovers before them, interrupting. Your father wishes to see you now, Madam.

Her eyes flare in excitement. What about?

–He didn't say.

For a moment Aditya believes she'll refuse the summons, then she smiles and he thinks he only imagined the reluctance.

–Don't forget the movie, he calls after her as she hurries in.

They sit in silence in the bright light. He wishes they were in the dark. Thunder mutters, coming nearer. A flash of lightning blinds them for an instant. I remained a few moments longer to listen to their laments.
  –When you're in love all you can see is the person you love. The world ceases to exist. Are you in love?
  –Yes.
  –Be careful whom you fall in love with, her mother continues. With the wrong person, it could be a fatal affliction.
  –Is Avanti wrong for me?
  –At this moment, no. What time's your film?
  –Nine thirty. Then I thought we'd have dinner. So she may be home late.
  She clutches his hand suddenly, squeezing hard, taking him by surprise.
  –Go now, she whispers urgently. Take her away, quickly. Then to an aide who is a few feet away, she orders: Tell missy it's time to go.
  –I'm not in that much of a hurry. We have time. Her tone and the hand still clutching his bewilder him. She is telling him something he can't understand. She wants to spend time with her father, as she hasn't seen him for some time.
  –Go, she says. Never be accommodating with a woman. You'll never get her that way.
  –It's only her father.
  –You believe it will be easier if it's another man? Like all men, a father can be as dangerous as any other would-be lover. Go into the house, grab her. Go.
  –I can't do that, he says, dismissing the threat.
  She lets go his hand and sits back, eyes closed so she won't have to see him. The aide returns to murmur that 'missy will come soon.' She smiles without any humour, knowing Avanti's reply.

■

Shakuntula is a beautiful woman with high cheek bones, almost almond light brown eyes and a sensual mouth. Her marriage was not an arranged one but an instant, love-at-first-sight one. A lightning bolt of emotion lit her heart and her senses when she saw her husband-to-be stride into the railway carriage she was travelling in while on her way to deliver her Master's thesis. Despite the turmoil of racing blood, she experienced a calm certainty that her love had finally arrived. His physical presence was overpowering and his eyes appeared to penetrate through to her heart, and down to her toes that curled up in anticipation. In that instant, she believed that love was a magic potion, a sip of it could tame a tiger, halt a rampaging elephant, calm a ravaging dog and cause a man to abandon his past and start life anew, changed beyond recognition through the power of love. She is a woman of many talents—she sings ghazals, dances the bharatanatyam, plays tennis and was a gold medallist in her university in physics, history, biochemistry and anthropology. She has a master's in political science but the science of politics would fail to interest him, as he bludgeoned his way to power. What good would the intricacies of ideology, the art of compromise, the craft of integrity be to him? Her husband forbade her to work at any of her skills or to use her knowledge.

Shakuntula never shows an interest in her husband's and daughter's political ambitions, in their hard work to fulfil these dreams. At one time, and she has forgotten when, she did. She is now a discontented woman who says little but who possesses dreams of her own, as far removed from politics as possible. She never speaks of them to her husband or daughter. They will not comprehend them. She is disappointed that Avanti has taken on her father's characteristics, ambitions, features, and his shape, if a gentler, slighter version.

■

Avanti is in the hall, hesitating. She hadn't wanted to accompany the messenger; she hadn't wanted Aditya and her mother to see her apprehension. The smile comes out to dispel it, and she follows the messenger.

She hears Aditya call out: 'Don't forget the movie.' He sounds husky with wanting. She would too, if she'd spoken.

In the entrance hall, below the chandelier, her father's aides mill around. They have the air of men used to waiting, familiar enough with each other to chat and laugh. They fall silent when she enters. As she begins to turn right to her father's office, the messenger stops her.

-The President says to wait in your room. He will join you in a minute.

They remain silent watching her climb the wide teak staircase. It has a landing half-way up, with a large window overlooking the inner courtyard. Two commandos sit on rattan chairs, smoking, guns on the floor. In summers, it is always cool in the courtyard. I follow, quiet as a mouse trailing a cat, and take my usual place on the small chair inside her room. Patient as an oracle awaiting a command.

Her room overlooks the courtyard. The commandos still smoke; she draws the curtains. The room is extravagantly large, an only child's room filled with its needs—a television, computer, audio equipment, shelves of books, favourite toys still kept from childhood. On the bedside table, a framed photograph of her father. He also hangs on the walls in the company of famous men and women. He looks at her wherever she goes in that room. She feels restless under his gaze. It could be the coming storm; the air is hot and heavy, waiting to ignite. She takes off the locket he gave her and goes to her cupboard. She had meant to hide it earlier; no one would ever see it. She doesn't want to either. Under a pile of clothes is her jewel case. It has a beaten gold cover and is the size of a hardbound dictionary. She takes the key from under the mattress and opens it.

'Ring-a-ring a roses, A pocketful of posies...'

A child's sweet voice sang the nursery rhyme. Avanti always imagined herself as Alice, she told me once. A pretty little blonde girl in a white frilly dress tied at the waist with a blue sash, white shoes and a red ribbon in her hair. The song stops when she closes the lid with the locket inside. She had promised her father to wear it forever. It is too early for a forever. Aditya's ring is still tied in her pallu. She slips it back on her finger. Fretting, she checks the time. Fifteen minutes have slipped by; she wants to see the Godard movie. She turns on the television. Her father's face springs out from the screen. He is on a dais somewhere, yet he is also downstairs. It is magical, he can be everywhere in an instant and she imagines thousands of homes watching him at this moment too.

–I believe passionately in the democracy we have created, he says. It's the check on unbridled and corrupting power...

She senses him before the door opens. She switches off the television a moment before he enters.

–Where's my princess? He speaks in a playful voice.

They do not consider me an intrusion on their privacy, such is my privilege. I am just another stick of furniture—a chair, a table, an unlit lamp—in the room. I only speak when spoken to, directly, and give the questioner my wise advice and guidance.

-I'm here.

-Why are you in the dark? He switches on the light and sits on the bed next to her. He draws back as if in surprise. You're not my Avanti. You're a beautiful woman.

It is their normal exchange, the flatterer and flattered who accepts the game they play.

-But I'm still you're princess, aren't I? She leans against him, breathing in his familiar odour. How comforting it is. She feels at peace.

-You'll always be that. He caresses her head. This room is always my oasis. No one ever thinks of looking for me here.

-They do, but I forbade them to disturb you when you are with me.

-What a clever girl. He shifts and stretches out. Give me ten minutes.

He sleeps in an instant. She watches over him. His hair is starting to grey, there is grey too in his eyebrows. Not too much, she would have liked to pluck the grey hair out. How she wants him to remain young forever, the hero of her childhood.

She hears the faint knock, rises quietly and tip-toes to the door. Mr Aditya says you'll be late for…, the bearer says.

-Tell him to wait, she shuts the door, cutting him off.

She returns to sit by him. If he says ten minutes, she knows he'll wake the instant ten minutes are over. If he is exhausted, the sleep will be deeper. She waits twelve minutes then leans over to whisper: Awake, like a princess rousing a sleeping prince.

-I've kept you, he says on the instant of waking. You were going out with your friend?

-It's just to the movies, there's lots of time.

He goes to the bathroom and we hear him splashing water on his face. He returns drying himself with her towel; breathing in her perfume. He drops it on the chair, turns to the mirror and combs his hair. It is full and thick, often falling over his brow.

-You like him, don't you? He watches her in the mirror.

-Oh yes, she says eagerly. We've been seeing each other for fifteen

years. We could marry one day... She reveals the ring on her finger.
-I didn't know it was that serious.

He keeps combing a moment longer, absorbed it seems, and then pats his hair into place, turns to her. There was always a touch of vanity in him. His kurta is crumpled from the sleep and he will change before he returns downstairs.

-I've been thinking. He takes her face in his hands, looking into her eyes, bewitching her. Will you come with me? Love isn't a career, power is. Love confines, it becomes its own prison; one person becomes your subject. Power encompasses a nation, it liberates your dreams. You've always talked about changing the State. If you believe in its future, if you want it to have a future, you must commit yourself to it. If you see injustice, you can correct it, if you see corruption, you can cleanse it, and if you have a vision people will follow you.

She feels the power of his words ripple down through to her toes. It always happens when she hears him speaking to the masses. He uses his eyes and his hands like a charmer mesmerizing his snake. Of course, I know it is to keep possession of her and deny the boy the love he craves for. Like any 'king', even one democratically elected to his throne, he is aware of the political implications of marriage of his only child and had approached me for advice some days ago. I quoted the *Arthashastra* to him as he had never heard of the masterpiece. This is what I say to him, even as Chanakaya had wisely advised the emperor: *Everything a prince does, he must first consider how it benefits the empire, or how it affects the empire. A prince's life is not his own. It is the kingdom's. How will a marriage strengthen the empire? What does the groom or bride bring with them? Wealth? Power? A kingdom? A political alliance? Will marrying make a friend of an enemy? Will it extend the empire? If the answers are 'yes', only then can the marriage be arranged.*

-You really want me? She needs affirmation, despite knowing she is the sole heir to his throne. He's never mentioned it before. Certainly, they've talked politics, it is his occupation and he sometimes tells her his secrets, which she holds tight. All along, he had been grooming her for the ascension when his time came to leave the world.

-I wouldn't have asked. Wouldn't you like to?

She tries to take a step away to give herself a moment or two to consider the proposition. Can I think about it?

–What is there to think about, Avanti? I can't waste any more time. I need you. You must come with me…

–Oh yes, I want to. She flings her arms around him and hugs hard. She knows what she wants for her state though her vision is different to his and she has never spoken of it to him.

–What about your friend? he whispers.

–You mean you want me right now? I thought…

–Now is always the best time. He untangles her arms and says softly, hiding the hurt of her rejection. But if it's inconvenient….

–No, no, it isn't. I'd better tell him I can't go out with him. But she doesn't move, dreading Aditya's disappointment. He is easily hurt, that is his passionate, artistic nature. She too is unhappy, she wants to be with him.

–Yes, do that, her father says brusquely, frees her, and leaves the room.

It was then that she knew he'd played his game. Aditya is an unnecessary impediment in his life and he has neatly disposed of him by forcing a choice on her. She had said her 'yes' too quickly, his wounded tone had forced it out of her, now she is committed to him. Yet, she also feels excited at the thought of being by his side, learning the secrets in his head, learning to be a politician. The news will not filter down through the television screens. It will happen live in front of her, as long as she is by her father's side.

She turns, almost in tears. I'm so weak. I want to go with him but I don't want to leave here now. What should I do? I want to be with Aditya.

I have to persuade and convince her, even as I guided the prince Chandragupta to the throne. When the Nanda king insulted me and banished me from his kingdom during a feast. I planned my revenge to destroy him and lay waste his family. We defeated him, eventually. Then we had an army, now there is only me. I must do the same. I told you the choice is love or power. This is your chance, take it. It is your destiny. How else can you succeed him unless you're closer to him? Power demands sacrifices, even wars. A daughter's love for her father should be boundless, it is worship. He is the sun around which she circles.

She slips off the ring and ties it again in her pallu before we leave the room.

THREE

HE HAS FRETTED and paced for a half-hour. Her mother could have fallen asleep; she hasn't opened her eyes. Her relaxed face looks resigned to the wait, she is used to it. He walks to the edge of the lawn and back. The band has dispersed, security guards smoke, ignoring him.

She catches up with him half-way, walks beside him in silence, head down.

-Let's go. He takes her hand eagerly.

She carries his hand to her lips, kisses it. I can't. I'm sorry.

He should've understood the kiss. It is damp with apology. He pulls away.

-Father wants me to go with him, she says. He says he needs me; I'm the only one he trusts.

-But you can't. You promised tonight...

-I know but I can't refuse him. She leans towards him but he draws back from the kiss that was on her lips. I'll be back soon, that will make it even better. I want you too.

-When? Will I have to wait for your next birthday? I should've listened to your mother.

They both look back. Her father is watching them, standing beside his wife, still distant from her.

-What does that mean? she asks.

He doesn't hear the angry edge. He's taken you away.

He walks away from her, hiding the unshed tears.

-If you loved me, you'd understand, she says, following him now, trying to placate him.

-I do love you, he says. You don't know how much. Please, don't go away with him. Stay with me. Run away...

-I can't. I'll be back soon. Wait for me.

-How long? Months? Years? He turns. He is in tears now. Once you go, you'll never return. Come with me.

He is trying to break the spell cast on her by the magician, unaware that it binds her too tightly. Love is not a powerful enough weapon.

–I can't. He needs me.

–I do too.

They are a foot apart but the distance is infinite. There is no bridging her stubborn refusal. Even without moving, she has already left him. He can follow but only on her terms. Waiting and waiting, the way her mother does. He has no intention of doing that.

–I love you.

How futile those words sound, all passion drained from them. He spoke them as a last temptation, as if love has the power to divert her.

–What happened? What changed your mind?

–I told you, she says impatiently. Father wants me to be his assistant. Isn't that exciting, aren't you happy for me? I'll travel everywhere, meet all those people he deals with. I could change the way the state's ruled. I could… She holds onto the ring, clutching it in one fist, not yet revealing her true intentions once she holds power.

–Become a politician, like him, he barely hides his contempt.

–No, never. It is a denial neither believes.

–Is that what you want? He asks suspecting her answer.

She evades it. I want to be his secretary. It's just for a year. He needs me.

–He could hire a hundred secretaries, he looks over her shoulder. He already has them.

–I won't be like them. And he needs someone to help him entertain.

–He has your mother.

–She hates the city. She hates parties. She hates politics.

–Did you tell him I want to marry you?

She hesitates, a moment too long. Yes, I showed him the ring. I still want to. You can wait, can't you?

–I won't. Goodbye, he says and turns away, understanding now the futility of love.

–Aditya, she screams as the thunder rolled above their heads. Here, take this as well, damn you.

He turns in time to see her throw the ring at him. It misses. He doesn't even look where it has fallen.

–I hate you, I hate you.

At that moment, the rain comes down, blinding him and blurring the night. All of us start running for shelter without even looking back. In a moment, he is alone on the lawn, soaked. A part of him, despite being emotionally gored, thinks this moment is cinematically perfect—but life often is like cinema.

When she threw the ring at him, she had been furious. He had been stubborn, refusing to give her the time she asked for. Now or never, he had said. Now or never, her father had said. If Aditya loved her, he would have waited instead of stalking off into the rain. Love is nurtured by patience. She has run under the porch, relieved that they will mistake the rain for the tears streaming down her face. The downpour is thick and Aditya disappears into it, as if entering a watery mirror. She waits, he doesn't step back out again. She goes in to the house and into an argument.

-No, her mother is firm and angry. I don't want her to go with you.

-No! To another's ear he sounds surprised but she hears the menacing undertone in that one word. Who are you to say 'no' to me? I am your husband. You do what I say, haven't you learned that by now. I wasn't asking your permission, I was telling you that she is coming with me. Do you understand?

-She can live here and work there.

-No. She needs to be at meetings, at dinner parties and receptions that you refuse to attend, travel with me. It's best for her to live there.

She doesn't retreat. Let her get married first, then she can go with you.

-No.

-Leave her alone. You're too…too…possessive of her…

-And you're over protective of her. She's my daughter and does what I tell her for her own good. What kind of a man do you think I am?

-A man, there is no other kind. A seducer. And I don't want her mixed up with politics.

-She loves politics and I want her to come with me. She leads such a cloistered life here. It's about time she met the people I have to deal with daily.

-She's just a child.

-She's a woman. I don't want her to just sit at home, get married and become another housewife.

–Like me? She doesn't disguise the bitterness.
–I did want you to be more involved with my life.
–I couldn't compete with your other love, her mother mocked.
–I love my State.
–I don't mean that. Power, she says. I don't want what happened to me to happen to her as well. She looks to Avanti by the door leading into the dining room. Let her find her own life.

A child's mind, even when it is older, is the kingdom both parents wish to rule. They make subtle forays into the virgin land, planting dissent, planting their love, erecting barriers against one another and sniping at each other across them. If the child is confused by these battles for possession, that is its misfortune.

–Are you saying it's my fault?
–You can be too persuasive when you want something, her mother says. She tries to change her tack, become less confrontational as she knows she won't win. Please, give her time. Leave her for another year so that she can finish her work.

He smiles with no humour. So you can have more time to dissuade her? Let her decide then. They both turn to her, their lives in balance. He looks past her. Where's your friend?

–Gone, Avanti says softly but the sadness doesn't touch him.
–And I hope forgotten. Now you've heard your mother would prefer you spent another year as an artist? Or get married and do nothing like your mother?
–She wanted to work but you refused to let her.
–And so will your husband, he snaps.

She looks from one to the other, confused by the choices, her mother's eyes pleading, near to tears, wanting to hold and hide her daughter away in the folds of her embrace. He is looking fierce, commanding her to obey him

–No, Avanti says, softly. I want to go with father.

Her mother turns away, an additional stoop to her shoulders now, knowing she's lost her child. She leaves for her refuge, the prayer room closing the door behind her. It is a room crowded with many gods—the Buddha rubs shoulders with the Christ and the Christ looks across to Mahavira who in turn stares out at Vishnu. Her sanctuary is religion, following all the spiritual masters in the hope of saving herself. They too drown men's minds in belief that they are the pathway to god. However, as I mentioned earlier, he does not exist, so they are only illusionary lanes to the end of the void.

-Well, you'd better pack, he says, moving to the main reception room.

-Where are we going?

-To the Presidential palace. I want to spend more time with you. He doesn't add he wants her to escape her mother's persistence. Her mother refused to move to that mausoleum when he became President, and stubbornly remains in this relatively humble home.

Before she goes up to pack, she takes a torch and walks back out into the rain. A commando begins to follow; she dismisses him with a flick of her wrist. She is aware all the aides and commandos are watching her. They must think her demented. She can command all of them, and the servants and the band, to crawl on their hands and knees to search, and they would have obeyed. Except they would have known what she was looking for. I know, and she searches in the wet grass, letting the rain wash over her, gather in puddles on the lawn. It takes her a full ten minutes to find the ring. She kisses it, staring out at the driving rain where she had last seen Aditya, and her tears mingle with the rain. She had been happy in the moment as he had cupped her breasts and now all she has are the melancholy memories of his loving caress. She returns to her room to change into a dry salwar kameez and I discretely withdraw to allow her that privacy, and to weep the love out from her heart.

I have a summons from her father. He is in the drawing room of the bungalow, furnished with heavy, dark chairs and sofas, rosewood tables neatly dividing the spaces between them. He sits on the sofa, and waves me to a nearby chair, on which I perch. Within whispering distance.

■

...the cows and goats are home...father and I stand on the dusty lane.... looking...expectant...dusk vanishes.....darkness...the night is to fear...thieves, leopards....mad lorries...sleeping cobras...the moon a curving slice of silver.... the stars revel in their beauty but don't light the way....I cry... 'Maan.... maaan...' My father... 'Kumari...Kumari...' lanterns and torches only glow at our feet...swaying...as many join us,....calling.....at dawn only we remain... staring into the rising sun...and the long lonely lane...father says 'she is

dead...' my tears cannot appease my hunger for her....then father says... as the sun burns us... now angry 'your mother.. runs away with her lover... taken in by her bright brown eyes... the curve of her cheeks... the suppleness of her body...' Midday...my tears still flow...the glare of staring hurts my eyes....the postman is coming with a woman...supporting her....I run... 'Maan...maaaa'...I cling...she is in a dream....her clothes torn....her face bruised...lips swollen...I waken her...she holds blindly...crying with me... clinging....my father waits...at the entrance...mother cries... 'I was coming.... passing a car...a man jumps...hits me...pulls me in...I scream...hits...takes me to a house...he does... things...' She cannot speak....her breath pants. 'Then...he carries me...car...drives...throws me out...' the villagers wait.... silence....looking to Father.... 'you gave...body...to him...you smile...dance... like always....and you tell me this story...cheap woman...go...' Mother screams....falls at his feet...he steps back.... 'Believe me... believe me...'... slaps her...cries... 'Prostitute,' he shouts, 'leave here and take that ugly son with you...useless...boy...wastes his time reading...cannot even look after my goats...' He goes in...shuts the door on us... The panchayat approves... guardians of a woman's chastity...my mother cries 'I will kill...myself...here.' I hold her... 'I love you...can you not...think of me...' She holds me...cries... and I give her strength.... We leave and my family dies...exile again...with each step...I swear to avenge...honour...the men laugh....at such a puny boy... my weapon is a ruthless mind. We walk...the heat a burden too...all day...through night....the town...her sister opens her arms...shelter us...I am Chanakya...working in a store...small kingdom...and guide this king...to wealth... inventories...cash flows....CCTV to spy on all in this State....I rise...manager....my mother strings jasmines...for women's hair...sitting by the road...she sees the election poster...vote for....cries out...pointing...' that is the MAN....that is the MAN...'

■

Beneath the silken exterior, he is steel, and ruthless. How else could he have climbed to power so fast and remained there? He began his career as a gangster and was proud of his profession, though he had had only middling success, and gave it up when he understood it was easier to plunder the state than rob a bank. You may smile in disdain- a gangster—but remember every emperor, every king, every prince elevated himself to royalty from his ancestor's bandit beginnings. He had inherited his skills from his father, whose ambition was to die a gangster's death in a hail of bullets. Unfortunately, on his way to a kidnapping, he stepped on the tail of a cat which screamed in pain and leapt up; startled, he fell and struck his head on a rock. As you can see, life is unpredictable and possesses a sly sense of humour. His only son expanded the family business into extortion, kidnappings, midnight robberies, scams, prostitution, gambling, murders, knee breakings, counterfeiting, protection. Oh yes, he has killed, snuffed out lives with the breath from his gun. If one believes the canards against the great leader... However, in a poor country there were limited opportunities, robbing the poor didn't make him any richer and the rich were beyond his reach, hidden behind the high walls of their palaces, surrounded by gunmen. He has a magnetic presence, even as he can attract, or repel, as he wishes. His fathomless brooding eyes, arched eyebrows, defiant jaw and passionate mouth... the striking face atop a wiry body—honed through wrestling for his college team as a place to pass the time in between his nefarious activities off campus. He won gold medals consistently, only because he would whisper threats to his opponents as they grappled. Those who ignored them, believing they were superior wrestlers, had fatal accidents. They were shot, stabbed, run over and fell off buildings. He was also president of the student union at the university and was never opposed in the elections during his ten years studying for a B.Com degree—which he finally passed by subtly threatening his examiners.

While the Emperor Chandragupta possessed a disciplined army with which to enforce his will on the people and against his enemies, her father had a fine body of thugs. Elections did not exist in my day. How can one trust the people to make wise decisions in a democracy? They are incapable of clear thought—narrow minded, selfish, prejudiced, ignorant, easily deceived and gullible. Surely, inheriting the throne is more economical than squandering lavishly on a gamble. A king should provide his subjects justice, law and order and honest governance but these virtues have long since been forgotten. Instead, her father sent out his army to intimidate, threaten the electorate and at the same time spend lavishly to purchase their votes. And where did he get such vast sums? Men called industrialists and corporates, dressed in funereal black suits, pristine white shirts with coloured ribbons hanging from their necks like so many nooses, were generous in their contributions. In exchange for special favours. (They had never heard of Chanakya as they were educated in the creation of wealth but not in knowledge of their world.) He used planes, trains, cars, bullock carts, autorickshaws, motorcycles for these campaigns. The opposition parties, despite their efforts at corruption and daylight robbery, could not match his resources. One by one, they retreated from his onslaught. He purchased print and television journalists for a pittance. They followed him around like lapdogs, watered with Black Label, fed biryanis and quartered in five-star accommodation. He was a swift learner and, taking my suggestion, knowing the character of the people, he paid off the opposition candidates so they wouldn't canvas for votes. He offered free food for the poor, a monthly salary for those below poverty level, less taxes for the rich, free cell phones/television sets/two wheelers/cars for all. How could they resist such lavish generosity? The raggedy people expected such behaviour and were happy to grant him whatever he desired. In such ways is victory purchased in any democracy. Avanti and I trailed him into the assembly on opening day and sat in the visitor's galley to hear his maiden speech where, again, he made many promises. Shakuntula remained at home, not even watching her husband on television.

–I was right in forcing her to choose? he asks softly.

–A king must never entertain second thoughts once he has decided. You were right to take my advice. I quote from *Arthashastra*: *The king must have no scruples, even when expediency compels him to be cruel*. Indeed, 'he who would be great must be cruel.' I did not elaborate that I too had given Avanti guidance in this matter of power over love. I continued: It is time for her to learn from you as one day she will have to take your place on that wondrous chair.

–She will forget him?

–Love is full of porous holes; it will drain away in time. You must occupy her mind and her heart will become obscured.

–It was good advice to separate her from Shakuntala. Her mother would do everything to convince Avanti to marry that boy, bear children and live in obscurity. She is an insurmountable problem in her determination to defy me. He sighs heavily, a man of passion who sleeps alone in a bed, apart from the occasional companion who shares it for a night or two before he tires of the woman, knowing she bartered her body for his favours and not for any genuine affection. He scratches his stomach and continues: If only I'd had a son...

–A son would only grow more impatient the longer he waits for the seat of power. History is replete with the murders of fathers by greedy sons. *As for sons, it is cynically affirmed that it is the nature of princes, as of crabs, to devour their parents. Therefore, they too, must be kept under surveillance and deprived as far as possible of opportunity for insurrection.* I add: Daughters are more patient, more respectful, more worshipful and will not harm their fathers.

It is a wise remark and even if I had the power to foretell the future, I would not have regretted any word spoken. *No one is to be trusted, not even wife or child. One might even say particularly wife and child. The harem must be filled with spies and agent provocateurs to get wind of the intrigues which were expected would mature in this superheated atmosphere.*

He checks the time. It's late, fetch Avanti.

I climb the stairs and through the partially open door I hear their voices. I am a practised eavesdropper, a necessary trait for a spy. Secrets were my chosen weapons in my past battles, as they are now.

–...You could've said no, Shakuntala says. The moment you said yes, there was nothing more I could do.

–You know I can't say no to him. I love him...Avanti is sniffling.

I gently push open the door wider. Her mother sits on the bed, Avanti paces, arms crossed tightly over her breasts.

–Of course you do, I'm not saying you mustn't. I want you to live here and not there.

–That's you wanting to protect me.

–You heard me, I wanted you to marry Aditya first.

–I'm older now and can protect myself.

–You think you can but he is stronger than you and you'll succumb, because you love him.

–You're saying it's my fault. Why didn't you fight harder then?

–I did what I could. I forced him to send you to boarding school just to get you away from him. You don't know what a rage he was in about that. I still have the scars. I told him the school was a status symbol and he succumbed to his own ego. Then when you returned in the holidays, you chose to spend time with him, and wouldn't come to me. Why not?

–He was more exciting, and he wanted my company.

–And I a dull housewife, a woman of no worth.

–He told me that you were cold to him, Avanti flares up. That's why he needed me. I thought you loved him and would be more of a comfort to him. You're the one who wanted separate rooms, you drove him away.

–He had long since turned away and blamed me as I couldn't have another child. I was only his womb, like all women are for men. Her voice is weary from the guilt that he has shifted onto her. You must stay here. Go and tell him you've changed your mind.

–I can't now. I want to learn from him. Who else can take his place, except me? If I refuse, then I will never get another chance.

Shakuntala rises. She goes to embrace Avanti, a farewell, but Avanti stiffens and steps back, arms still protecting her breasts.

–He's seduced you with his promises, even as he did me. Don't fall in love with love, as I did. I will miss you very much. Her arms drop to hang by her side.

When she comes out, I am around the corner, listening to her heavy footsteps fade down the stairs, back to the prayer room.

I knock on Avanti's door. She knows my knock, much lower down the wood that another man's, and calls out to enter. When I do, she has nearly filled a large suitcase with her fine wardrobe. She is composed, the tears washed away. Determined.

–No, no, no. No silk, nothing fancy. Always dress simply in cotton. Earthy colours. Blues, greens, browns, yellows, with simple borders. The masses won't vote for you if you wear silks and satins. And no jewellery. And no makeup. Look unspoiled. Your people want you to look wholesome. Virginal.

–How long are we going away for?

–The rest of your life.

FOUR

IT'S A SHORT drive to the palace, we're in the centre of a fifty-car cavalcade, swiftly racing through the night along empty roads, passing people sleeping on the pavements. The night sky is brooding over us, watching our parade, waiting to release thunder and lightning at such defiance of its mood.

My complaint is that this city, which did not exist in my time, is a place of terrible din, dust, dirt, debauchery and deviousness. Many empires have been consigned to the rubbish heap here and lie piled one upon another. However, this world is also filled with new places of worship called shopping malls, sterile glades of glass, steel, items of expensive value, and cinema houses where people flock to pay homage to their new idols. Our ancestors would weep to see that their descendants have lost all sense of the aesthetic. Even I cannot bear to look upon the brutal ugliness of glass, concrete and horizontal and vertical lines in this culture's architecture.

The city lies in the exact centre of the state, the beating heart. At its back, the mountains, and its face to the distant sea. Let it remain nameless, but be assured, like any capital it is venal, corrupt and dangerous. This state is an ancient land, vaguely shaped like a quadrangle with wavering lines for its borders, three rivers flow through it and its plains are fertile, depending on the rains. Other parts are stony and unproductive. In my time forests blanketed the land, abundant with animals and birds long since evicted from their habitats. The land is now bald as an old man's head. The state and the modern Raja of this age—politicians, corporates, industrialists—own most of the land; the poor are ejected at will should any covet their meagre holdings. The inhabitants look unchanged from my day and I see many familiar features among them.

The capital then was Pataliputra, a perfect rectangle, fourteen kilometres long and two and a half kilometres miles wide, rising at the confluence of the Ganga, Gandhaka and the Son rivers. Two hundred thousand citizens lived within the wooden walls of the jaldurga, pierced by sixty four gates. The streets were straight as arrows, east to west, north to south, at perfect right angles. The Emperor's land stretched from the blue waters in the east, north to the Himalayas, south to the low mountains and flowed west over more mountains across Khurastan (now Afghanistan) to the borders of the Persian kingdom. Caravans travelled freely from east to west carrying silks, spices, precious stones and bandits never molested them, but those who did hung like jackfruit from the higher branches of trees on their route. The emperor's palace, as splendid as that of the Persian king, Achaemenid's, was in the exact centre. Guards checked the entry of every visitor for within the royal apartments lay the armory and the treasury, overflowing with gold, silver and precious stones. In the palace compound were the public rooms, halls with hundreds of carved pillars decorated with silver birds and golden vines. In the wavering light of torches, they came alive, fluttering their wings among the swaying vines. All religions, Hindu, Buddhist, Jain, and even Greek, had freedom to preach their beliefs openly, and build their temples. That rich, grand city has been reduced to a poverty stricken town and all that remains of a great empire is rubble and overgrown mounds. It's the fate of all empires in this land of a people with fatal amnesia.

This Presidential Palace, set in a vast garden, is ablaze with lights. It rises like an icy cliff out of the darkness, appropriately intimidating, grand and befitting the occupant who rules the state. The architecture is Greek, Roman and British to reflect the confusion of the great empires of history; and air-conditioned in homage to America, which contributes such a cornucopia of comforts through its inventions. There are many interior courtyards and hundreds of rooms so I have acquired a GPS (a truly wonderful invention as in the past one groped one's way through jungles, along mountain passes and forded rivers, asking directions of the locals who more often than not deliberately misdirected one) to guide me through the maze of halls and corridors. In this dwelling, the President will have the peace and quiet to tutor his daughter in statecraft moulded according to my advice.

She sits on the bed in her new room in a dream-like state. She has willingly given her life to her father hours ago and waits to see what will happen to her next. Aditya is lost to her, replaced by this room. If she had chosen differently, at this very moment, she would have been in bed with him, in an elegant hotel suite, languorous from love-making. Instead, she is in a guest bedroom, a temporary arrangement. This room is large, the ceilings high as the sky and the marble beneath her bare feet cold as a grave. The bed is not her comfortingly single one that embraced her in sleep. This one is huge, appropriate for the size of the room, and is the resting place for the bodies of powerful people—visiting presidents, potentates, dictators, prime ministers, generals—who need much space in their restless sleep. The furniture is numbered, the numbers stating their ownership and location. The bed is PP54/2G. She has slept in the room once or twice before, only for a night, and had not minded then. Now, it is to be her home.

Her solace is her childhood friend, the privileged Monika, and they talk continuously. I only hear Avanti's side of the phone conversation, shrieks or screams of dismay or delight from Monika, as I hover in the background, holding a few pieces of paper in my hands, should Avanti demand to know my business there. But she is oblivious of my presence, and is wholly focussed on her conversation with Monika as she paces the verandah.

-He's a bastard, a fucking bastard. (shriek). He said he loved me and when I asked him to wait he fucked off, without even a goodbye. (shriek). What did we fight about? He wanted to marry me, yes he proposed. (scream). No, it isn't exciting...I told him to wait. (scream). I want to work with father. (scream). Yes, he wants me too and when I told Aditya, he walked out...I do love him... (scream)...I thought he loved me but all he wanted was to fuck me. Fucking men. I get married, I have kids, then what? I don't want to be a fucking reproductive machine for any man. Press the button and out pop babies and babies. I'll end up like my mom. (scream). Of course I texted him but he never replied...What should I dooooo?

Apart from their past, Avanti and Monika have another common bond—their fathers are the two most powerful men in the state. Monika's father is a noble in the President's court. I call him 'noble' although there is nothing noble in his character. He is *the* richest man alive here, his empire larger than the state as it flows out across the boundaries, over mountains and leaps over the seas. He inherited his money from his father, a wily man who rose to great wealth in the previous President's court. Such wealth humbles even the President and he has to obey the dictates of this corporate predator. Monika lives in a thirty-floor building of unsurpassed ugliness, furnished in the apex of bad taste that only money can purchase. It towers over the city and peers down at the slums at its feet. Her father is a portly, pudgy (I can never make up my mind) man, married to one equal to him in girth. Monika worries constantly that as she ages she will lose her youthful curves to the pudgy portly syndrome and end up like her mother. Her father never sees me, his gaze always a foot above my head. He dresses in dark suits stitched especially for his pudgy frame in London (where there are tailors of repute who can disguise his shape through cloth and cut), blue shirts and the noose around his neck. Her father and the President confer daily, dine together weekly and his private jet is always available for the President's use.

The women talk for an hour before she disconnects and collapses on the bed.

–I want to cry, she confides. I never want to see him or speak to him ever again. I hate him. Why couldn't he wait, what was wrong in asking that of him, if he loved me?

–You cannot have such emotions any more. You're the heir.

–Have you slept with a woman? She turns beseeching eyes on me, thinking of her lover.

–Many.

–Liar.

–A few.

–And it's good?

She seems surprised that I can manage to seduce women. Why not? I have a perfect body, muscular and strong in all the right places, a harmony of perfection from the neck down. I have spent more memorable hours lying between a woman's legs than advising the President.

–It always is. However, when we're...I hesitate. Fucking is an intimate word, an intimate act between lovers and she is my pupil and I cannot sully her with such a word from my life. When we're in congress, the woman only wants to gaze on the face of my beauty and not the other one that horrifies. It gives me a crick in the neck to keep the correct angle before her eyes.

She smiles, imagining the distorted coupling.

–But you never married?

–For a fleeting moment only. The bride came, arranged of course, seduced by the promise of my employed position. In the light of the sacred fire, when the veil was lifted, she saw the beauty and was wet as the monsoon, then petrified and dry as a draught at facing such a paradox—the delight at my beauty and the revulsion—she turned and fled, never to return. I was relieved. I glimpsed pity in her eyes. I do not accept pity, the cheap coin of compassion. I haven't the courage to face a woman willing to spend a lifetime with me. She must have a high capacity for suffering. I don't tell Avanti that my mother's moods depended on which side of my face she saw first on waking.

–Aditya is all beauty, she sighs.

–He abandoned you, remember. He could have waited. I want her to escape the longing and command: Sleep well and rise early. I give her my scrap of paper with her daily routine, written in an ancient hand and she squints at it, unable to decipher the language.

–Is it English? It looks like Sanskrit.

–It is English, I reply indignantly. But I know my hand continues to obey that cursive script. I prefer working with pen and paper, head down, watching the flow of words making their marks across the pages. It reminds me of my past when I composed the epic. If I had told my emperor that a language, the spoken and written word, has conquered greater territories than he can imagine, he would have laughed. Only armies create empires, he'd reply. But here in this new world, English, a language first spoken in an island the size of a flea on a dog's back, has captured the minds of the whole world. Its empire even greater than Alexander's.

–What does this mean?

I sigh in frustration. I had given her a copy of the *Arthashastra*, abridged, badly translated, misinterpreted, incomplete. I wasn't surprised. How can the original work of genius on palm leaves survive thousands of years and thousands of wars? But my prince(ss) wanted it on her Kindle. Imagine, that great work reduced to pixels to lie beside romantic novels and crime fiction, and not a paisa of royalty to the original author. I take back my notes from Avanti and read out my advice for my pupil: You must have self control and curb the senses: Lust, Avarice, Pride, Anger, Drunkenness and

Insolence against the four special temptations: Hunting, Gambling, Drink and Women.

-The last doesn't concern me; nor do the other sins in that book.

-You must not allow emotions to guide your decisions. Think every action through carefully and, if in doubt, consult your elders. Also, you must recruit your own spies. You...

-Why do I need spies? Today the word is Intel and father has countless intel agents.

-Intel?

-Intelligence. God, you're ignorant.

-Spies are not intelligent. They see, hear and report. It's not for them to use their intelligence and make decisions—that's the duty of the prince. Those men and women are loyal to your father. You need your own Intels whose loyalty lies with you, for one day you may need to know more than your father.

She bites her lower lip, doubtful about my subversive ideas but I have to protect her from the many enemies she will accumulate in her newfound position.

I warn her: You are teetering at the lip of the volcano of power, and if you're not cautious and watchful, you will be consumed in the fires.

-You're overdramatic, as always, she laughs and my over-drama at least has lightened her mood, lifted her from the despondency of lost love. She has an enchanting smile, and as it lights up her lips and eyes you can see its capacity for mischief. She brushes the hair from her eyes; it's long and lustrous and too glamorous. I must remind her to cut it short, neck length. Severe. But don't be taken in by those looks, she can be stubborn and determined once she is focused. As her advisor, my role in her life is to keep her focussed on what is important.

-Always look after your people and they will elect you again and again. Keep away from another man's wife. This doesn't apply to you.

She laughs. I don't know why you keep quoting this *Arthashastra* to me. I suppose because you're named after the author. Why not Karl Marx or Mahatma Gandhi, every one quotes Gandhi.

-But never follow his advice. Chanakya was a very wise man, I say with humility, and the *Arthashastra* teaches you how to get power, hold it and successfully rule a state.

–I bet he was assassinated.

–He followed the emperor, who renounced the throne for his son, Bindusara, whose life Chanakya saved; he then withdrew to lead a life of contemplation. He even stopped eating.

–Young girls do that today and it's called anorexia. It's fashionable to be thin.

–I prefer them buxom with cloves on their breath.

–If you're lucky. She yawns. I need sleep.

–Then you must wake early and study the files so you are prepared for tomorrow.

–But I don't have any files.

–I'm reading out what I wrote. She yawns, flicking me away like dust.

–Wait. Let me finish. Do not covet another's property; practice ahimsa, non-violence towards all living things; avoid daydreams, lying and expensive lifestyle; and avoid bad people.

–How do I do that?

–It will be hard in this world filled with such people. I have to hurry on as her eyes are starting to close. Before sunrise you must listen to the reports of your ministers, hear the reports of your spies, talk to the police and your finance minister...

–Intel, Chan.

She is young; she abbreviates. See what I am reduced to now—Chan—but she is the only one I permit to shorten my name; others have to respect me as Chanakya.

–Now go, she commands and points to the door.

But before I can obey, her father enters, wearing a silken gown gifted to him by a foreign ambassador grateful for favours. His breath is bitter from Chivas as he passes me to sit beside her on the bed where she lies in languor. He strokes her hair tenderly, then massages her neck and I think I can hear the purr of satisfaction. With his other hand he flicks me out of the room. Their gestures are very similar; father and daughter. I cannot prevent what is to happen between them; they are both following a familiar pattern. It is abhorrent but the practice ancient, even before my days. I do possess some morals, admittedly not many, when I guide a prince to power.

I slip out and use my GPS to guide me to my quarters, not as grand a room as hers but appropriately humble, among the palace officials and not the servants. There is just a narrow passage to my cot, the right size for me, between hundreds of books on science, history, politics, economics, philosophy, astronomy that I am reading to catch up with this day and age. I will never finish the reading in this lifetime. It's with a feeling of satisfaction that I lie back, knowing I have set her on the path to power but how she will wield it is something I ponder as I fall asleep. Power can be both cruel and benign—two faces of the same coin..

■

On my advice, she is allowed a few days to adjust to her new life; contemplation, I strongly advocate, is a necessary precursor to one's actions. However, her head is filled with what she calls music, plugs stuck in her ears, what chance for silent thoughts on her future. She spends her time sitting on the verandah that opens out from her room, staring at the rain, now so heavy that the garden is barely visible. I note how she clutches her cell phone tightly and frequently looks at it in longing. I know what she is waiting for and when she goes to the bathroom, I check her text messages. She waits for Aditya to reply to her brief message: I am sorry, Avanti. But he remains silent all day, too wounded and defeated to be able to continue. She calls Monika; Monika calls her. They speak about Aditya constantly and I have to discourage that continuous memory. I think it's best he never replies. Like many others, in my idle hours, I have explored the intricacies of the cell phone. I cannot tweet or FB or use the other means of pointless communications available to the young but I know how to block his name in her contact list. It's a mean act and I should be ashamed, but you must understand my reasons by now.

The second step I have outlined for her on the journey to power takes place a few days after. The rains have eased and her father takes us to the party headquarters, another sprawling bungalow embraced by a garden. It is little used, a mere symbol, but on this day it is crowded with ministers and party workers, the driveway clogged with SUVs, the standard vehicle for these hardworking men and women. They are tightly packed in the main hall which smells of roses. They carry garlands, all of them wrapped in cellophane, and make room for her father to ascend. His chair is throne-like with a high back and carved arms; it's also raised on a small platform.

Hanging on the wall behind the chair is a huge photograph of him looking out like an explorer viewing unmapped worlds. In a trance, she follows him to sit at his right hand, even as the Christian Jesus does with God. She is demurely dressed and smiles shyly at those upturned faces studying her minutely. She's no stranger to them. The artistic daughter whose paintings they have purchased at her occasional exhibitions and hidden in their cupboards. She knows the limitations of her talent and why she sells so well. She still worships art in the Louvre, the Met, the Tate, foreign names to me. But art, paintings or sculpture, were not shaped to hang in lifeless halls but in the palaces of kings, in homes or in places of worship for which they were created in my time. The party workers know why she is there and only wait for the announcement by the double-President, of the party and the state. At this time, he has barred the press who bay at the gates wanting to witness this historic event, and use it as a stick to beat him with. Nepotism is their cry, as if it's an evil. Nepotism! How else, I want to ask them, do empires last for centuries? By magic? It is safer for the child to mount the throne than usurpers who, through war or assassination, upset the calm of the people and the state. The state must remain free of the turmoil that democracy causes. The hall falls silent, cell phones are muted, as are the whisperers.

-I am here to introduce my daughter, Avanti, her father announces, to all you faithful members of our party. She has decided—she wishes to join the party and I would like for you to welcome her.

Avanti places her palms together and bows her head. The hall erupts with loyal cheers and clapping, fists are raised in salute, cell phones are clamped to ears as the joyous news is swiftly spread out to those who weren't invited to this gathering of the privileged. The noise startles her, even as a horse will skitter when it hears a loud outburst. Outside, we can hear the celebratory fire crackers.

Her father holds up his hand and silence returns. They wait breathlessly for his next words to confirm her position, cement it into their hearts and minds.

-As my daughter is inexperienced, he continues in his soft seductive tones that are cored with steel, she will need to work for the party and learn how it functions on a day-to-day basis. I believe the best position for her to observe and learn will be as President of the Youth Wing of the party.

She is taken by surprise at this swift elevation. I know she expected to start as a lowly worker, trudging through the poverty of her state, promising them salvation. She doesn't yet understand that an heir must be elevated far above the common herd. A prince must promote his offspring swiftly. All the Youth Wing of the party are men, with a sprinkling of women, in their fifties who have retained the magic elixir of youth through muscle and might and their devotion to the President. They are ecstatic that she is raised above them, as they understand the natural order of their world. Who else can follow the President? Not one of them is worthy, although they do dream. She has her father's name and that is credential enough to be fawned upon by the other party members. They see her as the continuity of their lives in power. When she lifts her head to the baying men and women, she sees the greed alight in their eyes. She doesn't need sexual wiles to seduce them. They fall under the charisma of her power-to-be. When I defeat her father, sooner or later, they will be hers; she can have them even earlier. Watching her, I know Avanti savours that thought, holds it as her secret as she moves among them. She knows at that moment the simple trajectory of her career—Member of the Assembly, Cabinet Minister and President, not of the Youth Wing, the State. Outside a thousand crackers explode in ecstasy and the din of clapping is endless. I push my way onto the dais, the advisor, to lean over to her.

–Adulation is an intoxicant, like wine, drink too much and you will become confused.

But she cannot hear me for the stampede to the dais by the faithful, unwrapping the cellophane from their rose garlands, scattering petals, crushing them underfoot and filling the hall with their perfume, as they jostle to garland their new leader. Each announcing his name aloud so she will distinguish him, or her, from the throng. I am pushed aside just as a wave sweeps away driftwood. I find a safe vantage point to observe the fawning workers bend to touch the hem of her saree. They would prostrate too, full length, but know the others will trample them underfoot. They would garland her father too but he is allergic to roses and accepts only their touching his feet.

–Madam, Madam, Madam, they call her as they smother her in roses. They cannot call her Avanti, (only her family, including me, can use the name) as this will be disrespectful and so she will be always known as Madam. It's spoken with reverence and love and flattery unlike other women known as Madams of brothels and beauty salons.

∎

Two years pass. Aditya is a fading memory, hopefully forgotten entirely, as she no longer mentions his name.

There are times when I am lonely in my new world, having existed in it for thirty years. I long for my past and when I suffocate from such longing, I escape from the palace on my scooter, and ride to the old city that has long been forgotten. I leave the privileged enclave of power and the generous avenues, shaded by trees, bordered by broad pavements, grid-locked with Mercs, Audis, Jaguars, BMWs, hooting and howling to unleash their power and roar along highways, killing all those who step in their way. As I travel east, the roads narrow like sclerotic veins in an ageing body, clogged with buses, pedestrians and autorickshaws. In my time, this part of the city, the only one which existed, was a village, a caravanserai for merchants with their silks. It hasn't gone away; the ruins remain, colonized by the poor who live among the fallen walls of palaces and forts, sleep on the floors of the hamams and defecate where royal princesses once bathed in pools of clear water. I walk among them, along the alleys and gullies, past havelis in which rajas once lived. I commune with the ghosts who haunt these halls, waiting for their resurrection. The people all know me, and I them, the visiting stranger passing among them infrequently, and they do not flinch at my sight as they have their own infirmities to nurse. I brush against them in the chowk, even as I did in the past, and they whisper their secrets to me. The streets in any city, anywhere, are full of informers, spies, Intel. I hear who has taken a bribe, who has bought a weapon, who speaks against the President, who supports him, who plans an insurrection. Nothing here has changed—the same faces, the same voices, the same secrets, the same wares—silks, satins, cotton, beads, silver, gold, fruits, vegetables, blended with the odours of spices, dust, sweat and shit. The hum of voices is a constant and the ancestors of the men who sit in their stalls under whirring fans, once trod the silk routes. Today, the silks and spices arrive in hand-pulled carts, are deposited on their doorsteps and they no longer travel to Cathay or Athens. I stop at the food stalls, taste a morsel of kebab, sucking on it until the flavour fills my mouth before I chew, savour the mutton biryani still hot from the cooking fires, cool my palate with lassi. Even the street dogs know me as they accompany me along the serpentine, crowded lanes snacking on the morsels I throw. If they could speak, they would make the best Intels as people give away their secrets within their hearing, but I also have other sources in the old city. On my way, I visit the home of the singer Akbar Khan, forgotten by the youth, whose ghazals on lost love enchant my heart with their melancholy lyrics. He lives in a haveli with his family, a small palace hidden behind high walls, with marble floors and painted walls and ceilings. His room looks out on the inner courtyard. As it's dusk, his many admirers have gathered to wait for his voice that will fill the room but no longer those halls that once welcomed him. He's near ninety, white hair, white beard, a wise, serene face, and, when the lamps are lit, he sings the ishq-e-majazi songs for us. He never sings ishq-e-haqiqi as he no longer believes in God. We're carried across mountains and deserts to find our lovers in shady gardens, beside cool waters, and we beg them return to us. In one song she does, in another she's dead. When he ends his small concert, we leave money at his feet, touch them too. He never sees us; he's blind. I leave him, replenished.

In this decaying past, there is also the present and the future, just two lanes away from Akbar Khan's home. The building is new, squeezed between two ruins, and I enter the internet café on the ground floor. Every booth taken by young men and women exploring a world beyond these walls. They are from the alleys and the tenements, mastering the world language, mastering the machines, and are the horsemen racing to the future, armed not with bows and arrows, but with a little mouse in their fists. In the next room are even more children of this new age, ears clamped with headphones speaking a dozen versions of the English language. French, German and Spanish too, and I marvel at their ingenuity. On one wall are six large clocks, with white faces, black hands, and red second hands. Beneath each, in black lettering, UK, Europe, Australia; America has three clocks to itself. They have sleepless eyes as they talk to Austin, Texas, Glasgow, Scotland, Melbourne, Australia, Barcelona, Spain. At the far end, on a raised platform is the conductor of this symphonic babble. Malini, in her fifties, shabby salwar kameez, sunken dark eyes, hair knotted in a bun, bare of jewellery. It's a pretence. She owns a farmhouse 20 kilometres outside the city, with an indoor pool and a three-car garage. Immediately below, is her daughter, Sita, and it is her I come to visit. She is a slight, twisted girl, one leg too weak to support her weight, her back bent sharply, as if someone broke it. Polio, the name of an ancient disease that afflicted many in the past, though now under control. Sita is an exception. She too sits at a computer and smiles when she sees me. Her eyes are round as marbles and she speaks a broken language that I have mastered, through patience and Malini's help. Sita passes me printed sheets, her week's work on my behalf. She is my hacker, not all spies work the streets, secrets are hidden now behind firewalls and Sita can sneak past, over or under, any wall. I scan through the papers—bank accounts of ministers and bureaucrats, (millions of dollars, sterling, euros and all of them with criminal charges for rape, murder, extortion, arson and embezzlement, dragging through the courts), email exchanges between them and the Opposition, each courting the other, police reports on crimes not to be investigated on orders from above. There is a mail for the President from his party leader on Avanti. I read it carefully, knowing the future before it is to happen, the better to advise her. There is a shredder and the sheets are reduced to tiny strips. Sita unplugs the memory stick on which she has also saved her 'research' and hands it over. It's warm in my fist and, if I had a larcenous heart, I could be a very wealthy man. I kiss the top of Sita's head, pay Malini and leave.

Secrets give me an erection. How can I leave without seeing Rupmati? She has named herself after the singer who bewitched a prince but this Rupmati cannot sing a note. Her laughter seduced me—especially the sweet smell of paan on her breath. She has a paan stand opposite the biryani stall and after that spicy meal, the diners cross to buy her supari paan. Even the spoiled youth of the city leave their Mercs and Audis on the outskirts of the chowk, and wend their befuddled way to her stall. Her speciality has a little cocaine, a little hashish, a little of this and that, and it is very expensive. She is a wealthy woman from her humble trade, owns the haveli, and rents out the rooms to tenants.

She stands at the door, hands on hips. So, my lover comes only when he has a hard one he needs to soften.

-I come every day whenever I think of you. I dream of you at night too and wake with such an ache in my loins.

-So you use your hand then and when it gets tired you come here.

-No, I came because I can never resist your beauty for long. I fight such a longing but then I succumb. I can smell your perfume, the sweetness of your mouth and I escape the office and race over here.

She laughs. How can I resist such a liar? I miss your expertise, I miss that knowledgeable tongue...

She draws me into her home. The first room is her storeroom. The air is pungent with the spices for her paan and filled with the jars and gunny bags of betel nut, cloves, cinnamon, nutmeg and coconuts. Each morning, a hand-drawn cart delivers fresh betel leaves. Beyond it, her bedroom is a museum. The walls are painted with many coloured figures, depicting marriages, religious ceremonies and folk dancers. There are flying blue elephants, prowling red tigers and nubile dancers in bright yellow. The paintings have faded over time yet the reds, greens, blues, purples are still vibrant, the characters alive with their expressions. The artist, as always, is anonymous. Against one wall is a steel Godrej cupboard and beside that the door to her private bathroom. A fan whirls overhead as we fall onto the divan.

She has a plump body and when she welcomes me into her arms her sensuous, passionate embrace sets me to dreaming of my own lost lovers while grateful for the present flesh beside me. In my time naming our sexual members was sweet—lingam, yoni, they were worshipped as deities, blessed with delicate oils, sandal paste, kumkum, perfumed with incense and lit by sacred flames. They are now toppled from their pedestals, reduced and contracted to these two new words—cunt, cock—with other equally commonplace variations.

-As you kept me waiting, you must go down.

-It's not a punishment, I tell her, as I slide my tongue down from her breasts, over the arching belly. You will not find another man with such knowledge in this art. My tongue does not only taste the sweetness in her mouth but the sweeter still perfumed one between her legs. I need to describe our founts of pleasure. Why else do I have a tongue? I tell her as she heaves in ecstasy.

Then when it is her turn to taste I tell her, the caress must be delicate to only brush the outer skin of the magnificent beast between my legs. It must not be suckled, as only babies do that, but constantly stroked from the tip to the base of my cock. Tongue tip.

At the same time as her tongue licks, she has to insert the middle finger, not the index, glistening with oil up my anus and stroke the interior. The mind evaporates with this double delight and the body teeters on the lips of the volcano just waiting to spew the hot lava into her eager mouth. What is fucking without delicate oils, food without spices? I bring with me a bottle blended by experts in the chowk and its formula is a secret but I can tell you a few ingredients: cloves, jasmine, cinnamon, a little red chilli, a pinch, tamarind and attar. The others remain a secret. Now I must caress the oil into her body, from the neck down, to her toes. Every inch. She slowly performs the same for me and then when we grapple with each other, we slip and slide on our hot flesh tantalizingly in and out, always balancing at the edges of frenzy. We play our games as we wrestle, her resistance my insistence, pushing and fighting to remain between her legs. And then, what is pleasure without pain, bread without salt? My pain arouses me when I am hung by my wrists and my cock beaten with a switch, a horse made to gallop faster and faster as it tries to escape the pain until the final sprint that ends in heaving exhaustion. Rupmati doesn't like to be hung but instead bent with her legs tied behind her, open and vulnerable to my strap on her brown sensual lips, beaten until the juices overflow and she falls unconscious. Her favourite lover is the teak dildo, oiled and delicately carved with erotic figures, to ceaselessly give her pleasure. Even I cannot compete with that permanent erection. Our sexual games vary, depending on the heights of our imagination and we vary them on each of my visits.

We part with an amicable kiss and the promise of my return as she caresses the wounded side of my face with tender fingers. I am renewed again, and I tell no one of my escapades, waiting for my next escape from within these suffocating walls.

FIVE

AVANTI IS DILIGENT in her duties as President of the Youth Wing, attending the office five days a week, conferring with her youthful supporters. She wants youth, not these elderly men and women, clinging to their positions; unfortunately, they won't vacate their various posts. She has her own Personal Assistant as no one can exist without a PA. It is a status symbol to be trailed by this man (never a woman) wherever she goes, notebook in hand, pen poised, cell phone ready. Ramesh is a gift from her father, plucked out of obscurity from some ministry. In his early thirties, he is thin as a fleeting thought, bespectacled, and appropriately servile and efficient. How he manages both puzzles me. He is wary and watchful of my position, but I quickly reassure him I'm not a PA and no threat.

-You must find another PA, I tell Avanti.

-One is enough.

-Ramesh is your father's eyes and ears. He will report everything back to him. He is the Intel man. Confide only generalities, and save your secrets for a man of our choosing.

-You're my sort of PA.

-I'm a man of thoughts, not action. You need an action man to do your Intel, perform duties out of sight of your father.

-And you have found him.

When Ramesh leaves the office for the day, returning to his humble home, we arrange to dine in a crowded restaurant where the common people gather. She is not recognized, yet, and still has freedom of anonymity. Vikram is my choice, also in his thirties, muscular, quick-witted, neatly dressed, unmarried. He needs work desperately as he supports a large family and I have known him since childhood. He has pestered me over the years for employment, and has survived on his wits—some theft here, some extortion there, but he needs steady work with a salary. We come to a swift agreement on the terms of employment; he will only work in the evenings when Ramesh has left and instructions will be given over his cell phone. Never again face-to-face, and Avanti is happy with the arrangement.

Vikram is also a distant cousin, a relationship I forget to mention.
-When should I use him?
-When you have the need. We also make him a party member in the Youth organization so he can keep an eye and ear open to discover who is loyal to you and who to your father.

Her father too is meticulous in grooming her. She learns etiquette, protocol, politics and power from the master himself.

At her first state banquet, he instructs: Now remember, as my hostess, people expect to learn my secrets from you. Make polite conversation, smile often...say everything, reveal nothing. Avoid issues, avoid opinions. Neither like nor dislike.
-That makes me feel so bland.
-People like bland. It deceives them.
-But you're not bland. You're full of fire...
-But not brimstone. They know me, not you. You'll learn. I'm proud of my princess. He caresses her head with warm familiarity as her lessons begin. Stand straight. Look them in the eye. The secret is to find one man or one woman in that audience and seduce them. The others will follow.

I am not invited to these banquets, much to my chagrin, as I love food. My only interest when she returns in the evening is to ask her the menu. You must understand that after sucking on star dust for more than two thousand years food it is the one experience I long for—a glass of water tastes of honey, honey of wine, bread like cake and cake like tandoori chicken. Sometimes she even eats (depending on the guest of honour) lasagne, fried noodles, chicken in red wine sauce—these international flavours fill my mouth with long. I discover choc-o-late, and begin to always carry a packet of this dark sweet in my pocket. I am a very slow eater as I eat with care, savouring every mouthful, a grain of rice, a bite of chapati, the seed of a tomato as if it is my last (and it could be too). I can write and speak reams on my longings. Once she has given me the succulent details of every dish, she then tells me whom she spoke to and on what topic. She is faithful to my suggestions, avoiding politics, to talk (depending on the day's news) about sport, celebrity gossip, medical marvels. She avoids art and books as her dinner companions, mostly industrialists, corporates, are ignorant of such refined subjects. But they are of use in her duties as President of the Youth Wing of her party. Her main work is to fill the party coffers; democracy is always a famished beast that needs constant nourishment. And it is to this end that she is learning to charm her dinner companions to donate generously in exchange for her father's favours: lower taxes, higher tariffs, lower tariffs, subsidies, monopolies. The party workers too must contribute monthly sums and how they raise it is of no concern of hers. Though it is the concern of the extorted shopkeepers, farmers, restaurateurs, cinema houses, any organisation. If her workers don't fulfil their quota, she screams: Out, out, out, resign your membership. She is ruthless and no manner of grovelling will make her retract her decision. Should a dismissed worker appeal, she snaps at him with the ferocity of a crocodile. In her temper, she is her father's child, face and voice so alike, indistinguishable, down to the way they clench their jaw.

–A prince must rule through fear, but judiciously, I advise after one such outburst. Remind them it exists and you can apply it. But not terror. Terror frightens but will also create an army of enemies who will haunt you. There is a thin line between fear and terror and a prince must walk the tightrope cautiously—if he wishes to live long enough to die a natural death.

–Stop telling me what to do, Chan, she turns on me, with the same fury. I know what I am doing. Mind your own business.

–My business is to lead you to power.

–Then keep your advice to that subject and guide me.

I retreat, temporarily. Patience. She is like a young horse that has the bit between its teeth and will gallop until exhausted. Art is a hard taskmaster and having flunked her, she now revels in her power. A ruler should be ruthless, as I have written earlier, but should be tempered. She is goaded to please her father, knowing how closely he studies the finances of the party as bribing the electorate, when the time comes, is inflationary. They speak hourly on their cell phones, exchanging information on the health of the state and of the party.

■

May I give you some advice? I ask, not out of humility, but to remind her of my position. She notes the sarcasm in my tone.

–Do I have to listen?

–Yes. Give your cell number to your party workers. This will

give them a feeling of importance that they can talk to you any time. A hotline to their President.
-Are you mad? They'll clog up my phone with their calls and I won't be able to talk to my father or my friends.
-Have a second one for them, specially.

I wonder whether she will take my advice. I wait a day, two days, a prince shouldn't be harried to make a decision, even if it may appear frivolous. There are more cellphones than toilets in this state, I've learned, and it is a symbol of importance to possess one, even if unable to pay the dues. She summons me, along with her youth party cadres, to the office. On her desk is a shiny new cellphone. She ignores my approving look.

-As I believe it very important that we keep in close touch with each other on important party matters, I wish you to contact me on my cellphone so that we can discuss any problems you might have. But, she holds up a warning hand to the wide smiles of inclusion into her private world, it is a secret number, exclusively for you, no calls before 9 a.m. and no calls after 5 p.m. You should keep your calls brief and I will always be happy to hear from you.

And she gives that exclusive number to the fifty chosen ones. When they leave, clutching their secret, Avanti sticks her tongue out at me.

■

In the passage of time, I have not forgotten Aditya, though Avanti never mentions his name within my hearing. I believe it is good advice to always watch for the enemy that can upset all your plans. He is diligently working his way up the slippery slope of filmmaking, a notoriously fickle business. As in an election, success depends on the voters, or ticket buyers—the queues outside a box office. He works as an assistant director to famous directors, eschewing working with his father, rejecting the mantle which would make his life easier. He left the city when she left him in the rain and travelled constantly to exotic locations—New York, Sydney, Paris, Rome—to make a myriad heroes and heroines dance and sing to admiring passersby, bewildered by these apparitions in their midst. He is reaching the point at which he will begin to direct but at the moment he is still a nobody and his name never appears in the press or on television linked with sultry, pouting actresses with ferocious manes of hair and large bosoms. I have my Intel watching him and I receive daily reports on his progress. I know the mantle of celebrity, a golden garment that dissolves at first failure, will fall on him soon.

Once a week I visit her mother. I mentioned it once to Avanti but she made no enquiries of my visit and showed no concern. She has cultivated her father's indifference, a form of love and flattery. Shakuntala is a widow in every sense of the word, a lone woman haunting a rambling bungalow looked after by servants. She wears the white of widows to emphasize her abandonment by her husband and daughter. She always welcomes me, I am the source of gossip about her family as she doesn't read the papers or watch television. At first, I'd visited her in the evenings, slipping out of the palace when there was a banquet or a conference, but Shakuntala was incoherent at those times. Her new passion, her only companion in her solitude, is a few bottles of Chilean Chardonnay. I enjoy a sip but never more as it dulls my mind. Dark clouds shroud her mind in the evenings. We discuss Avanti always, and her husband almost in passing, though I know she cannot escape the spell he cast on her long ago. It simmers, even though she has reached the shore of despair.

-How often do they see each other?
-Daily, all about politics.
-In her office.
-Yes.
-Only there?
-Yes. Where else? They're both very busy.
-In her bedroom? She is persistent. In his?
-I'm asleep and not patrolling the palace, I lie, persistent too. I don't mention their private meetings in more intimate surroundings.
-I tried to stop her leaving but she is under his spell, like a sleeping beauty but awake.

She sighs then, after the brief inquisition. I note a spark of derangement in her eyes, that comes and goes. My imagination? I advised my emperor: language can be so subtle, the meanings of the spoken word should be weighed and judged with great care, for it's the tone that has the inner meaning. There is an undertone of remorse, a fateful affliction that squeezes the soul dry, in the longing

that a mother has for the child who rejected her. And I am no comfort to her, only the conduit of this sadness.
 –How is my husband? Is he keeping well?
 –Yes, very busy, as you can see from...
 –I don't like to see him on television, a stranger speaking. Does he ask about me?
 –Yes, he promises to see you soon, but the burden of office is very heavy.
 Lies are a necessary balm for a wounded heart, although it gives false hope. Hope, even if false, is better than being forgotten. No medication can purge love; the sediment clings stubbornly to the walls of a heart. We return to her second concern.
 –I wish she had married Aditya. He is a good boy. A film director and an artist would make the perfect match. Does she still paint? I loved her work.
 –No. She has forgotten the sun-drenched room, facing south for the morning sun and the light that artist's desire for their work. The easel still stands with a half-finished canvas, abandoned mid-stroke, and other paintings are on the floor, their faces turned to the wall like so many mischievous school boys under punishment.
 –Do you hear from him?
 I answer in honesty: no.
 –I know he will return.
 Alarmed, I ask, mentally castigating my spy for false information: he is in touch with you? He says he will be back soon?
 –I have a sense he will. He loves her.
 If she had phrased it another way I would have believed her. How can one trust a woman's intuition, her power to foretell the future? More kings have fallen on their women's intuition than mangoes from a tree. She remains focused on marriage for her daughter, wishing only to fulfil any mother's duty.
 –What else do I have to live for but to see her married, and cradle my grandchildren?
 A young man emerging from the house interrupts us this evening. My spy has informed me of his presence. She met him at a discourse on the *Bhagavad Gita* held at a friend's house. He recited the enchanting slokas and ensnared her dispirited soul. Swamis are common as coins in a bazaar. He comes like a ghost into the dusk,

dressed in white from neck to toe, a garment like a gown afloat around his slim body. He has abundant hair framing an angelic face, the lips curve in a welcoming smile (as if I am a stranger to this household) and his eyes are wide and pale brown. Milky coffee. His nose, straight and long, divides the high cheekbones. The slope between his eyes and mouth give him a simian look, reminding me of a pet I had whose chattering disturbed my contemplation but who was still a small pleasure in my life. His eyes sparkle, as if sprinkled with stardust, attesting to his good-natured spirituality. Shakuntala looks at him with longing as he floats towards us and, when he is near, she rises, only to kneel and touch his lotus-like feet in Gucci sandals. His delicate fingers are be-ringed with diamonds.

-My guru, Jagdish, she announces in a tremulous voice, rising. Expecting me to also touch his feet, but I remain seated. She has found an addition to the many deities that hang in her prayer room and I don't cast any blame on her. The warmth of a human is more comforting than a cold, indifferent image that is deaf, dumb, blind.

He holds up a hand, a policeman of piety, to bless my indifference. I have heard much about you. He has a soft, chiming voice, like temple bells summoning his worshippers. Although there is a higher pitch, as if his balls haven't yet dropped. I also note his accent to be faintly American; I've heard the accent on television and can now distinguish one spoken English from another. He doesn't avert his eyes at my disfigurement, warned no doubt.

-He has just returned from America. He has many followers there and he's on his way to his ashram. You must have heard of him.

-No.

-It doesn't matter, he smiles, forgiving my ignorance. I know you and that is more important.

-He knows my husband is the most powerful man in the state.

-What good is power when he has lost his soul?

-My husband never had a soul to start with, so he has lost nothing. My daughter is not to be trusted. She sighs loudly. What a family to belong to.

-Everyone belongs to strange families, if we delve beneath the surface of their subterfuges, her guru comments.

The words do not comfort her. She needs more than language, more than the physical embrace to save her from despair. She needs love to strengthen her but she lost that many years ago, when she gave it away to the man she met on the train.

-I have one more duty to perform for this family—get Avanti married. Then I am done, I will be free of all ties to the family, she says.

-You are a comfort to Shakuntala and for that I bless you, the guru says to me.

He makes a gesture of blessing, cupping his palms above my head. It's time for my meditation.

He drifts into the garden.

-You should go away, I say to Shakuntala. I need to widen the developing rift.

-You're right. I will stay in his ashram for a few weeks. You should come too, it's in the mountains, away from all this. She dismissively waves away her present life. I will pray that Avanti will marry soon when I'm there.

I don't mention that Avanti's father too is concerned on that subject. He needs her to marry an ally, to protect his flanks and strengthen his coalition but she has stubbornly refused or ignored his suggestions about that particular suitor. A portly young prince of a politician, preparing to follow his portly father's footsteps. An unpleasant person with two rape charges against him winding slowly through the courts, confident he will be proved innocent of such horrendous acts. He has the money for a hundred judges. In my treatise, I wrote many shastras on this subject and can remember just a few: He who defiles a virgin before she reaches majority will have his hand cut off and pay a fine. If the virgin dies, the offender is executed. No man shall have sexual intercourse with a woman against her will.

When Avanti informs me of the possible marriage, I advise her: He's a good choice, marry him and this will strengthen your father's position. Of course, I have an ulterior motive. Aditya will then be unattainable. If he lurks like a thief in the shadows of her mother's memory, and mine, surely he is present in hers too.

-He's fat, she says. Disdain. Disgust. How would you like to get into bed with a fat woman?

-Ahh, if only I could experience such pleasures of resting on mounds of fat breasts and a fat tummy, it will seem as if I'm flying.

–You have no taste, Chan, she scolds me.

–Lying on a thin woman is like resting on a bier of sticks, all hard. I try to cajole her again, wear down her resistance. Marry, if only for the sake of it, as a single woman in politics is suspect. Voters like to see happy marriages and families. It's a necessary deception, like everything else.

–I won't marry fatso, she says in a schoolgirlish voice, and I expect her to stamp her feet too to emphasize the decision. Then she turns my advice back on me with the questions. Should a prince or princess marry a man who could possibly be more powerful than she is? You don't know that family at all, they will try to usurp the party from us and my rightful place beside my father. You tell me.

I bow to my own wisdom, though I dislike being reminded of it. You're right. Marry a man who is weaker than you are, and protect the party.

–Well go and find me such a man.

–What about a handsome young man from your crowd, the party people, your privileged friends?

–They are all rich and brainless. He would make me weep with boredom, as he'd only speak about money, expensive cars and malt whiskies.

–Then we must search, as it is important you marry. If necessary, take on a lover to help you pass the time until you find the ideal match.

I meant this jocularly. In a court, there is no better way to pass the time than to love, briefly, the delightful company of willing women who too know the desires of their lithe bodies. Sex is a contagion, once tasted, once explored, once sated, it devours the mind and the body.

–Chan, how can you even suggest something so...so disgusting? She is genuinely shocked. You have absolutely no morals.

She was incarcerated for many years in a convent school to give her the sheen of respectability, even as brigands anoint themselves as princes. Her mentor, Sister Benita, would have boxed both her ears and wrestled her to the ground for such lascivious thoughts. Sister Benita, a woman of sensual beauty, was a Belgian pole dancer who, while performing a truly lascivious pole dance for the Minister of Health and Welfare at a five-star hotel, had slipped off the pole, cracked her ankle and was rushed to the public ward of a government hospital, as her health insurance had expired. There, among the poor, the destitute and dying, she found salvation when a cripple tripped over a dead man's leg, fell on her ankle and restored it to health. Experiencing an instant miracle, she renounced the pole forever and entered the convent.

Avanti storms away with a toss of her head, indignation burning from every pore. I have never mastered woman craft, my wisdom is statecraft. I had planned to write a manual on sexual positions and erotic longings but my death distracted me. When Aditya was her lover, they fucked often, and her virginity was soon a dim memory. And now she is conveniently forgetting her father. Her maidenly horror amuses me. I know she blots her relationship with her father from her mind, from her conscience. I had an ulterior motive (as always) in making my suggestion—I was trying to break the spell that her father has cast over her, to save her from the watery grave that awaits such a love.

The following year, her love is rewarded.

SIX

HER FATHER SUMMONS me to the grand Durbar Hall of the palace at midnight. I was still awake, I sleep sparingly, knowing how precious time is, and was reading a history of the last thousand years. As I read the book, all that seemed to rise from its pages was a vast confusion of endless wars, as man seems never to have lost his appetite for killing. Empires rising and falling to the steady breath of passing time, leaving behind the detritus of their rule, crumbling monuments, dead people; kings come and kings go, many lacking their heads. I learned that even as corporates rule the state today, through the President, that a corporate once ruled here through a foreign monarch. This history tells me that the world is full of collisions, that actions started a day or even a century ago, move forward inexorably to impact nations and people—who are usually unaware that a juggernaut is about to destroy or deflect their lives. Actions performed by strangers, friends, lovers, enemies shape all our destinies.

When I am not reading and have some spare time I visit museums to learn about the past from artefacts, bronzes, sculptures, paintings, scientific discoveries. I explore too the mosques and churches. The mosques are peaceful with a sense of serenity, open spaces for man to follow his beliefs. The churches are more sombre, enclosed, and lit through the coloured windows depicting scenes from the Bible. And there too I feel the sacred. Like a GPS, they merely lead you on a different route to end up at the same destination—God. That's if you believe there is one. If these religions were practised in my time, the Emperor would have granted them space to build their places of worship. However, should any of these new religions disturb the peace of the state, on my advice, he would grind them into the dust.

I set my book aside and mount my electric cart, invented for a game called golf, and thread my humming way through the corridors and halls of the presidential palace. The Durbar Hall is glorious, the ceiling aglow with the richly coloured paintings of various deities, looking down benignly on the sole occupant this night. The hall measures twenty-five metres in length by fifteen metres in breadth; a long walk from the main entrance, high enough for a giant. On the walls, hang portraits of historical figures gazing out sternly, Britons and Indians too. The marble floor is scattered with richly textured carpets woven out of the finest silks. An eighteenth century Venetian chandelier hanging in the centre lends it an air of opulence, a place for feudal respect and much fawning. He sits on his favourite chair, with arm-rests like lion's paws. It is his favourite perch and on which he receives all his cabinet ministers, party workers, foreign dignitaries who come to pay homage, and the press looking for a photo op. Of course, it isn't quite a gaddi, like a Mughal throne or even a British one, but it radiates the same aura of power and vanity. The seat has a plump scarlet cushion which gives its occupant a divine sense of pleasure. It is sensual, a thrill rising up from the seat to suffuse his body, like an orgasm. The entire chair is made of gold and impossible to shift. Two smaller chairs are adjacent to his right for visiting presidents and prime ministers, not too near to suggest intimacy, but close enough to hear low conversations. On the wall behind him is a massive oil portrait of himself, splendid in a white kurta, sitting in the very chair he occupies now. The painting has to be included in every photo op to remind the citizenry that he is a permanent fixture in their lives. As always he is impeccable in his dress, mine crumpled from study. On a side table a half glass of Chivas with melting ice. His head sinks in thought, chin near his chest, but I still feel his calculating eyes on me. Dark, brooding, unreadable. All powerful men possess crouching beasts within them, even as my emperor had.

    The bearer opens a new bottle, the seal broken in front of him; the bearer drinks the first amber liquid. My emperor too feared poison, it's more insidious than an assassin's sword. I protected him by testing his food and drink by using birds, such as the heron, cuckoo and partridge—which are very sensitive to poisons—and also by tasting the food myself before he touched any dish. I even took the precaution of adding an infinitesimal pinch of poison to his food right from his youth so that he gradually grew resistant to it. The President waits, impatiently, while having his glass filled, then the bearer stumbles to his corner, intoxicated.

    -I am thinking, he breaks the silence only to allow it to return in a long pause. ...What do you think of my daughter's performance as President of the Youth Organization? Truthfully now.

To ask a man whose name means falsehood to be truthful is like asking a tiger to eschew meat. I am her mentor; *her* future concerns me, not his. I reply: In all honesty, I would say she has performed brilliantly, President. I have watched and guided her, as you instructed.

–I am thinking of testing her again. Do you think she has now had enough experience in understanding the party?

–She is as wily and devious as any of the party faithful.

–I want to promote her in some way. What about as President of the party, not just the youth wing. He sips his scotch, the golden liquid glazing his eyes.

–May I make another suggestion? He nods, unaware I have been waiting for this conversation. I already know the answer as my hacker has given it to me. It will bring me closer to his defeat. I am thinking of her standing for election.

–Do you think it wise?

–It will be a test if she has your charisma, I say. Always flatter the powerful.

She has a cat's smile when she hears the news from her father and I witness her throw her arms around him and kiss him. Not on the cheek or the forehead. On the mouth, and their embrace of power and themselves is passionate. I am just another piece of furniture in her room, now decorated to her expensive tastes; no longer a simple, young girl with artistic longings. The furnishings chosen from Harrods, Bon Marché, Bloomingdales, the pushcarts of the wealthy. She possesses a piece of plastic though it's called 'platinum', issued by a Swiss bank. Without even soiling her hands with paper notes and coins, she can spend 100,000 Euros. It's a gift from her father. It's madness to give a woman such an amount to spend. We know there is no limit to her necessities. She could empty my emperor's treasury within a day. Her new bed is not as narrow as her childhood one, but wide enough to accommodate another, if need be. Her curtains are muted pink, her beautiful dresser a foreign antique from another era. Bookshelves take up part of the wall, filled with political manuals, histories and biographies of the thieves and scoundrels who have ascended to being presidents, prime ministers, despots. They are her favourite how-to books. Otherwise she reads romantic novels, and sometimes leafs through books on art, large as granite slabs and as heavy; magical in their reproductions of Raphael, Da Vinci, Rembrandt, Picasso and other foreign names, at least one on M.F Hussain, remain imprisoned in her old room. Silken carpets protect her bare feet from cold marble and cover every inch of the room, an exorbitant expense. In my day, there were only rush mats on stone floors.

-Which constituency? is her first question. A true politician.

-A safe one, District 18, a lucky number.

Safe may sound comforting but her father is experienced in the wilfulness of the electorate who scavenge on the peripheries of power in the hope of improving their sorry lot in a state that shows no interest in their aspirations. That's another problem with democracy, your dependence on total strangers, not your vassals, as the wellsprings of your power. How can one truly trust them, except by manipulating the vote count; her father is an expert in this sleight-of-hand. I learn it is common practice in other democracies too, except more subtle.

-But you have… She snaps her fingers, trying to remember the present incumbent, a man pliable as wet rope.

-He has graciously decided to resign. I suggested it and he accepted, though it was expensive persuading him to give up a lucrative seat with big potential. But the money can be recouped quickly. Corporates have approached me for free land to set up industries, and mine the jungle for copper.

He has bank accounts in many names and shell companies (whatever they may be). American dollars, Canadian dollars, Singapore dollars, Australian dollars, euros, pounds, francs, kroner. He has yet to trust roubles. In my day the emperor's treasury was kept in rooms below the palace, guarded by a hundred soldiers, and the gold, silver, diamonds, rubies, emeralds were counted each day, thrice, to ensure there was no pilferage. When he travelled across his land, the entire treasury, carried by elephants, accompanied him, as to leave it unguarded would only invite an invasion from a neighbouring prince. Today, all that's needed is a pin code—a password to her father's wealth in distant cities. An honest politician, I have written, is a no-thing. It is by cleverness, divorced from all morals, that kingship is to be vindicated. To quote myself again: *He who shoots an arrow kills but one at best, but he who uses clever thoughts kills even the babe within its mother's body.*

–How much will it cost for the by-election campaign? Is there a budget? How many party workers can I deploy? Which newspapers, television networks, internet magazines, and social media networks do we control?

These are the practicalities a politician must take into consideration on the thorny route to power. It is not a poor man's sport. Avanti knows the way, she has learnt well from her father the deviousness required to ensure the seat remains safe.

–The party is flush with funds, he laughs, releasing her from his sensual embrace. Thanks to all your efforts. That's why I thought it's time for you to work more closely with me after the election. You'd like that?

–Oh yes. Those two words, spoken in happiness contain all the adoration she feels. She will no longer be a party worker, sitting in that old office, but will have her feet firmly on the first rung of power, legitimized by her election.

–You'll campaign for me of course.

He lifts his arms in resignation, letting them fall on her waist, a smile of regret, tender and loving: I will be too busy with the budget session and as you know we have problems with those insurgents in our jungle.

–You must punish them severely, she says passionately. They have no idea how hard you work for them. Ungrateful bastards. Let the police deal with them and you come with me. She hugs him, holds on to him as if he is a rock and he is throwing her into a stormy sea, alone.

–I wish I could.

–We can postpone until…

–No. He is naturally firm, rightly so but she doesn't know his reasons for her to launch her first election campaign without the warming shadow of his power. He wants to see if she can win without him and this will prove that his name is still the power behind her victory; should she lose, he will distance himself from her defeat. Any prince would be proud of such a tactical move.

She weeps softly at his rejection, and he consoles her, dabbing her eyes with a fine linen handkerchief, murmuring platitudes to comfort her.

–I'll be all alone, she wails. How will I act? How will I speak? What will I say to those people? I need your guidance.

–I'll be there on the cell phone, he consoles. You will have Chanakya to guide and advise you on all those matters. And take Ramesh to help with the other arrangements. He is good at such things.

–Chan! She looks at me with hope...

–And you'll have 'X' category security. I have spoken to our Home Minister.

–X!! Such dramatic dismay in just one word, surely a lost actor. She does show promise.

To add insult to injury she will only have a four-car cavalcade, only a dozen cops to protect her with their black weapons pointing in all directions. I fear them more than the crowds that will gather, peacefully. Y category has thirty cars while the President is YY+1 which means fifty cars, along with ambulances. The powerful and the rich must be comfortable in their travels and cause enough chaos in their movements to intimidate the people.

–A plane...

–No plane, no helicopters. Everyone must see you as you move among them, along roads, past fields, villages and towns. You must be earthbound before you become airborne. Chanakya knows this. He turns to me. Don't you?

–Yes, President. *A prince must show himself daily to his people to reassure them that he lives, as he is the heartbeat of the kingdom.*

–How many will I face in this election? I know it's a safe seat for the party but will they vote for me?

–Half a million. They will come out of curiosity, and you must persuade them that you should be their choice.

–Couldn't you just appoint me to the Assembly? I won't be good at this.

–Of course not, he taps lightly on her cheek, curbing his strength. Without a seat, how will you follow me? I don't want the press baying about nepotism and favouritism.

–Whom do we own there in the media?

–Any of them; all of them. They're cheap as whores. Pay them to write good things about you, buy crates of Black Label to distribute among them, feed them well, and they will obey. But be careful of one or two who are poisonous vipers.

In my day, the media didn't exist; only rumour-mongers who spread malice about the emperor among his subjects. My emperor was ruthless when he found them; he would boil them alive in large copper pots or his war elephant would crush their heads with one foot. They deserved their fate. There are not enough copper pots or war elephants to mete out punishments to all the people in the media who deserve them.

–I need you to win, and win well which is why you have a safe constituency. Then you can be with me always. He smiles: Seduce me with your speech; tempt me into your arms.

–I can't orate as well as you, you know that.

–Learn then, my speeches are on DVDs, as you know. You'll also have 10,000 party workers campaigning for you.

And with the promise of such an army, enough to conquer a small kingdom, he leaves us. They will be unleashed on an unsuspecting populace, cajoling, bribing, threatening. Avanti subsides on her sofa, frowning, then smiling and I know that she is an actress. She has what she wants, deceiving and flattering her father to think she needs him while she is happy to campaign alone and test herself in the cauldron of democracy. She knows if she wins without him by her side, it will strengthen her position.

–I want a map of District 18, she tells Ramesh over the intercom. He has been expecting that request and instantly appears at the door with the roll. Ramesh stands watching us as we study the map, I wave my hand to dismiss him back to his cubicle outside. He looks to her.

–Yes, you may go.

When he leaves, I remind her, as she can be forgetful: He is your father's spy and will recite every word we speak together. Even now, Ramesh tells your father you have asked for this map. This is when you use Vikram as your intelligence in District 18.

We lean over the map which we have unrolled on the table, holding it down with paperweights. Like any state, anywhere, there are three layers of people—the elite, the middle class, the poor. History may have shuffled the numbers since my day but the definitions remain constant. The elite will always be low in number as they do not wish for upstarts to join them in their elevated positions, and they will always remain in control, enriching themselves through devious means. The middle class has attained a certain level of comfort and will fight to protect that, aspiring to the elite that will never open its doors; the poor...the poor remain the same, hungry, uneducated, unemployed but Avanti must woo them, in their huge numbers. The elite will give her the money, the middle class always abstain, the poor vote. District 18 is 250 kilometres east of the capital and the thin black line travels from it to pass through the three large towns, fortresses of the middle class, before abruptly ending its journey, exhausted by the distance. There are approximately fifty-two villages within the district, less or more—the poor await their saviour, patient as ever for uplift. To the east of District 18 is jungle, rich with spotted deer, sambar, wild pigs and luxuriant trees. On this map, there is writing across this jungle—copper. And the corporates wait like vultures to swoop on the jungle to steal it. I recall a line from the *Mahabharata*: *Do not cut down the forest with its tigers and do not banish the tiger from the forest. The tiger perishes without the forest, and the forest perishes without its tigers. Therefore the tiger should stand guard over the forest and the forest should protect all its tigers.* But who listens to wisdom, even mine is ignored. She rests her elbows on the map, her chin in cupped palms, looking down at the flat surface of her possible constituency. She traces the borders with a finger then, rests it on the towns, villages, open spaces, the jungle.

-I've never been there, she says softly, more to the map than to me. You need more roads for a start.

-It will be hot, dusty and humid, I warn. Sweat vaporizes in such heat, only to re-emerge from panting pores, and the dust will layer you like powder, scented only with the smell of the poor.

-I wish father could just appoint me, instead of...she says petulantly, staring at the map.

-It will be good experience in learning the art of falsehoods.

-How many will be standing against me?

-The usual numbers, eight, nine or twenty. They all want the same power. There is no finer motive for lying and cheating. You must learn to lie better than them and you have the advantage over them. You're the President's daughter, you are in close proximity to power and can perform miracles because of that.

–What should I say?

–First, what you believe. This is for practice. Then say what you want them to believe. In this way, you will learn to avoid your true essence.

She jumps to her feet and climbs onto a chair, looks down at me, an electorate of one, representing the thousands who will watch her.

–My people, we must ask ourselves what has happened to our state. Her voice is thin and nervous, even in the privacy of her room. The elevation has already affected her senses.

–No. Never ask a question as they will then expect an answer and in that answer you will have to blame the President for the state of the people. But it's a good idea to blame someone else—the Opposition, world economy, the weather.

–It is the Opposition parties that are to blame for the problems, they refuse to understand that the economy is not working due to their continued clamouring against the President and his wise policies. Every effort to reform and reshape this country is met with resistance in the House. Outside, we have insurgents roaming the country with their guns, frightening people, robbing them of their hard-earned money. They claim to be your friends but they're not. In other democracies…

–Don't mention other countries as this will give people ideas when they go home and look up how those countries are doing so well. They'll Google…

–Not everyone can Google.

–Don't believe that. You must start making promises right from the first word.

–My people, it's time for us to fulfil our promises. Free food, free education, monthly salaries, otherwise the opposition will take away…

–No. Don't threaten or hector, be compassionate. Put life into your words—you're standing like a mechanical doll. Use your hands, your body, they're the instruments of rhetoric and seduction. Make love to the people watching you.

–Sex in a campaign.

–It always works. They're looking at a young, attractive woman, the men thinking it would be good to bed you, the women wishing they could look like you.

–Should I use Father's name?

–As often as you can. Our people are still ignorant, they believe in names. They've honoured him with their trust. So they will trust you too, as his daughter.

I set up a full-length mirror for her to perform in front of, and catch a view of myself. I don't look in the mirror even shaving this irregular face but am always caught by surprise at my reflection. My image here is clear, precise, perfect. At least, so I believe as I'm not certain whether I am looking at myself or at a total stranger. In my past, I saw only a blurred outline reflected in polished silver or in the still waters of a pond and I believe this is both magical and an illusion. Whom I see is not really who I am, it's just the outer image that is deceptive.

Avanti has the talent to be a consummate actor and she learns how to use her hands, her arms, express her emotions through her whole body. We make a list of promises for the poor, trailing them as a fisherman the hook in the flowing waters. Free food, thrice daily, free schools, free university, water piped to every home, free cooking gas, free cellphones for women (they always vote, just to get out of their hovels), free electricity, free air travel, free train travel, laptops for their children, guaranteed employment.

–Free liquor for the men, she suggests.

–Then you'll lose the women's votes, they have enough problems with drunken husbands squandering their money.

–The opposition will of course cry themselves hoarse that these promises will bankrupt the treasury. In one breath. In the other, they will promise free motorcycles, free petrol and diesel.

She is joyful in compiling her 'list of freebies', as she calls it. My emperor had no such largesse to draw upon. All he offered was justice, equal for all. But that's one promise Avanti cannot make; no one will believe her but will believe the other promises, as they are tangible, something they can hold in their hands if they ever get them.

The mirror doesn't give her the distance she needs to judge her performances. I am the cameraman, sound recorder, director. It's like films, creating a sense of glamour and goodness, an artificiality that doesn't ever exist except on the screen. After each shoot, we study the results on the giant television HD television screen in her room. She appears so large and lifelike, even the pores on her face are visible and we decide to hire a make-up woman to dust away the flaws, re-shape her eyebrows, trim her hair to a severe length.

–Now, we need to give you a new image. Just being the daughter of the President is not enough, I tell her one day, some weeks into our regimen to transform her into a political candidate of consequence.

–It is in this district, she insists. That's going to win me the votes. I don't need to add anything else.

–Voters like to elect educated people in the hope that the person has some intelligence. Not that education grants intelligence, only arcane knowledge, but a few degrees behind your name will sway them even further.

–I have a diploma in painting.

Ahh, we're getting there. She didn't finish her course, but she has created a diploma.

–They'll believe it's for house painting, furniture painting. You need…B.As, B.Coms, B.Scs. Even a master's in something. Economics. And you must have activities, social work, soiling your hands among the poor. You must show you belong to the people and not just the elite of this society.

–The press will find out.

–The press are like pigeons, feed them bread crumbs and they will swallow them.

She happily accepts my suggestions and we work together on her laptop creating a new persona for her—a splendidly educated, compassionate woman who can sing and dance the Bharatanatyam too. I want her to win, to distance herself from her father, as it will give her independence to make her own decisions with the power that falls into her hands.

I notice she makes no mention of her mother, despite knowing of my visits. I haven't seen Shakuntala for weeks now, as the tutoring of Avanti demands all my time.

–Are you going to tell your mother?

–I can't. I know what she'll say. She'll scold me, she never wanted me to be in politics. Then we'll row and I'll get angry and walk out on her. She'll read about it in the papers. You tell her.

I know she loves her mother which is why she fears her wrath. It is one of the reasons she neglects her. She remembers her mother's battle to wean her away from her father's seduction and the fact that she chose to walk away compounds her guilt.

It's a long drive and I leave very early. Shakuntala no longer lives in the bungalow down the road but has moved to Swami Jagdish's ashram, high in the mountains. The car leaves the plains behind and starts zigzagging up the ghat road, so narrow that we stop to allow lorries and buses to race down. Traffic stops often, and we wait for the jam to clear somewhere ahead. On one side, houses and shops tumble down the hills to the road's edges, on the other the front doors of homes and shops open directly onto the road, while the rooms behind hang in space, supported by slender pillars sunk into the sides of the steep valleys. A slight shake of the earth and they will tumble down like dice thrown across the table.

Waiting for the traffic to move, I see a small signboard, the lower half covered by a bush. In black lettering it asks two questions: *Who are you, God? Where are you, God?* Further questions must lie beneath. I cannot answer either question, despite my years of non-existence, as I did not find the god this board seeks anywhere. I am embarrassed by this to a certain degree. Especially as I was a Brahman once, a believer in Mahavir and am now an unbeliever.

As we climb higher, the drop grows steeper. I am not used to such heights and cling to the seat, my eyes shut, begging the driver to go slow, as I am in no hurry to die. On both sides are deodars, pine oak and sal forests, the air sweet with their perfume, clean and refreshing but pungent as spices. It grows cooler and I'm grateful it's still summer. We finally reach the ashram, turning off the road into a dirt lane winding through the trees. A small valley cossets the rustic buildings and tents scattered between the trees. A guard prevents me from entering until the guru himself identifies me. He is still in white, still capable of floating through the shadows and broken sunlight. The trick is to take tiny steps.

–We do not permit visitors, he says in his gentle, high-pitched voice. They disturb the tranquility of the ashram, disrupt meditation.

–Avanti sent me to see her mother. I am sure you'll understand a daughter's message of love will not in any way perturb her. Love is meditation too. It brings peace of mind, a freedom from concern and worry, tranquility to the soul.

I too possess a silken tongue to match any guru's. He frowns, thinking of escalating our exchange of such flowery thoughts but then decides against it, nods sagely, and accepts my presence. The guard steps aside and I enter this sacred place.

-Please deposit your cellphone with the guard, the guru says. It is not permitted as my followers cling to them as a child to its mother. As with other sins, abstinence is good for the soul.

She is not alone in this wooded glade. Dreamy men and women, caught up in the trance of spirituality, move soft as shadows or sit still as idols. There are white people too, among our brown ones, with blonde hair, red hair, brown hair, silver hair, eyes of blue, green and grey, shedding their unsettled lives like a snake its skin. They glance at me, attracted and repelled, their fragile calm exteriors rippling with unease. They still have a long journey before they reach their spiritual terminus. They look sleek and indulged. As we pass, they acknowledge their guru with smiles, pressing their palms together, bowing in homage even as his shadow touches them. I will make no comment on their belief in this guru, except the world even then was crowded with charlatans, as people need divine sustenance from man, not god. They want the human voice, the human touch to keep loneliness at bay. He leads me to Shakuntala, seated against a deodar, reading. She looks up and, seeing me, smiles widely. She rises gracefully. I have always admired her movements; she is so at ease with her body, like an athlete. Her face glows like the others' in this newfound solace. The frowns of worry, the wrinkles of loneliness are erased. Her eyes are clear, the seductive pale brown no longer distracted by the redness of despair. Her face has lost the puffiness induced by alcohol and there's a sense of purity and purpose about her. She appears stronger, both in the body and in the mind, for which I'm grateful to the guru. Now, she doesn't genuflect to him as the others, and almost ignores him in her focus on me.

-Chanakya, I'm so happy to see you. She embraces me, then stands back. You're looking well as ever. She turns to her guru who hovers like a watchful spirit. We'll need to talk in private.

-You must not be distracted from your meditation. Then adds firmly. Only fifteen minutes as his presence brings in bad vibrations of the outside world. He leaves, not floating but stomping his tiny feet at his casual dismissal.

We sit facing each other, the book between us. It's the writing

of her guru and I've no wish to contaminate my mind too.
  –How is my daughter? She sent you, didn't she?
  –Yes. She sends her love.
  –She could have it carried it herself. Why message it? That's what the young do now, just text their emotions with funny little figures.
  –She's well. And I see you are too? Are you happy here?
  –What is happy? Is there a definition? It's only a fleeting feeling we have. I'm content, let's say. I like the company; there are many interesting people here. It's better than living alone in that bungalow. You've come here for a reason. I heard he made her President of the Youth Wing.

I smile. News travels slowly here. That was a few years ago.
  –I wish I could see her. She must have grown. She speaks as if she last saw Avanti as a small child, not a grown woman. Now tell me truthfully which one of them sent you?
  –Avanti. She is going to stand for election.
  –And she couldn't tell me herself because she knows I'd dissuade her. She is naturally aggrieved at such a slight.
  –Scold is the word she used.
  –I've lost her. She sits in pensive silence, the glow fading as if the news is draining the blood from her face. When she was young, three, four, five years old, we were so close. She clung to me, and we seldom saw my husband, he was away so much. But when he returned she would run to him and throw her arms around him and while he was home she seemed to forget me. She took her afternoon naps with him and I should've known then but I closed my eyes. When he left, she would return to me but with less warmth, as if looking over her shoulder the whole time. And when she did look at me, she saw a woman who had done nothing with her life but sit at home. I had my masters in politics, history, I knew more than my husband and I was going to be a professor and teach the young that all politics is theft. But he refused to allow me that freedom. She doesn't cry; she accepts her fate though there is still defiance in her eyes, waiting for release. I pray it will happen for her one day. I tried but Avanti was so enamoured with her father and he promised more than I could. Banditry is in his blood and he is passing it on to her. She will become him, except as a female, and there will be no end. Genetically his DNA is bent as a corkscrew. I had prayed

mine would straighten it out in our daughter. She sighs again. I wish she had married Aditya. He's doing well, you know. He told me his new film is going to the Toronto Film Festival.

–He told you? You've seen him? He's come here? The man is haunting me again, circling us, knowing his conduit is Shakuntala and her partiality towards him. He cannot meet Avanti, not yet at least, not until victory.

–He wrote to me. We write each other letters. She giggles over this secret like a schoolgirl revealing love notes. You don't like him, do you?

–I do, I insist vehemently. I don't add, at a distance as he is a threat to my plans. I'm delighted to hear his film is a success. I must get a DVD. Do you have one?

–They're banned in the ashram. No gadgets, no liquor, no sex, no magazines, no television, no books. She pauses. I have no regret at such deprivations.

I am a consummate actor, as you know. I have already seen the DVD; it was sent anonymously to Avanti at the palace and I intercepted it. (I have suborned some members of the palace postal system to be my spies). She didn't need such a distraction. It is a good film, off-beat, artistic, the story of a young man who first emulates his adored father and then rebels against him and the violent confrontation between them that follows. It's disturbing, enlightening, partially autobiographical as Aditya did confront his father's work. But it isn't violent, as in his film, no doubt a wish, a fantasy, as we struggle against the suffocating chains our parents bind around us. Many children murder, metaphorically, their parents; only princes commit the crimes physically.

–Where is Avanti standing for election?
–District 18.
–It's a poor place. No doubt that's why her father chose it for her. I hope she'll work hard for the people and prove him wrong. She grips my hand, pleading. Tell me, what I should do? Or is it too late for her to love me again? I must do something.
–Be patient.
–Is that your only advice? Does he ask about me?
–Yes, always.
–Liar, even you, the expert, cannot convince me. She sighs. I

think about him daily. Not think. I feel more. I cannot cleanse him from my heart, no matter how much I try. Even in meditation, he flows into my mind, unbidden as if waiting to distract me. How does one get rid of love? It's a disease and I haven't a cure. Do you?

—None. Even time hasn't an antidote for such a sweet poison.

—I wish I'd had the courage to...to...have done something to him.

—You mustn't say such things. You are a calm and peaceful woman. Her ferocity concerns me. I have witnessed women in the emperor's harem slash out at a man's throat. A woman's heart can be as dark and perilous as an emperor's. She stares at me for a very long moment through those lovely eyes; something flares in them and then fades quickly, leaving me to imagine I glimpsed the rage.

—What do the people say about me? I'm not with my husband at all those endless functions.

—He tells them you are visiting an ashram. People accept that as a sign of your piety and understand how necessary it is to renew oneself.

—Is he still drinking too much?

—I see him rarely, only when summoned. He drinks, still.

Now with concern, leaning forward to grip my hand. Does Avanti drink too?

—A glass of Chablis, occasionally. A sip at dinner time. I don't. And this comforts her. But I am the bootlegger for her wine. The palace has a cellar in its bowels, deep and dark and chilly, the remnants of a past empire, where there are thousands of bottles of wine—red, white, rose, champagne—covered in dust and cobwebs; when Avanti makes a request, I mount my vehicle and hum away to the cellar to snatch a bottle.

—And no doubt each day my husband accumulates more power, more wealth. She sighs loudly, hopeless in her love. I knew what he was and tried to change him. My father warned me against this marriage but my love blinded me. He was very reluctant to give away his only child but, as you know, my husband has a persuasive tongue and a commanding manner. As a professor of history my father knew how the past always fashions the present and that my husband could not help himself. I had a choice then, you know.

—A choice! Just one? I would have thought a woman of your beauty and intelligence would have men falling at her feet.

She laughs. I discouraged them with my nerdy mind. There was one and I made the wrong choice in marrying the man I fell I love with. It would have been wiser to marry the man who loved me very much, except I didn't love him in return. Possibly in time, I would have. She smiles through her memories. He was doing his master's in...I can't remember in what now—and we had the same professor. So we'd meet monthly in our professor's office. He was two years younger than me, and quite handsome I thought then. He was slim, a bit too intense though, but he told me one afternoon that he was in love with me. He was so shy in that admission. I thought of him more as a brother, a good friend as we'd have coffee after our meetings in the college canteen. He played a lot of cricket but I think we talked mostly politics and the future. When you're young, those are your main concerns. He would look at me with great intensity through his spectacles. He had gentle brown eyes though when he became passionate in his talk they would grow darker, almost black. Now, when I remember Mayur, I wish I could've returned his love—my life would have been better.

-Different, not necessarily better, depending on whether his love was that of a young man and whether it matured. Every action has its own pitfalls. What happened to Mayur?

-I lost touch once I married. I don't think he came to the wedding though I did send him an invitation. I suppose that was cruel. He wrote me a sad, hurt letter swearing he'd always love me, no matter what. I think his passion was too deeply embedded. Not for me, but for his ideas. He's probably a professor in America now.

I was distracted for a moment trying to recall the face, form, the voice of one I had loved many centuries ago. In so doing I didn't pay enough attention to her tale of a vow made so many years ago by this young man which would have fatal consequences in the future.

The guard approaches, tapping his wrist on which there is no watch. We understand the signal and rise. Shakuntala embraces me tightly, her odour clean and perfumed as the air around us.

-We don't even know the time here, she laughs. We live by bells marking our days and obey them docile as sheep. Bells to wake up in darkness, bells to meditate, bells to end meditation, bells for meal times, bells for lecture times, bells for private guidance by our guru.

–It's like a good hotel. Is there a charge or does the swami generously support you all.

She laughs, even sounding like a bell. Of course, there's a charge. Nothing is free. Even on this pathway to heaven you have to pay the toll before you start the journey. She kisses both my cheeks, a rare gesture, as most prefer only the one. Give my husband and Avanti my love, tell them I pray for them every day. And I also pray you will guide her. You are wiser than her, and her father. You have motives I cannot read.

Avanti remains silent when I convey her mother's love, not out of indifference but reminded of her neglect. Her face wobbles between remorse and defiance, unable to settle on one or the other.

–You shouldn't have told me.

–Why blame the messenger?

–Now I feel all guilty and upset. How is she?

–Extremely well, at peace with herself. We discussed you and she is praying you will marry soon. That's her remaining wish. I don't add that the name Aditya came up in our conversation though I am tempted to see the reaction. Will she remember? Or recoil? I resist the temptation.

–You did tell her I was going to stand for election? What did she say?

–She wasn't happy. She only sees the influence of your father.

–She's unhappy only because father and I are so close, she says defensively. Adds defiantly. I do love her too but it's different. She was just a mother and didn't impose herself as Father does. He's... exciting and, and...

–Powerful.

–You're the one who advised me and I want to share that power, not sit at home like Mother. I can do things.

She closes the door on me to be alone with her conscience. I have no intention of informing her father about my visit; his spies have already done so. But not what we spoke about as there was no one within hearing in that glade. I will lie when he summons me to hear about our discussion. It comes soon enough.

–How is my wife? It sounds solicitous. He is in his usual chair, the usual drink beside him. His eyes dark with deceit, a natural trait of all princes if they are to survive their lifetimes.

–She is well and sends her affection to you.

–And what else did you discuss, apart from Avanti and me?

–Her daily routine, her belief in her guru, the usual, as her experiences are now limited.

–And him? Do I need to arrest him, imprison him? He isn't preaching any dissent is he?

–He is only another swami taking advantage of the spiritually bankrupt. He is content with growing rich as it costs a lot of money to save souls. They come from other parts of the world too.

His eyes fix on me. Should I trust you Chanakya? You spoke to her for fifteen minutes and that is all you talked about?

–A prince must trust no one, as I have told you before.

–Even Avanti? I love her, she is my heir, that is why I took her away.

I have proffered my advice and say nothing more. He has confessed and I am expected to believe him. Which I do. He dismisses me and as I walk away I feel the daggers of his eyes in my back, a feeling one gets used to in the courts of kings.

SEVEN

THE ELECTION CAMPAIGN will take two weeks. I suggest we make our first visit to District 18 anonymously. Other visits will have her entourage of 10,000 party workers marshalling the electorate to the maidans and penning them in. Apart from the driver of the SUV, we only have Vikram, our spy, accompany us. He is an assiduous informer who has spent the last week travelling District 18 to check the pulse of the people.

-What have you discovered? I ask.

He replies to Avanti. Madam, the people are unhappy...

-They always are, she says in irritation. What's their problem?

-The same. There are rumours that their land will be confiscated for factories, the jungle will be razed for mining. And there is no work. You must assure them the rumours are false. They will believe you because you are the daughter of the President.

-I can't make those promises. My father and his cabinet are the ones with the power to make such promises.

-Are the insurgents working with the people? I ask, more concerned about troublemakers. They are the rumour-mongers that my emperor dealt with severely and they exist in every society. They need to be contained. Or encouraged, depending on the emperor's use of them.

-Yes, many, Vikram says. They will be very active during your campaign, so I hear, as they want to humiliate the President by your defeat.

-Who is their leader?

-He calls himself Chay.

-You mean C-h-e.

-He spells it C-h-a-y.

She turns to me. Che Guevara, a Cuban revolutionary.

I have great gaps in my history of mankind , and it's a pleasurable experience catching up, especially as I didn't have to live through wars, pogroms, assassinations, more wars, holocausts, colonisations. I have only reached the French Revolution in my reading. I need to race on to catch up with a country I haven't heard of and a man now resurrecting his hero by giving himself the same name. Later, I find Cuba on our earth, a speck of dust, a mote in the great American eye. I bring myself up to speed on Che and think he is inferior to Robespierre although all revolutions are the same wheels turning through centuries to overthrow tyrant kings.

–Does he have any followers?

–Some say hundreds and others say just a few, Vikram shrugs. He does have weapons. AK47s, grenades, bombs.

–Who supports him?

–The people, they are neglected by the state and are forced to fall into the hands of men such as him.

–What does he look like? I ask.

In this day when all such information is on the web, I expect Vikram to pull out a photograph, downloaded from FB. Instead, he hands me a much folded sheet of paper. I unfold it and Avanti and I peer at a sketch of a man, exaggerated by the roused emotions of the artist who appears to have taken violently against his subject. The man in the drawing has a broad forehead, a bulbous nose, a cruel mouth, his hair spiky with rage. Large glasses circle his glaring eyes.

–The villagers gave his description to the police artist and he drew this.

Avanti shivers. He looks mad.

–This is useless, unless you have the same Intel from four or five sources and they all confirm the information, you cannot trust it. I crumple the paper into a small ball.

–Does he have a real name?

–He must have, Vikram concedes. But no one knows it. And I've heard he's well educated.

–You mean he can read and write.

–Well educated, Vikram says vaguely. Chay has spies everywhere, he adds.

–Are you one of them? Avanti demands.

Vikram is wounded. I am not one of his spies. I am your personal spy.

Avanti remains silent as we drive along the narrow black ribbon, swerving to the sandy edges of the road to avoid head-on collisions with trucks and buses that charge like bulls along the very centre of the road. We see the sign: District 18, and we're past it, and Avanti sits straighter as she enters her kingdom-to-be. It's her first ever view of this place. She has her map out and refers to it from time to time, it is neatly cut to page lengths and placed in a ring binder. She has been as meticulous as possible in her preparation for the visit—she has all the reports and accompanying statistics, compiled by the government. Unfortunately these are inaccurate, exaggerated, imaginative. The kingdom doesn't look promising—rocky, seeded with hundreds of boulders, dotted with stunted lantana, low uneven hills, dry riverbeds, broken bridges, more potholes than roads. Not even a goat in sight. Dirt lanes meander away to the horizon, the only path to those villages she must reach if she is to win this seat.

I have seen kingdoms more barren than this, sand and more sand to all horizons, and yet the prince prizes it, it's his land, his princedom, and the people his people. The people we pass, soon to be her people, wait patiently for buses or carts to transport them, while we race past in air-conditioned comfort. They are simply clothed, none brazen with any riches, poor as their neighbours. Children play their village games on the roads, parting to allow traffic to pass. She looks at them possessively, as being imbued with possibility as they will eventually have to vote for her. The sun is malignant as ever and dust films the windshields and windows. The towns are crowded, the streets so narrow that buses can barely squeeze past each other, garbage clutters the edges, the shops are small, selling cheap materials. The buildings lean at all angles of despair. A thin man, outstretched arm holding a cane, caught in mid-stride is elevated on plinths at every roundabout. So common are statues of Gandhi that he has been rendered invisible. The statues seem to be on the verge of breaking into a sprint, it would seem the Mahatma is trying urgently to escape the disenchantment of his people.

-But money was allocated for roads, canals, schools... she is saying to herself, studying the reports and the generous numbers, with many zeroes. All the zeroes evaporated long before they crossed the border.

Finally, we pass a few fields of rice, wheat, maize struggling to survive. We reach the capital of District 18, no more regal than the smaller towns we'd passed, jangling with noise and crowds, motorbikes and cars parked haphazardly. A banner stretched across the road

Warmly Welcomes Madam Avanti to Our Great City. Below it, a crowd of men wait, pristine in their identical new clothes, immaculate as her father, carrying party flags. It has three bands: red, yellow, blue, a streak of white lightning running through them. Ancient armies too marched into battles carrying flags and waving banners. The loyal party workers are here to meet their new leader-to-be, ensure their place in her sun early so they can share in her generosity.
 -I have to?
 -You have to, I advise.
 She climbs out to be garlanded, escorted to the hastily erected platform on which is a majestic plastic chair. Vikram and I remain in the car, not wanting to reveal ourselves though even that secret won't last long. I am known, if not seen by many. The district's senior party worker, a corpulent figure with a bison's moustache, welcomes her, speaking for an hour, extolling her virtues, making many of them sound as if she has descended, as in the biblical sermon, from the skies. Others speak too, each outdoing the other. Avanti looks petulant, angry, impatient. Suddenly, she asserts herself, scolding them and they fall subdued as chastised children. Madam has finally spoken. She has no speech for them, or the motley crowd which has gathered, blocking traffic. She rises and marches back to the car, slamming the door.
 It's a timely exit as a small homemade bomb explodes behind the chair on which she was sitting, raising it a few inches and then toppling it. Her stalwarts scatter, black smoke rises from beneath the stage. No one appears to be hurt, as there's no blood on the fleeing men.
 -Oh my god, I could've been killed, Avanti screams in the confines of the car. She is shaking from the near collision with death.
 -It was only a small bomb, Vikram says, pragmatically. It's just a warning from Chay. If he was serious, he would have used a much bigger bomb.
 -I'll deal with Chay when I win, teach him a lesson, she says severely, hiding her fear. What or who is he, really. Tell me.
 -Some say he's a student leader, a commie, others say he's just a villager causing trouble.
 -Has anyone seen him?
 -Only that drawing, Vikram replies. He's a ghost, a shadow. He

is tall, he's short, he's dark, he's fair, he's fat, he's thin, he's old, he's young.
  -The police will deal with him. She looks around. Where are the police?
  -Safe and well, I tell her, in their police stations. No doubt Chay warned them.

We drive on, the horn clearing a path through the chaos of still running people, garlands meant for her scattered along the dusty road. Many kilometres out, we see a lane meandering away.
  -I want to see a village, Avanti orders.
  -There's nothing to see, Vikram counters.
  -I support her. For me, cosseted for so many years in an urban cocoon, this will remind me of my beginnings.

We turn into the lane, bumbling over dips and humps, wandering in search of a village and finally we discover a small hamlet on the bank of a stream, with a fence of thorny bushes; the lane on which we are driving continues on past it, and ends on the horizon where the jungle looms. Our sudden appearance startles the inhabitants. They promptly flee into their mud-and-thatch homes and close their fragile doors. A cow or two, maybe a goat—their precious possessions—are all that are left to welcome us. The scene is no different from the days my emperor too descended from his gaddi to mingle with his citizens. I accompanied him often and advised him: emperor your gaddi rests on such naked shoulders and will fall unless you strengthen your people. They are the cows that give you milk, without them, there is no milk. He listened and acted, when he could. These people are as poor as my emperor's subjects, he would recognise them in an instant.
  -Is this all? Avanti murmurs, almost astonished, a wrinkle of disappointment, even dismissal in the curl of her lips. Her eyes, so like her mother's, are behind those dark bands of glass and I cannot see whether her heart is touched. I know she imagined a pastoral paradise—lush fields, happy people gambolling among shady trees, singing, dancing, overflowing with joy, fat on ghee and lassi. The poor are miserable company and I cannot blame them. Fate decreed their misery and is the fuel for their eventual rage against it.
  -What else can there be with such neglect? I start to open the door, as even Vikram does.

-I've seen the village. We can go.
-You should meet the people.
-I will when I campaign.

Finality in her tone. No debate. So we retreat as we all do when we look upon such destitution, leaving them to survive, if they can, until the next passing visitation, the whispers of promises, never fulfilled.

-*A state is only as rich as its poorest citizen.* Chanakya advised the emperor to call the poorest man in his empire to attend the council of advisors, to speak his wants and listen to them carefully.
-And did he?
-Yes. The proud advisors were unhappy to share the council hall with a beggar. The emperor told him to speak and he said: Hunger. Thirst. Shelter. Land. Work. Education. And he is still here with us. I wanted you to meet him but you are afraid. The poor have pride too, they don't want charity, though they will take it. They want work. Enrich them and the state will be stronger.
-It's not my father's fault, she says defensively, as we bump back to the road. I know he allocates huge funds for the upliftment of the people. I will tell him what I've seen. He will sack all the bureaucrats who have been ineffectual.

Even that has not changed. It's the natural character of all men to be corrupt, no less so the bureaucrats whom the emperor has entrusted with his power to administer his kingdom. I wrote then that out of a thousand functionaries in his kingdom, he would be fortunate to find one honest man. *Every public servant was subjected to tests such as only the most diabolical ingenuity could invent. He was tempted by love, by fear, by greed, by ambition, even by the obligations of his religion. If he did not succumb he must have been endowed either with more than human fidelity—or with superhuman cunning.* Then, my emperor was swift to execute the corrupt entrapped by his spies. In this day, they're elevated to high positions, along with their wives, children and innumerable relatives.

When we leave the district, and leave Vikram to continue his spying, I ask: Why didn't you meet the poor face-to-face?
-I cannot bear to look upon them and, you're right, I'm afraid. She stared straight ahead. No further discussion.

I understand her fear: our lives can touch, collide and shatter at any time and be catapulted into the abyss of poverty in a moment.

■

We campaign without pause throughout summer, a miserable time. The sun is raging, more vindictive than in my time or is that my imagination. She has her four-car cavalcade, her armed escorts. We have prepared well, she has her maps, her notes and her statistics. In the *Arthashastra* I do discuss the science of politics (*dandiniti*) and though 'democracy' did not exist then, in choosing a leader, my advice to Avanti is still relevant. I simplify the beauty of my language for her to understand in these modern times.

Although it is good to be honest and upright in your actions and in your language, it will be necessary also to deceive the people. I know leaders have performed great deeds, not through goodness, but through deceptions. And yet the experience of our own times has shown that those princes have achieved great things who made small account of good faith and who understood by devious means to better their opponents who believed they should stick to integrity and honesty in their actions. There are only two ways to fight this election: by following rules or by brute strength. Good men follow the rule; animals use violence. If the first doesn't work, use the second.

At the party headquarters in the capital, she has appointed booth captains for the 152 polling booths in District 18. She tells them, and the others, our well-thought-through plans for this age of instant communication and brevity: Every one of you must text everyone you know the message—Vote for Avanti. In turn, those people must pass on that message to all their contacts. Do this daily. And on Election Day, we must send a new text: Vote.

Her soldiers spread out like thieves, stealing people from their daily labours in the fields and along the road, from tea shops and buses, wherever they find them. They bundle them into lorries and transport them to every venue where Avanti is to speak. The 'supporters' are paid; food for the women, liquor for the men, some hard cash too for both; it is a break in the monotony of their existence and they are used to such outright bribery. It is to be expected and they would be disappointed if denied this largesse. They are generous in their support and no sooner than they are released back to their habitat, they are scooped up by the rival candidates, fed and liquored again. Most of her rivals campaign at the heart of their own small armies, with their own flags, banners, manoeuvring for power against the prince. Dusty battles for the love of the electorate are fought with sticks and stones, not bows and arrows or guns. This electorate is divided into vote banks—colour, creed, caste, religion, rich, middle class, poor, left wing, right wing—as if they are deposits of cash, accruing interest, and then withdrawn with the right pin code of promises.

Avanti is as resilient and determined as her father, whispering his advice over the cell phone. He has his Intel giving him up-to-date info so he can calculate his popularity from the enforced turn-outs. He keeps his distance, feigning indifference. She is just another candidate for the public's consumption. But caravans of money mysteriously criss-cross the district, avoiding the election monitor's averted gaze. She campaigns in the dust and heat of District 18, racing from one rally to another in her convoy, flanked by her worshipful party men and women. The crowds wait everywhere to see the daughter of their President, basking in the proximity of power. They spread like carpets on the hard earth; they stretch out along the rice fields, to the edge of the road, down to the river. Although not always. Sometimes only a handful gather at the smaller venues. The women shade their faces and the faces of the children in their arms with their pallus; the men with party flags. No breeze brushes these listless cloths. They listen to her intently, not stirring, the sun baking them darker. Corrals of casuarina poles tied with coir ropes pen them together in flocks of hundreds. They have filed into the spaces, shepherded by policemen with lathis, at dawn. The dust rarely settles. It hovers as a yellow haze over the landscape. Behind her on similar podiums in similar places, decorated with the party colours, are giant portraits of her father. Smaller ones of her, standing in his shadow. He looks down, benign and kindly, on her and the crowds; a constant reminder to her, and them, that he is their benefactor. Their king. Her speech rarely varies.

-My people I stand here before you not as the daughter of a great man but as one of you, a humble citizen. I see myself as the destroyer of your old life and creator of a new one. If there is injustice done to you, I will hunt it down and annihilate it, if there is corruption affecting the fabric of your lives, I will hunt it down and destroy the corrupt. If you are without food, I will create a thousand acres of rice and wheat to feed you and your children, and if you have no work, I will create a million opportunities for you to work and prosper. I will create roofs over your heads, schools for your children. I will give you free electricity, free mobile phones, free cycles, free laptops for your children. Because of who I am, I can do these things. They're not empty promises seeking your vote. I have the will, I will have the power. Vote for me and be prosperous.' She flings her arms to the sky. *People for Prosperity*.

It's a slogan I devised, *People for Prosperity*, and I am proud of it. A prince should never hesitate to lie to his people if he is to remain in power. Will they grasp my slogan's implications: Which people? Prosperity for whom? It is the slyness of democracy that nothing is defined; it remains opaque, depending on interpretation. Which people? The electorate who gather to listen, to vote. For whom? The elite, the privileged, to tighten their grip on power. Television and the newspapers publish polls daily, a democratic creation that befuddles even those who poll. It is, I learn, a science, not unlike astrology or alchemy. Imagine, my emperor sending out men to enquire from the populace how much they loved him. Or not. Ask the question. Count heads. One day she is ahead in these polls by a few points; another day trailing by a few points. This only spurs her on, driven by the desire to please her father and prove herself. She wants to sweep these polls, annihilate the enemy.

To gather Intel, Vikram and I attend the meetings of the other candidates to hear their speeches.

–My people, I stand here before you as one of you, a humble citizen. I see myself as your destroyer and creator. If there is injustice done to you, I will hunt it down and annihilate it, if there is corruption affecting the fabric of you lives, I will hunt it down and destroy the corrupt. If you are without food, I will create a thousand acres of rice and wheat to feed you and your children, and if you have no work, I will create a million opportunities…

They throw in HD televisions and train tickets so they are all on equal ground.

But should my slogan not inflame love in the hearts of her audience, and improve her poll numbers, there is another para to add to her manifesto. The other candidates have plagiarized her speech, even as she has theirs so they're all the same. Chay, the terrorist, the insurgent who could be commun-ist, social-ist, capital-ist, no one knows, lurks on the edges of the campaign and in the second week, a bomb explodes, more powerful than the one that toppled her plastic throne. The next day the media reports '100s injured, two killed.' The visuals are gory, blood scattered like rose petals on the clothes of the wounded, shrill young women standing beside them, shouting to the cameras. It is a necessary exaggeration, to strike fear into the viewer and the reader. No one died, a few had minor injuries.

Her father calls: Avanti, are you okay, are you safe?

She's delighted she's drawn his attention and, though wishing she had a wound for him to bandage and kiss, as he would when she was a child, she replies reassuringly, I'm fine. I was frightened though when it went off. And all that blood and screaming was also terrifying.

–I'll order the police to increase your security status to Y. Be careful. He disconnects. Avanti's security expands: Thirty cars, thirty guns. Her arrivals are now more dramatic, a chase scene from the movies as she races to meetings.

On television, the President is angry: In our vibrant democracy, we cannot allow a few insurgents and terrorists to disrupt the calm and orderly conduct of the election process. I am taking stern measures to restore law and order. The police are conducting an investigation into the bombing and will make arrests very soon.

–You have all seen and heard what has happened, Avanti tells the crowds. There are people who hate what I represent, they want to kill me to keep me from fulfilling the promises I have made to you. They want to silence me. I am not afraid, I will not give in to fear. I will continue to speak the truth, continue to keep my promises to you all. But it's not only me they attack with bombs and guns but also you, my people, who want to keep your freedom of choice, the right to choose the way you want to live your lives in peace and harmony.

Then, on my advice, she steps forward through the barrier of her guards to reveal that she is not afraid. See, she is brave, see she is ready to sacrifice herself to the terrorists.

A prince must use such attacks on his people to inject fear into their hearts. He always needs an enemy to keep his people subdued and loyal to himself. Fear is the wolf stalking the goats; they huddle together, looking to the shepherd to protect them. If the prince cannot find fear from outside his kingdom, then let him find it from within, they both serve the same purpose: to intimidate the minds of his people and render them docile.

When the campaign ends, we retreat to rest in the palace. Tens of thousands of texts have been sent: Vote, Vote, Vote Avanti. She is worn and thin, worried she has failed her father who does not come to comfort her or praise her. Yet. We watch the television, muted, and she leans against me tiredly. She has her glass of wine, the bottle on the table, and she sips greedily, wanting release from her own fears.

–Chan, I have tried my best. I must win. What does Vikram report?

Our private pollster roams the district. He says you have a good chance. The people like you and, as you're the President's daughter, they will benefit by having you represent them.

–What if I lose? She wails. The voice of a lover mourning the possible loss of the one she loves.

EIGHT

WHEN A PRINCE is defeated in a war, he is entirely alone. His soldiers die, flee or defect, courtiers vanish and even the harem disperses like so many beautiful petals blown by a warm breeze. But the prince has debts, money lenders clawing at him for what they loaned. Now, not money lenders, but the investors, corporates, industrialists, who will demand not just the principal plus interest but rewards far greater than both. Avanti also has debts, her party workers wanting their prizes. They will need patience but their reward will come—democracy has a thousand nipples to dispense sweet rewards, an empire only one—the emperor to give them sustenance.

The people queue faithfully, and fatefully, clutching their voter ID cards, some valid, most not. Endless. Men and women, separate booths, the old, the infirm carried to cast their ballot. Such hope brings tears of amusement to my eyes. How can they still believe that the machines inside those rooms, the buttons they press against a name, will be their salvation when they have performed this exercise throughout their lives and the results have remained the same? Self-delusion is the charming trait of humans, we will ourselves into the hallucination. And, like Avanti and a million others, we continue to watch the screen and listen to the experts, discussing the pride of democracy, each chosen for a conflicting opinion. They are bland, predictable, unimaginative, inarticulate and they too are a part of this delightful conspiracy, spun out at great length, like a spider's web entrapping the poor who fly into it. They think out aloud, speak their thoughts. Avanti will lose. Inexperienced. Callow. Pretty, yes. Presentable. Look at her hair. Look at her dress. Look at her arms, mouth, eyes. Her breasts. Daughter. Feudalism. Empty-headed. Failed painter.

We wait. Her booth captains report a record turnout, they have persuaded the people to vote but who knows if these goats will obey the shepherd's commands. The magic boxes are ready to disgorge their secrets. The count begins. All listen to the trickery of this new science of prediction—supposedly more dependable than reading the movements of the stars—as if a deity speaks. She's leading. She's not leading. Another is ahead. She is ahead. With each vote counted, experts project margins of numbers. I don't need to listen. I am her guru and know she will win; I guided her every move. The pundits continue to opinionate, mouths gasping like dying fish flopping on the sand. She wins by a landslide of 126,768 votes.

The victor throws her arms around me, squealing, screaming, deafening me with her joy. She dances, she sings 1-2-6-7-6-8...1-2-6-7-6-8. If I close my eyes as she sings I hear her mother's voice, yet when she speaks it's in her father's. 1-2-6-7-6-8 are digits to savour, she annihilated her enemies. And, if this was a war, the number of dead would be 1-2-6-7-6-8 bodies, left on the battlefield.

–I didn't think it would be so easy. Father will be so happy, she finally articulates, and looks to her cell phone which remains silent. But there are tweets pouring in from all her friends, her colleagues.

–You won without his help.

–His name helped.

–They voted for you, not for him. I am determined to separate her from her dependence on her father, and turn her against him. They love you, they believe in you, they want you, they'll follow you.

–I'm going to see him. He's probably too busy to know the results.

–When a prince has won, he must wait for his courtiers to pay him homage. He doesn't go to them but lets them seek him out. Wait. You have won by the biggest margin, even bigger than your father's, and he knows that. He will come.

She looks pensive, twisting a lock of hair. I wonder if I'd have won without using my father's name?

–Yes, you inspired your workers and the strategy of sending SMSes to the cellphones of voters worked. Now you have to build on your victory, gather your own followers. There are many who already believe in you. One day you will stand alone but...

–But? You can tell me the truth. You must always.

I smile. Me, Chanakya, speaking the truth! You will need to be financially independent. You must start now, and you must expand your spy network to every corner of this state.

–Yes, of course. Distracted. Waiting for the call. Twisting hair into knots.

We wait for her father's blessing. And wait. He is exerting his

power over her, the magnet drawing this filing to come to him. He too knows how a prince must behave. He wants her to approach, bend and touch his feet, acknowledge he is the true victor. She chafes, she frets, she paces, drinks wine. She wants to celebrate with the man she loves, yearns for his praise, only then will she believe her victory.
   -I must go...
   -No. Wait. He will come to you.
   There's a soft knock on the door and she runs to open it, hoping it's her father, waiting for the kiss and embrace. It is only Ramesh, humble eavesdropper.
   -Congratulations, Madam, he speaks softly, unctuous. Your father will be happy.
   -Where is he? Crossly, starting to close the door.
   -On tour, he says blandly.
   -Where on tour? Did he call and leave a message?
   -He doesn't inform me of his itinerary, Madam. And he would not call me. I am only your PA. I just wish to congratulate you and know you will make a wise contribution to the party and the state. If there is anything...
   -Nothing. Closing the door on his bowing figure.
   We fall asleep waiting. She on her bed, I on her sofa, too weary to guide my cart to my own bed. I have a deep sense of satisfaction that rises into my dreams. I am getting closer. I have guided the prince, as I had many times before, to the threshold of power. She has proved my faith in this first battle; there will be many more. The route to power is a long and dangerous journey, many men wait in ambush—including the father she loves—as she rises higher. He will watch her, even as the tiger watches the deer in the shadows. In my old time, the emperor would keep his sword ready as the victorious son approached, empty handed, after defeating an enemy, knowing how swiftly a treacherous child could strike, even while he (or she) entered the embrace.
   A knock, soft as a drop of water on a leaf, awakens me. It is past midnight; Avanti sleeps deeply, and, like all women in sleep, she releases her inner beauty to the watcher. She is dreaming of victory, savouring it in the small smiles I see playing on her lips. Then the frowns of disappointment at her father's deliberate neglect. I am good at reading the faces of sleepers, as it reveals their thoughts and

emotions. Every spy should practise the art. I lean over, my mouth near the delicate curves of her right ear, and whisper my shastras. I have an insidious voice, even as I have an insidious mind. In sleep, a whisper enters the deeper caverns of the mind and lodges there in the crevices and folds of reason and thought to guide the prince. Of course, he can ignore every word, that is free will, but it is my duty to keep repeating myself in the hope that he listens and acts accordingly.

–*In the happiness of your subjects lies the king's happiness, in their welfare your welfare. He shall not consider as good only that which pleases him but treat as beneficial to him whatever pleases his subjects. You must bring peace to your district and reflect its prestige beyond its borders. A prince must rule for the good of all his people, careful and clever in preventing treachery and you must keep a watchful eye over your people and the officials through whom you will rule. Your authority is a matter of divine right now, you have been chosen by your people and must not allow any doubts to intrude themselves such as may weaken the exercise of your will.*

She stirs, turns her head as if to hear me more clearly, and sighs. When she settles, I continue.

–*You must be personally mindful of this by an unceasing fight against the six enemies of a monarch: Lust, Avarice, Pride, Anger, Drunkenness, and Insolence. The government is to be regarded, literally, as the nitishastra, that is, the science of 'leading', and this needs constant consideration for those whom you lead. But the king is not the only element to be regarded. A kingdom needs six things in addition to the king, namely, Ministers, People, Fortifications, Armies, Treasury and Allies, though the king is the foundation and source. He is the embodiment of all sovereign authority, both moral and legal. 'Gods and kings are alike'. As all other footsteps vanish in the footprints of the elephant, so all other dharma (law) disappears in the raja-dharma (the royal law). But the royal law is not mere caprice. The king, as the protector of the people, must be punished (in certain cases thirty-fold) for neglect of the popular welfare.*

I straighten, listening to her breathing steady and serene. And think that kings are seldom punished, except by rebellion and executions. If only they read my *Arthashastra* and followed every word I had written, they would have kept their heads intact on their shoulders. Will she heed my wise words? I will have to wait and see, human caprice can take her off a cliff.

A second drop of water, now on the ground. I move softly to the door, step out and follow the messenger through the corridors, even in half sleep knowing where he is leading me, preparing my answers before I hear the questions. He waits, still as always, watching my approach across the great hall.

–Why hasn't she come to me? Petulant. Commanding.

–She was tired and will meet you tomorrow morning. First thing. As a proud father, you should see her, as the king you can be magnanimous.

–She won only because of me. Sipping his scotch.

–It is only and entirely because of you and your great name. Never hesitate in oily flattery, kings are never sated.

He smiles and even allows the pleasure of my flattery to touch his eyes, accepting my praise. I thought so and I'm happy you confirm that. And not because of those…messages…whatever they're called?

–SMS. No, of course not.

–Then who advised her on this stupid policy to win votes? Sharply. Petulant again. Yet worried.

–They were just games she wanted to play. I advised her not to resort to such tricks but she can be quite stubborn.

–She should stick to tried and true methods in campaigning, as I have taught her. I don't understand how she won with such a majority. How did she tamper with the voting machines? I'm told it is impossible.

–It is. But there are ways and I have no experience in that.

I hear the tone of jealousy; she has won by a much greater number than he ever has and this without booth capturing, destroying the machines, intimidating election officials. Those are the tried and true methods he speaks of now, the old route to power.

–She spoke very well, he admits, grudgingly admiring her fluency, her perfect imitation of his gestures, voice and tone. That is what he is praising now. Did you write her speeches?

–I helped her but she wrote her own, first in English, then translated. My command of language is hesitant. Sanskrit is sweet as a poem hummed in my ear. English is too guttural, too arrogant with its huge vocabulary and the trickery of its pronunciations. I am grateful that I lived 2,000 years before the English unleashed their language on the world.

—Who is this Chay? A bearer hurries to refill his glass, the ice melted and fresh squares dropped in.

He watches me with innocence, the President who surely has Intel superior to mine. I shrug. A man unhappy with the affairs of the state who believes it must be changed. I'm sure your Intel knows more.

—A madman. Ungrateful for what I am doing for the state. How can one please everyone? The police and special forces are searching for him and his followers. He won't last long. They have orders to arrest him but if he doesn't surrender, then they will have to eliminate him and his followers.

Eliminate. It's called an 'encounter', the meeting between bullets and a human body, though he doesn't use the word, he implies the extra-judicial killing of Chay. I approve of his actions even as I had advised the emperor—*A king must crush any terror threats within, and outside, his borders if he is to keep harmony among his people, and control them. The state must also suppress any radical and revolutionary ideals that can dethrone a king. Or undermine the state.*

—Who is supporting him? He asks, as if I have such answers but it is a rhetorical question. Outside forces, foreign hands meddling in the affairs of our state. They give him the bombs and guns, and money. He dismisses Chay with a wave of his hand. Avanti, he says. What do you advise?

—A king must elevate his son, in this case his daughter, and give her a grand title. All kings have done that for their children. And, as we see in other democracies, sons can follow fathers into the highest office, and brothers too, and cousins can follow the king. Power should remain within the family, if possible.

—A title, yes that's possible. He knows what I mean and broods.

—So I must visit her? he asks, breaking a long silence, chin on chest, drowsy as a beast.

—The king then shows he is magnanimous, that he truly loves his daughter.

He dismisses me, and I trudge down the halls to my own small bed, closing the door on the silence.

■

I am in Avanti's office, adjacent to her room, early and so is she, still flushed from victory, talking on her cellphone to her foot soldiers, congratulating them too. She is quick to learn, knowing all wars depend on the loyalty of the soldiers. Finally, she switches off the phone.

–I woke with strange dreams in my head and they confuse me, she announces, tapping one side of her head like a swimmer trying to dislodge water in the ear. I was moving among the electorate and they were cheering me. I saw myself as a sort of Raja and that if I vanished the people would also and I would be all alone. What does it mean? Am I a Rani now? Am I meant to behave like my father? But I have a feeling the Rani has other ideas. It's all confusing for me.

I wonder who will triumph—her father or Chanakya? I wait to see, not comforting her or deciphering the puzzle planted in her mind.

She looks at her phones, cell phones and land lines, a clutter of communication. Is he back from his tour?

–We must ask Ramesh.

–Why won't he come and see me? she asks in despair. He knows how much I need him and love him. Why is he treating me like this? He's waiting for me to see him. I shouldn't have listened to you. You give bad advice sometimes.

–He will come, I say. Be patient.

He finally comes, acting flushed with his triumph (through her), confident now that the people are enamoured of his rule. They throw their arms around each other, him whirling her off her feet even as he did when she was small, both engulfed in laughter. In the whirl, I see the hero and heroine in movies circling and dancing together. Singing. But they are silent, except for the laughter.

–I knew we could do it, Avanti. You and I will make a great team, we will work together. He stops then and holds her at arm's length, staring into her eyes, mesmerizing her. I have a special place for you too. We start with something small and once we have the cabinet's confidence, we'll move you up. You're a natural, and your mother thought you'd hate it.

–That's because she would have. She never knew me as well as you do. I was always a little girl to her but to you I was always a woman.

–Your room was my refuge from the world and from myself. He caresses her head, the hand possessive and heavy.

–What's my post?
–You'll be my Minister of Education.
She claps her hands. Minister! she repeats, knowing deep down that though this title is her reward it could also be the poisoned chalice.
She escapes to sit at her desk. What's your advice?
There is a faint flick of surprise at her escape from his embrace, then the smile, aware that she is experiencing the first flush of her power. It will pass.
–Know more than your bureaucrat, he says blandly. As a breed they're manipulative, and have their own agendas.
He is wise. He has banished her to the farthest outpost of his empire. She will live among the boulders and stony ground with little sustenance to maintain her position. 'Education' has a low allocation of funds, the corporates and industrialists will not visit her little jagir, as they see no rewards. How can they benefit from a few schools, the low salaries of teachers, whining children clamouring for enlightenment? So she will languish there until he is satisfied that she will be loyal and grateful, and move her closer to the centre. It's also a test to see if she uses the funds wisely. He holds the treasury and the police portfolio close to his chest. His closest associates hold the lucrative posts of telecommunications, infrastructure, mining, agriculture, where money floods into their pockets from corporates eager for the spoils.

■

Later that day, we triumphantly enter the party's offices. SUVs crowd the driveway, the building is bulging with bodies, the party workers overflowing onto the lawn. Banners: *CELESTIAL QUEEN. MONARCH OF THE MOTHERLAND.* They carry photos of Madam, holding them aloft as once soldiers carried banners into battle. Others have her photo on shiny badges pinned above their hearts. As she enters, a thousand crackers explode. Crows, parrots, mynahs, kites flap away in panic from the trees fringing the office compound, screaming their distress. I have sensitive hearing and wish I too could take to the skies. Even the shouts of 'Madam' by a thousand voices cannot be heard above the crackers. The air is acrid with sulphur and gunpowder, misty with smoke. They surge around her with their garlands and her head vanishes in this halo of roses.

As fast as she removes them, others rush towards her her with new ones. In between, they try to feed her sweetmeats, pushing them against her mouth, trying to force-feed her. They also feed each other as they are celebrating their own victory too. Fat mouths open and snap shut on doodh peda, rasgullas, jalebis, even as they make way for her to enter the building. She manages to reach the stage to stand under her father's portrait, sternly looking down in disapproval. Perhaps it's the angle of light or the angle of my imagination but he looks distinctly unhappy at this hysterical support for his daughter. His troops are defecting to rally under the prince(ss) as I knew they would. She gives a short speech, grateful for their support and all their hard work during the campaign. She says she won't forget it. She doesn't mention her new title; her father will announce that in due course. As she looks down at those adoring, fawning faces, I can see she has fallen in love with power. It has captured her heart and I pray it will not turn malignant.

I am chosen to accompany Shakuntala to witness her daughter enter the chamber of ultimate power. I'm surprised that she obeys her husband's command. The assembly building isn't the usual block of cement that has stunted the imaginations of the architects in this city. A thousand police surround this magnificent building. It is graceful, the roof curved, rising, and delicate as a bird in flight; the walls are marble and red sandstone; in the centre rises a perfect dome. It has the beauty and elegance of a space ship, and I almost expect it to silently levitate and float away. Long pools of water in marble channels reflect the building on all sides; neem, mango, tamarind trees throw their gracious shade over the lawns. The designer is a Danish architect and his work of art cost the exchequer a major fortune. The other surprise is that the President, a man with no aesthetic sense, commissioned this marvellous structure and watched it grow as anxiously as a parent watches its child. It is his legacy. The entrance hall is forty feet high, the ceiling filled not with images of gods but of the modern world in which we exist, tastefully executed by a Spanish painter. I wait at the arched entrance, high enough for a giant to pass under without bowing his head. The legislators arrive in their limousines, along with their security. There are eight curving steps from the earth to the entrance but, as they are busy men, and a few women, who have no time to lose, they take the escalator up and pass by me, unseeing.

Shakuntala's SUV finally arrives and I hurry down as the turbaned servitor bends to open her door. I have to jostle through the arriving guests, as I escort her to the visitor's galley, her beauty drawing many stares, and holding mine. She wears a black cotton saree with a heavy gold border embroidered with a paisley pattern. Her blouse matches her saree but she wears no jewellery. Her hair, just touched with grey, is tied in a severe bun. Meditation never quite contains the natural vanity in a person and she is now looking around defiantly.

–You look splendid, an empress descending from her chariot could not be more striking.

She smiles and takes my hand. Chanakya, you're a natural liar. But thank you.

–Never to a woman, unless it's necessary to achieve one's ends.

–You're wondering why I've decided to come. I wanted to see my family, what's left of it, in case I never return.

–Is that a threat?

She looks up to the high walls, curving like a woman's hips, as if seeing it for the first time. There are three layers of different stones—twenty feet of pale pink, twenty of marble and finally twenty of black cuddapah. They create a pleasing harmony and I especially like the roundness. Shakuntala had suggested the pattern to the architect to relieve the monotony of one stone and, in those days, her husband listened to her. She is remembering that.

–It could be, she finally replies with smile I cannot decipher. Meditation also opens new avenues of rebellion and needs to be encouraged.

Those passing by now come to pay her—the President's wife—homage and touch her feet swiftly; others hesitate and only press palms together in case the President misreads such obeisance and banishes them from the warmth of his power. She is proof that they are all a happy family and the rumours of their separation idle gossip. I lead her up the steps to the entrance, her beauty cascading over my poor form.

It's as we pass through the reception hall that I notice another visitor, pushing through the throng to fall in beside us. It is Aditya—looking keenly all around him with a filmmaker's curiosity.

NINE

THE PRESIDENT AND his daughter wait for us to approach, together accepting the homage of all those who are in the assembly.

–They look like a married couple at their reception waiting for congratulations, Shakuntala whispers, unable to suppress the bitter grief in her voice that she failed to save Avanti from her husband's lust. She is remembering her own hasty marriage, the flower bedecked bride, mehendi decorations on her hands and feet, smiling, happy, adoring, greeting well-wishers. I saw the video, many men in the reception line sporting dark glasses, like movie stars and test cricketers, carrying envelopes of cash.

–To win her, don't scold, use flattery, use promises, lie too, I tell Shakuntala. The same rules to win power apply to win love.

The opposition leader, an ancient man supported by two aides, stops to whisper in the President's ear. A whisper, as he has lost his voice through shouting and screaming frequently in the debating chamber. Despite his infirmity, he has a strong right arm and I have seen him hurl books, microphones and other objects across the aisle at the President who has acquired swift reflexes in ducking both physical objects and verbal abuse. The President is resplendent in his white kurta, and Avanti in her pale blue silk saree, the gold border weighing it down, a motif of silver flowers decorating the pleats. It's modest compared to the attire of the other ladies. She also wears the diamond earrings her mother gave her four years ago, her lips have a faint gloss. She looks confident with her new title, although it isn't yet public knowledge. She is watching her mother, and the President has to draw her attention sharply to the Opposition leader, who is holding out a bent claw to congratulate her on her victory, salivating at the thought of hurling erotic abuse at her in the assembly. I know he spends hours massaged by dark beauties though even their dexterity cannot arouse his dormant dick. I did give him a bottle of my special oils and wait for his report. Once his parched palm releases her hand, she leaves her father's side to receive her mother. So fixed is her intent that she sees neither Aditya nor me.

–I'm so happy you've come today, Avanti says, with genuine pleasure as she embraces her mother whom she hasn't seen for years. I'm also sorry I didn't come to the ashram.

–Chanakya said you have been very busy, Shakuntala says, a little bite of scold in her tone, and then in a wounded voice, I have missed you a lot and think of you every day.

–I think of you too, Mother. I'm sorry I didn't come to see you. I'm just busy and the ashram's so far away. If you had stayed at home, it would've been much easier.

–I'm meant to make life easier for you? Shakuntala is determined to lay guilt on her daughter, rightly so, but it won't win her back. She remembers my advice now and caresses Avanti's cheek. Forgiving. You do look so beautiful. Congratulations on winning the election. I'm so proud of you. I tell everyone in the ashram, she is my clever daughter.

–Thank you, Mother. You're looking even younger, so calm. The ashram is doing you a lot of good.

–Meditation is supposed to do that.

–We'll have lunch ....

But even as she says this, her mother is looking at her husband. I see the adoration, the disappointment and the hope all at once passing over her face like swift moving clouds. In his face is the admiration at his own judgement of beauty, although now disenchanted. Like all men, he is thinking: I possessed that woman once, I chose her, she was mine to do with what I wanted. Until I tired of her. He has noticed the other men glancing at Shakuntala as he moves to take her hands. She would have preferred an embrace, a kiss, even if not one with passion. He is smiling. The harsh flash from the official camera silhouettes them starkly. His smile fades with the light.

–You've not changed.

–You have. Your hair's all white. Chanakya never told me that. But you look the same, still domineering.

–Affairs of state. Chanakya take my wife to the VIP gallery and with that he dismisses her.

The wife wants to continue the conversation, her first meeting. He doesn't even touch her hand any more, just keeps his palms pressed together in greeting.

–I shouldn't have come. He doesn't even see me. I'm going back.

She turns, I touch her arm gently. Never reveal defeat, use it to your advantage. You're not dead yet.

-And how do I do that?

-You'll find a way. Watch, wait, act.

We move to collect Aditya, face-to-face with Avanti. Cold. Freezing. Staring at him.

-What are you doing here? Icicles in every letter, every word. I have never seen her in such a mood. She is remembering what she considers his betrayal of their love, hence the reaction.

Aditya has grown since I last saw him on a rainy evening so long ago. He's confident. He's unafraid. He's thickened. He's even taller. He looks a film director of some repute—well-cut jeans, a black silk shirt, expensive loafers, and two cell phones (on mute). A four-day growth darkens his face. An artist must have no respect for power. And he is amused.

-I invited him, Shakantala says.

-How could I refuse? I just couldn't resist seeing your baptism into power. Finally. You look...

-I think you should leave.

-Not again. Hands held up in mock horror. Besides, how can I just abandon your mother who invited me? As I was saying, you look...

Avanti turns to her mother. You should have asked my permission before bringing *him*.

-As the President's wife, I don't need anyone's permission Avanti. You can be cordial if not friendly.

-As I was saying, you look beautiful, Aditya continues. Even innocent, like that girl I knew many years ago. I thought all that power would have changed you.

-What are you talking about? All I've done is win an election.

-You know what we're talking about. And I am surprised you're not married...but that would've interfered with your ambitions. Your mother told me that she's been searching for...

-And neither are you.

He laughs, genuinely amused. How do you know that? I'm not as famous as you are, I don't appear in any newspapers for people to know my private life.

She glares, furious that she has stepped into a trap. She does know something about him. There is no anonymity left in the world today. All she has to do is Google his name and IMDB will offer his film credits, other sites his telephone number, FB his photos and his confessions.

—You're not wearing a wedding ring, she says triumphantly.

He looks down at his manicured hand, the nails polished. He has made a special effort hoping this confrontation would happen. A civilized meeting, a polite exchange of 'How are you? Fine', would have meant he was forgotten.

—Even if I was married, I wouldn't wear a ring. He pauses a long moment, looking at her, remembering their conjugal past. Perhaps I'd wear a toe ring to match my wife's, a statement of our equality.

—Good luck in finding her, she snaps, and turns to her mother. You shouldn't have talked to him, of all people, about me.

Her mother smiles happily, as she too understands the exchange. Surely, I can talk about my daughter to an old friend. I haven't revealed any state secrets have I? Will they arrest me as a dissident, a terrorist?

—My life is private.

—Power cannot be private. All I said was I wish you'd marry, whomever you choose. All a mother wants is to see her child settled.

—Married, she snaps, and that isn't the same as settled. I'm not settling for anything or anyone.

Her mother is determined not to be provoked, and she looks to Aditya then to me. A swift glance, unseen by Avanti. Aditya's mother talks to me about him. And she told me he was getting married soon.

Avanti spins back to Aditya. Congratulations. A starlet no doubt.

—A floozy definitely, an actress. Or is it an actor now? A woman of many wiles. Who else do I meet in my profession except the most desirable women? Men sit in the front rows whistling and jacking off, women in the back wishing they could be as beautiful and have such a bosom to drive their staid husbands mad. A film director's life is so hard and my mother wants me married and settled too.

—I'm one of those men, I say. Do I know your bride-to-be? Have I whistled at her? I sit in the front row.

—It's not yet finalized.

—Good luck then, Avanti says. She wants to say more, her curiosity consuming her but she won't release it in front of him. Poor woman.

I'll read about it in the obituary column.

-With our photos, he laughs. I'm sure the press will cover my wedding in full detail. I'll be in *Hello, Celebrity, People*. Maybe they'll even pre-empt the evening news and give the whole hour to me.

-Avanti, her father calls. The reception hall is deserted, apart from the family, and the legislators wait in their comfortable seats for the proceedings to begin.

Avanti obeys his call, turning quickly to join him. Marching. Her fists tightly clenched. Not looking back. Her father takes a fist in his hand and they enter the hallowed hall. Aditya and her mother watch wistfully, each with different emotions at the sight of the clasped hands—she with deep worry, he with longing.

-We must witness the event, I say, as we move towards the stairs, a bearer approaches hurriedly.

-Madam wishes your presence, he tells me.

I gesture to the stairs and follow the man past the guards into an outer room that leads into the chamber. The room is luxurious with sofas, a thick carpet to soften our footfalls. A photo of the President dominates one wall. On others, smaller, more insignificant in size, are pictures of his predecessors, looking wistfully from their frames. At the far end, a bearer stands beside a table with coffees, teas, snacks. Avanti is the other occupant, pacing and talking into her cell phone to Monika, who's in Paris, shopping. I eye the snacks and choose a samosa with a spoonful of chutney. It melts into my mouth, the spices and the aroma filling me with goodwill.

-I had such a shock when I saw him, I swear (shriek). Yes...he came with my mother he said...the last person on earth I wanted to see here...yes, still smug and arrogant as ever. He hasn't changed one bit. Of course, I asked him to leave but my mother said he had to stay. We talked about marriage then....no, not mine, his... yes, he's marrying some movie actress...I didn't even know those women married...who'd want to marry one...except Aditya... What did I feel when I saw him? I don't know, I was so confused and angry, still. I thought I'd play it cool, and I think I did until all this marriage bullshit came up...mother pushing me to marry anyone, even Aditya...but as he's getting married I'm going to get married too...who cares to....anyone, just to get Mother off my back and Aditya too... I don't care....I don't want to think about him anymore.

Never. Ever. Think. (She sees me). We'll talk later.

She stares at me, eyes now baleful as her father's.

–I told you, I don't want to get married. Ever. So don't propose to me.

She has lost her sense of humour and ignores my witty remark which reveals I have listened to every word.

–You knew Aditya was coming here today and you didn't warn me. I thought you were my friend and advisor...

–I didn't know your mother was bringing him. He just popped out of the car, and I didn't spot him in the crowd. I'm going to find out how they got together. I sent the car to pick her up only...

–You're lying.

–Normally, yes, if it suits me. But I'm not. I continue eating, biting delicately on a potato, a vegetable that didn't exist in the old days. Delicious. I too want to know what he's doing here.

–I don't. And I don't know whether to believe you or not. She wants to twirl her hair but remembers it will disarrange the style for this important occasion. I thought I'd behaved with great restraint when I saw him. Didn't I?

–You did. I wonder which floozy actress he's marrying. I am teasing her, reminding her of what she believes she will lose. It could be...

–I don't want to know. Just get rid of him.

–You can, quite easily.

–How?

–By marrying.

She flinches at my suggestion. Another politician's son?

–Aditya.

Unmarried. Spinster. Unwanted. She's thirty, a mere twinkle compared to my two thousand plus years. We're all only a blink in the universe. You can ask me what created that waiting room for souls and I can only quote the *Rig Veda*: *Who really knows? Who here will proclaim it? Whence was it produced? Perhaps it formed itself or perhaps it did not. The one who surveys it all in the highest heaven, only he knows*—or perhaps even he does not know. See, if there is a god, he's as ignorant as we are. Is god in the heavens that we look up to in our eternal search? Why would anyone or any being live in our restless universe that growls, whistles, sings, hums, roars, explodes

continuously, giving no one, even a god a moment's peace or quiet.
—Never, she says.

She dismisses me and my suggestion. Never, is her promise, not the final decision. She cannot see within herself yet, see what lies beyond the door that imprisons her. If I can unlock it, I will succeed in separating her from her father; free her from the chains of obsession. Already a link has broken with her victory and he knows she will one day be his challenger. All kings must fear their children. I will continue to drip Aditya into her mind with the patience of water drops on a stone. I opposed the match before, now it will benefit her. I wipe my hands on a napkin, she returns to her phone, tries Monika but her phone is busy as she spreads the latest gossip to their select circle of friends. As she waits, she frowns, staring at the door. Once she steps through the portal, power waits to possess her.

I climb the stairs to the VIP visitor's gallery and am ushered to the front row seats, a foot away from the balcony. I sit between Shakuntala and Aditya. There are not many with us in the VIP area; separated by a barrier is the press, indolent young men and women paying attention only to each other. The public visitor's gallery is deserted; the people have long resigned themselves to the lunacy in the chamber and have no wish to witness it. Shakuntala leans forward to search for her husband and child among the actors below. In contrast to the modern exterior, the chamber is panelled with rosewood—dark and exclusive—and the benches are rosewood too, with green leather padding, rising from the floor of the house to the rear, as in a cinema hall. An aisle, separates the rulers from the Opposition. The benches face the Speaker who sits elevated on a high dais and out of harm's way. I have seen the photographs of other such debating chambers, where the atmosphere is meant to reflect the solemn and wise discussions that should take place, but more drunken opinions echo in this chamber than in the local bars. I was the advisor to my emperor in his court, among other learned men, and we spoke gently and, hopefully, wisely, when he sought our advice. And when we disagreed with another we would listen respectfully until we were ready to marshal our arguments to refute the advisor. To raise our voices was to invite a stare of such intimidation that one's mind conjured the gallows in that instant. In the courts of kings, death always hovered in the wings. His decision was final.

Shakuntala straightens upon seeing her husband, distinguished by the circle of party followers fawning over him. They form an aura around him; when he moves, they move, never closing the space between them and him. A sun with his planets. Shakuntala sighs on seeing her sun, now much diminished in her eyes, still glowing softly in her heart, though she has struggled to extinguish it. We cannot yet see Avanti.

–He looks old, tired..., she whispers. He's not eating well, he's thinner.

The Speaker calls the chamber to order, and men and women, shuffle to their seats, carefully segregating themselves from the other parties. The first order of the day is to welcome the new member to such an august body and a turbaned guard goes to fetch Avanti. She enters. Pauses on the threshold. She looks small, diminutive, head bowed in respect. Now she crosses the floor slowly. They are all watching her progress, they are watching the future and it is in that silence that she appears to grow in stature. They all know the numbers. 1-2-6-7-6-8. A landslide, an avalanche, a tsunami. Their minds are playing mental gymnastics as they re-calculate their allegiances. There is a new power in their presence and they want to re-align themselves, also to be swept by the tidal wave of her victory at the next election. Her pallu will be what they will cling to when the time comes. The silence breaks when her cell phone rings, Monika calling back, and, embarrassed, Avanti fumbles to silence the cheerful chirping of a Bollywood song. It breaks the spell, the calculations are over and now the natural murmur of restless men and women who have better things to do in life than waste it sitting in the assembly rise from the tiered seats. She faces the speaker and reads the oath in a firm voice.

–I, Avanti, having been elected a member of the Legislative Assembly, do swear in the name of God that I will bear true faith and allegiance to the Constitution of India as by law established, that I will uphold the sovereignty and integrity of India and that I will faithfully discharge the duty upon which I am about to enter.

The Opposition leader has been waiting for this sacrilegious moment to arrive. He rises, shaking his fist at her, believing he will intimidate the young woman and hoarsely whispers the dreaded abuse: Nepotism.

The chant is taken up: Nepotism. Nepotism.

The Opposition leader's son, in the third row behind his father, shouts the loudest, joined by the sons and daughters of other older members. They know when the time comes she will not ally with them. She is their bitter enemy-to-be. Others who have done their maths (hopefully correct) rush out of the benches to surround and congratulate Madam on her momentous victory. The President doesn't move. He has been deserted, left solitary on the front bench. He is watching, watching. He knows too that the prince(ss) is reaching for the gaddi that he has kept warm for so many years. He could end up on a cold toilet seat.

-She loves it, she loves it, Shakuntala murmurs in despair. She is right. Avanti smiles and laughs, her face raised, and she seems to tower above those around her. She is searching the VIP gallery, her eyes skimming past me, her mother, settling a moment on Aditya. I lean forward to see his face—he is laughing, not with humour, but in mockery. Derision is open on his face, he recognizes farce. He is a film director and knows that all this is illusion, like the ones he creates with his camera, his actors, lighting, script, music. In fact, his hands are above the balcony, choreographing an orchestra of movement. They are the extras playing their parts in his film, to die in a hail of gunfire or a flood. She is watching him, knowing what he is doing, smiling. Victory. In the smile, she says: See, you have films, I have power. Aditya rises and claps, slowly, disturbing the VIP gallery and an usher hurries to quiet him. And then Avanti lowers her head to acknowledge her flatterers, her dissentors, before making her way through them to bow in front of the President. He acknowledges her and when her head is low enough and within reach, he touches it gently. They expect her to sit beside him but she moves up three steps and slides in to a bench.

Shakuntala rises, angry with me, looking down. It's all your fault. You encouraged her, you guided her.

-I only gave advice to the princess. She makes her own decisions. She had a choice, she made it. As easily as she could have made another. You have forgotten. Her father too forced her to choose between him and you.

-I've not forgotten. What is your advice to the vanquished one?

-The same as before. Watch, wait, act. There is always a moment

when power slips—even if it's from the grasp of a princess.
 -And will you be there to advise me?
 -If you wish, I will be there.
 We move along the row to the door that leads down and I allow her to descend, regally, first, showing no signs of her distress. An empress has seen her child anointed and is duly proud. Aditya falls in line with me.
 -How did you manage to come with Shakuntala? I know you've been in touch.
 -I was recceing a film in the mountains, and while I was there, I dropped into her ashram and she asked me to join her. The swami wasn't at all pleased to see me and to allow her to leave. He thinks all his good work will be undone in an instant in my depraved company. What do think of him?
 -Am I expected to think of him? I prefer not to. My mind exists on a higher plane.
 -Guiding Avanti.
 -That is my profession.
 -Chanakya, you have made a mess of my life, he says in good-humoured exasperation. It was painful to see her surrounded by more bad men than can be found in *The Godfather* trilogy, and throw in *The Silence of the Lambs* too.
 I have not seen the films he mentions. They are the signposts of his career. Although he makes no mention of it as we descend into the reception hall, I know he won *Un Certain Regard* for his film, *The Toy Boy,* at the Cannes Film Festival earlier this year. It's not in English so the title is misleading. I haven't seen the film, but I hope the director will send me a free DVD when he sees I am interested in films.
 -What's the film you're going to shoot in the mountains about? I know it's a trite question to ask a famous filmmaker but I am, as mentioned, besotted by this medium.
 -I can't tell you the storyline.
 -Who is the star? At least that can't be a secret for long in this country.
 -Siggy Chopra.
 Siggy Chopra!! At the mention of her name, my breath leaves my body and I have to hold a rail to steady myself. Siggy Chopra!

My fantasy. I've lost count of the times I have stared up in erotic worship of the most desirable woman in the world. She is thirty feet high, five across, and I'm not alone in my daily worship. Others come too, scrambling for that centre seat, to lust after her lithe body, the tummy flat, writhing in dance, heaving in passion. Her navel, as big as my open mouth, undulates to the rhythm. Her breasts, in the low-cut choli, are magnificent, swelling curves almost bursting out of the delicate material that encases them. I see a hint of nipples—I wish I could suckle them. In the 3D film, *Dharwaz Bis*, a thriller, her breasts float out of the screen and I reach up to caress them, along with a thousand other palms. Her face, her face—the lips have the pout of sexual promise, the curves reflecting the very shape of her yoni and I can imagine it moist and delicious as her mouth. Her nose is slim but only flares at the nostrils, defiantly teasing her man; her pale brown eyes always have the twinkle of a thousand affairs. Her skin is milky honey that I could lick out of a saucer. When she wears short skirts they barely cover her bottom and like those breasts they promise excitement; she can twitch each cheek to the beat of the music. Her thighs are strong enough to hold any man who rides her and crush him with desire. Watching her films were the times I was most happy, not out of a sexual longing, but experiencing the beauty of this huge woman. There is no happiness in sex itself; it is a physical act, a brief pleasure, followed by the languor of the kill.

Happiness is as brief as a wisp of breath, fragile, lasting a few seconds then vanishing. Think the thought 'I am happy' and you have driven it away. I cannot say I was happy often. There were times, sitting cross-legged at my low desk, composing my shastras in the flickering flames of my oil lamp on a warm, pleasant evening, I would raise my head and smile, believing I was happy and even in that act of acknowledgement it fled my being. I can only recall happiness as a feeling of transcending the body, a levitation of the spirit. Love isn't happiness, it's more a physical feeling centred in the heart and the mind, and thinking on love doesn't banish it. It can last a day, two days, a lifetime. I will die between Siggy's legs. A Saudi prince offered a million dollars for a night with her, according to rumour, and it is the only time I coveted wealth. We men are not alone in our worship. Young women, older women, spend lavishly to reshape their lips, their breasts, their noses, their navels to resemble the goddess of sex that they all wish to be. Sex is in the eyes and they can't change that with a surgeon's knife. One such specialist volunteered to perform his skills on my face but I declined. Let them all see my imperfections, I told him. They are not hidden away as in others, disguised by your knife.

–Siggy Chopra!!! You must invite me to the shoot; I have to see her in the flesh, smell the perfume of her long black hair and even just touch those exquisitely shaped hands and those long, delicate fingers.

He laughs. The magic of cinema. Of course, you can come to the shoot.

I cannot shut out the envy in my voice. Is she the one you will marry?

He keeps laughing. Chanakya, if I could trust you, I would tell you. But for that secret, you must somehow persuade Avanti to have dinner with me one night. Just the two of us, not you too.

I am cautious in such bargains. I need to examine the action, and then the consequences. This one has promise but will it work to my advantage? Yes, I want them to meet, to talk, to hold hands, though my pupil will show reluctance and distrust my motives. He is a film director whose fame is growing but does he have the magnetism to draw her away from her father. If this fails, then love of power will prevail and there will be no second chance. I need a guarantee but there are none in life. I take a step further into the future, examining possibilities and consequences in this eternal game of chess. I see possibilities far away, a collision of desires that can change the future. That is my art, to manoeuvre people to the positions I want.

–Is that too much to ask? Aditya asks impatiently. We have reached the steps, Shakuntala stands waiting for the driver to open the door, waiting for Aditya to join her; she is in a hurry to escape this place and retreat to her sanctuary in the mountains.

–I will try my best but only after I've been on the shoot and touched Siggy's hand, held it for a moment.

–Done, he says and we shake hands before he gets into the car with Shakuntala. She smiles at me, then stares ahead as the car pulls away. I follow dreamily, on foot, wanting only the privacy of my bed, my room so I can close my eyes and be with Siggy.

TEN

MINISTER AVANTI'S OFFICE is a few streets away from the secretariat in the assembly complex. Her ministry is banished to a low, two-storey decrepit building, as far as possible from the power centre. It needs several coats of paint to hide the naked brickwork. She has the first floor, the Ministry of Culture the ground, both hives of lethargy. Her bureaucrats welcome the new minister and lead her to the office of the Minister of Education. It is spacious, a desk of polished teak dominates, with four telephones of different colours, but no files; the minister's chair thickly padded and tilts back, should she need a quick nap. Behind it is the President's photo on the wall, in front a row of straight-backed chairs with hard seats for secretaries and supplicants. To one side of the room is a sofa, two armchairs covered in green fabric, and a coffee table for more informal meetings with visitors. A few cobwebs remain on the windows, and the walls are yellow with water stains.

-Bring me the files, Avanti orders her secretary.

-There are none, Madam Minister. He is a kindly looking man, slight, quite tall, large spectacles framing his face. Behind him are the lower ranks and their gaunt faces are hungry for bribes, they're starved of their rewards in this posting. They hope the President's daughter will flush in the funds that can leak into their pockets.

-We had a minister but we have not seen him for two years. He stays at home. The secretary leaves the meaning unsaid, and sighs, wishing he too could remain at home and not waste his life in this empty-coffered ministry.

-A policy statement, I suggest.

He looks at me in doubt. Should he answer me, acknowledge my presence, demean himself? He must consider protocol. He looks to Avanti.

-Policy statement, she confirms.

The first secretary informs the second secretary who informs his assistant and finally the peon goes to search for this elusive document.

-Do we have an annual budget?

–Yes, Madam. There is a budget but no money.

Silence descends. We wait. The peon returns, wiping dust off the file with a grimy rag. It passes upward to reach the first secretary who gives it a final clean and places it reverently on Madam's desk. She waves them away and when they have filed out, opens the file.

–He knew this ministry had no money, no power, she fumes at the President, skimming the slender document. Big plans. Two thousand new schools a year, free schooling for all children, books and laptops. Ten thousand teachers. She closes it with a weary sigh and swings her chair around to look out of the window.

–Now what do I do?

–Your first action must be to recruit more spies. Not just for District 18 but for the whole state. You need Intel on what is happening below the surface.

–What for? I'm not planning a coup.

–In case you do. I'll get Vikram to search for reliable spies though I know such men don't exist. The more you have the more you can cross-check.

–And how much will that cost?

–Good spies cost and they're worth the cost. But you pay only for reliable Intel.

–You're quite paranoid about spies.

–It's best to know what is about to happen to you before it happens. The world is full of assassins and you're now in a position of power. With power comes dissent, discontent too.

–Do what you have to then.

When the phone rings, she checks the time. 11.30. She picks it up, listens and answers. Send him in. Her first visitor is the noble, the second most important man in the state—Monika's father.

–Remain seated, you're the Minister. When a supplicant appears before a prince, he must remain standing, and it's always wise to disarm them. She sits on the edge of the chair, looking at the door.

The noble enters, pudgy, portly, his expensive suit the usual black, the crisp blue Egyptian cotton shirt and his noose. A matching silk handkerchief peeps out of his jacket pocket. His presence is flattering since usually his VPs and managers meet with ministers and bureaucrats, while he remains far out of reach. Behind him, his personal assistant, a young woman in her mid-twenties, with lips and a nose resembling Siggy Chopra's. Her breasts make me catch my breath—she has out-sized even Siggy. She wears a dark suit too, her pink shirt unbuttoned to the top of her breasts. She carries a leather briefcase with gold clasps.

-Congratulations, Avanti. He crosses the room, hand extended to reach across the desk. Avanti is on her feet.

-Thank you, Uncle. She crosses the expanse of her desk, allowing him to embrace her with familial familiarity. Let's sit over there. They take their places on the sofa. The assistant hovers, forgotten. I take an armchair.

-You know Chanakya.

-Who doesn't? I am dismissed, just another ancillary in her life. He looks around the office. Disparagement. Condescension. His office, I've heard, not seen, is the size of a tennis court, wall-to-wall carpet, a bar with every kind of liquor available, furnished with only a sofa and chairs. He doesn't sit at a desk.

-It's an honour to have you as my first visitor, uncle. Coffee? Tea? This is a government office, no malt whisky.

-No, no. I only came to congratulate you and wish you all success in your position.

He glances to his assistant. She immediately takes out a package from the briefcase. It is wrapped in gold foil and tied with a red ribbon. It is her handiwork. She holds it out to him and his pointing finger deflects the gift to Avanti.

She takes it with a Thank you, Uncle.

They are watching, expecting her to open it now, in front of them and she unties the ribbon, unwraps the foil to reveal a blue velvet box. She opens it. A lady's gold Rolex watch, studded with diamonds, curls around a raised mound of yellow velvet. It is an expensive bauble and she smiles with another Thank you, Uncle, and sets it aside.

He lifts a hand and his assistant opens the briefcase again and passes Avanti a slim folder. Monika's father is a very cautious man. I note he touches nothing, not wishing to leave even a fingerprint as evidence of his presence in this room. I have learnt about this magical identification method from watching films and television, detectives dusting surfaces and finding the criminal through a tiny print. This forensic science fascinates me, crimes unravelled through

microscopes, blood samples, DNA, heat tests, bullet casings, chemical solvents and too many other ways for me to want to commit murder.
–I am aware that this very important portfolio is underfunded, Monika's father says. And I only want to help educate our young children. They are our future. These are just suggestions I had in mind. With your help, we can make this ministry do great things.
Avanti opens the folder. Skims through its contents. Turns a page. Unfolds a map.
–You see, he continues, leaning across the sofa, a fat finger pointing to a place but not touching it. In District 18, there is a jungle on the eastern border. My engineers have surveyed it and there is a huge deposit of copper beneath it. We need to explore further and start mining in the near future. Your father wanted me to discuss this first with you, as that is your constituency. My company will build all the schools in District 18 and pay the salaries of teachers. Whatever else you require, just ask. He looks to his assistant, a cue.
–All the funds will of course be channelled through your office, she says, almost in a whisper, bending lower and revealing more of her breasts than any man can bear with equanimity.
–I will study this and get back to you…
–Oh, that's not necessary, he says. It's only for your information.
–Chay and his followers live in that jungle, I remind Avanti.
He ignores me to address her. Your father assures me that he will take care of this Chay, a good-for-nothing, very soon. He's sending a special task force to flush out the vermin.
Chay disposed, the noble rises, he's a busy man. The meeting is over, and he expects the familial embrace from the minister, which he receives graciously, and then she accompanies him to the door. She has left the file on the table and I peruse it swiftly—many zeroes follow many numbers; I cannot even begin to imagine the value of the wealth to be stolen from under the feet of tigers, elephants, hyenas, cheetal, sambar, gaur, wild pigs, the thousand trees nesting a hundred varieties of birds. Where will they all go? To that distant, invisible land of extinction, crowded with the exiles of all the ages. Monika's father would be dangling by his necktie from one of those trees if my emperor had read this document. In economics, a word that did not exist then, I advised the emperor there are always two courses for revenue and you must choose judiciously. The land

can be exploited for immediate gain only to regret it later as the relentless desert claims it. Or be gentle in your greed so that it will continue to feed your people for many generations to come. The more you take from the people the more insecure your throne. My emperor always listened to wise advice. Only so many trees felled in a jungle for firewood, only so many elephants captured for the wars, and then the jungle would be left in peace to regenerate itself.

Avanti returns to her desk, scooping the file from my hands on the way. She sits to study it, head down. Silence. Finally, she finishes, closes it, smiling.

–It's very generous of Uncle to fund the department. We can build a few schools and hire new teachers. There's more than enough.

–There's never more than enough and I wonder how much will finally reach the children.

She flushes at my innuendo. You yourself said a prince must first look after his needs.

–After his people's needs. I repeat my shastra as people are forgetful: In the happiness of his subjects lies the king's happiness, in their welfare his welfare. He shall not consider as good only that which pleases him but treat as beneficial to him whatever pleases his subjects.

–We have enough, she says, firmly ending the discussion.

I don't allow her to. You must oppose your father.

She is shocked, she is nervous, she pulls back as if I'd spat. I can't do that. He'll be furious with me.

–You're afraid of him. A princess can't show that and it is the convention that princes challenge their fathers. At first. You retreat later but reveal that you're your own woman. Kings no longer kill their sons in this age.

–He won't kill me but he'll stop talking to me, and helping me run the ministry. I'll lose him, she ends in a wail.

–You have your own power, the people who voted for you. Besides, how can your father lose his love for you?

–When he gets angry with me, he slaps me and says he won't love me. I love him and couldn't refuse him when....

It's the child who has emerged out of the woman, despite her imprisonment, in this drab confessional. I suspected that, though some days I'd not see her until dusk, so the marks had time to fade. The cheeks remained tinged, the spirit subdued by sorrow. Such love is not new; it was there in my time and before that too. Even then, I disapproved but I only interfere in the affairs of state, not in the affairs of families. I am only surprised that this confession comes now, in this office of power. Power frees one of subterfuge; it is answerable to no one. She flushes, she turns away in embarrassment at this confession that escaped out of her mouth, and now cannot be recalled. It hangs between us, the pain and suffering so visible in her eyes.

I rise and circle the desk to stand beside her. Her face remains averted from me. The light is muted behind those heavy, green bureaucratic curtains and the room is too full of gloom. I leave her side for a moment to draw them back, dust motes float on to my clothes. The sun dispels the permanent dusk, it's harsh yet uplifting. I return to her side as she blinks at the rich polish of her desk now visible, reflecting her.

–It is time for you to assert your independence. You are sitting in a seat of power and you won it all by yourself. He may claim victory but it is only through you and not because of him. Believe in yourself, Avanti.

–It's easy for you to say.
–It's easy for you to do.
–You've known, haven't you?
–Yes.
–Mother knew, she did nothing.
–She was as helpless as you but she fought to keep you away from him. Love constricted her mind and her emotions. I know she loves you.

–I know that. Sharply.

–Then distance yourself from your father. We'll do it gradually, we'll be subtle. Avoid meetings, banquets, dinners. Be unavailable in the evenings. Better still...

–Get married. There is a tragic look in her eyes. Then she straightens, recalling her position. Now, soon as Chay is cleared out of the jungle, Uncle can begin mining. I'll try to stop it and then allow it. I have to do this to challenge father. We need copper desperately if we're to grow our GDP and our GNP. Look at what other countries are doing.

GDP, GNP and other abbreviations baffle me and I ignore their meanings. Let them do what they want. Chay will fight.

–He'll be defeated. The special forces will clear him and his men out.

–Not easily. He knows the jungle.

–That's my father's concern and the sooner it happens the better. We won't get any money until Uncle can start mining. If you're so enamoured with Chay why don't you go and talk to him? You're the big advisor. Tell him he hasn't a chance and to surrender his weapons. He believes he's some kind of a Robin Hood.

–Robin Hood! Who is this Robin Hood? I'm aware of gaps in my knowledge and I am eager to hear what she will say about this man.

–I forget you're ignorant at times. He was an Englishman who stole from the rich and gave the money to the poor.

–It's a fairytale then, and not a real king.

–It's a true story.

–It can't be. No Englishman would do that. And no matter what the nationality, the state steals from the poor to give money to the rich. How else can a king maintain his rajas, his army, his court? If he stole from the rich to give to the poor, he would have an insurrection in his court.

–Whatever. I give you full permission to meet Chay and discuss his surrender. The sooner the better.

–Why me? I have to protest this arbitrary decision, sending me into the tiger's den.

–From our Intel Chay hates politicians, loathes the police, detests industrialists and our babus. That leaves you. You're neutral. She gestures for me to take the chair opposite and I sense the interrogation to come.

–Well, what did he say?

–Chay? I tease her.

–Aditya, for god's sake. You did speak to him, didn't you?

–Oh yes, we spoke. I scratch the stubble on my disfigured side where the razor can't clear the crags and crevices of my skin, pretending to recall. Oh yes, he told me he's starting to shoot a new movie up in the mountains and…he has Siggy Chopra playing the heroine. He's going to let me watch the shoot and introduce

me to her.
 -Chan, she shouts. I don't care about Siggy Chopra. Then a deep breath, almost a sense of impending defeat. Is she the movie star he's marrying? She is beautiful.
 -She is oversize stunning. When I saw her in *Dhanvaz Bis* I...
 -Is he going to marry her? Another shout.
 -He didn't tell me whom he's marrying. Could be another movie star but if I was him I'd marry Siggy.
 -Did he... Madam Minister speaks slowly...speak about me?
 -In passing.
 -Just in passing? Nothing more?

I haven't forgotten my promise to Aditya of a dinner with Avanti but she needs subtle persuasion as her pride will not capitulate that easily. I will put words into his mouth to soften her for that invitation. He's proud of you and thought you looked so seductive standing among those chamchas. He said you looked like a movie star, stunning and glowing like one. And you're exactly the way he remembers you and nothing has changed. He also remembers meeting you outside the convent school to eat ice cream at Shandy's ice cream parlour. He said that Häagen-Dazs vanilla was your favourite.
 -Butterscotch. She smiles at the memory I invented. The passage of time recreates scenes in the past that never existed but if described, can become as real and true as you want them to be.
 -He wants you to visit the shoot.
 -No, I won't. Not if Siggy Chopra's there. And you won't have time to do that either as you're going to meet Chay, remember. Or are you afraid of entering the jungle all alone? Take your Vikram with you.
 -Politics is far more treacherous than any jungle. I've crossed jungles deeper, thicker than this sparse one. And I think I can manage both assignments. What do you want me to tell him?
 -I don't want to see him again.
 -But you've not seen Chay.
 -Aditya, Aditya. You're so dense at times.

Aditya is the prayer of love on her lips, longing to escape and express itself. And it will soon...

■

Siggy calls me, I can hear her siren voice in my dreams and even in my waking moments. That is the problem of returning to the world of the flesh, it distracts the spirit from its true calling and leads us astray. Chay is entrenched in the jungle, he'll always be there. Siggy won't wait, she's on a flying visit, and I'll only see her again thirty feet high. Dressed in my normal black kurta, I look immaculate in the mirror, depending on the angle you view, and I know she will flinch when she meets me. It's a natural reaction. I have read the fairy tales, as you have too, of beauties and beasts, of princesses and frogs who fall in love. I expect nothing like that will happen. My happiness at seeing her will be enough for me, that moment will pass too once I look into her eyes. See, even as I think of this expectant happiness it dissolves into doubt. It's an interminable journey into the mountains, the winding ghat roads again affecting my equilibrium and I hope I'm not sick when I reach the film location. It is beyond the ashram, higher, in the colder regions with a view of snow-capped peaks, the horizon jagged like a hundred daggers.

We pass the diesel generators, silent for the moment, and fifty or so men, a few women, moving lights, reflectors, all the magic that creates our illusions in the cinema hall. Some distance away, cooks are preparing the lunch and snacks, stirring darkened pots over gas flames till the smell of food overcomes the perfume of pine. A young man awaits my arrival, he is a third AD, and, averting his stare, leads me through a tangle of cables and extras sipping chai, eating vadais and samosas. They fall silent, my presence unsettles them. Film people are superstitious and they quickly look away in case I carry a curse which will affect this movie. Aditya is beside the camera, in conference with his director of photography, Kumar. They have collaborated on many films, won many awards. They look at the script, look to the mountains, look around, both framing scenes together, then panning the shot. Just beyond them, teetering on the edge of a slope is the set—a village, a dozen homes huddled together. The walls are made of stone, the roofs are narrow logs and tufts of wheat stalks, dry and brittle, peep out between the roof and the walls. It looks authentic but when I tap the stones, they're hollow.

I wait, scanning the crowd, looking for my Siggy. There are trailers parked to one side, doors closed, the abode of the stars. The male lead is BKW, only his initials are needed for instant recognition and he is paid a fortune to act with Siggy. It's their first pairing and, if the magic works, they will work together in other movies. Can BKW match Siggy's screen charisma? I will wait and see. Aditya turns and notices me and I am elevated among the curious eyes by his warm smile, the familiar laugh of affection. He takes my hand, leading me to his director's chair and when I'm comfortable, the AD brings him another chair, then returns with chai, vadais, samosas.

–We're just setting up. It's a morning shot. Siggy is coming out, then walking down that slope to fetch water...

–The story?

–It's a woman's story. She was once rich, even powerful, a tycoon of sorts, who has lost all and has to return to her village. The man who destroyed her, that's BKW, has fallen in love with her and wants her to return and marry him. So she has to make a choice—to remain in this simple life where she's happy or return to the turmoil of urban life with a man who harmed her. She's insecure about his love. That's it. You'll pay to see it?

–If you're making it, of course.

–Or because of Siggy?

–The added bonus. You shooting in 3D?

He laughs. It's not an action thriller so you won't see her tits sticking out of the screen.

–Did Shakuntala visit you?

–She came yesterday, just to get out of the ashram I think. And to see me. The shooting didn't interest her, she wants to see the finished film. He turns to the AD. See if Miss Chopra is ready for a rehearsal?

He hurries to the trailer, knocks. Aditya takes my hand and rests a finger on my pulse.

–Just keep your BP under control when she comes out. Now that I'm about to fulfil my part of our bargain how's your part coming along.

–Why do you persist?

He takes his time, looking away to the mountains for an answer. I wondered why I loved her. Why her and not another? It puzzles me as I suppose it has both men and women for an eternity. Here I am working with a woman whose beauty and smile seduces a nation. I love Siggy's laugh, low and throaty, I love the flicker in her eyes when she looks at me, I love the curve of her mouth, and I love the perfume on her skin. Yet, I don't really love her as whole. I want to, but you can't command and summon love from a bleak heart. There was no closure, between Avanti and me and that must happen. We've known…okay loved…each other since childhood and that's hard to forget. I remember how happy I felt each time I saw her. When you're that young, you believe that you are destined for each other. He glares at me. Then you came along.

–No, I was only an advisor, not the instigator. You'll be having dinner with a politician.

–You make it sound like a disease, he laughs. As long as she isn't like her father. He studies me a long moment. Is she? I hope to God not.

–No. Though I want to tell him how can I foretell the future. I don't know what's in anyone's heart. In my previous existence I loved Suvashini, daughter of the courtier Shaktar. She chose to become the mistress of Rakshasha instead of being with an ugly man, and splintered my heart.

–Can she help change this state, get rid of those corrupt old men with bankrupt ideas? He charges back. So, our bargain?

I pull out three envelopes from my kurta pocket, find his name scrolled in gold lettering on one and pass it over. He opens it.

–It was to be a quiet dinner, not this, he waves it around, irate.

–It's the first step, after that the dinner for two with candlelight and sitar. You meet Avanti, just friendly chat, at her father's seventieth birthday party.

–Who are the other two invitees?

–Siggy and BKW. I don't mention that I blackmailed the clerk for these exclusive invites. He was fucking his secretary and I threatened to inform his wife, a vengeful woman capable of sticking a knife in him while he slept.

Aditya checks the embossed card with its gold lettering. It's next week. Siggy'll be here as we have some more shoots for her. BKW won't be, he has a dance number to shoot on the Golden Gate Bridge and leaves the day after.

–Then just you and her.

Even as I say 'her', the door of one of the trailers opens, and a woman walks down the three steps. Her feet are fair as lotus flowers, bare too, toes caressing the earth with each step, unpainted and natural. A faded blue, patched skirt, cheap cotton, falls to her ankles. As she approaches, a beam of sunlight silhouettes her legs through the thin material. She isn't wearing an under skirt, only white panties and the perfection of her legs as they glide along stops my breath. Her hips float from side to side, as if suspended in air. Her breasts are snuggled within her faded and patched choli, rising and falling with her gentle breathing. The neck rises from her shoulders like a column of water, smooth, cool, the neck-bones delicate as flutes. The chin is the tip of a heart and the lips, slightly apart, soft as rose petals, reveal her teeth, perfect rows, white as an egret's wing. There's the familiar flare of her nose, and I envy the air that slips through it into her body. In this light, her eyes are almost green. The lashes fall to protect them, and it's as if the sun has vanished momentarily; the eyebrows are perfect arches and one rises in query, just faintly wrinkling the expanse of her forehead. A thousand sparks of the sun light her hair. She is looking only at Aditya, a silent complicity of sensuality in the smile. A woman can reveal her secrets with just such a glance and now when I look at Aditya I see his smile embracing her as if they have been apart for many years.

When he rises, I rise too, and he takes her outstretched hands into his. Then turns to me, as he draws her closer. Siggy, I want you to meet my friend, Chanakya.

Her full radiance shines on me as she puts out both her hands to take first one of my hands and then the other and warm them between the pliant softness of her palms. She is a slight woman, taller than me, but not by thirty feet. And not as youthful as she is on the screen. She is in her late twenties, with faint lines around her eyes and the corners of her mouth. She draws me into a secret assignation through those mysterious eyes, that disarming smile and the gentle squeezing of my hands. She makes this promise to all the men she meets but I am not at all disappointed. How else can she project her magnetism on the screen if she did not practice it in real life? It is not an act, it is her natural self, the seduction within the innocence of her smile. She has a child's manner in her wish for acceptance. Yet she is aware of her power. Remember what I said earlier: *There is nothing more powerful in the world than the youth and beauty of a woman.* And looking into her eyes, I don't see them flinch at my appearance; I am as normal as any other man.

–Chanakya, a beautiful name, she speaks in a husky, low tone, a breeze caressing leaves.

–My…my…pleas…I cannot believe that I of the fluid tongue and thoughts stutter like a school boy in front of a headmaster. My …pleasure to fin…ally meet you Miss Chopra. I have seen all your films.

–Poor man. They were all terrible, except this one. And it's Siggy. She turns to Aditya. Are you ready to rehearse?

–Not yet. He's making a notation in his script.

–Then I'll take Chanakya with me down to the stream. It's boring sitting in the trailer.

–Be careful, Aditya warns Siggy, looking up. Smiling. Chanakya is a dangerous man, very amoral, and he can ruin your life if you get too close to him.

She laughs and I feel the vibrations in my bones. Then she draws me close and those sensual orbs of firm flesh press into me. I could die now, with no regrets. I love amoral men and he'll teach me all the tricks. She releases me from her heavenly body and the world is so much the poorer to my vision. Still, she holds my hand, guiding me down a path.

–Will you ruin my life?

–Not if I can help it. But how can I tell this vision-in-a-peasant-costume that even I cannot predict how I will use her for my ends. The invitation card lies in my pocket.

Her lotus feet are unmindful of the pebbles and stones as we make our way down. She is carefree now, looking around at the deodars, the oak trees, pine, alive with tits, leaf warblers, flycatchers, tree creepers, nuthatches, rosefinches accentors, redstarts, pipits and that most beautiful of mountain birds, the grandala. She whistles to them, almost a perfect imitation of a warbler; they reply, and I don't know whether they recognize her calls. The air is cool, scented, heady and we have left the set some way behind. We cannot see the mountains clearly for the trees and the sun. The sun dances on the water; the stream sings its own melodies. She sits on a low stone and sinks her feet into the water, laughing at the cold caress.

–Take off your chappals, the water will fill you with energy. It's magic water all the way down from the high mountains.

How can I refuse? I dip my feet in, the water is not cold, but icy, and I feel my feet losing all sensation but as long as her legs brush mine, I shan't move.

-Where are you from?
-The plains, far below.
-I was born not far from here.
-I thought in the city.

She dismisses my belief. Oh, that's all in the press. They make up stories about me. I was born in a small village. She points to the mountains. There, under that peak. I was four when my parents moved to the city. Do you see Lakshmi in that mountain?

She leans closer so that my eyes align with her arm and follow the finger into the distance. Smoky clouds drift between the peaks and fall at their feet. No matter how I squint and try to conjure Lakshmi out of that ice, snow and rock, I can't see the goddess who stands guard over her village. Gods, after all, live only in our imaginations and if she believes she can see her, then Lakshmi is there.

-Do you?
-Yes, I think so. Reluctantly, I part from that exquisite arm.
-My father was very poor and he worked as a labourer first, and then learned to drive an autorickshaw. He worked hard to send me to an English school. He wanted me to be a doctor. I failed him; I wasn't clever enough for that.
-He must be proud of you now.

Her eyes darken she shakes her head. He died when I was nine in an accident. Some big shot's car smashed into his auto and raced on. The police didn't even try to find it. What was another autorickshaw driver to them? I wept for a whole year.

I hold her hand, an inadequate condolence for a long ago death.
-Who raised you then?
-My mother. Who else? She first worked as a domestic in a house but the man and even his teenage son harassed her. So she quit and learned to drive an auto too. The other drivers were very kind and helpful, as they knew my father. She's now back in our village, building a small home.

Gradually her eyes glisten again, surfacing from that melancholy memory. I know the press say that my father was the chauffeur to the producer Prem Malhotra and that's how I got into films. That isn't true at all. I was playing Sita in a school play and Mr. Malhotra came to see it as he had donated some funds, and he was the guest of honour on that day. That's how the producer saw me and cast me as the younger sister of the star in his new movie. My grandparents too are still in that village and I return once a year, heavily disguised, so the press don't chase me. No one in my village has even seen cinema so they only know me as the village girl who left home years ago, and returns once a year.

–Your life sounds like the movie you're making now.

–That's why I agreed to do it. Aditya will make a great art house movie. No song, no dance numbers and I had a good reason to come to the mountains. She takes my hand, palm up, pretending to read the lines in the shifting, shadowy light filtering through. She is still a girl, not the woman I imagine on that giant screen. I see the secrets in your eyes and deception in your hand.

I try to take her hand, palm up, but she makes a tiny fist. I don't want anyone to know my future, I don't want it spoiled. Why does Aditya call you amoral? What does it mean?

–Aditya didn't tell you about me?

–No. He just said a friend would visit the location shoot. Not to me. To the AD, and I overheard.

–I am an advisor. Political power is amoral, and I advise on that.

Her eyes open wide. I have impressed the movie star. You advise the President?

–Avanti.

–Oh. She pouts, splashing the water with her feet. She pulls up the hem of her skirt and reveals her exquisitely shaped legs all the way to her thighs. I'm not sure I like Avanti after the way she treated Aditya.

–It was a difficult choice. Sometimes, I advise the President, if he asks for suggestions. Would you like to meet him?

She smiles. I would love to. He's such a handsome man, with that greying hair and wise face. I doubt he wants to meet a movie actor.

I note she is modest, she doesn't call herself a movie star, which undoubtedly she is. She is capable of stopping traffic, even starting a riot. I take out the envelopes, and pass her the one with her name on it. She opens and reads it carefully. Once, twice.

-He's invited me!!! Oh yes, I'll be there. Will you be my date?
-Aditya will be there too. He's your date.

She puts an arm around me, draws me to her, and kisses both cheeks, planting delicate lips against overheated skin. I return those kisses to her cheeks, inhaling the perfume of her warm skin, testing my lips against the soft flesh. If only… She draws away, that embrace, so brief, will remain in the memory of my skin for a long time.

-I suppose he'll be with Avanti.
-Yes.
-And her mother? She is a beautiful woman. I met her and really liked her. I read that they live apart.
-She spends some time in an ashram, not far from here.
-I know. She's lucky. I want to return to live here. Then I'll be truly content. I don't like my life, I never aspired to be an actress. Every man I meet only wants to fuck me, so he can boast to his friends 'I fucked Siggy Chopra'. They're all blind to everything about me beyond my body and my face. Women too want me to sleep with them. It's the same everywhere—London, Cannes, even Hollywood where there are a thousand women more beautiful than I am. And I don't think I'm beautiful. I'm just a village girl whose real name is Rachna Das but the producers thought I should have a snappy name—Siggy Chopra. She's make-believe. I want this to be my last film. I have enough money to build a small house at the foot of the mountain and I'll just sit there and meditate. She laughs, dryly. I'll be a sanyasan and everyone will forget Siggy Chopra. There'll be others after me; there always are, just waiting.

The AD slips and slides down the slope, nearly falling over in his urgency. Miss Chopra, we're ready to rehearse.

She rises. The dream, the contemplation returns to hiding. She smiles down at me. I never told anyone this before. You're a man who keeps secrets. I can tell you would also like to fuck me. Don't be embarrassed. I refuse always. You have a young face, and ancient eyes. Aditya and all my co-stars are all young men.

-I'm over thirty, nearly forty.

She laughs. Too young. I want to fall in love with my father, I suppose. Over and over again. Now I have to play Siggy and it can be boring—rehearsal, then a wait, then the cameras roll and roll. Aditya won't start shooting yet, so you can stay down here awhile.

She returns the invitation. I don't have a pocket in my skirt, give it to me later. She follows the AD up, swinging those liquid hips. She takes the enchantment with her, leaving me saddened. Even the sun has shyly slid behind a cloud and the forest is darker. I didn't want to hear her confessions, I wanted to believe in the glow of stardom, although I am aware it is dulled and tarnished. Such fame, built on physical beauty, is fragile, wasting away even as the flesh ages. She is wiser than the others who are wilfully oblivious to the darkness that will consume them. A part of me is disappointed, although I know I could never hope to slip between her sensual legs. I wonder if she enjoys sex, knowing the intent of every boastful man. She is the prize to be coveted, won and held aloft, as winners do their trophies in sports. I wonder too whether she will fulfil her dream and withdraw from her glittering world. I can't feel my feet, yet I don't lift them out. The water is silvery now, still musical. I hadn't seen flowing water until I was five, as the only well was five hundred metres away and water came to my house in a plastic vessel, carried on my mother's ample hip. It shone in a corner of our single room, more precious than gold, diamonds, platinum—we drank sparingly. I would lean over the vessel, inhale the sweet, cool perfume, and dip a finger in for a drop to bless my tongue. In my earlier life, I had three clean rivers in which to bathe and drink my fill. Now, in the city, the river is thick, slimy, stinking as it struggles through the narrow banks to reach the sea. I throw a stick into the stream and watch it bob and float away. The water twists and turns it, and traps it against a rock. Then it's freed and is swept from sight around the bend. I travel with it in my imagination as it negotiates other rocks and hurtles down the steep incline, sticking against the bank, tugged free again as the water carries it on. Somewhere distant it hurtles into the river, broad and powerful, past women washing clothes, their bodies, their vessels, men their cattle. It will continue on to finally flow into the sea. And from there across the world to end on a distant shore where people speak a different language. A piece of driftwood, gathered by young children and when dried, heaped onto the flames to cook an evening meal. Its journey over, its purpose fulfilled. Or, if I walk downstream, I will see it held firmly in the roots of a tree. Its destiny changed by a whirl in the current.

The rehearsal is over and the cameras ready to roll when I

climb back up to the location. Aditya sits apart, staring at a video screen. The AD shouts the magic words at the lift of his directorial hand: Silence, sound rolling, camera roll, camera rolling, action. Siggy emerges from a hut, stretching and yawning away sleep, carrying a vessel and moves languidly towards the slope down to the stream. The camera, on tracks, follows her, until she takes the first step down. Cut. That's a take. Siggy returns, smiling. There are close-ups to be shot, reverse angles. I have yet to see BKW, who remains in his trailer. Aditya barely notes my presence as he confers with his DP, and I signal to Siggy, in her canvas chair, as makeup artistes work on her, that I will leave the invite in her trailer. She blows me a kiss.

It's a small room, with a single bed, a dresser and an open closet for her clothes. I place the envelope on the dresser table, inhaling the perfumes of her powder and scents. I cannot resist touching the crystal containers and caressing the costumes hanging in the open closet. I want to leave my fingerprints, proof that I was here, in Siggy's trailer, and carry away as many intimate memories as I can on my fingertips.

On the way down, I stop the car at the entrance of the ashram. The same guard watches my approach. He knows my intent and is ready with his refusal: It is meditation time and no one is permitted to disturb the devotees.

–I can wait. How long will they meditate?

–An hour, two hours. He is a surly fellow, clean shaven, bald too, though young, wearing holy colours and a fine line of contempt.

I leave; it's getting dark. The road down is dangerous at night. I didn't fear the tigers or elephant herds or dacoits that patrolled those dark paths in my time. But here, at dawn, you'll witness the night's carnage of crashes, smashes, overturned lorries.

■

Since she has Y-category security, cops surround the building now. They patrol the entrance with their AKs, they lounge on benches, doze in the shade of a neem tree. Beyond, the compound is deserted, an air of high inactivity, compared to other ministries through which money flows abundantly. I have an identity pass, encased in plastic, with my photograph. But before I pass their scrutiny, I notice a young man sitting on the opposite pavement. He's in his early thirties, neatly dressed in jeans and a white shirt, thin, rimless spectacles accentuating the gaunt face. Beside him is a tin trunk, the size of a carry-on case. One arm is draped over it protectively.

–Who is he? I ask the nearest officer.

He shrugs. I don't know. He wants to see Madam Minister. We told him he cannot. She is too important to see someone like him. Then he adds bitterly. And he has no money.

–He could have a bomb in that case.

–As long as he blows himself up on that side of the road and not this side, he can sit there as long as he wants. This is a democracy.

It's a busy road. Cars race at high speed to jump the traffic lights at the far end, although the speed limit is 30 kilometres per hour. The pavement is crowded with pedestrians teetering on the edges, wanting to cross. In Pataliputra, twice, I was nearly run down crossing the street and in one shastra suggested a speed limit for chariots, horsemen, elephants, bullock carts and handcarts. The man looks forlorn but patient in his posture. He interests me.

–Get me across the road.

–Who are you to order me?

I pull out my cell phone. If I call the minister, you will find yourself in the jungle with the special forces searching for Chay tomorrow morning.

In this state only influence persuades the authorities to function and the police officer doesn't hesitate any more. Reluctantly, dodging cars, he lumbers half way across the street and holds up his hand to stop the cars so I can pass. I squat by the man.

–Who are you?

He shakes his head.

–What do you have in the box?

He looks up at me, with a slight squint. What's wrong with your face?

–I'll tell you if you tell me what's in the box.

–I can't. I can only show it to Madam Minister, she is the one sent down from the heavens to bless our lives.

He's another worshipper, though not a party man. The case is locked and he tightens his grip around it.

–It could be a bomb.

–It could be.

—If you show me, I can ask her to give you an audience.
—I will wait. A stubborn man. But I cannot risk leading him into her presence without the police opening the box.
—Just sit here then.
The police officer helps me back across the street.
I walk into the Minister's office to find her at her desk. She has done away with the bureaucratic decor, the room has been refurbished—the curtains are pale yellow imprinted with roses and green stems, the sofas are adorned with plumped pillows, vases with fresh flowers are on the coffee table and the room is perfumed with jasmine. Her desk is cluttered with files. She dominates it, and the room, no longer the neophyte but a woman of importance.
—There's a young man across the road…
—I know. I refuse to see him. He could be an assassin. Her voice too has changed. She speaks with an authority and confidence she lacked before, even as president of her party's youth wing. She has her title, she has her bureaucrats, but she has no money.
—Aren't you curious about the box?
—No. Abruptly she asks—Is he going to marry her?
—He didn't confide in me. I just wanted to see how they make films. It takes away a lot of the magic and…
—Her. You met her?
—Briefly. She's a lovely girl, and innocent.
—No actress is innocent, they're all whores.
—I don't think Siggy is one, despite the publicity.
—Marriage?
—He didn't say to whom.
She pretends disinterest, though she wants to strap me down and burn me with hot irons to get whatever information she can out of me.
—Chay is an increasing problem. The police can't even find him. As if there are a hundred jungles he's hiding in. We can't get any mining investments until this man is finished off, one way or the other. I told you to go and meet him and make him a deal. Instead, you go off to watch films.
—And what do I offer Chay?
—Money. What else?
—What's my budget?

She bites her lower lip, dainty teeth protruding. Start low, a few thousand. He's only a villager. Then maybe a hundred thousand or two. No more than that. But first use your persuasive tongue to get him to lay down his arms. I guarantee he will be pardoned.

-A prince should not negotiate with money. Only arms.

-The arms aren't finding him. So offer the money.

ELEVEN

I OBEY MY prince(ss) reluctantly, I am not thrilled by the prospect of endangering my life by seeking out this Chay. A wild man in the jungle, nursing anger and hatred for the state, of which I am now a representative. I've no wish to swiftly depart the world I'd just re-entered, there's much more for me to learn and see before I'm returned to the abode of bored souls. My only companion is Vikram, silent in his unease. As a spy he prefers anonymity. Wisely, he will escort me only to the edge of the jungle, and abandon me there to meet a guide who will take me to the hideout.
  -What did you tell this guide about me?
  -Your name and that you're not a government person. Just an advisor.
  -How did you make the contact?
  -Through a tribal in the bazaar. He didn't say he knew Chay but could pass the word through the jungle. It took a week before he confirmed that Chay had agreed to meet you. Alone. The guide will be one of his men.
  -Where are the police combing?
  -Far from where he is.
  -Do they know what he looks like now? Or his real name?
  -No. Still nothing. He's a shadow. They say he always has a scarf covering his lower face.
  -There have been encounters. You sent me reports.
  -Chay did blow up a police jeep, killing five cops. In turn, they killed a few tribals, claiming they're Chay's people. But they weren't. It justifies the cops' presence. The tribals have fled deeper into the jungle. They're trapped between Chay and the police.
  -When I do meet him, and if I remain alive, will he negotiate?
  Vikram shrugs. I hear he's a man of strong principles. He is determined to overthrow the state and bring in a just and compassionate government. He claims he's not a communist but a socialist, democrat reformer. He searches through his shabby leather bag and pulls out a crumpled pamphlet. This is his manifesto, if

you want to read it. It's about thirst, hunger, shelter, land reform, employment and education.

—I have seen it, I murmur and return it to him.

Finally, we turn off the narrow tarmac road, and drive along the previous dirt track we'd followed with Avanti months ago. We reach the dismal village. It appears abandoned, there's not even a goat in sight and the thorn fence has disintegrated. The mud walls are cracked, broken apart in some places, and the thatch has caved in.

—Why have they left?

—They were ordered to leave. The mining company's acquired all the land.

Monika's father is an impatient man; he cannot wait to suck the glitter from under the earth. He is confident the President will obey his command. If he gave a small bauble to Avanti, what did he give the President? I will get my hacker, Sita, to find out when, and if, I return alive.

—Why didn't you tell me this?

—I thought you knew since you're with Madam Minister.

—Yes, of course. I will, for the moment, grant her ignorance, as her father doesn't confide all his actions to her. In future, tell me everything.

—I need more help. I can't do all this spying myself in District 18.

—We're working on that, I console him.

We drive on past the village. Other villages we come to have been similarly abandoned. The empty landscape is depressing. Not that it was fruitful for the peasants but it was their home, their roots deep in the soil, now uprooted by a company.

—Where have they gone?

—To the city, where else. The government has promised they will be resettled, Vikram says, not with any hope, as we're both aware of many broken promises.

Eventually, the jungle rises like a fortress wall before us and the lane becomes a footpath vanishing among the trees and the wild undergrowth. When the engine stops, we hear the silence; it's waiting for me to enter and I hear its steady breath. We have arranged that Vikram will return here daily at noon and dusk, if I am ever to return from the meeting.

—Where's my guide?

He points to a rock with a birth control slogan splashed on it. This is the place. He'll be along soon.

And with that reassurance, he jumps back into the car; I watch it turn and leave. I find shade under a tamarind tree on the very edge of the forest, and settle down to wait. If by dusk there is no guide, I will walk all the way back, and not spend a night out here. I have spent nights, lost in jungles in my past, and in the darkness up in the trees for my safety. My thoughts wander to my past. I spent many lonely days during my exile, wandering from village to village in search of enlightenment. Then my given name was Vishnu Gupta and I became Chanakya, the falsehood, and, until I found Chandragupta I had time to think upon myself, decipher a reason for my existence. We explore the inner cosmos of ourselves, always searching for who we really are and, like the universe itself, are lost in the vast spaces that exist within us. We reinvent ourselves, day by day, like Siggy and me, without knowing who was that first creation, that long lost child hidden under layers of illusion. We keep moving away until we find the stranger inhabiting us and wonder where he came from and whether he was waiting for us all along. And on our deathbeds, we reach back for the child but never find him, it's too late and he's long forgotten. 'Who are we?' is our final thought.

The heat, the hum of insects, the rustle of small creatures in the jungle, lulls me to sleep. I wake at dusk with a gun pointed at my head. Another gun is aimed at my chest. They're AK47s, barrels grey with age. The fingers on the triggers and the hands holding them are small, delicate and, when I start to rise the two young women take wary steps back. They wear salwar kameezes, patched, faded, the green colours long washed out, and their dupattas cover their faces, up to their eyes. Like orthodox Muslim women, the dupattas cover their heads as well. They gesture: raise your hands, turn around, embrace the tree. I obey. I'm searched, my cell phone confiscated. It had GPS to track me, and now they've switched it off. One walks into the jungle, I follow, the other falls in behind me.

-How far?

No reply.

-How long? Many days, a few hours? I'm hungry.

No reply. Do they understand? I know they do from the brief flicker between them when and I first made an effort to talk to them, but they prefer silence.

When we have walked a little way into the jungle, they force me to lie down and then crouch on either side, staring out at the dirt road, restlessly scanning the landscape. They're waiting to see if I am followed; they're professional and they're patient. A half hour passes before they rise and allow me up.

The woman in front walks nimbly through the undergrowth, following an invisible path past great trees, roots rising like the prows of ships. The jungle is warm and humid, as a woman's body pressed against me. I feel its breath on my skin. Above us a tribe of langurs, with black faces and silver coats look down in judgement; a sow, followed by her young, scurries away from us, a mongoose slides swiftly across the path, a peacock glides to a branch further away. We pass the stones of a ruined fortress, I look up, and, in the fading light, I see the walls crowning a high hill. Who was the great king, who left behind this legacy of broken stone? A placid lake lies at its feet, surrounded by high grass, and, on the far shore, a herd of cheetal is approaching cautiously. The point animal walks ahead of the others, its ears twitching for the predators. They show no fear of us. Yet, the jungle teems with dangers and every animal, bird, reptile, insect, even the blades of grass and those thorny bushes, those great trees and vines battle ferociously to remain alive. Nothing changes, except their world shrinks until it's the size of a prison cell.

It grows darker, the moon bathes the ghostly trees and bushes in a faint white light. The women keep moving and I feel my un-athletic legs tiring. I have looked back a few times and the woman behind is missing, then she reappears, hurrying to catch up. She has been checking to see if we're followed.

-Rest, I announce and sit in protest. Surprisingly, they too sit, watching from a distance, whispering, giggling to each other. They're lean and fit, scarcely panting. When they judge I have rested enough, they prod me to my feet with their guns and I stumble on, following the woman in the lead. When pale dawn begins to light our way, darkness descends on me as they slip a black hood over my head. One takes my hand, her hard fingers entwined in mine. We walk slower, she guides me along some kind of a pathway that snakes through the jungle. When I trip, she is strong enough to steady me. We stop after what seems like many hours. She removes the hood and I wince at the sunlight. The camp is temporary, a few makeshift shelters constructed of branches and leaves. About twenty young men and women sit around. They are all masked. Near at hand are their weapons, some AKs, others ancient .303s. Above, standing on great boulders, two sentries are watching us. I sit, I lie back in the shade and, in an instant, fall asleep. When I wake, I find a man standing about a foot away, looking down on me. His lower face is masked with a scarf; there is a brown cap on his head. He bears no resemblance to the sketch I've seen of him. My cell phone is in one hand. In the other, fitting comfortably into his fist, a machine pistol. He scrolls through the contacts list on my phone.

–Who sent you? Don't lie. I will discover that somehow and kill you if you're lying.

His voice is commanding, the growl of a tiger's warning. He wears faded green trousers and a pale brown shirt and, like the tiger, would be hard to find in the sun and shadows of the jungle.

–The Minister of Education.

–The President sent you. All the ministers are just the puppets of the President.

–No. The Minister...

–She's his daughter and an even bigger puppet I hear. She has a special relationship with her father.

–Who told you that? Shocked such news was known even in the jungle.

–Everyone knows. He squats down, and taps the machine pistol against my temple. Why you?

–I'm not a politician, a policeman, a bureaucrat, a journalist... What else? I can't think with you tapping my skull. They chose me as a neutral person. Do you hate neutral people too?

–The most, they're uncommitted, living fat, comfortable lives. Like you. What is the fine state offering me this time?

–Money.

–The only means of communication among the corrupt. Money talks, money whistles, it sings and dances and everyone falls down in worship of it.

–What do you want then?

He takes out a folded sheet of paper, unfolds it reverently, spreads it out and hands it to me. I recognize a lot of his demands are unchanged from the manifesto I am familiar with but there is more in this neatly typed sheet. My demands have not changed for the most part; they have largely remained the same from the start. I wish the state would at least respond to one or two so I can remove them from the list. Instead, it grows longer by the day.

I could recite most of the demands on the sheet of paper I hold in my hand from memory. Instead, I pretend to study it. Return of stolen land to villagers and tribals; schools for every village, with teachers; drinking water; irrigation; roads; employment; job training; homes; a just government; withdrawal of police patrols; the cancellation of mining rights in the jungle... I sympathize with these demands after all, in this avatar I too was born into the ranks of the downtrodden. I feel him watching as I read. His eyes shift from one side to the other of my face.

–You are Chanakya?
–Yes.
–I am Chay.
–After Guevara?
–After Chai, tea, my favourite drink. Since you're named after a wise man, have you read the *Arthashastra*?
–Skimmed what has survived of that great work.
–I have read it.
–So, you too wish to become a prince.
–No. To learn how to overthrow a tyrant and know the rules of good governance. In the *Arthashastra*, Chanakya advises the prince to crush all rebellion in his kingdom. Do you advise the President the same?
–I advise the prince to treat his people justly; by so doing he will not have rebellion in his kingdom.
–But Chanakya writes that wealth and wealth alone is important...
–He added that charity and desire depend on wealth for their realization. And in the happiness of his subjects lies the prince's happiness; in their welfare his welfare; whatever pleases him, he shall not consider good but whatever pleases his subjects he shall consider good.

He laughs uproariously, as if I am a comedian. His troops also laugh, though they have not heard the exchange. He stops laughing. Chanakya's prince was Chandragupta, a compassionate man, who had the wisdom to listen. Chanakya taught him how to gain power, ruthlessly, but he used it for his people. The President and his corrupt cabinet only listen to the bank notes counted by their machines. This state has no compassion; greed is its only motivator. Has the President ever listened to your advice? Be truthful.

-Not always. But I am not his advisor.

-You advise the daughter, the Minister of Education, who will never educate the children, never build schools, never hire teachers.

-Give her time. I can persuade her to act with good intentions. Now can I ask you a question? He nods and I continue. Why are you here in the jungle? I believe you're an educated man.

-I started doing a doctorate, he says indifferently. I left it unfinished. Death always paves the way for a revolution. The state killed someone I loved and respected.

-Who was that?

-No one you'd know, no one you'd mourn.

-And you want revenge.

-No. Academia lost its charm for me. What good is learning if you can't put it to use? I worked alongside the man who inspired me. We wanted to help the villagers and the tribals to improve their lives, to live among them and teach them better methods of farming, harvesting. I'm not an agronomist but I read up many books before I began my work. Then the state intervened—they took away the land to build a factory and the jobs went to outsiders. There was no compensation for those evicted. My mentor led a protest to the local collector. They arrested him for sedition and imprisoned him. He died in prison. The police claim it was suicide, I know it was murder. I took up where he left off, and now they want me for sedition and revolt.

-I have another question. Why did you attempt to assassinate her? Twice.

He laughs. Chanakya, Chanakya, I didn't set off any bombs, though the police blame me for them. I don't attack innocent people. Even in the *Arthashastra*, Chanakya advises the prince to use a threat of some kind to keep his subjects loyal to him. Like goats to a shepherd, he wrote. This time, I'm the wolf, next time the state will find another wolf. And you saw the results. She was given Y-security and the President gave a big speech on how dangerous I am. She

won the sympathy of the voters.
 -I just needed your assurance.
 -But I need more than that. How will you stop the mining magnate, the great friend of the President, from ripping apart this jungle for his precious metals?
 -I have advised the President to preserve the jungle.
 -He listened well, he says sarcastically, and acted immediately, confiscating village lands, driving away the tribals from the jungle. We're going to fight the mining company and we'll fight the state. He leans forward, his face close to mine. Tell me, Chanakya, how would you advise me to get power.
 I pull back, look around at his ragged 'army', his soldiers so young and inexperienced. What will you do with this power?
 -Read my list of demands. He taps it. Everything is in there.
 -I cannot advise you to overthrow the State. I can advise you to gather an army, equal to the State's army, weapons equal to their weapons and then encircle...
 -I have read the treatise. After his defeat by the Nanda king Chanakya suggested that as you eat a chapatti, eat away the outer portions first and then the centre. I am at the outer edges of this chapatti.
 -See, you already have his advice then. Who arms you?
 -Friendly neighbours.
 -Pakistan? China?
 -Friendly neighbours. Every country interferes and encourages insurrection in its neighbours. Chanakya wrote that a prince must always think of conquest to acquire a greater empire. He needs to create fear either from outside or inside to hold his people. He removes his glasses and rubs his eyes. He can barely see without them and peers at me closely, again searching my features as if he can read secrets in them. Will this Chanakya guide the Minister of Education and will she listen?
 -I am certain. I don't admit to the uncertainty, remembering her mother's despair that she too could have inherited her father's twisted genes.
 -You are close to the President's family.
 -I offer advice only to the daughter.
 -And you know her mother?

–Well enough. Why? And I wonder whether he read my mind a moment back.

–Where is she?

His new line of questioning puzzles me. I came to corrupt him, negotiate his surrender with as much money as he needs. Also, I expected more a discourse on his ambitions, a lecture from the guerrilla leader, and then, possibly the bullet. Why does he ask about the mother's location? And if I tell him where Shakuntala is, will he assassinate her?

–I can't tell you that.

–I won't harm her. His voice is gentler now, the growl a purr of persuasion. I know she no longer lives with the President, and that she is in an ashram in the mountains. Is she happy?

–Content. I need to know his thoughts behind this interrogation. He's slim, muscled from his hard existence, but suddenly I am certain, I know who he is. He sees the recognition dawning in my eyes.

–You know who I am?

–I think so. You're Mayur, the young man from her college days.

When I recognise and name Mayur, he sits back on his heels, contemplating me for a long moment. In his eyes, I see the memory of the young woman he had loved, who was stolen from him by another man, and his misfortune that she didn't return his love.

–She told you my real name, she still remembers me then. His voice and eyes smile. What else did she tell you about me?

He signals and one of his men bring me a clay cup of cold tea, and two guavas. He has accepted me, for the moment, and I accept his hospitality. I demolish the guavas in a few bites. They are delicious. Then I drink the bitter tea. No sugar.

–She doesn't know Chay and Mayur are one and the same man.

–You're the only who does, he says in a flat voice, and I sense a note of menace.

I hurry on. She said you were in love with her, and wanted to marry. Apart from that, nothing more than that she hadn't loved you.

–She would have, if he hadn't captured her. He sits finally, legs crossed but he doesn't lower the scarf covering his face. The gun remains on his lap, stays pointed at the centre of my belly. I met her in college when we were both doing our post-graduation in political science. Her thesis was on the economics of spousal abuse and mine

was on the economic history of state violence against its subjects...
—She told me that too.

He doesn't notice my interruption. Our professor was the famous political economist Chandrasekhar. You must have heard of him. He was a great professor. But she was my distraction from the very first day I entered his class. She was so graceful, beautiful and her smile lit up the room. I was included in her smile, although I realized she barely saw me. I was just a skinny young man, in threadbare clothes, and cheap chappals on my feet. I spent most of my money on books, not clothes or food. I was too shy to speak to her for the first few sessions although we sat side by side, taking notes, discussing our course work. She would do most of the talking. She was very bright and I remember how meticulous she was with her footnotes and her sources. Well, I was too, because I wanted to go on to do my doctorate, become a professor like Chandrasekhar.

That was my ambition, and I knew that Shakuntala's father was also a professor. I dreamed of proposing to her and she happily accepting me. When you're young daydreams nourish you, you walk around in a daze thinking of a woman, a profession, a home. Happiness. I was always happy when I was in the same room as her, and unhappy when she left it, taking something of me along with her without being aware of it. After a month of my tongue-tied presence in her company, she asked me: why don't you talk to me? Don't you like women? We're not bad people, we can't help it if we're women, we were born this way, even as you're born a man. She was smiling and I knew she was just teasing me, trying to bring me out of my shell. One day Shakuntala suggested we have coffee together after class. I'd never sat alone with a woman, certainly not someone like Shakuntala, at a table in a café. Other students looked at me with envy. As always, she did the talking while I listened. Over that first meeting, I learned about her parents, her schooldays, friends, sports. She played tennis for the college, and said she had thought of turning professional but knew she wasn't good enough. We had sport in common to start with. I played cricket, I had such a passion for the game and she knew nothing about it. Nothing. In this land where cricket is a religion that surprised me. So I slowly began to teach her about the game. I even persuaded her to come on Saturday afternoons to watch me play. I was so nervous that I was bowled out by the first ball.

I looked forward to classes and coffees together as we began to open up about ourselves. My father wasn't as educated as I was. He was a clerk in the office of an insurance company with secret ambitions of being a writer. Until his death, nothing he wrote was ever published. I still keep his scribblings as he was a man of ideas despite his humble profession. He was the man I told you about, the one I followed. After retirement, he went to teach in the villages and inspired the people to rise against the injustices of the state. I worked alongside him, proud of him and when he was murdered, I took up his cause.

He was speaking now with the passion that only love can summon from the distant past; it was this that was making him open up about his life for this stranger who, by chance, knew the woman he'd loved. I believe no one else had ever heard his story before, not even his companions in the jungle. He had held it as a secret in his heart. It nourished, yet it depleted him as he dreamed of what he had lost, but it warmed him that he had had the capacity to love.

–I believed one day we would marry, all I had to do was ask her. I wanted to wait until I had my employment in the university, and was no longer just a penniless student, hopelessly in love. I knew she sensed it. It was just a matter of time. Time. Time cheated me, it had other plans. He came into her life and stole her away from me. I was sick with rage, sick with my discarded love and I wanted to kill him. But I was also rational enough to know that he was too powerful for me. He was a strong young man, arrogant and, as you know, a gangster. He moved always with his thugs, now all of them ministers in his cabinet. I wouldn't have had a chance and they would have killed me. He knew about Shakuntala and me and he watched us.

He falls silent a long time, head down, ashamed of the powerless stripling he had once been. I know she loved me, yet contemptuously he coerced her into that marriage. I wanted to kill him even then, but I was powerless. I began to spend hours exercising to build up my muscles and strengthen my body. He flexes a bicep to prove his strength. I had a foolish fantasy, that I would wrestle with him and break his back.

–She invited you to the wedding.

—It was cruel though she didn't mean it. She thought my love was just affection, a liking for her, a friendship over coffees. I did attend the wedding but I stayed at the very back. I saw her covered with silks and garlands and jewellery and knew that I could never have afforded such a grand wedding myself. She saw me standing at the back and I saw the sadness, the helplessness in that look. She loved me still, I saw it in her eyes, but she was frightened of the man standing beside her. I left before the rituals were finished.

Memory plays tricks on all of us. It's like wet clay that you can mould into any desired shape to fulfil a fantasy, to recreate a better version of what occurred so many years ago. We believe that what we wanted, what we yearned for in, that mysterious zone below the surface of our thoughts, lie the dreams that we create which, after the passage of years, rise to the surface. Yes, that is the way things happened, our newly minted dreams say, and we convince ourselves that was how things were. Aren't our fantasies more comforting than the heartbreak of reality? Shakuntala loved me, she was sad at her wedding. Our eyes met, hers filled with tears. Isn't that better than Shakuntala not loving, Shakuntala with a bride's happy smile, looking at her groom with the adoration of a worshipper, not even seeing the shy young man at the far end of the hall, staring at her with worshipful eyes? I've seen the video and the photographs of that day and saw only the glow of marriage on her face. I fully understand the deceptions we entertain and I have sympathy for Mayur. Even I, Chanakya, can misinterpret the past. I am grateful that those who knew me—my emperor and friends—are not here to contradict my memory.

—You didn't think of marrying another woman?

—I did marry a tribal girl, and I loved her in my own way. She was a gentle, sweet woman. But she died in childbirth. I am now celibate. His voice is wry. I have no luck with women. But to return to Shakuntala, after she married I tried to return to my studies but my mind was in tatters. I was consumed by thoughts of retaliation, I turned to the gun.

—So it's personal, not political.

—All politics is personal. I disagree with his governance. We must remove him from power. In the treatise, Chanakya advises cutting off one hand for corruption. Or was it both hands?

–One. But then he only needed to advise one man. The emperor chose which hand to cut off.
–This state would be littered with millions of severed hands.
–And populated with one-armed men.

I smile, his eyes return the smile. He rises, my audience is over, and when I stand he shakes my hand, and then embraces me. When you see Shakuntala, tell her I still think about her. You must not tell her who I am or where I am. I will never approach her.

Despite his many denials, he is saying the opposite. I see the possibilities ahead.

They hood me again then and I feel the hard woman's hand hold mine as she leads me out of the encampment into the jungle's maze. I find Vikram waiting for me when I emerge from the jungle. He has smoked a whole pack of cigarettes, the butts scattered around him, evidence of his patience. He has brought parathas and chana dal, and while I eat, I tell him about my meetings, with no mention of Shakuntala. I tell him about my attempt to bribe Chay (I pronounce his name differently now)—the man is determined to liberate his people and fight for their rights.

■

On my return to the office, I notice the young man sitting in the exact same spot on the opposite pavement. Once more, the police shepherd me across and I squat in front of him.
–You could die here before she sees you.
–Then it's my karma to die here.

I could get the police to wrench the box from this infatuated man and force it open. Yet, I like the way he waits with such patience. Besides, I am always wary of setting in motion actions that I cannot predict. The police could beat him up, imprison him, even kill him, and then they will inform their superiors that Chanakya ordered their actions.
–What do you do?
–I'm an artist. His voice is haughty with the pretensions of the artist.
–Painter?
–Yes.
–Singer?

–Yes.

I rise, cross the road and enter her office to find further feminine touches added in my absence. Paintings on the walls, flowers in many more vases. Her desktop is cluttered with more files.

–I didn't expect you to return alive.

–He tortured me and I escaped.

–I can see that, she says sarcastically. What does he look like?

–I didn't see his face, he kept it masked.

–Well, did he accept my offer?

–I didn't make it.

–Why not?

–Money won't work for him as it does for others.

–Then what did you talk about?

–His revolution and his demands. I hand over the sheet of paper to Avanti but tell her nothing about Mayur and her mother. She reads Chay's sheet of demands carefully.

–I can do the schools but not all the others. They're not in my power.

–You can tell the President that you want him to stop the mining, for a start.

–I can't, she cries out. I can't. He'll be furious. He's committed and he'll be very angry with me if I go on about that. I know what you're going to say, so don't.

She then hands the list of demands to her PA, Ramesh, to pass on to her father. From there, it will vanish into a file. And be forgotten.

TWELVE

MY ANXIETY: WILL he come? Will he bring Siggy? It's a cool evening, the garden glows with lights that hang down from the branches like luminous vines. A sitarist accompanied by a tabalchi plays evening ragas under a distant awning. Tables covered with white tablecloths dot the lawn, a lotus floats in a silver bowl in the centre of each, white plates, embossed with the Presidential seal, await the arrival of snacks and, beside them, starched white napkins to cleanse greedy mouths. Waiters, splendid in white uniforms and purple turbans, move among the chattering guests with silver trays of nimbu pani, lassi, aam ras; other guests queue patiently to greet the President on his seventieth birthday. They are the specially chosen ones, and they clutch those gold embossed cards with their names imprinted on them. It isn't love that has brought them here; it is the power that magnetizes them all. They form a jumbled line waiting to touch him, murmur their greetings to him, and leave their gift. His ministers are all present, lumbering up to him in turn. Men of incalculable wealth, I think, remembering their worth from files I'd had hacked. They bring their wives, regally bedecked in 24-carat gold, studded with diamonds, emeralds, rubies and draped sarees and salwars of the most expensive silk. Monika's father too waits dutifully in line, along with his portly wife. Monika will soon be a clone of her father. She is in Rio on her month-long honeymoon with her husband, Nikhil. Of course, she did not invite me to the grand wedding. Her husband's father owns a cell phone company, an airline and a few television channels. He is a step behind his brother-in-law, similarly attired, except he's taller and slimmer, matching his wife's height, though not her beauty. Her wrists groan under the weight of gold bangles, heavy as handcuffs. One arm, I think, chopped from the elbow, would feed ten villages; one be-ringed finger a family for a year. Though marriage has united the two families, the tycoons are adversaries for the coveted title published in *Forbes* magazine—Richest Man in the State. Their worth is calculated in a phoren currency, more valuable than our own worthless one, and more envied. Monika's father has the slight edge at five, the cell phone tycoon at four point nine; the numbers followed by nine zeroes. We invented the zero for mathematics and just see how we abuse it to measure vulgar displays of wealth. My emperor commanded his rajas to share part of their riches with their people and he always ensured they did. He did not want unrest among his subjects because of the selfishness of the nobility. These rajas all come bearing gifts, wrapped in joyful colours, and also garlands of money (only high value notes), roses and sandalwood.

The President sits on a regal chair, not the one from the Durbar Hall—it's too heavy to shift—but a lighter replica. As always he's dressed in a white kurta. Today, he has a rose pinned above his heart, a rare gesture. He accepts each gift, each garland, and passes them on to a minion, who stacks them on a table. On a side-table beside the President is a glass of nimbu pani. Avanti stands beside him, a hand resting on his shoulder when not lifted to namaste a guest. She too is in silks but the gold ornamentations she wears encircling her throat, on her ears, and wrists are not ostentatious. She is a person of the people. She looks shy as she greets each visitor. I stand two steps behind her, my right arm in a sling. Her father, impatient, bored, thinking of his Chivas, sips his nimbu pani. The whispers flowing from the security gate break the hum of respect for this happy celebration. It grows louder into a buzz as it reaches us. An event is happening beyond our vision. I know what it is. Siggy Chopra has arrived. Men and women in the privileged queue turn away from the President, forget he exists, as her name becomes a continual whisper among them: Siggy, Siggy, Siggy.

-What's happening? Avanti asks me.

-I'm short, I can't see above their heads.

-You're vertically challenged but you're not surprised. Then the name is in her ear too. Who invited her? She turns on me, quick as a leopard. You did, didn't you? You had no right....

-She's with Aditya. How else to entice him here? She is no threat, not to you or Aditya.

-What's happening? The President asks, stirring from his lethargy, straightening from his lounging posture, almost coming awake for this event now. There is a limit to the amount of flattery that even a king, can absorb in one evening.

Beauty has its rights over power. It straightens the shoulders and pulls in the stomachs of elderly men. The queue wavers, gives way, wanting Siggy to brush past them as she heads towards the hosts. Siggy doesn't need the glow of gold and diamonds, nor of silks. Her smile, the glance in her eyes, the undulation of her hips—these are enough. She wears her village-style costume from the film but not worn and faded. A black skirt with a gold border and a black blouse patterned with gold stars, revealing cleavage that forces men on to the tips of their toes. Her dupatta, a pale crimson, also threaded with gold leaves, falling from her shoulders, barely covers them. A small gold chain around her neck, two gold bangles around her right wrist and small diamond earrings outweigh the gold on all the women. She is acting the star now, but it is the village girl inside her who's looking around with great curiosity, acknowledging each greeting with a smile. She, Rachna, is about to meet the President, she is moving among the elite of this land who bow to her in passing as if she were their queen. Even they scramble in their expensive suits for visiting cards for her to sign and return, the women passing her scraps of paper dug out of their Louis Vuitton clutch purses.

Aditya, in a black kurta and churidar to match her ethnic attire, strolls beside her. They're not holding hands. He walks in her shadow, almost unnoticed. In his turn, he barely notices those parting before his companion but is looking straight ahead. A slight smile now when he sees the one he has come to meet. Avanti too is not looking at Siggy but is watching Aditya closely—his hands, his eyes—do they stray from his side, does he whisper intimacies in her ear, does he reach out for her hand. Then her smile widens, laughter simmers on her lips. She is happy at this deceit I'd played on her, and she is ready to welcome the gatecrasher. Aditya raises a mock salute as he comes nearer; she waves her fingers. They have forgiven each other, the past is too powerful an undercurrent in their lives. I admit my eyes are moist with the success of my manipulations of their lives. Can she live with love; can he live with power? I have not forgotten my advice to Avanti—love is watery. But water also has the power to submerge and wear down rocks. I never underestimate its power to flood and create havoc. If Aditya holds steady, he will become my wedge between her and the President. He can draw her away to find a firmer foothold on the first step to the gaddi. The President will oppose her love for Aditya, even as he had done so long ago. But she must take him on. How else can she become the Empress?

Aditya pauses a moment, Siggy by his side. He must greet Monika's father, after all he once belonged to the exclusive clique that surrounded Avanti. He introduces Siggy, and the noble's plump hand now moves to smother the beauty's small one. He smiles and I know he stutters, all men are helpless before those eyes filled with erotic promise. But Siggy is distracted, she is looking towards Avanti. No, it's not Avanti she is looking at. The President sits upright, he even runs a hand through his white hair, still abundant; like any schoolboy he wishes he had a comb in his pocket to make himself more presentable. The beast in him rises from its lethargy and now radiates the power. I confess that I did not see the possibilities of their mutual attraction in my endless calculations. I had invited her so I could crow that I could summon Siggy to this event. So you see how an innocent action set in motion accelerates in unforeseen directions over which one has no control.

I have skimmed Newton's *Philosophiæ Naturalis Principia Mathematica* and read his three laws. The only comment I wish to make is that while these great minds theorized about inanimate objects—metal, marbles, planets, stars—as a philosopher I believe these laws also apply to the human heart and mind. 1. Every object in a state of uniform motion tends to remain in that state of motion unless an external force is applied to it. Until you fall in love, you live your life calmly with no expectations. 2. The relationship between an object's mass m, its acceleration a, and the applied force F is $F = ma$. Acceleration and force are vectors; in this law the direction of the force vector is the same as the direction of the acceleration vector. (I had read Aristotle's great work, translated into Sanskrit for my benefit by Megasthenes, the Greek Ambassador to the Imperial Court). Aristotle preceded me by many years and was Alexander's tutor. Obviously, Alexander did not learn anything from the great man (who also wrote on 'ethics' and 'politics'), especially the importance of good governance. Who listens to us? In his work, *Physica*, which I recall hazily, he wrote: *Of things that exist, some exist by nature, some from other causes... Each of them has within itself a principle of motion and of stationeryness—in respect of place, or of growth, and decrease, or by way of alteration...* I cannot recall the entire text but essentially he believed there was only velocity if there was a force. Newton states that an object maintains its velocity until a force acts upon it. As he postulated: 3. For every action there is an equal and opposite reaction. In physics, there is an equal and opposite reaction but in love such a reaction is totally unpredictable. It is neither equal nor opposite; it can skew sideways, in unforeseen directions.

I remember Siggy confessing to me her interest in older men. She is now approaching the most powerful man in the state. An older man. He rules and ruins lives, unlike my emperor, who only endeavoured to serve his subjects. The President believes his subjects must serve him.

–Who were you smiling at? the President asks Avanti.
–Aditya.
–Do I know him?
–Yes.
–From where?

She doesn't reply. He can wait, even though she hears the querulous tone in his voice. Another guest steps forward.

–Who is that woman? he asks, a tremor in his voice, an eagerness that he tries to hide.

–Which one? Avanti is playing his game, watching him now, reading his intent. She is frowning.

–The one with your friend. What's his name?

–I just told you. Aditya. She speaks firmly. It's Aditya. Don't you remember him?

–Of course, but he is not distracted by her sharp tone, her accusation of his deliberate forgetfulness.

Before they can continue bickering, Aditya stands in front of her, smiling. When he takes her hand, I see in her eyes the touch of his mouth on hers; fresh as only memory can make it, and the passion that abruptly ended. His eyes too reflecting the arbour, the rain, the ring, suppressed for so long, come alive.

–How are you? He laughs. I never got the chance to congratulate you when…

She laughs too. It is a shy woman's laugh, uncertain. Those behind look on with envy. She is bestowing her blessings on Aditya. No one else exists for them and, if I was a director, I would mute the hum, silence it, and move closer in for the two-shot. The lovers finding each other after years of acrimonious separation. But will they reconcile?

    –Congratulations on your Palme d'Or.

    A smile, a gentle correction. I'm elevated. It was *Un Certain Regard*. I deserved it, finally. Another man would have been modest but Aditya has never been humble about his talent. Have you seen it?

    –No, not yet. I haven't had the time.

    –Ahh, the affairs of State. You're obviously thriving. You still look wonderful.

    –Thank you. Her cheeks turn coppery with the blush. So do you.

    –Chanakya!

    I have to pull back from them. It is Siggy calling, standing just beyond them, extricating herself from her admirers. She holds out both her hands to welcome me into her embrace. Others received one hand, lightly, then swiftly removed. This is why I invited her, for this moment of glory among the powerful and the wealthy, to be smothered in a familiar embrace. A friend, a lover, possibly, let them be envious, as her arms enfold me and pull me in to sink my face between those lovely breasts. She knows what she is doing too, letting me smell the perfume on her warm skin and have my cheeks pressed against her tits. I wish the embrace to last an eternity but she releases me and I look up at her eyes, sparkling mischief. She holds me at arm's length.

    –What happened to your arm?

    –I'll tell you later.

    –I know, you fell off someone's bed. Then she leans in to whisper. Introduce me to the President, please. I want to meet him.

    He is forgotten, usurped by the presence of this exquisite woman; to make matters worse, his daughter is distracted by the man she loves. I take Siggy's hand possessively and approach the President. He rises slowly, his movement the uncoiling of power—much like an emperor rising from his gaddi and imposing himself on those surrounding him.

    –My President, I wish you to meet Siggy Chopra. She is a film actor.

    Siggy laughs, brushes her hair from her eyes, a gesture that has seduced millions. She puts out her hand boldly. To my surprise, the President appears shy. Beauty's power humbles even powerful men.

The lechery in his heart breaks to the surface of his eyes, and sinks without a trace. Only I have noted it.

-It's my misfortune that I've not seen your films, Miss Chopra. But it is a pleasure to meet you. He takes her hand, holds it, looking down at it and then finally into her eyes. He sees that his presence mesmerizes her too. Now, I know what I've missed in life. Which of your films should I see first?

-None of them, she laughs, and turns to me, still holding that shy hand in hers. The one we're shooting now, don't you think Chanakya? The others are...action movies.

He turns to me. Chanakya can advise me then.

He still holds her hand, and she is allowing it to rest there.

-Yes, President. I am jealous that her hand remains in his, her eyes remain upturned.

The queue awaits behind, and he looks past Siggy and sees those impatient faces. Gently, reluctantly, he extricates his hand from her small, soft one. I know too well even her hand can heat up a man's heart. Regally, he lowers himself back into his great chair. The intimate moment has passed but I know that the arrangements have already been set in motion. He beckons to me.

-Arrange a showing of one of her films and invite her to it, he whispers.

-I'll inform your secretary.

-I can do that myself, he says, barely suppressing a snarl. I've asked you, as I can see how friendly the two of you are.

Enchantment, like happiness, is short-lived. It leaves a bitter sediment in my heart. As he commands me to bring her to his private theatre where he can exert his power over her, the memory of her breasts pressed against my face is extinguished. Ah well, that is what happens when an external force is applied to an object. As I turn, Avanti, bringing Aditya to the throne, confronts me. Women have extraordinary peripheral vision and she knows what has passed between her father and Siggy. She is upset and unsettled, uncertain how to deal with this interaction.

-Father, you remember Aditya. She ignores Siggy standing beside me.

-It's been some years, sir, Aditya says, as a frown forms on the President's face. It is meant to humble him. It is an act; he's not

forgotten. He'd been the enemy.
 –No.
 –We were friends when I was younger, Avanti says, emphasizing each word.
 –Happy birthday, sir, Aditya says, not wanting another family altercation.
 –Ah, yes, the impetuous young man. And what have you done with your life?
 –He's one of our famous film directors, Avanti snaps.
 –I've so little time for such pleasures, her father says silkily.
 –I know you have more important work than watching movies.
 –Hey, remember me, Siggy nudges Aditya. She steps in front. I'm…
 –Of course I know who you are, Avanti says. You're more beautiful than your photographs.

The compliment is sincere, Siggy's radiance commands it. Avanti doesn't feel dowdy beside her, even though she had jealously watched her progress through the crowd.
 –Thank you. You look so much like your lovely mother.
 –Where did you meet her?
 –She came to the location. She's so kind and gentle.
 –And Siggy's stunning on screen, Aditya adds quickly, to divert the dialogue.
 –Aditya told me he knew you.
 –That was a long time ago, he says. We were kids.
 –Not quite, Avanti says dryly.

They withdraw, making room for the queue to continue forward and pay homage. Even as the President and Avanti play their roles, they barely notice the faces or hear the compliments. They are watching the other two—Aditya and Siggy—mingling in the crowd, moving further away. In between courteous conversation, she watches them.
 –When does this end? the President is petulant again, he wants to escape.
 –Why? Isn't this a great birthday party, Avanti says. Just look at the famous people here. Even Siggy Chopra, the movie star came to wish you. Isn't that something?
 –An empty-headed woman. He accepts a rose garland from the Minister of Communications, a man who is heavy with riches but so ancient he can barely walk; two aides support him. He wants to

speak to the President, his fount, but the President turns him away.
    -I wasn't talking about her head. A snap, sharp enough to bite the head off a scorpion. She's just an actress, you should see her movies.
    -If I get the time.
    -She met Mother and thinks she's lovely. She does this deliberately, to remind him of the other woman, the discarded one.
    -When did that happen? He is surprised that this little encounter has escaped his Intel. He'll deal with those incompetent spies later.
    -At the location. Didn't you invite Mother to celebrate your birthday?
    -I'm sure my secretary did. Bland, indifferent, smiling now at another supplicant, grateful to be momentarily spared his daughter's hostility.
    -But you made sure Siggy Chopra was invited.
    -I didn't know she was on the list, I barely knew who she is before tonight.
    As I am not the one people wish to meet, I search for Aditya and Siggy. I find them easily enough, seated at a table, surrounded by fawning courtiers. The movie star, Siggy, continues to play her role—still signing scraps of paper, napkins, visiting cards and accepting compliments while Rachna seems to be captivated by a man with a gangster's heart, in the same way that Shakuntala had been. I want to tell Rachna to run away, return to the village at the foot of her mountain and remain there. Power will entangle her in its coils and it can devastate her life if she is not careful. He has already ruined the lives of three women, what is a fourth—I'm not even thinking of the multitude of others too insignificant to matter. Siggy puts her hand out to take mine.
    -Thank you for inviting us. I'm so excited. I met the President and shook his hand. And he talked to me. I mean, can you believe it? Rachna, the villager, sitting now in the Presidential Palace gardens. I must tell my mother.
    -It sounds like a movie, says Aditya indifferently, then turns to me. Knowing him, I presume there was a purpose.
    -Yes, and we must discuss that later, before you leave.
    -Now you have to tell me how you broke your arm, Siggy says. Which bed did you fall off?
    -It wasn't a bed. I tripped over a rock in the jungle as I had

a hood on my head and couldn't see where I was going. I had forgotten the magnificence of nature, a jungle isn't the same as a village in the valley. You're still going back there?
-After this shoot.
-How many days? I worry. I want her to leave this very night.
-A week, at the most, Aditya the director answers. And now you're going to tell us why you were in the jungle with a hood over your head.
-I went to meet Chay.
-The insurgent? they chorus, and I have their attention.
-I prefer the word 'dissenter'. It was for a discussion and I can't reveal what it was about.
-What's he like? Siggy asks. Is he very dangerous? Did he threaten to kill you?
-No, nothing like that. He's just a man who wants justice for the people.
-I'd like to make my next film on him, Aditya says. Fictional.
-We need someone like him for our village too, Rachna, the village girl says in a voice filled with longing. There's so much wrong there and we just don't know what to do.

While another fan slips across a scrap for her to sign, I make a note in the little book I carry around always. It's to jog my splintered memory, mostly, trying to remember what I had written so long ago. I write an address, draw a map, tear out the sheet and slide it across to Aditya. A movement of secrets meant only for him. I write on another paper and wait for Siggy to smile away an adoring fan and give it to her.
-You want an autograph too her she laughs. Or would you prefer a kiss?
-The kiss. And your phone number when you have the time.
-You dating my star? Aditya rises, checking the time. She needs her beauty sleep.
-The President wants to see one of her movies and hopes she'll be there too.
-He does! She makes a face. I don't want him to see any of my movies. They're too embarrassing. But I'll be there after, with my director and you.
-He wants to see it tomorrow. 6 p.m.

She turns to Aditya, pleading. We'll finish the shoot by then, won't we? Say yes, please.

-He's certainly impatient. He takes her by the hand and says pleadingly. Say no. Don't go.

-Why? I want to meet the President properly. Not standing in a queue. She detaches her hand, smiles sweetly. I'll fall sick at four o'clock, if you say no.

He turns to me. You tell her Chanakya.

-Go back to your village, I tell her, though not with conviction or urgency. She is not my prince. Power, I told you, is ruthless. She will draw the President away and free Avanti who is finally rebelling. Siggy is the wedge between them.

-Not before I meet the President. Her tone is stubborn now.

-She should go then. It's not often, never in fact, that he wants to see a movie.

-I don't like it, Aditya warns Siggy. Just be careful.

-I can look after myself. She is beginning to sound indignant.

-Not against monsters. He turns to me. Will Avanti be there too?

-Of course. I'll see to that.

He smiles. Then we'll finish by four. But we'll start earlier.

-I don't mind, she laughs.

As he rises, he leans over. But this isn't the bargain.

-I will keep my word.

When they move, the thinning crowd parts for the star, the whispers following her dying out as she leaves the palace. The remaining guests shamble after her, the glitter gone from their lives and the palace loses its lustre. The lights dim, a signal for the end of the celebration. The gifts and wilting garlands are carried away. The President remains on his throne, and a bearer, waiting in the shadows for this moment, hurries over, carrying a silver tray, a silver bucket of ice, a bottle of Chivas and two glasses. He opens the bottle, breaking the seal, and pours a chhota peg which he sips, then swallows. He remains upright and when enough time has passed for any poison to bring him down in writhing agony, he fills half a glass, drops in ice cubes and passes it to the President. In future, I must check that the ice isn't poisoned. We didn't have such cold pleasures in my time.

Avanti stands behind her father, massaging his shoulders. He

appears to purr with pleasure at her touch.
   −God, I hate these garden parties, listening to the drooling prattle of fawning fools.
   −I thought you quite enjoyed the evening.
   −I did? I must have missed that moment.
   −You found her fascinating. You couldn't take your eyes off her. She looks better in her photographs. I suppose that's all clever make-up.
   He cranes around, smiles. You mean the actress. I thought you were above such catty comments.
   −You mean it's unbecoming a minister? She presses down hard on his shoulders.
   He winces. That hurts. Gently.
   −Sorry. But didn't you think she was beautiful?
   −In an actress-y sort of way. I'm surprised you remembered that childhood friend and invited him.
   −I didn't invite him. Or her.
   −I thought you did.
   −No. But he is famous. I do have to keep in touch with that real world. And it wasn't exactly my 'childhood'.
   −He did walk out on you.
   −It wasn't his fault. He didn't have a choice.
   He rises to escape the strength in her fingers. In her smile I see the seeds of revolt; it's a beginning, and I will develop that further. The bearer carries his glass along with the tray and follows him into the palace, tailed by his security. Avanti twirls her hair, still standing at her spot and, instead of obediently following him, sits down on the vacated throne. She bounces up and down, then leans back. It's too deep and her feet dangle in mid-air.
   −I've never sat on this before. It's uncomfortable.
   Her action is that of a child taking an adult's place, unaware that this is her first contact with the seat of ultimate power in this state, to sit on the throne still warmed by a king's bottom. She will remember this moment long after and believe it can be her rightful place.
   −You will need a smaller one. I speak softly into her left ear, as the cleaning staff hovers around and who knows for whom they spy. I think you must meet Aditya privately. Every time it's in public.
   −But where? I'm too well known, even if Aditya isn't.

–Yes, your photos are in every newspaper and magazine, on hoardings and on the lapel badges of the party. We can't do five-star, four-star or even one-star.
    –He can come here.
    –So the whole palace knows. Your father will interrupt, as he has done before. I know a place and I can take you there.
    She manages a smile. On your scooter?
    –Why not? Or do you want Y-category announcing your arrival. You'll have to wear a helmet, what better disguise.
    –When? And I don't want you hovering around me.
    –I don't hover. Indignant. I spy, and I promise I won't this time.
    –What were you and father talking about?
    –He wants to see one of Siggy's movies.
    –He couldn't take his eyes off her. A quiet rage and a hurt in her voice. With disgust. He's too old for movie stars.
    –No man is ever that old. After the movie, we have dinner.
    –Just for him and her? And the hurt is almost visible in her voice. I can see the smoke of anguish in the air.
    –You should be there too.
    –I don't want to watch him drooling over her. She's near to tears, wiping her eyes with her palms, trying to get rid of the pain.
    –It's important that you be there. Never reveal enmity to the king until the princess is certain that she can win the throne.
    –I don't want it. And I won't be there.
    –Aditya will be there too, I tell her slyly. And you must live your own life now, you must follow your heart, your love for Aditya. Don't let him stop you again. Will you come?
    –No way, she rises, then changes her mind with a smile. But I'll be there for the dinner. Neutral ground, and then we'll see if I want a private dinner with him. And with that she strides away.

■

From advisor I'm reduced to major-domo. See how swiftly power can slip through one's fingers; it happens to every prince, and his advisor, eventually. As Avanti refuses to organize the evening, the duty falls on my frail shoulders. I buy the DVD of *Dharwaz Bis*, as it's my favourite—I can sit through it a dozen times. The palace's movie theatre is dusty, the air stale; it hasn't been used for years.

It can seat twenty guests in recliner chairs with holders for scotch and kebabs. I have the staff clean, dust, vacuum, polish and scent the air with bottled perfumes. And then, I choose my favourite menu for dinner. We'll start with mulagathani soup, a British dish for which I have acquired a taste. Followed by daniya murg, a chicken dish heavily flavoured with coriander; along with pepper fry lamb chops. As for vegetarian items, there will be paneer saag, dal makhani, green salad, naan. For dessert, butterscotch ice cream, to prompt a fading memory, and rasgullas for my own palate. Apart from the Chivas, we'll have chilled French Chardonnays and Chilean Sauvignon Blancs. I've read that red wines don't suit our spicy foods but I'm no sommelier. The formal dining room with its long table that can seat a hundred guests is too big and intimidating. You're watched over by dozens of dead eyes staring hungrily out of oil paintings—viceroys, governors, soldiers, great mughals, little mughals, ex-presidents—and the chandelier too bright for intimacies. The chairs too are heavy with red cushioning and straight-backed. They are for the bottoms of visiting presidents, prime ministers, dictators and financial rajas. The second dining room seats fifty but it's a gloomy place with teak-panelled walls. The one adjoining the President's suite is too intimate, seating four or five—it is mainly used by the President to entertain his close confidantes. The room stinks of secrets, intrigues, crimes planned, it is regularly swept for bugs—electronic and natural. In my day, the emperor would hang these men so high that even the vultures could not pick at their entrails. It makes me melancholic to contemplate what is happening in my country, and I hurry out. I prefer the oval dining room that overlooks the garden through French windows. It seats ten at the most and the lights are couched in wall brackets so they glow softly. There are landscapes on the walls by local artists—mountains and rivers, hills and jungles—I find them calming. I will place the President at the head of the table, with Siggy to his right, Aditya to his left. Avanti beside Aditya and I have invited myself to sit beside Siggy so our shoulders brush. The chairs are dark teak, cushioned in grey velvet, with armrests. They encourage a guest to relax, lean back in them. I have the gardener cut roses, cannas, crocuses and lotuses for the centrepieces. The bearers who follow me are impressed with my immaculate planning for this event, and suspect an ulterior motive, as I never get involved with such chores. Surprisingly, I enjoy it as this is also a set, like the private chambers of the prince, where plans are laid and executed. I think about music, a mix of ragas and ghazals to stimulate conversation and defuse hostilities.

At 5.45 p.m., the guests haven't yet arrived. I wait in the theatre and only the President with a secretary enters, looking around puzzled.

–Where are Siggy, Avanti and the director? He won't use Aditya's name.

–Avanti's still at the office, and apologizes for being late. Siggy and Aditya are shooting. They will be here for dinner.

–Let's see this film.

He sits in the front row, I at the back, and the film begins. Once more, Siggy enchants me but I'm trying to watch the President too, and wish I was beside him to study his face. He leans forward whenever she is on screen, examining her minutely and hungrily as I do. So large, so desirable. Then he sits back when the hero appears and Siggy disappears. It's a crime story but since he knows more about crime than any screenwriter, he pays no attention to the plot. He leaves abruptly. The secretary and I sit through to the end.

At eight, Siggy and Aditya arrive and I alone am there to greet them, and lead them through the maze of corridors to the reception room adjoining the oval dining room.

–How many rooms? Siggy whispers. For today's occasion, she is wearing a saree of pale purple silk, a pink choli, both woven with gold motifs. Her petticoat is tied so low, the saree pleats are just in line with her pubic hair; it is to court madness to gaze at the expanse of her perfect stomach with an emerald lodged in her belly button.

–About a hundred or more. I've not counted.

–I'd get lost here.

–Watch where you are leading us, Aditya warns me as I try to walk sideways so that I don't miss her undulations. He's in jeans, a black shirt and a fawn sports jacket, a director's uniform these days.

To impress her, I detour to open the doors into the darkened main reception room with the President's real chair at the far end.

–I've only seen this in photographs, she whispers, wandering in to look up at the chandelier, the frescos on the ceiling, then around at all the paintings.

–I need a drink, Aditya deliberately breaks the spell of power, not wanting her here. And reminds her. We have an early schedule tomorrow, Siggy.

–I know. Just let me enjoy.

The small reception room, adjoining the oval room, is furnished for informality: armchairs, sofas, side tables and Mughal miniatures on the walls. One wall has a shelf of ancient books. I play barman. He has a Chivas with soda, and isn't aware he is the poison tester for the new bottle. Siggy sips a nimbu pani. We talk about the day's filming while we wait for our hosts to make an entrance. The President arrives, striding across to welcome Siggy; as she rises he takes her hands in his.

–I enjoyed your film. You're such a good actor. I just couldn't leave until the very end.

–Thank you, sir.

–Sit, please. You'll have a drink? Good. The usual for me, Chanakya.

There is no faithful bearer so I pour a burra peg, plop in ice and hand it over. He appears not to notice Aditya, sprawled in an armchair, failing to rise at his entrance. The President sits next to Siggy and, surprisingly, talks about the film knowledgeably. His secretary had remained to make notes and write up a flattering critique, a detailed plot line, as well as a list of Siggy's other movies. When he wishes, the President can mesmerize, as a cobra a mouse, and he gives Siggy his full attention. Aditya scowls at me, tapping his watch, he is thinking about the shoot, about Avanti too, as he cocks a thumb in question. As if on cue, Avanti sweeps in, making an entrance as confident as her father's.

–I am sorry I'm late but I was trapped in the office. She wears a pale blue salwar kameez and matching dupatta. Her throat is encircled by a simple gold band. Her hand is out to Siggy. You always look so lovely, Siggy.

–Thank you. I feel a bit overdressed…

With a glance at that tummy, Avanti says, I wouldn't say that. She is determined to be gracious this evening and I'm grateful she did listen to my advice. She turns to Aditya. Thank you for coming. I know how busy you've been with your new film.

He rises to take her hand, and they clasp each other a moment longer than necessary, looking at each other appraisingly. Maybe you'll get time to visit the shoot one day.

-I must, she sits beside Aditya and I serve her a chilled Chardonnay.
I'm wondering, as they make small talk about films, at what time I should serve dinner. I avoid all invitations to dinner parties in this city as the host always serves the food well past midnight; since I don't drink, I have to wait until the drunkards are ready to feast before I can vanish swiftly into the approaching dawn.

-We'll have dinner, Chan, Avanti says, reading my mind.

We take our places at the dining table, bearers hover behind each chair. I expect the conversation to continue but silence descends upon the diners. They pick at the food. Avanti watches her father and Siggy with sharp eyes. She catches the exchanged glances and smiles, the small flirtations, as his hand sometimes reaches over to tap hers. He talks softly. She knows her father's powers to seduce, recognizes every gesture and the smallest flicker in his eyes. I should've sat Avanti and Aditya at the far end of the table, the President and Siggy in another room, and eaten my dinner in the kitchen.

-I wasn't aware you liked films, sir, Aditya tries to break the enchantment.

As if aware for the first time of Aditya's presence, he turns. The smile remains, the eyes change from seduction to a snarl.

-I haven't the time. It's a frivolous pursuit.

-Watching films or making them? Aditya can match him.

-Both.

-They can be frivolous and honest too. People enjoy films about gangsters, especially those that end with the hero killing the villain.

-It happens only in films. Dismissive. Turning back to Siggy.

-Real life does follow art.

The President has dismissed the upstart and pays no further attention. The secretary enters, humbly, almost doubled in apology, to distract the President with a whispered message and a slip of paper. The President rises, bowing to Siggy.

-You must excuse me, some sort of a crisis I have to sort out. Chay is causing problems again. He takes her hand, holds it and, with great reluctance lets it slip away as he strides out of the room. Urgency in every step for us to witness.

-I'll be back. Avanti rises too, her food untouched.

-Another crisis? Aditya enquires.

–We'll see soon enough.

–Great dinner party, Chanakya, Aditya turns on me after Avanti's left.

–I wasn't the host, just the director, and, as you know in films, even the best shots can get lost in the editing room.

–Do we wait for the President to return?

–Avanti said she would.

–Where's the loo? Siggy asks me.

–I had better show you the way.

I lead her out, down the corridor, pointing out the landmarks for her return journey. Do you want me to wait?

–I'm a village girl, I'll find my way.

–I hope so.

Aditya is finishing his butterscotch ice cream and sits back while I finish dinner.

–How far is the loo?

–Round the corner. I don't offer to escort him. By the time he returns I've finished a plate of rasgullas.

–She's not there.

–You went in?

–How else? We must search for her. She can get lost from the trailer to the camera.

–She said…

–I know village girls, but even they get lost in the jungle…

We set out to search for Siggy. Passing attendants shake their heads to our question and our fruitless search eventually takes us to the palace entrance.

–Have you seen Siggy Chopra? Aditya asks the armed guard.

–No. No one has left.

–Fuck, fuck, fuck. They arranged this. I know he's fucking her. I know I shouldn't have brought her here. She's gone with him. She'll fuck anyone over fifty, it's her father fixation.

–It's a common failing in this palace.

–I'm leaving. Tell Avanti…

Even as he mentions her name my mobile calls me with a sweet ghazal.

–It's Avanti. I listen. Her voice sounds muffled and angry. She is suggesting a private dinner tomorrow.

–It had better be private, just the two of us.
I assure her it will be and disconnect.
–You have a date, alone, as promised.
The smile fills his face. Thanks. What's your advice or is your wisdom only on how to acquire power?
–Also on love. Be tender, love her as you have always. She has suffered more than you.
–I know, and the smile vanishes. Her mother told me. As he leaves, he adds, When you find Siggy send her home.
–I will.

■

Avanti wears a black salwar kameez, the gold pattern on it very similar to what Siggy wore at the birthday party. She always looks splendid in black and knows it. I have a helmet for her and help her slip it on before we even step out of the side door of the palace. She is anonymous now, another secretary leaving for the day.
–You do know where we're going?
–Of course. I can't tell you, it's a secret.
–You're sure Aditya knows where it is?
–I gave it to him in writing, with a map of how to get there. And a key to let himself in.
–I'm mad. Should I be doing this?
–Of course you should. Don't doubt yourself. You do want to see Aditya.
–Yes, I do. Now with steely determination.
My scooter is one among many in the long shed. When I wheel it out, I see the doubt in her eyes.
–How do I sit on this?
–Like a horse.
–I've never ridden a horse.
–Become one of the people.
When I start the scooter, she straddles the back seat and holds my waist. I believe it is the first time we have had such close contact. Our positions define the relationship. I try to remember whether I had touched my emperor, held his arm or helped him up a step. It had happened once or twice when we were planning our military campaign against the Nanda king. The young prince stumbled and

I steadied him. Otherwise, I kept my distance. I knew then one can never be intimate with the powerful, and they must always remain aloof from such familiar contact with those beneath them.

-Where are we going? I hear the concern in her shout, as we cross the borders of her privileged enclave, the familiar wide roads, the avenues of trees and the grand bungalows on either side, past the police outpost protecting the elite from the chaotic city that now looms ahead.

-The old city.

-There are no good hotels there.

-But great food. Don't worry.

We enter the old city, and the noise, crowds and overwhelming traffic engulfs us. She holds on even tighter as I manoeuvre around cows, dogs, handcarts, food stalls. I thread through the chowk and merchants raise their hands in greeting as I pass.

-Who are they waving to?

-I don't know.

I pass a BPO office, cross Rupmati's lane and go down another before I stop and switch off the engine. Avanti climbs off, a bit unsteady from the unusual posture of clinging with knees and arms.

-I don't like this. She starts to remove the stifling helmet.

-Not yet.

The building is narrow, about twenty feet wide, two floors, squeezed between two crumbling havelis. It is an illegal construction but no building inspectors venture deep into the old city. I open the door with my key, switch on the light and welcome her in.

When the door closes, she removes the helmet. Whose place is this?

-A good friend. I don't tell her that it is my humble home, my only investment for old age. Its furnishings are simple: a divan, a bolster pillow, a low desk, surrounded by many books. In the centre, neatly laid out on the Kashmir carpet is a white tablecloth, on which are plates, side plates, wine glasses, scotch glasses. A bottle of Chivas and a Chilean Sauvignon Blanc stand guard, liberated from the Palace wine cellar. A plastic ice bucket sweats next to them.

-It's not much.

-Enough. Behind that door is the bedroom, with an attached bath. A local restaurant will bring dinner at nine o'clock. I have chosen the food.

She opens the door at the back, looks in, and smiles. There is another divan, large enough for two persons, with plump pillows and a patchwork quilt filled with down to keep one warm. Aditya is asleep on it, still with his shoes on. I know the day's shoot was cancelled. I had questioned my palace spies and they told me that Siggy left just before dawn broke. I'm certain Avanti's spies gave her the same report. The star complained of a headache—I'm aware that love making does leave a woman languorous, and prone to such aches. Apart from supine Aditya, there are clean towels and a bedside lamp. Also, a clothesline strung across the room to hang one's clothes on.

She hesitates, the smile drained by nervousness. I know this is an emotional threshold. Can she step over it and enter a new life? If she does, she will escape her father. For what? An old love or should I say, lover—it's best to be precise—who has waited patiently. She's afraid, knowing how fragile love can be. Is she remembering what I had spoken of long ago—on love and its watery foundations? I need her to take that step to help set her free. When she starts to close the door, half turning away, I stop her.

-You have to awaken him. He's the sleeping prince.

-And I'm the princess? She manages a smile.

-Yes. A gentle push and she takes the step. Call me when you're ready to leave.

When she enters and closes one door, I open another and am back on the lane.

I plan to while away the hours with Rupmati. She's waiting.

-I heard Siggy Chopra spent the night with the President—is her greeting as she embraces me to whisper paan breath into my ears.

There are no secrets in this city.

-You know more than I do.

-Liar, she says with an affectionate cuff and half carries me over the threshold to her divan. Our first fuck is one of frenzy and desire, our bodies hungry for the great release, followed by the slow, loving fuck of true pleasure. We don't have time for our games and our toys as I'm uncertain when I'll get Avanti's call. I fall asleep with a woman to one side, the phone on the other.

Before dawn breaks on this new day, Avanti summons me. She waits inside, lying on the divan and her face is aglow with the night's love-making. The food is half eaten, a forlorn tandoori-chicken leg with two kebabs on either side. The wine bottle is empty, and a few pegs have been poured from the bottle of Chivas. Avanti smiles and finally rises.

-Aditya still asleep?

-He left early, in a dreamy voice. The shoot.

I pile the plates outside the door; the streets dogs will have a feast. She follows me, putting on her helmet before stepping out into the pale pink light caressing the city.

-We're going to be married, she announces as she mounts my scooter.

THIRTEEN

AVANTI'S ON THE mobile in her office, laughing and listening, whispering endearments. Lovers speak in a child's language, with giggles, sighs and loud laughter. Children understand love better than adults, which is why we regress when we fall in love. They know the happiness of receiving it and also the pain and disappointment when it is withheld. Love is the control adults use to discipline their young. She clicks off.

–I want to see my mother, Avanti announces, standing at the window, looking down. She can just about glimpse the patient young man through the branches of the neem tree, still sitting on the opposite pavement.

–Will you still recognize her? I feel guilt, I too have neglected her.

–Chan, I don't need sarcasm. She turns. Not angry, the smile hasn't worn off; it remains in her eyes if not on her lips. I want you to come with me. I must tell her that I am to marry Aditya and I want her blessings and her presence at the wedding. It will be bad luck if she isn't there.

–Have you informed the President? Note how I formalize and distance the relationship between them, not wanting to use a familial word to remind her.

–No, not yet. She twirls her hair in worry. Should I? He won't be happy.

–Only after you tell your mother. She is the one who will be the happiest that you're marrying Aditya. She wanted that all along. We leave now?

–Tomorrow. Aditya wants me to watch the shoot but I don't want to because I'll have to see her.

–She isn't to blame.

–Oh, a woman can't say no?

–To your father?

This brings a flush to her face. I told Aditya the reason. He'll come here for dinner tomorrow night after we're back from seeing Mother. I'm hoping he'll agree to live with me in the palace.

–Never invite an artist into the heart of power. He'll disturb and question and bring nothing but chaos. Find another home, and distance yourself from the palace.

–I suppose you're right. I'll talk to Aditya.

She sits at her desk, now covered with files and sheets of paper. I lean over as she opens them, following her eyes. There are drawings of buildings in the files.

–They're the schools we're building.

–You've started? I mentally cross off one of Chay's demands.

–We have to put out tenders for contractors to bid on. You know that.

I uncross the demand, knowing this lengthy process can take years and by the time the winning bid is accepted the money would have mysteriously evaporated.

–You have the funds?

–Of course, though not as much as I wanted.

–How many villages will eventually get these schools?

–We start with ten.

The architecture is not inspired and the buildings look like matchboxes. Four walls, and a roof. The room doesn't look large enough for even ten small children.

–Give them more space, more classrooms, and don't forget separate toilets for boys and girls. Also playgrounds. And where will you build these schools?

–On village land. My officials have already earmarked the properties.

–Have you seen them yourself? Do they exist?

–I'm the minister, she says in a huff. And I don't need your interference.

–One more suggestion. Never trust your bureaucrats.

Avanti points to the door and I follow the finger. It opens before I reach it and Monika enters in a cloud of perfume, in tight jeans, a low-cut blouse, her Louis Vuitton bag and two cellphones in her hands. Like a wave, she flows past me, not even noting my presence; to her I'm just another chaprasi. The vanity of wealth surpasses even the power of princes. Before Avanti can rise from her ministerial chair, she is engulfed by arms, smothered in scent, has her ears assailed by shrill screams of joy. Monika is no longer the slim, curvaceous girl I last saw years ago. Already the outlines of her mother are emerging like a ghost from within her—the hips are broader, the tight tummy rounder, the face slowly swelling, the thighs thickening (straining her Rodeo Drive denims) and even those once-slim arms are weighty with flesh. Poor girl, she cannot escape her genes.

Avanti disentangles herself from the hug; in her office she prefers to be formal.

–I thought we'd said lunch.

–This is lunch time, Monika almost shrieks with joy. Finally, finally. I don't believe it. You and Aditya, I can't be any happier. She speaks in American, Indian and other confusing tongues. I can't wait until one o'clock; I want to know everything now. This minute. She looks around. But not here, she adds, in a 'yuck' voice. I've booked a table at the Five Seasons and I want us to get there early before the others join us.

–Others?

–The gang. You've not forgotten us. I know how important you are but you're still the Avanti we all know. C'mon. Let's get out of here. She's pulling Avanti out of the chair, dragging her across the room. She has her overweight mother's strength.

–I have work.

–That can wait, Monika says dismissively. Daddy's delighted to hear the news too. You must tell us what you want as a wedding gift.

I know she's the go-between for her father and Avanti, she will negotiate the terms, the payments and the daughter will be as ruthless as the father. The gift? A BMW, an Audi, a Lear jet, whatever, to smooth the passage of the destruction of a jungle. Though Avanti's just denied telling her father, she knows the grapevine has been activated— Monika has told her father, her father will call to congratulate the President on the upcoming nuptials, offering all the support he can command to make it a memorable and joyous occasion.

She's a force that Avanti can't resist. She grabs her handbag, a utilitarian one of woven brown leather, large enough to hide a file or two, and her cell phones.

–When did you get back? she asks Monika as they pass me.

I don't hear the answer. The door closes. I wait until they reach Monika's limo and then follow them on my scooter. Aditya's shooting in the city, not far from the office. Some exteriors, before the final interiors, of a penthouse apartment. He could build a set but he believes in verisimilitude in his work. Every shoot draws the crowd and the police have blocked off the road. A cordon of them now holds back the mob, wanting to catch a glimpse of Siggy Chopra. I manage to wriggle through the hot, smelly, sweaty bodies, and get to the front row. A gleaming black limo is parked on the cleared road; the background is a skyline of glass and concrete glittering with wealth. To my right, a residential high-rise with balconies, a few spotted with curious onlookers looking down. I wave to Aditya but he doesn't see me, he's conferring with his DP. Fortunately, I've caught the third AD's eye and he comes over to let me into the hallowed space.

-What's the scene?

-Siggy drives up to the camera, climbs out and goes into the apartment block. That's the home she's going to abandon to return to her village. She'll dismiss the driver, give him the car as a gift...

-Where's Siggy?

He points to the trailer standing beside the generator truck. I thread past cables, reflectors, the crew sipping tea and tap on the trailer door. Her make-up girl recognizes me and though she smiles, she doesn't open the door more than a crack.

-Tell her it's Chanakya. The door closes and then opens wider for me to slip through.

Siggy, lounging on the couch, tosses aside a film magazine with her on the cover, smiles and holds out both her lovely hands to draw me in; I kiss her on the cheek, she plants two on mine. She's wearing cream pants and the matching jacket is on a hanger. Distractingly, all she wears on top is a bra; I feast my eyes on the expanse of stomach on which I yearn to rest my head.

-At least you're not mad at me. Aditya was furious. But I couldn't help it, he's such a wonderful man. We're going to have dinner tomorrow night. I mean, Rachna is having dinner with the President.

-And Rachna screwed him.

-Siggy Chopra was who he wanted, not Rachna the village girl. She's astute enough to separate the two. I told you my preference in men.

-How long will it last?

She shrugs. We'll see. He wants me to live with him in the Presidential palace but I don't want to. Not yet. He'll find a penthouse for me. But I'm not sure I want to do that either. She sighs. He's so forceful.

–Do you still plan to return to your village?

–I do. Eventually.... He's a very lonely man. His wife left him to live with her guru...

–He had Avanti.

–But she's his daughter. Then she snaps. I know what you're going to say. I know him, he'd never do that to his own daughter. It's his wife who has told all those lies, she's the one to blame. She didn't want to screw him. He told me he has had other women. How could you have been taken in by that witch? I thought better of you.

–I thought you liked her when she came to the shoot.

–That was before I knew anything. He wanted more children, a son, but she wouldn't give even that to him. And you know how important a son is in our society. He wanted a man to succeed him. She claimed he was to blame. How can she say that when she wouldn't go to bed with him? She sits up, more agitated. And it's Avanti's fault too. She should've married long ago. What's she now? In her thirties. And as long as she stays single, everyone will believe what her mother says about the President.

So Siggy still doesn't know Aditya intends to marry Avanti! Has he kept it a secret from her to show his displeasure? He shouldn't be angry though, he should be grateful to Siggy for freeing Avanti from her father's influence. I must work harder to widen that chasm.

–And what will your mother say when she hears about this?

She laughs. I don't tell her everything and she won't hear anything in the village. I'll return, I promise. I know you're worried for me.

–When it's time to leave, you must leave and not look back. If you do, you'll forever be imprisoned in that penthouse he has promised you.

A tap on the door reminds us that there's work to be done. The hairdresser peeks out again and the third AD whispers: Rehearsal. Siggy stands, stretches, she doesn't ask me to leave, yet. Her dresser hurries in and helps her into the shirt, the make-up girl powders, touches up her lipstick, the hair dresser combs and brushes those shiny tresses. Siggy shrugs into the jacket and it fits perfectly.

–I'll see you again, she gently brushes the side of her face against mine so as not to mar her make-up.

–Yes. As I watch her leave, I think even if I personally find it distasteful I must fan the flames of the President's infatuation with her. Women are one of the six enemies of a prince and have caused the downfall of innumerable kings.

I watch her climb into the limo, it backs away and then at a signal, moves towards the camera. The chauffeur jumps out, scurries around to the open the passenger door, bows and Siggy emerges, immaculate in her suit. She strides towards the apartment block and enters. She returns a moment later to stand, arms folded across her chest, and listens to Aditya. The distance between them, emotionally, can be measured in metres. He points. She returns to the car, it backs up. The camera rolls as it comes forward. The driver jumps out, opens the door. A long moment, and then Siggy climbs out more regally, talks to the driver, hands over the keys and leaves him bowing as she strides to the apartment block. Filmmaking is a wearying profession, two takes, three takes, five takes, a puzzle of images fitted together later. Siggy comes out, passes Aditya and returns to the trailer. He turns to watch her, smiling to himself, and sees me. He crooks a finger and I go across to him.

–I just want to say thanks.

–Just that?

The AD hurries over with two chairs, directors do not remain standing long between shots. We sit in the midst of confusion and watched by the crowd.

–I did what you advised. You're a man of many parts, not just an expert on political power.

–I have been in love too. In fact, I am planning to write a treatise on the subject.

–You should. We had a wonderful evening, okay night, together. The wine helped her to relax. We talked, we had a lot of catching up to do. Not so much about what we'd done with our lives, but with how we felt about our long wait to get together. She wanted to know why I hadn't married, what with all the beauties in my life. Of course, she meant Siggy, among others. I told her that I had had affairs but a director is a centre of power too, in his own small world. I was never sure whether the woman was screwing me for love or for my power. I confessed that, with her, there had always been something special. We'd loved each other since we were children and that love was embedded in my bones, my blood, my heart and I couldn't shake it loose. She told me of the various alliances her father had tried to arrange for her, political connections but they had all come to nothing as she couldn't bear the thought of being with another politician with ambitions. He paused a long time, turning over their conversation in his head. She did admit to her father's early obsession for her, his demands that she couldn't refuse as she both loved and was intimidated by him. If her mother had stood up for her, she felt she wouldn't have had to undergo such a trauma.

–Poor Shakuntala, she was as helpless as Avanti.

–I said that too, she reluctantly agreed but she needed someone else to blame than her own weakness. The man's a monster.

–All kings and politicians are. They are prisoners of their power.

His grin is ironic—I love the daughter; hate the father. We'll make great in-laws.

–When do you plan to marry? Don't wait too long, the magic can wear thin.

–It won't. As soon as she tells her mother, we're ready to get hitched. Have you seen Avanti?

–This morning when she was on the phone to you. She's happy, she reminds me of a child again.

–I feel like that too. It felt as if I was meeting someone new and exploring the life of this stranger I loved, yet hadn't met before. He takes out his cell phone. I'll call her.

–She's having lunch with Monika and gang.

He winces, and puts the phone away. I can't stand spoilt brats with too much money.

–You must not live in the palace.

–I don't want to and you must convince Avanti. I want her as far from her father as possible. We can live in my farmhouse, it's three kilometres out of the city.

He is not the only one with a farmhouse beyond the city limits. Avanti owns a large one, and also a few apartments and many bank accounts that he knows nothing about. They are not in her name but in fictitious ones—just like her father, his ministers and every

important politician.
 -I have my studio there. Come and see how I cut this film. It's only a half hour ride from her office. Avanti and I agreed we'd meet again at your place tomorrow night when she gets back. You'll have to bring her.
 -Now I'm reduced to being a chauffeur.
 -Power demands many sacrifices.
 -I advise on it, and don't seek it. I'll bring her. Maybe you should buy her a scooter as a wedding present.
 -She won't need it then.
 The AD hurries up. We're ready for the first interior in the foyer, sir.
 Aditya rises. Why didn't you marry the woman you loved?
 -She was a beautiful woman, her skin cool from the mountains. But my physical flaw repelled her.
 -We'll have to find a bride for you, he laughs.
 -You don't need to. I love myself too much and don't want to share that with anyone.

■

Avanti and I leave early the next morning, pale peach sky spreading over us to the horizon. The eight racing motor cars, three in front, four at the back, all with flashing red lights, of her Y-category escorts, break the peace of the sleeping city. Guns poking out of many windows, so everyone knows that a VVIP is on the move. As will her father who, for all I know, is watching us sneak out of the palace. Her father will know our destination through his Intel, even as I know through my Intel that he waits impatiently for Avanti to tell him—face-to-face—that she plans to marry the film director, Aditya, her childhood lover from whom he had prised her away. But Avanti is making him wait, even as he made her wait to congratulate her on her election victory. Her excuse is natural, her mother should be informed first, as she will have to plan the wedding ceremony. That is her conscious decision. In her subconscious, she wants to postpone the confrontation, maybe even until the day of the wedding. So she can be sure he won't interfere with her plans. He holds the paternal power to forbid the marriage, and she is unsure whether he will use it.

–Tomorrow night, she whispers as she doesn't want the driver to overhear.

–Yes, I have my orders.

She is happy and sits back, already in his arms.

When I travelled into the mountains to visit her mother and the shoot, it took several hours. Now, we are flying along the road, emptied of traffic, police every mile, shooing off trucks, cars, motorcycles, bullock carts, cyclists, so that no one hinders the VVIPs passage. You can see why power is seductive—even in such a minor way. It only takes us four hours to get to our destination. We arrive at the barrier to the ashram and the special forces leap out, guns ready, and wait for Avanti to descend.

She looks at the ashram, the bucolic calm and quiet, now upset by the arrival of such potentially disruptive forces at the gate. She takes in, with a look of disapproval, the rustic cottages and tents nestled in the woods. The simplicity of such an existence is beyond anything she can imagine. The birds, who have been disturbed by our arrival, settle down in the branches and continue to sing. I miss them in the city where we see only parrots, crows, pigeons and mynahs.

–How could she stay here so long?

–It takes time to discover your inner peace. She seemed happy enough in this place.

–I hope she'll be happy to see me. I know, I know, she grumbles that I haven't visited, but to be honest I didn't want to be scolded by her nor did I want to fight with her. I thought staying away would help us both.

–Tell her you're marrying Aditya and that will defuse any squabbling.

The warden at the gate isn't the same man but another of the chelas performing this duty. He is staring at the guns and beyond to the line of cars and jeeps. He looks back at the other chelas huddled together, nervous too, at this disturbance of their meditation. The real world has descended on them, reminding them that all escape is temporary. The Swami emerges from a cottage, finally, followed by a young European woman with yellow hair and a dishevelled dress. I scan the inmates and can see no sign of Shakuntala. She is probably in hiding, fearing her husband has sent for her to be dragged out of this retreat. The Swami floats up, unflustered, and sees me first and then Avanti.

-You are upsetting my ashramites with all these guns and cars. What is the meaning of this, Chanakya? Will you please leave?

-We've come to see Shakuntala. Could you please tell her we're here. From his slow smile, I sense this is a foolish request.

-Sister Shakuntala is no longer with us.

-Where has she gone? Avanti demands.

His shrug is subtle, a mere shift of his shoulder. I don't know. She left. Everyone is free to go and come as they please.

-I want to search the place. Avanti steps forward. She wouldn't have left here.

-Do you have a warrant? You know the law, you have to have a warrant to search this place.

-The police can break the law if they suspect wrongdoing.

I intervene as I can see that Avanti is about to order her men to storm the ashram. Let us enter, I say gently but persuasively.

-There's no wrongdoing here. He steps aside. You and Avanti may search, but not those men with guns.

-When did she leave? Avanti asks, when he lifts the barrier and we both enter the compound.

-A week, maybe ten days ago. He falls in beside us. Time here is immaterial, and we do not count the hours and days.

To contradict him, a bell chimes, and the somnambulant gathering obeys the call and drifts away.

-What's the bell for?

-Lunch, he snaps. I meant time as a measure of our days on earth.

-As long as we eat on time, we'll last.

Avanti is preoccupied. She had summoned her resolve to see her mother after so many years, braced herself for the conflict, and now she can't find Shakuntala. We follow him into one of the cottages—it's furnished with two divans, bolster pillows, a small locker with a lock for valuables. The tents too are as sparse. We pass the kitchens where the chelas are queuing up for saag aloo, chana dal, a salad of tomatoes and cucumbers, rice and chapatis. Each person holds a stainless steel plate and a spoon; they remind me of inmates at an orphanage or a prison. They take their food and sit at long trestle tables, white and brown, young and old; the whites sit at one end, the brown at the other. The only thing all of them have in common is the look of benign condescension. Too soon, we're back at the entrance.

-You think he murdered her? Avanti asks in anguish.

-I don't think so. I turn to the Swami. How did she leave here?

-By bus. There's a local bus that goes into the city twice a day. That's how my followers come and go. We don't have taxis.

-Did anyone visit her?

He smiles. As you know I don't welcome visitors, including you and...he waves to the security....and them.

-A friend? I persist.

-There are days I'm not here so I've no idea if she has seen any friends.

-She must have discussed the reasons she wanted to leave you, her guru.

-What we talk about is sacrosanct. I do not divulge such conversations.

-Like a lawyer.

-More like a priest, he counters sharply. She is welcome to return when it suits her.

-Where could she have gone? Avanti is near to tears.

The Swami smiles slyly. She could have gone home. Didn't she call? Or doesn't she have your cell phone number?

Avanti doesn't hesitate. She slaps the Swami hard, to little effect. Suffering is his calling and this is nothing, he continues to smile. Only the chela guarding the gate witnesses the event, and he will keep his silence. The others are feeding their physical hunger. The Swami smiles, sweetly, and turns away. I climb in beside Avanti, and once more the motorcade roars into life. There is one person who knows where we can find Shakuntala—the President. He has his Intel here, watching her constantly, she is still his wife, his chattel, and he will not give up possession. She believes she's free but he will never let go of her. I blame myself for not having a spy here too.

-What do we do now?

-Go home, she may be there.

-Where else can she go, if not home? Another ashram, you think?

-Another guru.

-Who?

-Just a thought. My cellphone plays the ghazal, interrupting her.

Apart from spies, only three other people have my number—the President, Avanti and Rupmati. It's a spy from District 18, reporting. I listen to all the details that she whispers hurriedly. The woman, unnamed for security reasons, is the wife of the local provision store owner, a dissatisfied lady with expensive tastes who always needs money for her village extravagances.

–Chay, I say as I disconnect.

–You're saying my mother went to Chay? What rubbish!

–No. Chay's IEDs blew up a tractor, a lorry of mining equipment and also a jeep of policemen escorting them into the jungle. Two dead, three injured. It happened an hour ago. The President has announced an emergency in District 18, and is sending in more special forces to capture Chay. The money for the schools came from Monika's father? You agreed to allow him the mining rights.

–Some of it. She is evasive. Not all. We need it for the schools and teachers. When I passed on Chay's demands, Father said it was too late, he had signed the MOU and the mining company bid was the best he'd had.

–Only one bid?

–It was the best.

–What was the bid?

–I don't know, she snaps, and it's none of your business.

–It isn't, as long as you haven't benefited too.

–I haven't.

She claims innocence but her silence condemns her. I do despair it's in her blood as her mother had predicted, and I cannot cure such an illness. A prince must be above such vices, as I have tutored her before. Then I had a prince who listened, now I have one who pretends to. I blame her father, she fears his anger, his rejection of her love and silently accepts his vices as she did his use of her. Once parted from him, I believe, she can be a wise ruler.

–We must get rid of Chay so that we can continue getting funds.

–What he is fighting for is for the good of the people and to protect the jungle from rape and pillage. The state should reward him, not punish him.

–He has killed.

–The state drove him to it. I gave you his grievances. If the state even meets one or two of them, he and his followers will be more amenable to reason. You must negotiate...

-I sent you to do that, and you came back with a sheet of paper.

-You should have then sent back your own paper. A dialogue should have started between him and the state. I quote from the *Arthashastra*: *A king should rule for the welfare of his millions of subjects, cautious and dexterous in preventing treachery, watching over the conduct of subjects and officials.*

-That may have worked then, not now. You told me that Chanakya wrote that a prince must crush all dissent for the good of the state. Don't deny that.

-I don't. But only after negotiations fail. Your army is moving in without such a discussion, and it can cause a perpetual war within the state.

-Once they capture Chay, it will end.

-There will be others, I predict gloomily and fall silent. Injustice is such fertile soil for revolts against the prince and unless he can correct the wrongs, the rebel will never give up the fight.

The gates to the bungalow are closed and a blast from the police siren summons the chowkidar at a run to unlock and swing them open. The bungalow seems abandoned, the silence oppressive once the engines of the vehicles are switched off. The front door is open. I follow Avanti as she hurries into her old home. A bearer materializes out of the darkness, adjusting his turban, backing away as she hurls herself from room to room.

-Mother, mother...she calls, as if her voice can materialize Shakuntala out of the still air. She runs upstairs, still calling, a lost child, searching for comfort and security now. She wants her mother desperately; she can't marry without her blessing, without her presence. She needs to draw on her mother's strength too, Shakuntala was defiant enough to escape her husband's grip, if only to retreat to an ashram; nevertheless, an act of rebellion. This marriage is another one. I remain downstairs and, out of instinct, open the door to the prayer room. Shakuntala is sitting in the midst of her deities. The air is smoky with incense. Her face is calm and there's a slight twinkle in her eyes as she comes out, closing the door gently behind her. She's wearing perfectly ironed jeans, faded from many washes, and a loose white shirt. She looks youthful in the uniform of her college days. Her only jewellery, the silver rings on her toes. She notes my smile.

–I can still fit into them. I lost weight on that veg diet. She looks up. Was that my long lost daughter calling me? What does Avanti want?

–Let her tell you. Why did you leave the ashram?

–There's only so much meditation, contemplation, prayers and silence one can take. How long can you talk about god and salvation over breakfast, lunch and dinner?

–Did you believe in the Swami's teachings?

–For a while. He was the rope thrown to a drowning woman, and he pulled her to shore. I found what I wanted, an inner peace. A better understanding of myself.

–You're fortunate.

–I worked at it. I feel replenished now and, if I need my swami again, I know I can always return. My husband had diminished me in my own eyes—I allowed it to happen because I loved him and hoped to rekindle his love. Now that I mention him, how is he? I've lost touch and I'm grateful for that.

–Your husband's well, but I haven't seen him of late.

–So, you're busy making Avanti into a clone of him. Is that your excuse for not visiting me?

–I was busy and I am guilty of such neglect.

–You're forgiven. You helped me find myself too when I told you all my secrets. It opened a path for me. She smiles at me, wags her finger under my nose. You're a man who keeps secrets well but they do leak out when you least expect.

–Did you have any visitors?

–What kind should I have had?

–Friends.

She says non-committally, a smile in her eyes. I didn't want to see friends just for the sake of friendship. You know the Swami is strict about us observing the rules. Friends disturb our tranquillity—and I am quoting him. Her tone is gently mocking, her belief in him has evidently decreased.

We can hear Avanti opening and shutting doors, then track her steps to her old room. She opens it, enters, and it's as if she's vanished; silence. She must carry that key always on her person, along with the one for her music box. I imagine she is lying down on her childhood bed, reliving memories that were always waiting for her return. The same softness, the same ceiling, the same toys, books, paintings, even the odours will be familiar. The doors are opening in her mind, and she is passing through them in her sleep, and in her dreaming. The past is patient, it doesn't forget.

Shakuntala and I stroll out onto the verandah and sit, contemplating the garden together. Dusk is falling silently on the distant trees, gathering them up slowly, drifting nearer and nearer. The birds have taken note of the dying day and are flying swiftly to their nests, calling, chattering, singing. I wonder as I've done often whether they are exchanging the day's gossip. This time of day evokes memories of my childhood—the dust settling with a sigh, the cows and goats slowly returning to the village after a day's grazing on sparse grass, shepherded by children grateful to be home, the smell of dung cooking fires, my father and other elders gathering under the peepul trees to discuss the day's events. The lights come on behind, square patches fall on us, and onto the lawn.

-Avanti's woken up, Shakuntala says to herself. A mother's instinct about her child is rarely wrong. The bearer, unbidden, brings in a tray of tea and biscuits. I haven't eaten all day and eat a few of the biscuits, drink some tea.

Avanti comes out; she's changed her salwar kameez for an old one that was hanging in the cupboard. I note it is tight around her waist. She looks down at her mother, her mother at her, no words are exchanged as they examine each other. I wonder who will speak first. They have both changed. Avanti has put on a little weight; her mother, though still youthful to look at, has lines of age shadowing her eyes and mouth. Her hair is greyer.

-You look exactly the same, they say in unison and laugh.

Avanti leans down to embrace her mother, kissing her cheeks, and then bends to touch her feet. Shakuntala returns the embrace, returns the kisses, understanding her child's need. In her newfound equanimity and strength, she no longer feels the need to scold Avanti, she will accept whatever her daughter needs.

-I was thinking of how much I love you, then you drive up, Shakuntala says. You must have read my thoughts. Let me look at you, stand in the light.

Avanti smiles and moves for the light to frame her from head to toe, and then turns slowly like a model on the ramp.

–You have changed, you're so much more confident. Have you grown taller too?

–No, mother, she laughs. I think I'm just standing straighter. I used to slouch. She draws up a chair close to her mother and sits. You've changed too, you look wonderful. And you are serene. She takes her mother's hand. I've come for your blessing, and your permission...

–You're marrying. Finally. Shakuntala laughs, holding her daughter's hand tightly. I've waited so long for this day.

–Chan told you? And she looks at me accusingly.

–He hasn't said a word, he keeps secrets better than anyone I know. I can see it in your eyes. You're in love, it shows. You're glowing!

–It's the lights.

–Whatever. Are you going to keep me in suspense or shall I ask Chanakya?

–I'm marrying Aditya.

Shakuntala leans foward to pull Avanti into a loving embrace, holding her, rocking her. In this hazy light, with the shadows playing on their faces, they look so alike. Avanti's has taken on the contours of her mother's younger self, and the resemblance to her father is blurring. At times, and we don't know how, our features are fashioned by the parent we esteem and love more. As she ages Avanti will become her mother.

Shakuntala gazes into her daughter's face. Finally, finally. What a relief, for a moment I thought it would be a politician's son. It wouldn't have mattered if you were happy with that arrangement. I love Aditya, he's grown so mature and his films show a lot of promise. I know you love each other, you always have since you were children.

–You've seen all his films?

–One or two—the ashram banned frivolous entertainment but now I intend to catch up on all of them. Bring him here, when he gets the time. And you too. You'll stay for dinner? And she turns to the bearer, lurking in the shadows. Dinner for three. How did you two get together after that argument in the assembly?

–Chanakya played match-maker.

–What a talented man! Not just an advisor in how to get power but also to win love.

–It helps if the people involved are already in love.
–What made you decide after so long?
–Oh, we saw each other again at Father's birthday...
–I was invited. A personal invitation delivered by a police escort. I didn't want to celebrate his birthday.
–...and thought we should meet privately. Avanti isn't about to reveal all the reasons that drove her to the decision, and makes no mention of Siggy.
–Have you told your father?
–Not yet. I wanted to tell you first, it was very important to me.
–Thank you. Then adds, with a wry smile. He probably knows already. I wonder what he'll say. He never liked Aditya, and you're defying our lord and master. But he must not sway you; you must escape into your marriage. She pauses, embarrassed and apologetic. I tried to stop him molesting you but I wasn't strong enough—he had a brute's strength. You are his only heir, and he wanted all of you, not just your mind.
–I blamed you at first, then I realized that you did try to stop him. But I must take some of the responsibility as well—I wanted his love all for myself and didn't want to share it with anyone. She holds her mother's hand tightly. I don't want him in our lives any more.

Shakuntala sighs. You don't know your father well at all then. No one leaves him. He is the one who leaves them. And what he possesses is his forever.

–He'll leave me alone, she says defiantly.
–Does Aditya know?
–Yes.

They hold hands, like children, drawing strength from each other, thinking that with such a union that they can, and will, defy the President. They are both aware that he is not a man who can be defeated easily, he will strike hard and ruthlessly to break their bond and crush this rebellion. After all, did I not advise my prince that he must be ruthless in his actions if he is to remain in power and, if necessary, kill the son who rises against him. Even as I will advise the daughter that if she is to survive, she will have to kill the father to win the gaddi. Corpses of fathers and sons litter history, the victor settling into the seat of power, wiping his bloodied hands on the dead man's clothing.

The bearer announces dinner, and I leap to my feet, my stomach growling. They rise more slowly and I wait for them to sit at the table before joining them. I have every intention of concentrating on the food—a simple meal—dal, a subji, chicken korma, chapatis.

–Let's talk about the wedding, Shakuntala laughs, shaking off her sense of foreboding. It will have to be a big one, considering who you are, and all the people you know.

–Not too big, I hope.

–It will have to be, I comment between mouthfuls. You are a minister, your father the President. It can't be a small family affair.

Avanti makes a face at me; the child of the bedroom has accompanied her down. That's only for the reception.

–Two receptions, I say. One for the family, friends and ministers, the other for your party.

Her mother is laughing, listening to our exchange.

–Party! There are thousands.

–You must invite them, they will expect that. This is their reward too, and you must include them. They will work even harder.

–And all my spies too?

–They will remain invisible. Ignoring the sarcasm.

–Can I interrupt this dialogue on power? Shakuntala asks. She turns to Avanti. We should set the date? I'll consult the purohit to find an auspicious day.

–I thought the swami would have cured you of that superstition, Avanti laughs now, she too is anxious to lighten the mood.

–It's custom, and we must follow that. When?

–In a month's time. Aditya will have finished a rough cut of his film and will need the break.

–A month! That's too short a time for something so big.

–A month, Avanti is stubborn. She doesn't want to give her father enough time to create trouble. Once the invitations are out, he will have to concede.

–You must draw up the guest list, get the invitation cards printed almost immediately. We'll have it here and not in some hotel, there's enough space in the garden. I'm going to need help, then. I can't do all this alone. Your father will bear the expenses too, you should tell him soon.

–Shouldn't you be the one who talks to him? Avanti counters, not wanting to find herself dissuaded by his smooth tongue, his eyes drawing her back into his embrace.

–I will. Chanakya can come with me, he can be my advisor too. She turns to me. Will you make the appointment with my husband? I prefer to meet him in his office in the assembly.

The dinner passes quickly as they discuss the wedding. Avanti checks her watch, she's tired now. She kisses and hugs her mother and then we step out; the motorcade is impatiently waiting to race their minister back to the palace.

–I was in your bedroom when I was searching for you, she says to her mother. You were packing?

–No. I hadn't yet unpacked from the ashram.

–Stay a while, Shakuntala says to me. You can spare him?

–Of course. She takes my hand. Walk me to the car, we need to talk.

Watched by her mother and the security men, we stroll away. She's leading me to the arbour, drawn by her memories of that night. We sit on the stone bench, looking out at the house.

–What should I do? she is nearly in tears.

–Marry Aditya.

–I know that and I will. I must. I love him. I mean now. I don't want to return to the Palace, I know he'll be waiting and once he's in my room there'll be no escape. She shifts and squirms, already imagining trying to escape his grasp, shutting her ears to his whispered seductions.

–You have your phone?

She holds it up.

–Call Monika, go and spend a few nights with her. Catch up with each other. Of course, your father will know where you are but you're also out of reach. Once your mother has informed him, then you can return.

–What if he refuses? You know, he can refuse. He can force me to marry someone else.

–He hasn't succeeded so far, I remind her. She needs to be confident and courageous if she is to stand any chance of freeing herself from her father's domination. And I will need to help her by anticipating her enemy's moves and setting in motion actions that will counter his. A battlefield, like a chessboard, is always fluid and we will need to grasp opportunities wherever they present themselves.

-He can refuse to pay for the wedding too, she interrupts my train of thought. Then what will we do? All those friends, guests...

-Also, call Aditya and arrange to meet in the morning. I'll pick you up on my scooter but don't say anything to Monika.

She claps her hands. I knew you'd think of something. What is it?

-I'll tell you tomorrow.

My reward—a kiss on both cheeks. With another hug, we return to the driveway and she steps through the open door of the car, and the darkened windows shut her away.

When the last tail-light disappears beyond the trees and the throb of the engines fade away, I return to join Shakuntala in the verandah. The sky is hazy, and the stars barely visible. There is too much light from the city. In my time, we learned to read the stars for our religious rituals. In my past, both in the other age, and in the village, I would lie in the blackness and watch the movements of the stars, and the planets. There were twenty-seven constellations, seven planets and twelve signs of the zodiac in my time. We only had our eyes, limited in their vision, to map our heaven. Since then, with telescopes and satellite cameras, our knowledge of space has increased exponentially, yet what I knew then is the foundation for this science. Have you considered that even the universe could be puzzled by its *own* existence, and searching for its creator? It wants an explanation for why it came into sudden being in five seconds, when it had been sleeping peacefully for an eternity. Who, what thing, what power, opened the stopper and woke it from its hibernation? So, now it races in all directions at the speed of light ($c=299,792,458$ metres per second), searching for that thing, that force, that power, that culprit which released it from its confinement to wander in infinity. For what purpose?

-Were you packing?

-Yes. She pauses, takes a deep breath.

-Where were you going? Returning to the ashram?

-No, another journey. You met Mayur, she says quietly. You never told me that.

-But he told you. I'd known all along that Mayur was the one who had visited her in the ashram. He promised he wouldn't try to find you. I didn't tell him which ashram you were staying at.

-Well, he found me; he has his own network of spies.

-He came to the ashram?

-No, he sent a message through the postman, and we met in the village up the road. She laughs at my surprise. We're not prisoners in the ashram. We go to the village to buy a few necessities. There's a small Shiva temple. On Fridays, it's crowded with devotees. We met in the temple, surrounded by the faithful. He recognized me immediately. He said I hadn't changed one bit since our college days. I didn't recognize him at first. He's such a strong and confident presence now. While the others chanted and prayed, we talked. We spent an hour in our 'payers' and when the devotees drifted away, he did too. I doubt my husband's spies would've noticed him; they were watching only me. He knows how to be invisible.

-Did he tell you who he is now?

-Yes. Chay.

-Then you hold a secret only you and I know. You have the advantage over me, you know his face too.

-I never thought he'd become such a rebel. I note the admiration in her voice. We did discuss politics over our coffees. Everyone does at that age. We planned to change the world, overthrow our corrupt government, save our environment, dreamt of a new social order where everyone has an equal chance for happiness. But that's what it was—just talk. We find a comfortable niche for our lives and settle into it. Her laugh is dry. And I went off and married the very man who we now plan to rebel against.

-*We?*, you're packing to join Chay?

-To explore another life. I'm not sure yet. I said I'd visit. I'll stay in a nearby village. I want to see what kind of life he leads. Don't you ever think what your life would be if you had made a different decision at a tuning point in you life? If you had done this, and not that, you could be a different person, in a different world. I think of parallel universes that science fiction writers speak of—I don't think they exist, not in the universe but they do here on earth. One life stopped, the other continued, and yet I can see where the other life could have led.

-But, you didn't love Mayur—not then.

-Love, she spits out the word. It's such a deceitful word and emotion. Love sucked me in, I thought it would sustain me throughout my life. I don't *love* Mayur, I don't trust it any more. I liked him a lot then, and still do. I've led a futile life until now, and I want to make better use of it.

I smile. I don't see you carrying an AK.

She laughs. I don't want to. I'm incapable of killing anyone.

-Chay has killed.

-I know. So has my husband—but both for different reasons. My husband for power, Chay for change in the social order. She smiles, sighs. I am drawn to such men for some reason... But killing and fighting need not be the only ways to bring about change. I thought, with all my education, I could at least teach the tribal and village children. Even the basics of reading and writing, so they have a tiny advantage in their lives... Chay said you were against him.

-No, I am not. I told him that if the state is unjust he must overthow it, even as Chanakya returned to overthrow the Nanda king. But he needs an army. And a just man to rule in the king's place. In the eyes of the state, he is causing discontent among the people...

She flares up. The state created the discontent in the first place and he is only channelling it against the state. The state is always the first instigator of rebellion through either corruption or draconian laws or misrule. Which side are you on?

-Chay knows that I'm on the side of just rule. I told him that the duty of the state is to protect itself, which is why it will try to kill him. I advised him on how to fight the state. I reach over to hold her hands, pressing them as I warn her. The President won't be happy that his wife defected from an ashram to a revolutionary, his enemy.

-I won't be his wife by then. I'm filing for a divorce.

-He'll never give you one. I get up. I'll set up your meeting with the President.

-I know you won't betray me. I'm going to unpack. I'll leave after the wedding. She kisses me on both cheeks.

When I finally reach the palace, having found an autorickshaw and paid an extortionate fare, the security guards inform me that the President is waiting for me. All I had desired was a bath and my bed.

FOURTEEN

MY BEAUTIFUL SIGGY, wrapped in a diaphanous gown, sits cross-legged on a chair at the right hand of the President. They can hold each other's hands across the small divide. The Chivas has moved to the left side, alongside a chilled Chablis. At no time did Shakuntala ever occupy such an exalted position in his life. Nor did Avanti. Siggy lives now in the penthouse promised to her by the President, my spies tell me, and a chauffeured car awaits her every convenience; both paid for by the state. The President has reclaimed some of his youth, rejuvenated by the passion of this beautiful woman. The lines and creases around his eyes and mouth appear to have faded a little, and each time he looks at her his hard, watchful eyes soften. How many times have I to warn the prince about women, and, what I see is the action unfolding.

She holds out both her hands to take mine, her special greeting for me, and draws me into an embrace.

-I haven't seen you for ages. Where have you been?

-Busy as ever, the President says sourly, watching us.

-And you're still here, I say.

-Well, when we finished the shoot, and the President invited me to stay on as his guest. How could I refuse? She looks to him and blows a kiss.

-We have to talk politics, the President tells her and, taking her cue, she rises without a murmur. She pecks my good side and then plants a soft kiss on his mouth. He watches her all the way out of the room. When she has left, escorted by a bearer to where her car awaits, he slouches back in his chair. A bearer fills his glass and retreats.

-Where is Avanti?

-At Monika's. They hadn't seen each for a while...

-They had lunch a few days back.

-They needed to discuss plans. Women have much to talk about, it's in their nature.

-She has yet to take my permission to marry that fool, he

shouts. When is she planning to do it? I am her father. The longer she delays the more reluctant I am to grant it. She is being devious, says the master of deceit.

–It's your custom, isn't it, for the mother to discuss the marriage proposal of the child with her husband. Avanti wants to follow tradition.

–Do I have to see my wife? His voice rises another notch. It's disconcerting to see the President's anger—he has always been a man in control of his emotions. She left without my permission to stay in that crooked swami's ashram. She didn't treat me with any respect. A wife must obtain her husband's permission to go away for such a long time. She made a fool of me, everyone knew she'd left me. She should've stayed at home if she didn't want to live here. I knew when we married she'd cause problems with her higher education, her ideas and her degrees. She framed her certificates to remind me constantly how clever she was. I destroyed them to remind her that paper is worthless.

–You did love her?

–I wanted her when I saw her on that train. His hands reached for the jewel, picked it up and stowed it into his pocket. And just like that she was his possession. After we were married I hoped she'd give me a son. Instead, I have a daughter and she didn't want another child. Not from me. She hated my touch barely a few weeks into our marriage.

–She has always loved you.

–You are a consummate liar, Chanakya.

–Not always. Her love remains but…we both look at the vacant chair, recently occupied by Siggy.

–Siggy's very special, is all he says. No admittance of love, a word reluctant to slip past his lips. We're not here to discuss her. You're the one who encouraged Shakuntala to join that ashram.

–I never encourage, I only advise. Avanti followed you and again on my advice she stood for an election and won. I deliberately remind him of her landslide victory.

–And you advised her on this marriage proposal?

–It was her choice.

–I wanted her to marry Hari's son. Why didn't you advise on that?

–It wouldn't have made a good political alliance. His father could shift his loyalty as easily as ghee off a hot pan, and take Avanti with him.

He reflects, nods. That's possible. When do I have the honour of my wife coming to see me in supplication?

-When you give her an appointment.

-And if I decide not to give my consent? I never liked that man, a film director, he spits the word. His only true rival for Avanti who has now come back to claim her love, taking it away from him.

-A good one too.

-I don't like being defied. He broods a long moment and then pronounces judgement. I want Avanti to ask my permission, I want Avanti here. I don't want to see her mother.

-I'll advise them to meet you together then. You'll consent?

-I didn't say that. I will not give my consent. She must marry another politician, I need alliances to strengthen the party.

-Then why should she see you? You can send a message, refusing your consent.

-Because, he shouts. I want to see their faces when I refuse. And if they hear of what I have just said, you'll pay dearly, Chanakya.

-I will not say a word about our discussion, sir.

He dismisses me, and I make my long way back through the maze to my room.

■

He makes Avanti and her mother wait for two days before granting them an audience. I have kept my silence, even though I see the anxiety in their faces as they wait. The meeting is scheduled for noon. I am to accompany them, despite my protests. Shakuntala wears a beautiful pink cotton saree and yellow choli, and only the toe-rings to remind her husband they remain married. She has made other efforts as a reminder, with a touch of lipstick, in the shape of her eyebrows and a dust of powder to her cheeks. Avanti is in a salwar kameez, dark grey, with her favourite paisley motif woven into the fabric. We do not enter through the grand main entrance but are directed to a door on the right of the building that leads to the ministerial offices. Mother and daughter are escorted to the private elevator, and wait for me. I have to pass through three detectors and, each time I do this, I think that one day I won't appear on the other side. It could be a portal to return me to the infinite. I join Avanti and her mother at the elevator which will take us directly to the top floor. When we get there a waiting peon takes us down a corridor, past the closed doors of his First Secretary, Second Secretary, and the third, before we reach the end. We wait in the outer chamber of the President's office, along with a male secretary who never looks up from his computer screen. A buzzer sounds and he hurries to open the door for us; he still won't meet our eyes. I've never been to this office; it's large and airy. The windows are floor to ceiling and through the curtains, I catch a glimpse of the city stretching out all the way to the horizon. I can imagine him standing at a window, looking out on the empire that lies at his feet. Avanti too must have stood beside him, holding his hand, gazing at her inheritance.

We have entered the circle of power. This is how it felt to enter the private chamber of my Emperor. Power permeates the office of the ruler. His desk is rosewood, the size of a table-tennis table. There is nothing on it besides a phone and an open file. Thick carpet mutes our footfalls. There are a few photographs of the President with important visitors on the walls. The President sits at the desk, head deliberately bent to study the file in front of him, which he pretends to read slowly. We remain standing. There are sofas and coffee tables to one side of the office but he makes no gesture for us to sit, make ourselves comfortable. This isn't a family meeting but a gathering of strangers. Finally, finally, he looks up, feigns surprise, and then leans back in his enormous padded chair. It's too big, even for him. He offers no hospitality, only hostility in his distance from his wife and daughter.

–Well, what do you want?

Shakuntala smiles at his games, she no longer fears the bully. She speaks formally. We've had a marriage proposal for Avanti and I have decided to accept.

He ignores his wife, not even sparing her a glance, and addresses Avanti. And who is this proposal from?

–You know the boy…Shakuntala starts to answer.

Without shifting his gaze, he speaks sternly. I am talking to Avanti. Who is this proposal from?

–You know very well who the boy is. Aditya. I've agreed.

He closes his eyes, pretending to be in deep thought. He wants them to wait some more, feel the flex of his power as father and husband. He opens his eyes, thinking that his silence would have unnerved them, but there is serenity in both faces.

-I won't give my consent to this marriage. I don't like this boy.

-He's not a boy, he's a man, and a very successful one too.

-I don't care who he is. You heard me. It is a no. I want you to marry, but someone I choose, and not your mother.

-I didn't choose, Shakuntala says mildly. They chose each other.

-It's still no, he speaks to Avanti. It's as if his wife doesn't exist. You may leave. I'm very busy. He bends forward to look at the file, hand hovering over the phone to summon a secretary. Impatience in the bend of his head, his decision final.

Unexpectedly, Avanti takes a document from her handbag, a single sheet of paper, carefully folded in three. She unfolds it, the crinkle of the paper the only sound in the room, forcing him to glance up. Once she has unfolded it, she slides it across the desk, within reach of his hand. It's a photocopy of the original, which is in a bank vault.

-What's this? He pushes it back.

-Read it, Avanti commands, and this surprises him.

He snatches the paper, skims it and looks up. His face squeezes in rage. How dare you defy me? I will annul this civil marriage immediately.

-We'll end up in court, as only the court has the power to annul a legal marriage, Avanti says calmly.

He smiles now, a thin movement of his mouth, then the lips open wider to laugh, revealing those sharp teeth. The court! The court! My daughter, of all people, believes in the court. I can bend it to my will.

-As can I, she says defiantly. We'll have a traditional wedding in a month.

-I refuse to give permission.

-For what? Avanti asks. The marriage? I'm already married as you can see.

Shakuntala too opens her bag, and brings out a sheaf of papers. She pushes it across the desk, on top of the civil marriage certificate.

-That's an estimate of the expenses for the wedding. Please

arrange for the funds to be available.

–You put her up to this, he begins to shout at her.

–You've noticed me. For a while, I thought I was a ghost standing here. No, I didn't put her up to this. Aditya and she decided to get married, whether you gave your consent or not. She points to the document. As you can see, I'm not even a witness.

–You knew I would refuse, he snarls venomously. A pulse in his forehead beats furiously. Chanakya, you told them.

–I said nothing to them. And I am not a witness either. I am as surprised as you are. A falsehood.

I didn't add that the civil marriage was my idea—the only sure way to get past the President's inevitable refusal to grant Avanti permission to get married. I had accompanied them to the registrar, who had grown nervous when he realized whose marriage he was going to preside over. There were a few couples before them, dressed in muted finery, nervous because they were crossing boundaries of caste, religion, language and community to marry in secret for love. The registrar had hastily beckoned Aditya and Avanti to the head of the queue. Two of my spies witnessed the ceremony, then melted into the city as swiftly as they had appeared. Once married, Aditya borrowed my humble scooter and, with Avanti behind him, wove his way to my home in the old city to spend the day and night.

The President looks ready to rip the papers to shreds. He decides not to, then crumples everything up and throws it to the side. He knows they are only copies of the orginals.

–My party workers have been informed about the date of the wedding, Avanti says implacably. I've told them that you are delighted, I've had a thousand congratulatory SMSes, and I'm sure you'll receive congratulation messages soon.

He goes quiet, understands how comprehensively he has been defeated. He doesn't rise when we leave; his fury charges the air. I should have reminded him of my shastra: *No one is to be trusted, not even wife or child. One might even say, particularly wife and child.* I know he will work on his revenge.

The women are solemn on their way down, they do not exult in their victory. I have warned them to be careful of spies. We keep our emotions in check in the car too. It is only when we're safely inside the house, the doors closed tightly, that mother and daughter hug each other, laughing joyously, astonished by what they have pulled off.

–Be careful, I warn them, even as they giggle and re-enact every word and gesture of their encounter with the President in that intimidating office.

–Yes, you're right, Shakuntala says. We know what kind of a man he is. The gangster lies just below the surface.

As we continue to celebrate, we hear a car pull up at the front door. The bearer opens the door to admit two men, both young, muscular, wearing dark glasses, jeans and tight t-shirts. Each one carries a new Samsonite suitcase and without any greeting, places them beside Shakuntala. They turn and leave and, through the open door, we see the silver Audi Q5, driven by another man who looks almost identical to the first two. Once his companions are in, he accelerates away fast.

Shakuntala sighs, looking at the cases. I didn't expect a cheque from my husband for the expenses.

–Don't tell Aditya, Avanti begs me. He'll go absolutely nuclear if he knows about this.

I grip the handle of one and find I can't lift it. Cash is heavier than I thought.

■

Only her close female friends, and Aditya's sister and her friends, are invited to the mehendi. Muslim women, using slim sticks dipped in the different coloured hennas, create their temporary masterpieces on human skin. Eventually, the patterns will fade. As the bride, Avanti is first, and then her best friend, Monika, followed by the others.

All week men have been busy in the garden, building a platform 1.5 metres high, 6 metres wide and 2.5 metres long. It faces the wide expanse of the lawn, which will be filled with plastic chairs for the thousand guests who are expected. On the platform, they construct the marriage pandal; four pillars as the corners of a square, within it a smaller square, two bricks high, for the sacred fire. The stage and the pandal are decorated with thousands of flowers, roses and orchids flown in from Malaysia. The marriage ceremony is set for precisely 6.11 a.m., as calculated by the purohits. Four of them will perform the ceremony. The bride will be woken at three in the morning to have her bath, and then she will be dressed in her wedding finery, adorned with the family jewellery. Avanti's hands and arms are alive with peacocks, and her feet are covered with roses and green vines vanishing up the hem of her red silk saree, the same one Shakuntala wore on her wedding day. None of the female guests can match the glittering wealth that adorns her, though they bend and shuffle under the weight of jewellery fashioned from gold and diamonds.

At 5.30 a.m., on the day of the ceremony, Avanti is seated on the platform, facing the fire and the guests. Behind are her mother and father, neither looking at the other. Shakuntala is smiling as she fusses over Avanti, setting the saree to fall correctly, adjusting the clips holding the jasmine in her hair. Monika is beside them, doing her bit. There are other busybodies, fussing around or just strutting their importance, including Aditya's two young nieces. Weddings are chaotic celebrations. The President stands alone, his eyes are distant, looking out over the guests, his face stern and unyielding. Alongside them are Aditya's parents. His father is a tall man with a gentle, artist's face, the shape of his eyes and nose reflected in Aditya; his mother is slight and round, a pretty woman with a firm chin, a wide mouth given to easy smiles and in this, I see Aditya too. They are both at ease with Shakuntala but the President remains a stranger, a hostile in-law. We can hear the groom approaching, his entrance heralded by frenzied drumming of the tabla players. He comes riding a white horse and wears a pale blue sherwani woven with silver feathers, and a matching salwar; his head in a silk turban. He resembles a Mauryan prince. Behind him are his male relatives, and friends, delivering him to the bride's home. He will 'resist', but they will drive him forward. He rides easily, and dismounts without any help, to mount the stage, smiling at Avanti as he takes his place beside her.

The fire, agni, flickers in the morning light, and the purohits start the ceremony exactly on the auspicious minute. They chant the shlokas in my mother tongue, Sanskrit. The words have not changed over the last one thousand years, nor have the rituals. They bring tears to my eyes. I wait for the saptapadi, the seven steps that the bride and groom will take around the sacred fire. At a signal from the purohit, tabalchis beat the tablas furiously, the conch makes a loud, mournful sound. The couple rise and Avanti's right hand takes hold of Aditya's right hand, and they circle the fire, stumbling over the litany spoken by the purohit: 'We have taken the Seven Steps. You have become mine forever. Yes, we have become partners. I have become yours. Hereafter, I cannot live without you. Do not live without me. Let us share the joys. We are word and meaning united. You are thought and I am sound. May the night be honey-sweet for us. May the morning be honey-sweet for us. May the earth be honey-sweet for us. May the heavens be honey-sweet for us. May the plants be honey-sweet for us. May the sun be all honey for us. May the cows yield us honey-sweet milk. As the heavens are stable, as the earth is stable, as the mountains are stable, as the whole universe is stable, so may our union be permanently settled'. Avanti leads six rounds, then Aditya leads her for the seventh before they sit down again.

    -Finally, Aditya whispers, bending down, his lips brushing her head. I never thought this would ever happen.

    -This time it will be worth it. I can't wait.

    -Love does take its own sweet time. I wish we could leave now.

    -You're always so impatient. Just keep it in your pants.

    -It has a mind of its own. I do love you.

    -As much as I do you. We'll never part again, no matter what.

    My attention wanders as I hear a murmur spreading through a section of the crowd nearest the entrance gate. Two security men, in plain clothes, and ill-fitting grey suits, flank Siggy, who has just made an entrance dressed in full movie-star regalia. Neither Avanti nor Shakuntala sent her an invitation. The President is smiling now, this is his revenge, he has planned her entrance at just this moment. Siggy looks nervous, I've never seen her so unsure of herself, she looks around at the assembled guests, searching for support. Our eyes meet and I feel for her. I can leave her standing there, helpless, or I can go to her assistance. I turn to the stage. Aditya and Avanti have seen her too. They frown. Shakuntala hasn't seen her yet and I wonder whether I can escort Siggy out of public view, hide her in a back row. But the President has other ideas. He beckons for her to come forward; no one can resist that powerful summons. Shakuntala catches the gesture, sees who it is but doesn't recognize the movie star. Not yet. The wedding is far too important to pay attention to a lovely woman standing some distance away. I hurry over to Siggy, take her hand, lead her to the back but her security detail is trying to move her into a front row—in order to comply with the President's wishes.

-Let go, she hisses at them, and when they keep trying to persuade her to go with them, she simply turns away, and follows me. I didn't want to be here, I swear. He insisted I had to be otherwise...

-What? We find two seats as far from the stage as possible. The people in front turn to stare at her, readying themselves for her autograph, for a photo, for a chance to talk.

-He...threatened he'd destroy my career....hurt my mother...I had to come. Please, please tell Shakuntala and Avanti that. She grabs hold of my hand, leans over to whisper. I have to get away but I don't know how. Help me.

-We'll have to wait. Not now.

-I know you told me, warned me, to return to my village. I should've listened but I couldn't help myself.

I'm watching the ceremony, more familiar rituals, but I focus on Shakuntula. She stiffens visibly. She recognizes Siggy; she knew about the affair. Siggy is just another woman in his life and she has long been indifferent. She stares at her husband's cold smile; he has his revenge on her, the woman who deserted him for a swami, who defied him with this marriage. Shakuntula turns back to her duties, her smile more fragile but she won't give him the victory of tears. She has her duty to perform, right to the very end. Once the ceremony is over, the President bends to congratulate the bride and groom, only with a few whispered words, no warm embrace. He descends the steps, and makes his way down the aisle towards us. He passes and Siggy rises to follow, glancing back at me, desperation still in her eyes. He takes her by the elbow to reveal his intimacy with the movie star, and guides her to the waiting limo. The ceremony is over, the fire flickers and dies, the guests rise to shuffle out to their waiting cars.

Shakuntala goes into the house, followed by Avanti, who plants a kiss on Aditya's cheek.

Shakuntala is sitting in the living room. She is crying, dabbing her eyes with the edge of her saree, smearing her make-up.

-He humiliated me in front of everyone. Her tears are not of pain but fury. I want to kill him. Why didn't you tell me he was going to bring her? Shakuntala demands. You know everything and keep the wrong secrets. I want to kill her too.

–He forced her to attend. And I didn't think he would bring her. You did know about her.

–The whole state does. But to bring his woman to his daughter's wedding, for god's sake.

–Most of the guests were shocked and uneasy. Even princes should behave with propriety on such important occasions. The bedroom is the field for such marital battles.

–He's not a prince, I told you before.

Avanti returns, having changed into another saree, most of her jewellery removed.

–I'm sorry he did this. He insulted me too. I was furious, and so was Aditya. She embraces her mother, wanting to squeeze the pain out and take it into herself.

–It was just so childish and vicious, Shakuntala says.

–He is not going to stop, Avanti says. I'm sure he'll bring her to the reception.

■

He does. It's at seven in the evening, the bar has been set up, the cooks are busy preparing dinner for a few thousand. The musicians play in a far corner, barely audible. Avanti is in a blue saree, once again decked with jewellery, and Aditya wears a suit and tie. He watches as the President arrives with his escort. He gets out first, stops to chat to a guest, keeping us in suspense before the other door opens and Siggy steps out. She is more assured this time, and as resplendent as ever, she walks beside the President to take a seat in the front row. The President moves to stand beside his wife on the stage. I think Siggy has accepted her fate, to be a pawn in the conflict between him and his wife and daughter. She accepts compliments, signs invitation cards. A long queue forms to the left of the stage, of guests bearing gifts for the married couple. Hands are shaken, palms pressed, gifts given and the guests exit stage right. It's an endless procession which will be repeated the next evening for the party faithful.

The day after the final reception, the married couple flies away to Venice for their honeymoon. It's a watery city for lovers and I explore it on Google Earth, following the canals out into the sea. It's not far from the plagiarist Machiavelli's hometown. One day, I hope to travel there but, for the moment, I retire to my home to begin my new treatise on democracy—my advice to a prince who wishes to attain power through the democratic system. In my original advice to the prince I had suggested assassination, a sword in the belly, a dagger in the back, employing spies and even torture, to make the path to the throne swifter. But this is no longer advisable. In a democracy, the art of assassination has to be more subtle and revolves around the destruction of the rival's character—a well planted lie, a distortion of his or her words, an assault on his beliefs. The sole necessity for the democratic prince is not an army, not weapons, but wealth. Once he has amassed enough wealth, mostly by foul means and many promises, then he can leap from the pyramid of money and promises into political office. He should form his own party, and recruit his followers with promises of wealth through contracts, commissions, kickbacks and high office, even as the prince offered plunder—gold, horses, women—to his soldiers as their reward. These are my observations from studying the many books I have accumulated, watching television documentaries and drama series, and guiding my prince(ss) to her current position.

I start on my treatise, laboriously writing it out by hand, not on palm leaves but on white, ruled paper. A day later the President's secretary calls me.

-You are to meet the President in one hour.
-What about?
-One hour, and he disconnects.

I mount my scooter, thinking there are no secrets in the digital world. All firewalls can be hacked. At the assembly, I follow the security routine and am finally, after another hour in the outer office, ushered in. He sits at his desk, staring at me as I cross the broad expanse of carpet. There is a document on the desk which he slides across.

-What is the meaning of this?
-It's a petition for divorce, I say, after quickly skimming it.
-I know that, he snaps. How dare she file for divorce? I will never give it. And where is she?
-Home? I haven't seen her since the marriage.

–She's not home. She's not to be found. You must know where she is? She confides in you.
–Not really, sir. Perhaps she has returned to the ashram?
–No, she isn't there either. She's vanished.

FIFTEEN

THE HOUSE STAFF swears she went to sleep one night, and at dawn the next day, had disappeared. They had searched for her when she did not appear for breakfast. They had knocked on her bedroom door for half an hour and, when she didn't respond, peeked in. The bed was made and her suitcase stood beside it. She hadn't died in the bathroom. The chowkidar swore he hadn't slept a wink all night, and no one had passed him. The President's spies questioned the cops guarding the roads, but no woman had passed them. As she didn't own a computer, there wasn't a hard disk for them to examine to decipher her secrets, no firewall to break. She didn't have an identity on the internet, no Hotmail, no Gmail, no IP address. No Twitter, or Facebook account. She didn't even have a cell phone on her to leave the telltale electronic trail.

Shakuntala clung stubbornly to a different age, she didn't want such clutter in her life, she learned to keep her secrets from her child and from her husband, even her friends. Was it deliberate? She knew her husband watched her constantly and only by avoiding the use of modern technology could she remain hidden from his probing. The police raided the ashram at dawn while the chelas were still sleepy, dreaming of their imminent salvation. The police lined them up and questioned them individually in the swami's office. Where is she? Did she tell you where she was going? Whom did she meet? None of them knew anything. She was a lovely, calm, helpful lady. Whom did she see? Only us, they each replied. They arrested the swami for laundering foreign currency and imprisoned him. It was a false charge but that is not something that has ever worried our police. They beat him up, and kept asking him the same questions, over and over again.

–You're her Guru, she must have confided her innermost thoughts to you.

I heard through my spies that he denied it through bloodied lips. He told them: I only teach people to meditate, to free their spirit through their belief in God. The only way to reach Him is to concentrate on nothing and He will find you. I tell them that through His guidance they must find their true destiny. We discussed workings of destiny for many hours. I don't know whether she found her destiny. Even a cracked rib fails to elicit anymore out of him.

I reluctantly admire his fortitude, salvation will soon be his. No one has seen her in the train station, the bus station, the airport. Her passport is still in the top right-hand drawer of her dresser, along with all her jewellery. His spies comb the city, search the villages, but no one has seen her. The President's fury is unabated, he wants to take out his frustration on someone but doesn't know whom to blame.

Two weeks later when the happy couple return from their honeymoon, aglow with love, good food and the magic of that watery city, there's still no Shakuntala. I meet them at the airport to give them the news.

–Did someone murder her? Avanti asks, in a panic. I know by 'someone' she could only mean her vindictive father.

–No body found so far.

Avanti's VVIP motorcade waits outside the terminal, and Aditya winces at the prospect of travelling in it. He would prefer to take a taxi, even a bus. But by circling the fire seven times, he has accepted Avanti for who she is, and now reluctantly climbs into the limo to sit beside her. I take the front seat. Instead of following her directions to the farmhouse, their new home, like arrows the cars shoot straight to the President's office. Security clears us and we follow the familiar trail into his office, where he stands in front of his desk. An unusual position for him.

–Where is your mother? The President demands of Avanti, even before she has crossed the room.

–I don't know. I've been away. Or didn't you notice. Even if I knew, I wouldn't tell you.

This only enrages him more and he even thinks of hitting her but thinks the better of it when he notices the belligerent presence of Aditya by her side. He stops his open palm an inch from her face as Aditya is ready with a closed fist, unafraid of the bully.

–In any event, why do you care? You have your actress.

–She's still my wife, he says flatly. And if you do communicate with your mother tell her I will not give her a divorce.

–How wonderful! Aditya says, goading his father-in-law. Why

not give her a divorce? You can divorce and marry Siggy, she's a lovely woman.

-Keep out of this, he warns.

-I am family now.

He searches his daughter's face, trying to penetrate those light brown eyes as if she's hidden her mother inside them. I know he wants to divest Avanti of her portfolio as punishment, send her into the desert of back benches in the assembly. But that would be too risky, it would reveal the rift in the family, and cause a rift in the party too. Her followers might defect to support their martyr. With state elections looming the President needs her support. They both know their politics. He waves us away and goes around the desk, and settles into his chair. The audience has ended, and we leave. This time, the motorcade takes us to the farmhouse and we wait until it has left, and are in the privacy of the front room. I've not been here and I like the simple furnishings—divans, bolsters, low tables and rugs scattered across the parquet floor. The paintings on the walls reflect Aditya's excellent sense of aesthetics—landscapes, portraits, charcoal sketches, oils, water colours. There isn't one photograph of him with the stars he has worked with it—these are probably in his study.

-You know, don't you? she asks me. We have our spies.

-No, I don't. A falsehood. A woman should always have a secret place in her heart, or outside her daily life, to which she can escape. Shakuntula entrusted me with hers, and I will guard it.

-How's Siggy? Aditya asks when Avanti goes inside to unpack.

-I haven't seen her since the wedding. I tried to visit her three days ago, but they wouldn't let me into the building.

■

The months pass. I see Aditya's film at a private theatre. It is brilliant, moving, sad. Siggy mesmerizes on-screen, not with her sexuality but her vulnerability.

A few weeks later, Aditya calls Avanti's office from Berlin when I'm visiting.

-I won the Golden Bear. He can barely contain his excitement and his pride and I can hear him across the desk.

-Oh darling, I'm so proud of you. Congratulations. It deserves every prize, including the Oscar. Now, I have exciting news too.

I'm pregnant.
—You are? He shouts and we can hear his whoop of joy. I'll come home now.
—No, finish your tour. There's still another seven months to go and I'm fine.
—If you say so. But call and I'll return at once. I love you so much.
—And I love you too. They disconnect with many kisses.

He had wanted Siggy to accompany him, but the President refused her permission to travel.
—She's not well, one of his secretaries informed Aditya.
—What's wrong with her?
—Not well, is the only reply. But my spies in the apartment building—cleaners, the maintenance man, electricians, the postman—report there's nothing physically the matter with her; apparently she remains indoors, staring out of the window all day. I promised to help. I can't call her, as his spies will track the number. Siggy's cook, Meena, can call me though, and she reports that Siggy will be going to the Plaza Mall soon, if I want to meet her. She will have high security. The mall is crowded, the fashion outposts of London (Harrods), New York (Bergdof), Paris (Chanel), Rome (Louis Vuitton), Milan (Rinascente). I try to mingle with the crowd, but even a half-blind spy would recognize my distorted features, but that's simply a risk I'm going to take. Siggy enters. Her escorts are two men in suits, familiar figures. She wears large dark glasses, a headscarf half covering her features and a loose kameez. Whenever she enters a store to browse, her bodyguards wait outside until she emerges with the shopping bags which she passes to her minders. When she enters a third store, I slip in through a second entrance and move parallel to the racks she flicks through.
—Siggy!
—Chanakya! I'm not supposed to see you, you troublemaker.
—I was passing by, I lie, and spotted you. You look well.

She looks back, the men are watching the passing women outside. We keep walking to the far end of the store.
—I saw the new film, you are brilliant in it, the ending brought tears to my eyes.
—Really, you loved it?
—Really.

She laughs. I'd give you a hug but my minders will spot you. Instead, she blows a kiss across the silk gowns.

-Why didn't you go to Berlin with Aditya? The audience would have loved to meet the star.

She's near to tears. I really wanted to but he didn't want me to leave him. He's a very lonely man and I think he believed I wouldn't have returned. I swore I would but…

-Are you going to act in any more films?

-Definitely. I've had so many offers and I'm thinking about them.

She stops to run her hands over blouses, comparing colours and makes a face of dismissal.

-You were very upset at the wedding. You wanted my help to return to your village.

She laughs. I was a bit hysterical, and exaggerated. No, I'm fine, I really am. I'm with a man I love. Back in the village, Rachna will probably be with a man she has had to marry through an arranged marriage. He will dominate her, she will have to screw him, whether she likes it or not, cook the food, fetch water from the river, work in the fields, bear children. I suppose Siggy is also controlled but she doesn't have the drudgery of labour to deal with, and she actually loves her man. Her life is better than Rachna's. Besides, it's too late.

She flattens the outline of her loose kameez to reveal her swollen tummy. That beautiful belly is now carrying the President's child.

It's still a secret, she whispers. My mother will be here for the birth and then I will return to the village with her for three months, as is our tradition. She blows me a long kiss and wanders away.

Two women pregnant, two women racing to have their child. All conflicts begin within a family and then engulf those around them, rippling further out to bring down nations and civilizations, if they are kings. The President will be a father and a grandfather. Siggy will become Avanti's stepmother if she marries the President, and grandmother to her child. See how we humans complicate relationships by falling in love. There will be two heirs, and I am aware from experience that such an event will bring more discord into the family. With two sons, in those ancient days we could expect war; with a girl and a boy, there could be a truce, though women too have ambitions for the gaddi, even as Avanti does.

Shakuntala begins fading out of our memories and our lives.

She has not contacted her daughter despite their closeness in the months before the wedding. Avanti is desperate to find her as she must be present for the birth of her grandchild. But that doesn't seem likely to happen, as no one has seen her in months. Thin air. I listen to my spies' reports on Chay. He is gathering more and more supporters and he is constantly attacking the mining company. He calls his movement Insurgents for Action (IAC). His newest initiative has been so effective that it has brought to a standstill all efforts to raze the jungle. Monika's father has demanded the President launch a bigger offensive against the 'terrorist'. Until Chay is stopped, he will stop his contributions to the President's finances. Not to mention Avanti's. That amounts to many millions, lots of zeroes.

Avanti stands at her office window, one hand on her back to support the weight in front, the other clutching the cell phone on which she is speaking to her husband. The baby is due any moment now. Aditya phones every hour to check, ready to catch a flight back from wherever he is. He will be present at the birth of his child. She blows kisses into the cell phone and disconnects.

–Monika's father can't withhold funds, we've signed the MoU. I spoke to him but he says that until the insurgents are wiped out, he won't invest. I talked to Monika too but she says her father's the boss. She isn't being helpful at all. We have built only half our number of schools. See...

She points to her desk. In the file are four colour photographs of square buildings, set against a barren landscape, another surrounded by trees, a third next to a well, the fourth with cattle passing by. Printed on the back of each is their location.

–Those are the finished ones.

–Who won the contract?

–It's in the file.

I leaf through the file and find the name—Waverly Constructions—a grand name for such a humble project.

–Have you seen them?

–Not yet. I'm in no condition to travel into the villages. I will go after the birth. We must stop Chay first. Go and speak to him again.

–It didn't do any good the first time. He gave me his demands, you passed them on. The state made no effort to start even a dialogue with him. It's important to talk with the enemy, gauge his determination, his strength. And compromise.

-I can't talk to him. Not in my condition. She is staring down at the man, on the pavement, still clutching his box. He sits there, even in the rains, waiting patiently for Avanti to summon him. She points down at the man. He's driving me crazy. Get him up here and then we're rid of him. Make sure there isn't a bomb in the box.

-By now, it should've gone off.

His long vigil is over when I cross the road, escorted by the cops, to take him up with me. He smiles in delight and stands up, he's even leaner upright than sitting and, when he picks up his box, he lists to that side. Cash? Gold? His dress, shirt and trouser, clean but faded, attest to a genteel poverty. He has spent years waiting to see Avanti, I wonder what obsession consumes him.

-Thank you, thank you, he murmurs, as we dodge across the road.

Security is very reluctant to let the box through, but he refuses to open it. We wait a half-hour until a sniffer dog is found, a golden Labrador on a leash. It walks up to the box, sniffs, and promptly loses interest. It wags its tail at me.

-See, there's no bomb, I tell the cop.

-I don't mind if he blows you up but the President will be very angry if anything happens to his daughter. And I can't blame it on you 'cause you'll be dead.

-He won't blow us up.

We move past security to the lift.

-What's your name?

-Jugal. And you're Chanakya. I will not harm her, I swear. He pats the box. It is a gift.

-Will she like it?

-Possibly.

-And once it has been delivered, what will you do?

-Return to my native place and back to my work.

-As an artist.

-Yes.

We enter Avanti's office, she is still by the window, back to talking about her baby-to-be with Aditya. We wait until she's finished, then she turns, smiling.

-He's returning tomorrow, he can't wait. Then she frowns at Jugal.

-Avanti, this is Jugal.

Jugal drops the box and rushes forward. Avanti tries to step back but her back is already against the window. I reach out to stop him; he falls flat. He prostrates himself full length.

-Madam, I thank you for giving me this gracious audience in your revered presence. I have nothing but worship for your great being, you are a gift from the heavens for the people. You are the Princess of all our hearts...

-Thank you. Avanti says, cutting him off in mid-flow.

I half lift him by his shoulders and manage to get him upright. He stands with his palms pressed together, whispering to himself.

-Show the minister your gift.

He kneels beside the box and takes out the key that hangs around his neck. He unlocks the box slowly, and takes out an object wrapped in saffron silk. Tenderly, he carries it over to the desk, and gently puts it down.

-Remove the cloth.
-That honour must go to Madam Minister.
-You sure it's not a bomb?
-It is only my homage to you, Madam Minister.

Avanti approaches the package cautiously. With thumb and forefinger, she holds the edge of the cloth and unwraps it. There are many folds. Finally, we see his gift.

-It's...it's beautiful, Avanti steps back to admire the work.

The carving in black granite is forty centimetres high, about twenty across, and is a perfect likeness of Avanti. It is the work of a talented sculptor—she looks straight ahead with determination, yet with a slight smile on her lips. I go closer and see that he has studied her closely, from the shape of her ears to the arch of her neck; even her hair looks as if a breeze could ruffle it.

-It's beautiful, Avanti says. Isn't it Chanakya?
-It is a work of art. Congratulations.

Jugal beams.

-I want to buy it. Whatever the price.

Jugal is shocked. Madam Minister, it is my gift to you. I want no money. I just want your blessings.

He kneels and Avanti gingerly places her hands on his head.

-Thank you for such fine work. I'll arrange for your transport home.

I lead Jugal out of Avanti's office, and leave him with a secretary to make all the arrangements for his journey back home.

Inside, Avanti is looking intently at the sculpture, circling it. She touches it, tentatively, then more possessively she strokes her stone hair.

■

A week later, Avanti gives birth to a boy child. She's in an exclusive, no-expenses-spared private room at the Ladbroke Hospital. Aditya films every moment of the birth. He wants me to watch it with him later but I decline, I've seen it all before. I was present at Bindusara's birth and had to cut open his mother, Durhara's, stomach to extract him from the dying woman, seven days before the delivery date. It was her misfortune that she ate a portion of Emperor Chandragupta's food that was poisoned.

Avanti's perfectly formed baby weighs three kilograms. Soon enough, the President sweeps into his daughter's room, and looks down at the prince, his grandson, sleeping in his mother's arms. He is looking for a likeness of himself, the mirror of proof in this just born baby. He circles the bed, as a king will a wounded foe. He stretches out his hand to touch Avanti's cheek. It's not a caress, not the loving gesture it had once been, this is as impersonal as a doctor's touch. He is the conqueror, after all.

–Congratulations, he murmurs.

–Isn't he beautiful? She looks down at the tiny human, eyes shut in blissful sleep. Aditya lifts his camera and films the movements of the President.

–He is going to be a very handsome young man, he says, with Avanti's mind and hopefully some of my talent.

–Another film director, the President says in a mocking tone.

–Or a future President, Avanti corrects him, knowing his thoughts too well and deliberately whispering the threat.

–Possibly, he says and pads out of the room.

When she is sure he is out of hearing, she calls me. You must tell Mother, somehow, that I have my baby. I want her to bless him; I can't live without that.

–It will be in the papers tomorrow. She'll hear about it and will find a way to get in touch.

–But will she come and hold it? I want her to stay with us,

and help me.
  -Then you'll need to return to stay in the bungalow with her for three months.
  -I'm happy to do that. She turns to Aditya. You won't mind, will you?
  -I will miss you but she should be with you. She should have been with you even before the baby's birth.
  -God only knows where she is, Avanti cries in despair. I pray she is still alive.

There are enough distractions for her. Monika sweeps in, bearing her gift for the baby, a gold rattle. Though she's been married longer, she remains childless, and frets and worries as her parents want to hold a grandson, gift him the empire her father's building. Envy tinges her chatter as she looks down at the baby.

When she leans down to kiss Avanti, she murmurs, just loud enough for my curious ears: Speak to your father. My father is going to pull out as Chay blew up another truck and also a drilling machine. The workers are frightened and refuse to work. It's your district, it's your people who will suffer.
  -Father is sending in the Panther Attack Force. Chay won't be a problem for long.

■

Eleven days later, in the same hospital, but in a different suite, Siggy has a boy who weighs 2.9 kilograms. If one were to calculate who should mount the gaddi on existing numerical data, Avanti's son has the edge by eleven days and 100 grams. But, as the son of the President, Siggy's boy will be the direct descendant. The nurse tells me that the President spent much longer with the mother of his son, and that he held the baby in his arms and placed his lips on its forehead, anointing it with his acceptance. He took Siggy gifts too, orchids and roses, and a diamond necklace. For his son, he filled the hospital room with stuffed toys, teddy bears, stuffed tigers, even a tricycle. He obviously expects great things from this child. Two commandos stand guard outside her door, night and day, and only the cabinet ministers are on the list of those welcomed to visit the mother of the President's son. Those who are loyal to Avanti risk their portfolios, to visit her briefly. In and out in seconds. The others walk past her room, not even daring to turn their heads. With the elections now looming, they have minds as devious as mine and even as they bear their gifts to the babies, they are calculating which one, Avanti or the President, could return them to their sinecures. Ancient rajas behaved in such a manner too, thoughts of power constantly preoccupied their minds, even thousands of years apart. I count five Avanti supporters, twelve for the President; nothing is ever firm in politics.

–So she has had his son, Avanti says when Aditya leaves the room for a coffee. How will that affect us?

They had the baby's naming ceremony yesterday. Bharat is eleven days older. Now they're just babies, but they'll be adults before you know it. There'll be conflict.

–I know that. I asked a question.

–This is a democracy and you must promote your son as your heir when it is time, and ensure he has the money to fight the elections. Train him from the moment he can speak. If this was in Chanakya's age and his prince asked for his advice, his answer would be simpler: Kill him. Now.

She doesn't flinch at this, even seems to consider the possibility, a little smile on her lips. I should have lived in that age, Chan, and had you by my side.

–Politics is the same whichever the age. Even today, politicians are assassinated. In some countries by bombs or guns, in others by secrets and lies.

■

A few days later an envelope with no name, and no return address, arrives. Avanti opens it, instinctively knowing who it is from even before she unfolds the scruffy piece of paper.

–Mother, she says and reads.

My lovely, darling Avanti. I am so happy that you have a child, a son, I hear, and only wish I could be by your side to look after you both and help you through these difficult days. I have, again, failed you as a mother. I am so full of excuses, aren't I, but life seems to have conspired to make me this way. I have performed a long puja for my grandson, and pray daily that God will guide him in this hard life. I cannot tell you where I am because of your father but one day I will visit you and hold my grandson in my arms. I wish I could predict that day but the less I say the safer it is for me. Be assured that I am well, and contented. Finally, I have found a use for my life, and am not wasting it away in a bungalow or a palace—an accessory for my hated husband. Yes, I feel only hatred for him now. He discarded me when I was no longer of use to him. I wish I could understand love, it remains a mystery how I loved such a man for so long. Now, that love has curdled, and I cannot get rid of the bitter taste in my heart. Of course, he has his mistress, Siggy, but I feel no jealousy at all. But I am sorry and sad for her to be entangled with such a man. I know too well what he wants from her—a son—who will be his heir when the time comes. He never ever liked women, and only used us for his own ends. But we won't go into that again. I am helping my people and have found my calling. Finally, I am putting to use all those years of learning and those useless degrees in many subjects. I am not in another ashram. Initially I found my stay there helpful but towards the end I found it stifling, filled with selfish people only seeking their own salvation. I hope the police won't intercept this letter which is why I cannot tell you how to write back to me. But I will write again, and keep writing and will somehow hear about how my grandson grows. I pray too that one day I will see him, and you, and hold you both in my arms. With all my love and blessings for your son, you and Aditya.

-When will she come? Avanti cries, holding the letter to her breast and then kissing it. None of us can answer her. She wrote it some days ago. She doesn't know of Siggy's son.

Aditya asks the chowkidar: Who gave you this letter?

-A chhokra. The boy said some man gave it to him, and paid him to give it to this house.

-I'm going to write to her too and tell her everything until the letters reach her. I also want copies of all the photographs of our baby for her to see.

-And how and when will she get to read your letters? Aditya says in concern, comforting her. She's hiding somewhere.

-Chanakya will find her, he has his spies.

■

Aditya decides to celebrate, once Avanti is safely home, nursing her beautiful Bharat. He chooses The Amethyst for our lunch, a restaurant in the city centre, patronized by those with enough money for Italian fare—pastas, spaghetti, risottos, zucchini. My taste runs more to dhabas, parathas, kebabs, dal, in the old city but this is his treat. The place is spacious with booths and separate tables, dimly lit, with a giant TV screen on the far wall. The air is cold as winter. Four men sit in one of the booths and we take the next one; Aditya sits with his back to them. From their dress—ties, pressed trousers, formal shirts—I take them to be corporate types, ambitious men aiming to become Vice Presidents or even Presidents of their companies. They are celebrating some corporate triumph with tall mugs of beer. Aditya orders one for himself, I drink water, and study the complex menu. I'm happy to experiment with foreign foods, from time to time, but am ignorant of the dishes of the Italians. Aditya chooses spaghetti and mussels for me, a prawn and tomato risotto for himself. He settles back, stretching out his long legs, lounging back in the leather seat. My feet don't touch the ground.

He laughs good naturedly. God, it's stressful having a baby. I feel as exhausted as Avanti. Do you have children?

–Not that I know of. But I do have advice even on children. Treat your kids like darlings for the first five years. For the next five years, scold them. By the time they turn sixteen, treat them like friends. Your grown up children are your best friends.

–I'll remember that. Another quote from the *Arthashastra*?

–Chanakya wrote fourteen books. Not all of them were about politics. Politics stains every moment in our lives, whether it's about power or even a family relationship. Look around, every relationship you see is political. There is some self-interest behind every friendship. This is a bitter truth. Friendships are love affairs not consummated in bed but in classes, bars, on playing fields, on long journeys and they fill the void of loneliness that we all experience in this life. Friends are often closer than family and we share our deepest longings, thoughts and secrets with them. The bitterest betrayals are not between lovers or families but friends. They are our companions on this journey and when they vanish into dust and ashes, we know our own time nears. They are the last milestone we pass before the end.

He looks around at the other diners, many are women, stylish and wealthy, heads close in chatter.

-If I was here with Avanti, security would fill this place, patting down everyone. I love Avanti, but being married to a minister is a real pain in the ass. Even when I go to the toilet at home, there's a commando peering in to see if my dick is loaded.

-The prince, princess, must always be kept safe from an assassin.

He studies me, the low, romantic lights obscure my face partially. He only sees the scarred side. Sometimes, he smiles, I don't know whether to believe you or not. He leans forward to whisper. About Siggy's child. How do you, learned guru, interpret that?

-Problems in the years ahead. But we're celebrating, let's talk of other things. Have you started your next film?

-I'm waiting for the script. I'll tell you what it's about. What happens when one parent dies, and the living one remarries? The lives of the children are radically changed. I am working on parallel stories. In the first one, the mother lives and they follow a pattern of life already laid out for them. In the other story the mother dies and her death alters the lives of the children under the stepmother.

-It's complex. Death is not the end, it is the beginning of actions. It always alters the pattern of the lives of those who survive it. It is an action that has long repercussions, unknown to the dead person that can impact the lives not just of the children but their children and grandchildren, friends, lovers too. It is an avalanche that flows over graves and pyres and we can never predict when it will finally come to a stop. The children are always aware of the immediate consequences of the death and the re-marriage.

-Yes, that's what I'm trying to portray. It will make a wonderful film and I'll... He stops suddenly, and leans back, half turning his head. He's heard a line of conversation from the next booth. The man directly behind him, neatly combed dark hair, gelled into shape, is laughing and telling a story.

-...I get a call to visit her office, and it's late evening for the appointment. The minister is sitting at her desk, looking stern. When you enter, on the right side of the room, is this stand with a carving of her. You know how one has to act...crawl a little and say nice things. We chit chat for a few minutes and then she signals to her secretary to come in. When he does, I hand over the briefcase with the money and she slides over the contract for Waverly Constructions to build the schools. She's as bad as her father...

Aditya moves swiftly. He rises, turns and grabs the speaker by his neck and brings him down onto the floor. The speaker is too surprised to resist at first and lies there bewildered as Aditya strikes him in the face. I manage to pull Aditya off his victim, even as the other three tumble out of the booths to aid their companion.

-You're a fucking liar, Aditya shouts at him. A fucking liar. She'd never do something like that....I'm going to kill you...you fucking runt...you...

The lips of the man Aditya attacked are bleeding, his glasses are broken. He is furious, as are his companions, but just before they pile on to Aditya, I manage to pull one of them aside and whisper into his ear.

-He's the minister's husband. You want to end up in prison?

-Shit, he says, Shit. He spreads the word to the two men next to him. Together they now turn from Aditya to their injured friend, begin talking urgently to him. As they talk I can see the anger evaporate from the man who was attacked. He looks almost ill, knowing his career could end this moment. Quickly, he presses his palms together, panting hard, and bows low, to Aditya.

-I was just telling stories sir, the man pleads. Nothing like that happened, I swear. I was joking. I have never met the minister in my life...I swear on my mother...I never meet such powerful people... I was just trying to show off...you must please believe me...you know how we all talk...I swear I have never met the minister...I know a friend tried to pay her and she threw him out of the office and he told the lies just to get back at her...we all know she is a most straightforward, a good person.

-She's not like her father, Aditya says angrily. She'd never dream of taking money.

-Yes, yes, the others say. Our friend can't hold his drink, he was showing off. He has a problem. We'll take care of him.

-Please, I beg you, don't tell the Minister, the storyteller begs, almost in tears.

-Get out of here, Aditya says.

They're enormously grateful he's forgiven them. Each one steps forward to warmly shake his hand and hurry out of the restaurant. The other patrons have watched all this unfold. The women at their tables recognizing Aditya from the movie magazines, have their cell phones out, they are already reporting their version of the event. *Film Director Beats Up Innocent Man.* I worry that it will be on Youtube within the next few minutes, FB too. Aditya sits down, takes a long sip of beer. There's a bruise on his left cheek, which is starting to swell. One of the men must have managed to land a punch.

–It's amazing how quickly a gentle person like you can turn to violence.

–He got me mad with his comments.

–You had to protect your wife's dignity. You did right.

–Don't tell Avanti.

–She'll know even before you reach home.

–Does she? he demands.

–Does what? Though I know what he means. I must speak a falsehood.

–Take bribes, is she corrupt like her father?

–Not in my presence. But she's in politics, the party needs funding for the coming elections.

–I don't care what the party needs, he snaps. I don't want her name bandied around in this way by such men.

–A person should not be too honest. Straight trees are cut first just like honest people are the first ones to get screwed. You are not naïve, Aditya, you know even in films, there are a hundred ways of accounting for losses and how money vanishes. Isn't that also another kind of corruption?

–But I am paid only to direct, the producers…

–Are just artistic politicians.

The waiter, wary now of a man with such powerful connections, carefully places the dishes in front of us. Aditya stares at his, almost with loathing, and pushes it away. I need to eat, taste this exotic dish. The mussels are slippery and soft as a woman's tongue, and the spaghetti strands difficult to carry to my mouth. They slip off my fork, and I want to grasp them with my fingers but in such an exclusive restaurant I note everyone eats only with the gleaming cutlery. They are also watching our table discreetly, hoping perhaps for another burst of drama. This time their cell phones are ready, the daggers of instant reality. *Director Throws Food at Waiter.* The waiter, a young man with high cheekbones, slicked down hair, wearing a white shirt and black trousers, stands at a safe distance.

–Let's get out of here, Aditya says.

I drop my fork regretfully, and follow him out to where the concierge is. He pulls out his wallet.

–No, no payment, the manager, an elderly man, tall, slim, with red-framed glasses and a shaven bald head, waves away the offering. Compliments of the house.

–I don't take complimentary meals from anyone, Aditya says. He drops a few notes on the counter and we're out in the harsh light and the heat.

As we walk into the house, Avanti waits with Bharat at her breast, feeding him.

–I heard what happened.

–Your spies are fast.

–That's why I have them. Please, Aditya, don't believe a word of whatever you heard. This is a city full of rumours and you're going to hear many more about I did this or that, how I've made millions… She pauses to help Bharat burp. What did he say, this man you had a fight with?

–He claimed you take bribes.

She laughs. And you believed that? Who was this man?

He laughs. I didn't get his name. We were too busy rolling on the floor.

She studies his face. You better put some ice on that, pointing to his cheek. Should we call a doctor?

–I don't think it's that serious. He leans down to kiss his son, gently strokes his head and the baby looks back at him in contentment. I'm going to get some work done.

–You do believe me, she pleads.

He stops, lost in thought. Of course, without turning, and continues on his way.

She waits for the door to close. Who was that man? she demands and I hear the note of menace in her voice.

–He's with Waverly Constructions.

–I'll be talking to them soon, is her threat.

As always, in this political household, the television remains on, though on mute. She needs to keep abreast of the news, even though most of the reports are exaggerated and unreliable. One of the channels flashes a 'Breaking News' banner, repeating it continuously to hold our attention. The newsreader emerges through the banner and the commercials.

 –The President has just announced that the elections will be held in six weeks' time.

 Her fists clench. Sometimes, I want to murder the President. Then she flushes, embarrassed at what she has blurted. No, I don't mean that, I don't really want to kill my father, but he does drive me mad. If he wasn't my father I might've. Do princesses kill their kings?

SIXTEEN

-YES. PRINCESSES AND queens take to murder as easily as princes and kings. They can slit a throat faster than a snake's strike, but mostly prefer pouring poison down unsuspecting gullets.

She waves my comment away. His timing is deliberate. He knows that in the next six weeks, what with a newborn, I won't be able to campaign hard. He wants me to lose.

-Use your cell phone, use FB, Twitter, contact all your faithful party workers. You have the database of all those who voted for you, now you must use that. You must get started today, not tomorrow. The President will campaign the old way, on the road, flying here and there, giving his speeches to lorry-loads of voters. His thugs will coerce the people to attend every rally.

We watch the news for half an hour, my stomach queasy with unsatiated hunger, thinking of what I could find in the kitchen. There are many pundits to talk about this snap election, they believe the President could lose and that's why he wants to hold them early. This won't give the Opposition enough time to stitch together a coalition.

My cell phone plays its beautiful raaga, but the number is unknown. I listen to the voice of the caller, and instantly recognize it. I pass the phone to Avanti.

-It's your mother.

-Mother, where are you? I have to see you. You must hold Bharat. He's beautiful...She stops when she learns the reason for the call. Of course I will, but we must meet to discuss it, Mother. It can't just happen over the phone...

Shakuntala disconnects. Avanti says frantically... Mother, mother... She's gone. I don't even know from where she called. She frowns, staring down at the phone before looking at me sideways.

-What did she want?

-She's going to stand as an independent candidate in the election. She wants me to support her. I said I would. He's going to be furious. She's laughing, thrilled that she's going to see her mother soon. We'll be together and I will teach her how to campaign, the way you taught me. I'm sure I'll get the same number of votes if not more since I've built those schools and roads...She sees me frowning, doubt writ large as a billboard on my face. What?

-That won't be a wise move. You must think carefully before you make an alliance. You must ask yourself: will it benefit me in my quest for power or in holding on to power? Will this alliance harm me? I see no benefit for you in an alliance with your mother. As an independent, your mother won't even get her deposit back and, if you align with her, the electorate won't vote in such large numbers. You'll force your party workers to choose between you and remaining with the ruling party. They need to fill their pockets too. You're challenging the President too early. You must wait to see how he performs. The people are unhappy with his corruption...

-As they will be with me if I'm linked to him. As an independent, I can distance myself, Mother and I can offer an alternative.

-Your mother's only electoral advantage is that she is the wife of the President, and everyone knows that they have separated. It won't even get her one vote.

-I want to help her, Avanti says in despair. I must. I want her to win. It will teach him a lesson. I know he's a very vindictive man and will do anything to punish her. Mother and I will remain his possessions until we die.

Ahh, here's my princess once again confronted by the need to choose between the power of love or love of power. I have invested much in her, guided her to this point in her political career to defeat the President. Now she wants to relinquish power to help her mother. As much as I love Shakuntala, I know the reason for her decision: the deep hatred for her husband. She will campaign against him, she too possesses secrets about his wealth and the misdeeds of his past life. She knows the gangster, the thug, and will speak out about what skeletons he hides. She is risking her life in doing all this. The prince must protect himself against an enemy, which she has just become.

-I promised...

-Break it. Unless her presence benefits you, don't align yourself with your mother.

-I can help her with money then...

-How will you explain that? She won't accept money she knows has been made through corruption. She wants to present a clean image and people will immediately question her source of funding.

–Can I at least meet her?

–Yes, you can but not for political purposes. Just mother and daughter, with the grandchild.

–She's going to be very hurt.

–The princess must have no scruples, even when expediency compels her to be cruel. Your mother will understand.

She remains stubborn, her instincts overpowered by the love for her mother. I'll see what Aditya suggests, she adds.

She leaves, carrying the baby, whispering to it as it sleeps, filling its dreams with her love. I check my cell phone and call the number. It is switched off, a disembodied voice announces. Whose phone did Shakuntala use? The number remains on my phone and I wonder whether my hacker can trace it. As I slip it into my pocket, the raaga plays and I think it's Shakuntala again, using another phone. It's the President's secretary.

–He wishes to see you. And disconnects.

Avanti returns.

–Aditya says I must work with my mother. We must fight him together. The people will believe in us.

–You will lose together. Aditya's a fine film director, not a political advisor. He believes in ethics and honesty, neither of which exist in the world of politics. I don't tell him how to make his films, and he shouldn't be telling me how to guide a princess to power. My last word of advice before your final decision—consult your party workers. If they will work for you and your mother, and leave the party, then you have a chance. If they decide they will stay in the party, then you will be alone.

–But with you advising us, how can we lose?

–To quote from a famous book: *A prince without an army is a lost cause. Even his harem will desert him for another more powerful prince.*

■

The President waits for me in the Durbar Hall, not with a glass of whisky in hand but a baby in his arms. He is looking down at it with tenderness and wonder as it sleeps. Siggy sits, legs curled under her, in the chair and she too gazes at the child. Neither notices my entrance until I stop a few feet away. We are not alone. Behind Siggy is a nurse and, sitting humbly on a dhurrie on the floor, a woman in faded clothes, youthful-looking still who looks around her uneasily. A vacant chair stands next to her, but it is clear she prefers to sit on the floor, I find that admirable. I can see from the woman's features that that is where Siggy inherited her beauty.

-My mother, Lakshmi, is still very shaken, Siggy says, as she introduces us. The President sent a helicopter to bring her here, and that scared her. But it's so convenient; it took her just an hour to get here. By road, it takes days.

In the throne room, my prince too sat with his son, Bindusara— the baby with a drop of poison in his blood—in his arms. The President wants his son, who is awake now, to absorb the magnificence of this room, remember it as his heritage that he will claim when he is of age.

-Come and see him, Siggy says. Isn't he beautiful? She echoes Avanti's very words. They are the love hymns of every mother.

The President holds him out, not willing to relinquish the child to my arms, and I see some of his resemblance in the child's forehead, his ears, and the nose that already flares in pride. The baby's eyes, the curves of his cheeks are Siggy's, as is the softness of his lips. He looks at me with a baby's intent, seeing both sides of my face, considering and comparing the perfection and imperfection and deciding to accept such disfigurement as normal. Whose characteristics will dominate this tiny one's life? Will the gangster take possession as the baby grows older, or the wily politician, manoeuvring his way through kindergartens, high schools and colleges, knowing his destiny from the moment he is able to understand his lineage? Or will Rachna, the village girl, with all her simplicity and sweet nature, take possession of his heart?

-What is his name?

-Asoka. Tell us, will he be great?

-I'm no astrologer. He has the lineage but so have many princes who died with knives through their hearts.

-I'll protect him with my life, Siggy says fiercely, almost snatching Asoka from his father. She holds him protectively. The President kisses his son on the forehead.

Your uncle Chanakya will bless you, my son, Siggy says.

I bless the baby, with a kiss on the cheek, not wanting to touch the same place as the President. He is superstitious and could believe that I have erased his love with my touch. Siggy leaves with her son, followed by her mother and the nurse. We wait until they have left, and the bearer brings out the Scotch, glass and ice. The President's eyes are hostile when he turns to me.

–My wife is standing for the election. She is doing this deliberately to humiliate me because I won't give her a divorce. And because I have a son now which she could not give me... You must dissuade her. She will listen to you. Where is she?

–I know as much as I've heard on the news. Surely, your spies can find her.

–They haven't been able to. But you must know where she is. She confides her secrets in you. Who is supporting her? Where has she been hiding all this time?

–These are secrets she kept.

He leans forward, his face darkening, a pulse beating in his temples. Chanakya salah chutia, I will imprison you for insurgency and sedition, if you don't tell me. And they will beat you until you confess what you know. Obscenities flow freely from his lips. The gangster rising to the surface in his anger.

–Prison! I have to smile at his menace. I died over two thousand years ago and existed in dull eternity and all he can threaten me with is prison! With torture thrown in as hors d'oeuvres. I am beyond fear of death and of life hereafter.

He gulps his drink down and holds out the glass for more. This prince is restless in his anger, he knows that Shakuntala holds some of his secrets confessed in the early years of his love for her. She won't have forgotten; she will reveal them in her campaign. He will deny every truth as the bitterness of a discarded wife fabricating lies. Will he assassinate her before she speaks? That would be my advice but I don't offer it to him. Shakuntala is all too aware of her husband's villainy, and hopefully has taken precautions.

He breaks the long silence. You will be advising my daughter, as you did before?

–If she requests it.

–She will, she knows how devious you are, and I do too. It would be best if you refused and retired. You could become a very wealthy man if you did so.

-I am wealthy with my few possessions. Too many zeroes only clutter one's life with worry and high BP. I make him wait a bit, then say, She has asked Avanti to ally with her.

-When did she say that?

-No matter. Mother and daughter against you will make a formidable coalition. They could win.

-Who will finance their campaign? he shouts in anger. No one's going to waste one rupee supporting them, as they know I will win again. And when I do, I'm going to punish the bastards who thought of giving money to my wife and daughter. I'll destroy them, bankrupt them, imprison them for sedition and corruption.

-I'll pass on the message.

-Has Avanti agreed to this coalition?

-She is considering it very seriously. She wants to fight on her mother's side. She loves her mother very much, and wants only to make up for those years of neglect.

-You will guide them?

-If I am needed.

Another swallow, another pause, and I can read his mind even from this distance. He is remembering a number—126,768. The margin of her victory. It looks like an insurmountable cliff, which could rise higher. She is young, she is new, she has built a few schools, a few roads, hired teachers. Her only failure—to contain Chay—but that is as much his responsibility, being the President, and controlling the police.

I speak softly into the silence. Then choose her as your heir now.

I leave him to his drink, knowing he is savouring the victory over his wife, who will be alone as soon as he separates her from their daughter.

■

The carved bust of Avanti now adorns her office at the party headquarters. It's on a higher plinth, one of marble, new, shiny and polished. In the centre of her forehead is a saffron tilak mark, and a fresh garland hangs around her neck. Fresh petals are scattered around its base in homage, creating a circle of pink. Already, they worship her stone image. The youth wing workers are waiting for her visit, excited at the prospect of the coming battle, knowing that their leader will lead them once more to victory. They are whispering higher numbers among themselves—a 200,000 margin, with ease.

Avanti arrives with her Y-security, and her workers part to make way for her. She is carrying her baby and is followed by a nanny, a nurse, and a peon carrying the baby's necessities. She intends to take the child with her on the campaign trail. She takes her place at her desk, and asks that only the seniors of the party remain as she wishes to consult with them. The doors are closed, and the chosen dozen, dressed alike in white kurtas, with the party colours edging their collars, and party badges stamped with her profile, wait for her to speak.

-As you know, my mother is also standing for the elections as an independent candidate.

-Yes, yes, they chorus, frowning, worrying, already a step ahead.

-She wants me to join her in a coalition against the President. I wanted to hear your advice before I decide on the matter.

The dozen glance at each other, wondering which of them will voice the concern that is exercising them all.

-What is your decision, Madam Minister? A hesitant whisper from one.

-I am considering the coalition with her but I haven't yet decided... My mother wants my help....

-She is standing in District 10, the President's constituency.

-She won't win it, says another of her workers.

-She could, if I work with her. And all of you as well.

-But, Madam, we will have to leave the party. The President will expel us all.

-You will be with me...

-Yes, yes, but we will be going up against the President and we know he will be very angry with us. We work for the party too...

The sirens scream, announcing the President's motorcade, interrupting the discussion and relieving the youth workers from making a decision. They back out of the office hurriedly, leaving Avanti alone to greet their leader.

-He did this deliberately. He knew I'd be in this meeting, Avanti says irritably to me.

-You should go out to greet him, otherwise the faction will split.

Even she has to push through the mob to reach the far end of the hall. The President has already taken his seat, the single chair on his right remains vacant. He gestures, the crowd parts and Avanti mounts the stage to sit beside him. They don't look at each other.

-As you all know, we're always ready for elections and this one will be no different from the previous one. Through our dedication and hard work, we have dragged this state out of debt and brought it to great success. The people know of our unstinting efforts to serve them and they will vote us back into power, so we can finish what we have started. The Opposition is in disarray, they don't even have a leader, and they will foist many scams on us, but we know we have ruled with compassion and honesty...

His speech is long, and is made longer still by many interruptions as his party workers cheer frequently.

-My wife is standing as an independent candidate against me, and this breaks my heart, as it is clear she has been misled by her advisors. She is a woman of great character and strength and my affection for her will never change, despite the lies that her advisors will force her to speak against me. Do not believe her. After the election, my wife and I will reconcile as our differences are not insurmountable, least of all something like this.

They cheer as they are all family men and, even though most of them ignore their wives, outwardly they remain happily married. I know many possess a mistress, even two, and they are justly proud that their President's lady love is Siggy Chopra.

-My daughter... He stops, the words remain hanging in the silence. His timing is perfect, the solemnity in his tone and the gravity in his face befit great actors. All politics is drama, whether the emperor is facing his commanders or the President his followers. They're waiting for him to pronounce judgement, what will be the sentence for the daughter they are aware is planning to defect, to betray the party, and join her mother?

My daughter, Avanti... A long pause. He doesn't turn to look to his daughter. She too is holding her breath like all the others. I know what she is thinking: Should I pre-empt his judgement, rise with dignity and leave the stage, leave the hall, walk through the silent throng into political oblivion?

-My daughter will no longer hold the position of President of the youth wing of the party.

The groan of pain is sincere; they can all envisage a potentially cataclysmic split in the party ranks. Avanti stiffens, her disgrace is near now. She almost starts to rise. The President holds up his hand, silencing groans, and cell phones.

He turns to her, and bows gravely. Avanti does not react.—She has proved herself to be a very able minister, and she will campaign alongside me as the vice president of the party and she will also be, when we win with a landslide, the vice president of the state. He pauses. She is young and beautiful and a woman of great talent.

The President's announcement is followed by a thunderous cheering, even the ministers seated in the front row stand to applaud their wise leader's decision. There are rapturous sighs of relief from all her faithful. Avanti too knows the art of drama, she waits for the cheering to stop, for the ministers to settle back into their chairs. Now, her workers hold their collective breath. Will she refuse? Will she insist on joining her mother?

She remains sitting, glancing just once to the President, then looks out to the workers.

–I'm grateful for the President's trust in me and I will do my very best to ensure that we win this coming election with a landslide. I will work as hard as possible beside the President and all of you.

Her acceptance speech, is greeted by sustained applause. Fire crackers explode in the compound. Avanti stands. She bows to the President, her palms pressed together, and then to the party men and women. Then, like a sanyasi on a pilgrimage, head bowed, she passes through the parted ranks of the faithful and makes her way to her office. Her youth wing faithfully trail her. When she gets to her office she apologetically closes the door on them, and explodes.

–Why did he have to remind me with that comment about my beauty and imagination? God, he's a bastard. He still thinks he owns me, soul and body. He knows how to humiliate me.

–The others will not understand the comment, I say.

–I don't care about others. You're an 'other' and you know what he meant.

–But you've accepted his political offer, in public.

Her anger dissipates and a smile emerges onto her face. Yes, I have. I want to be the vice president. I want to see whether I can win even more votes than he does. She sits back and laughs, her eyes alight with the power conferred on her. She is the princess who will challenge the king, she wants that golden chair, she longs for the worship of all those men who serve the party. She imagines herself in the centre stage, not with the President's photograph staring down at her, but her own image.

–Until you ascend the throne, you must continue to maintain absolute humility. Especially, where the President and senior members of the party are concerned. Court them all. They must be disarmed.

–I know, I know, she says impatiently. I also know my father can change his mind and I could go back to being a junior minister tomorrow. Or even a back bencher for that matter. What will I tell my mother? She's going to be very disappointed.

–It can't be helped. You have to remain with the party if you want to rise higher.

She groans and lowers her head to rest it on the desk. Then she looks up and says, Aditya'll go crazy. He wanted me to support my mother. He hates father as you know and thought together we'd defeat him. What do I tell him?

–He's an artist and idealistic. He doesn't understand how vicious politics can be. Perhaps what you should tell him is that you are being strategic. Tell him, once you win you'll turn against your father. You'll have more power then. Call him, tell him before someone else does.

She presses the speed dial button on her cell phone. Listens and disconnects. It's switched off. I'll text him so when he switches on again, he'll call me. She sends the message. I noticed you're not congratulating me? I know, you whispered the suggestion in the President's ear and he did this to split me from mother. I'll still support her, secretly. I want to meet her. She should be easier to find now that she'll be electioneering. And she still hasn't seen her grandson.

I open the door and am nearly trampled by her eager party men, each wanting to be the first to congratulate her.

–Madam, Madam… congratulations, you are truly a great leader…

She silences them imperiously. We'll be working together now, and I want us to win by even bigger numbers…

∎

The President's constituency, District 10, is bordered by the sea on one side, and spreads twenty-five square kilometres inland. Years ago, as an adolescent, I came to see the sea. I touched the frothy waves, drank and spat out a mouthful of salt. The waves were the tablas to the flutes of running water, a continuous beat, rising and falling to their own rhythm. I watched for hours, thinking of the countries that lay beyond the horizon, the same waves touching their shores. I imagined if I stood on tiptoe, I could glimpse a foreign land. At night, the sea would whisper, then its mood would change and the waves would rise like monsters from the deep pounding the beach and driving us children running back in fright.

District 10 is wealthy, offices and parks line the broad four-lane avenues, and in the residential areas, grand apartments rise in every direction, all with private pools and gyms. Beyond the city limits lie the factories that manufacture cars, cell phones, spare parts. The President has nursed his constituency with care, ensured it has power, good roads, low taxes, all the gifts that corporates long for. What can Shakuntala offer to tempt them away? The poor have their free television sets, their cell phones, rice cookers, mixies, laptops, the middle class low taxes. The district is awash with the party colours, every spare wall plastered with images of the President. Avanti appears in the posters too, set to one side, as if looking over his shoulder. Great banners are strung across the roads, billboards larger than houses praise his wisdom, generosity, compassion, honesty, strength, handsomeness, beauty. In whatever free space they can find, the Opposition have plastered images of their heroes to challenge the President. But the state belongs to him, and he is the presence that dominates everywhere.

Where can I find the independent candidate Shakuntala in this flood of electioneering, this chaos of democracy at work? I call my spy, Vikram, and he directs me towards the edges of town. They have banished her from the centre, where the people gather, to a dusty maidan. An old temple rises in the background, the gopuram painted in a thousand cheap colours, disguising the works of great craftsmen. Alongside a wall that borders the maidan, spaced at equal distances, are three stumps etched into the brick for the boys to play cricket. Mango and tamarind trees bend their branches to give them shade from the afternoon sun. In the centre of the maidan is an open-topped ancient SUV, battered and dented. About a hundred men and women are gathered around it. A few are elderly, white-haired men and women, but the majority of those clustered around are young people armed with their cell phones, lifted high to record her speech. Surrounding the small crowd are fifty policemen, armed with lathis, led by a superintendent who is on his cell phone as well as listening to Shakuntala. On the outer circle of the crowd are four or five tough-looking men. The cops know who they are, they banter with them. The toughs too have their cell phones out, they are awaiting their orders. The President could fill this maidan with a 100,000 people in no time at all should he so decide, but it is clear that he is going to pretend to be gracious towards his wife.

Shakuntala is elegant in a pale green and pink salwar kameez with a matching dupatta. She is a lot slimmer since I last saw her over a year ago. I like the calm with which she speaks to her few listeners. She treats them with respect and lets them know that they are important to her. Her back is straight, her gestures minimal. Somehow, she conveys the impression that she will win this election, steal the constituency from her powerful husband. On the SUV, standing behind her are two young women, also in salwar kameezes, and I recognize them as the two guerrillas who had escorted me to my meeting with Chay. They are unarmed. Even if Chay is among those listening to her, I wouldn't recognize him but I am certain one or two of his men are amongst her security.

-...You know who I am, I am Shakuntala. I am the wife of the President and I am standing as an independent candidate to challenge his years of corruption, misrule and tyranny. I know him too well, and everything I tell you comes from personal knowledge. What I am about to reveal to you is a sordid saga about the misuse of power, corruption and a host of other crimes. Corruption starts from the top, not from the bottom. The President is corrupt, his cabinet only follows his example, and it is from here that the cancer spreads through the bureaucracy and everywhere else as well.

But before I go on to give you details about the President's worst excesses, let me tell you what I stand for. I will not promise to give you televisions, cell phones, goats and cows. I don't have the money for that, but I can promise you that I will give you a clean and efficient government. In the happiness of your lives lies my happiness, in your welfare my welfare. I will bring good governance to this district and reflect its prestige beyond its borders. If you elect me I will keep a constant watch over the affairs of this state and on the officials through whom I will rule. Those who are found guilty of misrule or corruption will be not only dismissed but also prosecuted. I will enact laws that will punish them with a minimum of ten years in prison and confiscate all their wealth, whether they are bureaucrats or fellow politicians. My authority derives only through your vote for me and as such I represent your wishes, your hopes and your dreams. Government is to be regarded as literally *nitishastra,* that is, the science of 'leading', and this needs constant consideration for those of us who lead. And should I fail you, I too must be subjected to the laws of the state and punished for neglecting my duties...

Her voice is firm, musical, and she holds the attention of her listeners. I know her words, they are from my own works, though she embellishes them with the demands of today's poor for land, education, forest rights, schools, jobs. She has been well trained by Chay and has learnt how to speak by watching the President. She attracts more young men and women. The crowd has swollen to over three hundred, there are more trickling through the gates, crossing the dusty ground, and the police are growing restless; so are the young thugs on the fringes of the crowd.

-I do have proof of the President's corruption. I will release the information, account numbers, banks, property holdings, when it is time to...

-LIES....LIES...the thugs start chanting, pushing and shoving. They have received their orders. The students, taken by surprise, fall back before their onslaught and then start to fight back. Soon, there's a melee of bodies, grappling and falling. The police rush in with their lathis...

-STOP IT...Shakuntala screams, and as her voice resounds through the speakers mounted on the SUV, it brings everyone to a halt. Before the thugs can resume their assault on the onlookers, she says in a quiet voice. I must thank you all for your patience in listening to me. On Election Day, remember my name, Shakuntala and press the button next to it. My symbol is the key that will unlock us all from the prison of this present government. I will continue campaigning throughout the district.

The students crowd around her when she descends from the SUV, and show signs of their support. They want her itinerary, so they can pass it on to other young people. I wait for them to disperse, the cops remain watchful, though they are relaxed now that the meeting has concluded. The young thugs hang around, they will follow her from venue to venue, and the President will unleash them if he feels more threatened.

Shakuntala hugs me, and kisses me on both cheeks. I have to see Avanti and my grandson. Where can we meet?

–Not in the open as you know he's promoted her to vice president…

She winces as if I've slapped her. I didn't but I'm not surprised. He knows how to split us. He has years of experience. How can she resist such an elevation to power? She is still her father's child. She checks her watch, then confers with the two young women. They recognize me with faint smiles. I have two more meetings today. We're staying in a lodging house. Can the vice president meet me there, with my grandson?

–I'll arrange that, as she wants you to see him too.

–Did I speak well? she asks as she climbs into the SUV.

–You've learnt from him.

–And you, I know you must have recognized words from the *Arthashastra*.

–Chanakya is finally rewarded two thousand years later.

I lean through the window to whisper. How is Chay?

She confers in whispers with the two young women and then gets out. We stroll side by side, silent and watchful, towards a mango tree and sit on the stone bench in its shade. She covers her lower face, masking her mouth with her dupatta. She has learnt that spies use listening devices that can pick up conversations a kilometre away. Her voice is low, muffled.

–He wants to meet with you, just to talk.

–After the elections I'll wait where I did before and the girls can find me. Why did you reveal yourself for this election? Did Chay ask you to?

–We decided together. He doesn't control me, like my husband did. We talk, we agree, we disagree, and laugh together. For the first time I can say I am happy, most of the time. When I look back to my past, I wonder what I would be now if I had married Mayur and not the President. I think my life would be the same as it is now, living deep in the jungle and fighting beside him. If only... She smiles. Two words but so powerful. It wasn't meant then but it is now. I love Mayur. No, not with the passion I loved my husband, the insanity of such love affects one's whole being. My love for Mayur is quiet, it's gentle, it's filled with comfortable silences, it's a peaceful love. When we move, we hold hands. My husband never once held my hand, he walked ahead as if disowning me. I admire Mayur for what he is and for what he is trying to do for the people who believe in him. I cannot ever say I admired my husband, I was ashamed of him, yet I loved him. It can be confusing, I know. We have no settled home, we move at night, and the tribals welcome us. Often I remain in one hamlet for a few weeks. I teach the children and the adults, men and women who want to learn. It's just the basics, the alphabet, how to read and write, arithmetic, hygiene and diet. I took a three-month course on midwifery in the town under another name and now they call me for every delivery. So many women and babies die because there are no medical facilities in the jungle. Mayur is not a communist or even a socialist. He's a justice-ist, I call him. My husband will destroy the jungle to get at the copper. What happens then to the tribals and their rights to the forest, what happens to the animals, the tiger and the elephant, the deer and wild pigs, the birds and mongooses? Where do they go? To heaven? Is there such a place for them too? If God has a place for humans, why not for animals, birds, reptiles too, to name a few?

-Maybe, if he exists, he has a place for them, as far from man as possible. How will you defend yourself if the police find you?

-I'll fight alongside Mayur and his small army if he needs me to. You know he's taught me how to shoot, and given me lessons in unarmed combat but, oddly enough, he doesn't want war, if he can get justice through peaceful agitation.

-But the President doesn't want to talk, he needs an enemy and it's Chay. He can frighten people using Chay as a threat. Besides, he's been paid too much for the mining rights.

-That's what I thought. Mayur just wants the mining to stop, and then he's willing to discuss the other points in his manifesto.

But we will continue to resist until then.

She rises and we walk slowly back to the SUV. One or two cops have lingered by the entrance, waiting to see what she will do next, and follow her to the next venue.

-Be careful, I warn her. Now they know where to find you and they are following...

She smiles. I've learnt the art of being invisible when I have to. But this evening...

I whisper my warning. —Don't release names of those accounts and banks.

-Why not? I have to fulfil my campaign promise, and I will.
-He'll kill you. You saw his thugs, they'll do it as a favour.
-I'll risk that.
-I'll bring Avanti. Both of you are stubborn as donkeys.

She laughs. I find it easier to tell you about my life than Avanti. I love her but she's his child still.

■

-I'm going to get her to take the money, Avanti says. She covers her face with her dupatta, holding Bharat, awake and curious, in her arms. I carry a briefcase, heavy with cash. While her Y-category security guards the front doors of the five-star hotel, we slip out through the kitchens in the rear. We take an autorickshaw to the end of the road, and walk the hundred metres to the Kissan Lodging House. According to the signage it's a strictly vegetarian establishment. The exterior of the lodging house is pitted and spotted, the paint peeling. It's a façade, for the interior is spotless and the walls are freshly painted. The dining hall on our left, furnished with long steel topped tables and plastic chairs, is empty, the evening meal over. We make our way up narrow stone stairs.

Her mother waits on the landing, the flickering neon giving out barely enough light to see but her eyes are riveted on the bundle in Avanti's arms. Shakuntala reaches out and Avanti happily hands Bharat to her. Shakuntala lifts her grandson up, laughing at him as he appears to smile down at her. Then she brings him down gently to kiss his forehead, then both his cheeks, lingering, longing kisses. It's only when this ritual is over that she frees one arm to welcome Avanti into her embrace.

-He's such a handsome baby, Shakuntala says. He has more of you and Aditya, no sign of me or his grandfather in the face, yet.

Avanti starts to cry. I'm so…happy to…see you, she stumbles with her words.

-Then why are you crying? I am happy too and I want to sing and dance and laugh, it's exhilarating to see you and Bharat at last.

Avanti cries even more. I've let you down, again.

Shakuntala shushes her daughter, rocks the baby to calm it, it is showing signs of distress at seeing his mother weep. Shakuntala says: Don't cry over that. We both know him too well. He'll do anything to keep us apart and he offered you the prize. You had to take it. You're my Trojan horse in his fortress, and I know that one day you'll inherit the Presidency. She looks over to me, the rest unsaid, a prayer that she will be different from her father. Come into my room.

The room has barely enough space for a cot. Her escorts are sitting on the floor, heads together reading the local newspaper. They rise and leave and I follow them, after placing the briefcase on the bed. The girls and I sit together on the stairs in companionable silence. They smell of sandalwood and jungle moss and look somewhat alike, heart shaped features, light brown eyes, around the same age too.

A half-hour later, Avanti comes out, followed by her mother, still holding her grandson, fast asleep. As they begin to say their goodbyes, Shakuntala says,

-Take back your money, I don't need it.

-It's my donation to your campaign, Avanti protests, as she takes Bharat back from her mother. It's not Father's.

-Where did you get so much?

-Mother, I am a politician, people donate…

-Keep it, I chip in, that's my advice when money is offered. Use the money to feed children, buy medicines, books, if you don't want to spend it on your campaign. Money has no politics.

-Chanakya has good advice, as always. She kisses her grandson, then her daughter, and then watches us carefully descend the steps.

SEVENTEEN

BETRAYAL, LIKE LOVE, is an emotion, a feeling, a sense, not a thought. It can be set in motion for the love of money, a price paid for the information; it can rise out of jealousy, envy, dislike, suspicion, even hatred. It can be an inadvertent betrayal, a whisper spoken, and overheard by the enemy. It can be a deliberate act to punish the victim-to-be.

Those of us who live in democracies and wearily vote for the poor choices presented to us, know of the chaos, the lies, the juggling of poll numbers, the demarcation of constituent boundaries, the fixing of electronic voting machines. And then the silence as we wait for the results, the instant polls predicting first one, then another as the winner. Power is about to change hands, no it isn't. Yes it will, no it won't. Avanti does win her district, this time with 201,000 votes. But, there is to be a recount in District 10, as five missing electronic voting machines have been miraculously found. My spies are good, if not quick in their Intel, and I find my way to Shakuntala to warn her about this new development.

Shakuntala and her companions are early at the Election Commissioner's office, waiting for the recount to finish. It's a temporary office in a school, sandwiched between a petrol station and a supermarket. The President cannot stay away, and materialises with his full security. Shakuntala and he stand apart in the compound, separated by the cops, his supporters in their hundreds, her young followers almost matching his numbers, so tremendously has her popularity grown in the course of the campaign. I slip through them to stand a foot behind, and tell her what I have heard.

Without turning, she replies—Yes, I've heard that too. And he now knows I am with Chay.

-That was bound to happen.
-Of course.

The wait is interminable. The gathered hawks turn the cameras on the President and then on his wife. He smiles, he waves, filled with a victor's confidence. To show them that he is a gracious man, and holds no vindictive feelings towards his challenger, he walks across and puts an arm around his Shakuntala's shoulders. Shakuntala, trying to play his game, does not recoil, and slips out of the embrace as naturally as she can after a minute or two.

–So, he says in a low voice, a hand half covering his mouth, you've disgraced me. You are now the lover of that terrorist Chay.

–He's not a terrorist. He's an insurgent; all he wants is for you to stop destroying the jungle out of your greed.

–All you've done is humiliate me. First, that crooked swami, now this terrorist.

–Insurgent, she repeats.

–Where did you meet him? How did you meet him? He can barely contain his fury.

–You should sack all your spies. I went online and found a matchmaking website. I wanted a rebel, as I discovered I was one too.

–You don't even know how to use a computer.

–Since we're talking about Chay, I have a message from him. He is willing to surrender, but only on the condition that you cancel the mining. Otherwise, I will continue my campaign against you, and so will Chay against the mining company.

–That's if you even get a couple of votes, he boasts. You must return to the house. I will not tolerate this insulting behaviour any more. You're behaving like a whore.

–You're an expert on that subject too. By the way, congratulations on the son your mistress has given you. As for me, I don't want anything more to do with you. Just stay away from me. Oh, and I should say that dyeing your hair was a mistake. With your white hair you looked distinguished, now you look a sad clown.

–I will stop all police action against Chay when you return to the house.

–And the mining?

–That can't be stopped. We need to make progress...

He's about to continue when the Election Commissioner, a balding, elderly man, with friendly round features that match his paunch, comes out of the building. His committee follows him. He holds a printout of the final tally of votes in his hand. In the silence that greets his appearance, I hear only the crows in the trees.

–I will be brief, as I know you all have been waiting since the morning, he speaks in a gentle but firm voice. The President has 100,118 votes....

The President grins, holds his arms up high and his supporters jump up and down, cheering him. The Election Commissioner holds up his hand, the crows speak in louder irritation.

-Shakuntala has 100,068 votes. The candidate of the main opposition party polled 31,200 votes, and the two other independent candidates have lost their deposits as they only won 20 votes each. The President wins by fifty votes...

Shakuntala stretches her arms up to the sky, her young supporters lift their cell phones high, the gadgets their symbols of near victory. The margin is wafer thin, another recount and the President could lose. His face grows dark, a frown spreads across his forehead, his eyes are wide with disbelief. His wife is snapping at his kurta and my revenge is nearing. The news sharks surround them with their cameras and microphones. They are young, attractive women with high-pitched voices, shouting questions above the rising dismay of the President's supporters.

-...Mr President to what do you attribute the erosion in your share of the vote? Mr President, how will this result affect your coalition? Madam Shakuntala, will you be demanding a re-count? To what do you attribute your resounding success in this election? Will you form a coalition with your husband?

Shakuntala grabs hold of my hand tightly, whispers urgently to me. What should I do?

-What do you want? Power. You have it now.

-No, I don't want to be a politician, there are enough in this family. I want him to stop the mining and meet Chay to discuss his other demands. That's why I stood for election.

-Threaten first, then negotiate.

-...Madam Shakuntala, will you be demanding a recount? The margin of the President's victory is only fifty votes? If so, when?

Shakuntala smiles sweetly, not answering any questions but turns to her husband and holds out her hand. It takes him by surprise and gratefully he grabs hold of it.

-I wish to congratulate the President, she smiles. However, I need to discuss any future moves with my advisors.

-We must talk, he whispers, while continuing to smile for the cameras. He says out loud, I congratulate Shakuntala on her campaign though she made accusations against me which are untrue and fabricated. Victory doesn't depend on margins but on the numbers. That's all I have to say for now.

They refuse to answer any more questions and walk back to the school, trailed by their followers. The Election Commissioner stands firmly in their way.

–No candidate is permitted to enter, he announces and doesn't flinch from the President's malignant stare.

He turns, feeling humiliated by this bureaucrat, vowing to transfer him the moment he takes office again. He asks Shakuntala to accompany him in his limousine.

–Chanakya comes with us, Shakuntala says, as the security opens the door for her.

–You afraid of me?

–No, I need him as a witness, she quips as she enters the car. If you'd campaigned with Siggy, you could've won another thousand votes, then you wouldn't need to be so nice to me!

He follows her, fuming at her remark. I slide into the front passenger seat.

–Will you ask for a recount? he asks.

–I won't if...

–Tell me your terms. Although I know with a recount I could win by a larger margin.

–You could, but then you might not. You're a gambler, and you know the odds.

–I'm listening.

–Cancel the mining concession, Chay will surrender and you'll not harm him in any way, and you will meet him at the negotiating table to discuss his demands.

–Agreed. He has spoken too quickly. I know he will not return the money he has received for the concession, merely offer the business tycoons who provided the funds other means of recovering their money—power, telecommunications, infrastructure, land—there are countless ways to plunder the state. Chay will surrender and I will meet with him to study his demands. However, I must warn you I'm not promising to agree with your lover's every word.

–Good. Now announce this to the press.

–I have agreed, he nearly shouts. Don't you trust me?

–Definitely not. You make the announcement otherwise I demand a recount.

–Now, I have my terms. Once I have met your lover, you will then return to live in the house. You will never see him again.

How will she meet this demand? He is asking her to leave the man she loves. Chay is her mirror, she looks into herself each time she sees him. In exchange for what? To live with a man she detests? And play the role of the docile wife again, when she has discovered such hidden spirits of courage and defiance? Love is as vicious a weapon as power; it can gut the heart, wrench it out and stamp on it. She looks stricken. How will she live without him? It will be an existence, the breaths in and out, the sustenance of food, the heart slowly pumping the blood, hearing, seeing nothing, just the wait for death. A lonely one.

–Why? she whispers, more to herself. You hate me, I hate you.

–Because I possess you. You think you hate me but I don't believe that, you can't stop the love you had.

–You are insane. I tell you how I feel, and you won't believe me. Then we must be equal in our terms. You will never see Siggy or your son again.

His heart isn't watery; it's set in the concrete of power. He is quiet, calculating his odds. He looks out at the crowd awaiting a decision. He can gamble, set his goondas to fight pitched battles but they can lose. Powerless, he will have no room to manoeuvre, to enrich him with even more power and wealth. If her life will be barren, so will his, trapped in the same house, as he will have to vacate the grand palace, step down from the gold chair and allow another to warm it.

–I will never see Siggy again but not my son. He stays with me, any court will grant me custody and I will take him by force if necessary. He is your son too, as I am his father. He smiles coldly. He will keep you company, along with your grandson.

–Children are no substitute for love. They're only painful reminders of its loss. Where is Siggy now, by the way?

–She and Ashoka are leaving this afternoon, along with Siggy's mother for her village. She'll be gone a few days. When she returns I'll tell her about our agreement.

—I agree, Shakuntala capitulates. Chay will surrender only to Chanakya. No police, and a neutral, unarmed committee to accept the surrender.

—Fine.

They leave the car through separate doors, back into the glare and the hum of the waiting crowd.

—Did I have an alternative? She asks me, as her husband strides ahead, victory implicit in each step, to face the press and his followers.

—You could have gambled too, beaten him in the recount by a narrow margin. Destroyed him. But, if you'd lost, you would have lost any power to negotiate. He won't live forever. Then the agreement is void.

—He might live forever, the bastard.

The President smiles into the cameras. He says, Shakuntala and I have had a long and fruitful discussion. I have listened to her, and to the voters, and I must bow to their wishes. The mining in the jungle of District 18 will be halted immediately, and will never continue. I have conceded to negotiate with Chay and find common ground to work together for the betterment of all the people. That is all I have to say for now.

He steps away from the microphone and Shakuntala takes his place. She says simply: I have consulted my advisors, and we agree that a recount will only delay the democratic process of which we're so proud. There will be no recount and I congratulate the President on his victory. I have nothing further to add.

His fawning supporters and the press engulf him, the victor. Shakuntala, the loser, is abandoned, now a cipher in this political game. Her shoulders slump, she is thinking of her future. If such an imprisonment can be called that. She turns to hide her tears.

—As much as Chay, I will miss the children I was teaching, miss the poor people I worked with for so long, she says miserably to me. I'll miss the jungle, the simplicity of that life. I had some worth, now I'll be worthless. Can I trust the President?

—No. Never trust the prince as he tightens his grip on power. Warn Chay to be extra cautious.

The ringing of my phone interrupts our conversation. It's Avanti, excited. Can you believe my victory margin? It's incredible. I can't believe it.

–Congratulations. Aditya must be happy.
–Not so happy. You know he dislikes politics more and more. Listen, is mother still there? Oh god, if we had worked together, she could have won, beaten him, crushed him. I have to talk to her.
–That's what I was hoping would happen. But equally both of you could have lost. It was not the time to challenge him. That time will come. I pass the phone to Shakuntala; she moves out of earshot. A little while later I hear her voice raised in anger.
–You've no right to tell me how to live my life. When have you ever stood by me, listened to me, loved me? Answer that first before you tell me how ashamed you are about my relationship with Chay. Sometimes you sound like your father...she lowers her voice, and continues to talk animatedly into the phone.

When she finishes talking to Avanti, she returns the phone to me and says, That was about Chay and me. Why should a child know everything about the mother she's neglected for so long? She's behaving like her father.—shock, disbelief, how could I do such a thing? But she's happy that I'll be coming home...I'm off now. I'll make the most of my last few days with Chay and my people.

We return to her lodging house, her home for the last few weeks. What little she owns is in a large cloth bag, the two girls possess similar ones. They're made of coir, hand woven in a village, with flower patterns on their sides. There's an air of nervous watchfulness about these two girls, they're attuned to danger. Shakuntala remains calm, though she too is aware that her husband now prowls even closer, more vindictive as a result of his humiliation at the polls. There's no telling what he might get up to. I have people on the lookout for trouble, as the women get ready to leave.

My phone vibrates and Vikram whispers: No one is around, come quickly. When the three come out of the room, at my tap on the door, they are no longer women but young men, swaggering in jeans and baseball caps, a loose jacket disguising their upper bodies. We take the back stairs, out into a dark, narrow lane. Vikram is waiting there in an SUV.

–I'll see you when you come with the committee. She blows me a kiss, and the old vehicle rattles away into the darkness.

■

I learn the next morning that, far to the north in the foothills of the mountains, the helicopter carrying Siggy, her son and mother is reported as missing. No wreckage has been discovered so there is hope, and an army of cops and volunteers are starting to comb through the forests and hills in search of it. I have never flown, never wanted to leave the earth. Being of an ancient age and superstitious, I believe men should crawl, walk, run, march or ride. Leave flying to birds, spirits and demons, the sky is their battlefield. The President is unavailable for comment. I hear from my palace spies that he has locked himself into his suite and will see no one, not even his daughter. I cannot imagine him mourning Siggy, he weeps for his son, the heir, the gift he received so late in his life.

A week later, the delegation to receive Chay's surrender assembles. I have no wish for this sort of responsibility but cannot betray Chay's trust. The President's Chief Secretary has picked the members of the delegation, all but one of them, people of integrity: Ex-Justice Malhotra, long retired from the bench but a man held in high esteem; Sunil Pande, an ex-chief secretary of government, though still an advisor; Sushila Menon, who works with tribals and village children, a woman of strength and dignity; Kamala Dhavan, the editor of an environment magazine who knows this jungle well. There are two others—P.S. Sood, a portly man, with heavy spectacles, thinning gray hair, a firm mouth.

The Home Secretary is holding the binder with the terms of surrender and the amnesty. A simple document but impressive with the gold seal of the state on the letterhead and the President's illegible signature below. 'I, the President, accept the surrender of one Chay, aka Mayur, and grant him amnesty for his subversive actions against the state. I also authorize my representative, the Home Secretary, to hold talks with him to discuss his suggestions for the betterment of governance and mutually agree upon them for the good of the people'.

The second State representative is the Deputy IG of Police, Sambit Bose, a young, handsome man, stiff in his starched khakis. His face starched with his authority too, and a neatly clipped moustache. I read an eager weakness in his eyes.

-I am here only for your protection and I am, as agreed, unarmed. But I do have my walkie-talkie and cell phone to summon help, if need be, to protect the party from any attacks.

He holds out both arms horizontally, as on a cross, expecting me to search him. I pat the sides of his upper body, then down the outside of his legs. He looks down in amusement. Otherwise, not another policeman in sight.

Our plan is simple: we will drive to the jungle, I will enter it alone with the escorts that Chay will have sent. I will meet him to discuss the terms of his surrender, and, if he is in agreement with them, we will jointly return to meet the delegation waiting to receive him. He will be unarmed. The press will wait at a chosen venue to interview Chay, briefly. He will start negotiations with the Home Secretary which will last many days in a secure, secret location. Meanwhile, the President continues to remain in seclusion, as there is still no sign of the helicopter that vanished.

Our motorcade leaves the capital at dawn, and by midday it reaches the outskirts of the jungle, where the road ends. Around the road, spreading out on either side, lie the corpses of many machines, yellow bulldozers, black lorries, steel grey drills, like so many slain dragons. I see no waiting guide to lead me into the labyrinth.

My cell phone sings and when I answer, a voice commands: Two kilometres east, switch off your phone now, leave it behind. He disconnects.

I obey the command, switch off the phone, leave it and climb out, telling the others to wait. The Home Secretary hands me the thick binder. I walk on a winding path along the jungle's edge, frequently looking back. No one follows. The heat hums around me, and the landscape I am passing through is deserted, there is not even a lone villager ploughing a field in sight. I know I am being watched and try to see if I can spot the guerrillas in the shadows of the jungle. Nothing. The trees sigh longingly for a slight breeze. After I've walked for about a kilometre, two young men, faces masked, step out from behind the trees, guns at the ready. They check to see that I am not being followed, although it is clear that they have been shadowing me ever since I set out, and then beckon me to follow them as they plunge into the jungle. I am not blindfolded this time, but the path remains torturous and twisted, the trees tower above us; their sturdy trunks would provide cover in the event of a a fire-fight, I note to myself. Like the girls, the men do not speak to me. When we reach the ruined embattlements of the fort, we climb slowly, past broken steps, fallen embrasures; trees have entwined their roots over fallen pillars, their carvings, barely visible. The bones of rajas, ranis and their many soldiers and servitors lie beneath my feet.

We reach the top of the hill where Chay awaits us. He hands me an earthenware cup of water, and I drink the offering. For the first time I can see his whole face. A strong jawline, a thin and bony nose with flared nostrils. By contrast, his mouth is sensual, curved lips. His movements are economical, and I sense his tension. He does not resemble that sketch of a frightening man that was my first impression of him. We demonise those we fear and cannot see, and they become our Satans. Shakuntala waits in the shade of a banyan, its vast shade sheltering forty to fifty people. Some are masked fighters, the others are tribals and villagers. Their faces are solemn and concerned. They are thin as the bamboos that grow so abundantly in this jungle. A boy stands on a battlement, scanning the terrain below with binoculars. I go over to Shakuntala to embrace her. She's trembling at my touch, the worry, near to panic at the coming loss, deep in her eyes.

–He'll be safe?

–I have been reassured about this more than once. But I've taken some precautions of my own. He was supposed to meet the press at a hotel in town but I have asked them to come out to the jungle to witness his surrender when I call. I've not told the committee, or the cop, that the horde will descend the moment I call my spy.

–Which cop? Chay asks.

–Sambit Bose. You know him?

–An ambitious man. Is he armed?

–No. I have the document for you to read. I hand it over but he doesn't open the binder immediately. In the negotiations, you will need to make some concessions.

–Which ones do you advise?

–Shakuntala has wrung the major ones from the President, the mining halted, your surrender. You must cling to forest rights for the tribals and the schools. For the moment, concede the roads, medical care, power. They can come later. With schools, you will have more educated children and adults to take up the cause.

He reaches out without turning and finds Shakuntala's hand waiting to hold his. The grip is tight, almost painful. And I won't see her again. I didn't want to give her up not now, not ever, but she convinced me to. We'll talk all day on our phones until the moment he dies. I thought of what you'd said, we don't have enough of an army to nibble around the state chapatti, and we can fight for years with little gains. But because of Shakuntala's success in the elections, we finally have some leverage, a new set of idealistic followers. We have believers out there among the young. At least I can talk to them, carry her message about the rights of people, fighting corruption, saving our jungles. Who knows? We may even reach the heart of the chapatti together and bring in the change from the inside. And who knows what the future might bring? I could even stand as a candidate at the next election.

He opens the binder. He reads the brief document carefully, trying to discover hidden meanings behind every word. Finally, he passes it to Shakuntala who goes through the same exercise.

He stands up. Let's not waste time. I can take one man with me?
–Not armed, it will give them an excuse.

He looks around at his followers, all anxious to accompany him. He takes his time, searching until he stops at one of the men who had escorted me. Vishnu.

Vishnu removes the scarf masking his face, a gesture of freedom in that swift movement. A youth in his early twenties, uneven teeth bared in a smile, the beginnings of a sparse moustache on his upper lip, a shy beard longing to be bolder. He hands his weapon to his companion, relieved of the weight of that power.

–What if….something….happens to you? asks one of his young female followers.

–If it does, then you will all become me. He summons a man from his band who comes to stand beside him. He is masked, around the same age but stockier, stronger than Chay. This is our co-commander, he says to me, but doesn't mention his name. Chay raises his voice and addresses his followers. You will follow what we've all learnt. You will recruit others too, as we must continue our fight, even if I am no longer with you. I am dispensable, you're not. If all goes well and the negotiations are successful I will return and then we will surrender our weapons and return to leading peaceful lives. If not… He laughs grimly. You will have to work the chapatti strategy, spread out to surround it and work inwards until it collapses.

He moves to embrace each of his companions. He holds them tightly, they have spent years together and they are not just combatants but friends, deepened by their love for each other. And then the others, men and children, women with folded hands. Even the young men cry in his embrace, the women weep, holding tightly to his feet, embarrassing him, not wanting to release their leader into this new unknown. But, it's a decision they have all agreed to.

He turns to me. Call the press; we'll be there in an hour. He kneels to search his worn blue backpack, and brings out half a dozen cell phones. They're cheap, not the expensive ones I see advertised in the newspapers and magazines.

–Do they work here?

He laughs, and it's such a pleasant sound in the melancholy stillness. The government very kindly erected many towers so it could track our calls, and the police use them too to talk to their wives and children. He checks one phone. We use different SIM cards for each call we make. Here, this one is unused. But make the call quick, disconnect and shut it off.

I call Vikram. Bring the press to meet us one kilometre east of the road in an hour. Disconnect. Switch off.

They all want to accompany Chay to the meeting place along with their guns, but he stops them. Stay here. I promise I will return and contact you all. Once we reach an agreement, we can return to our homes and villages and lead normal lives once again.

Chay doesn't look back as we begin to walk out of the jungle, but Shakuntala does, waving with one hand. The other clings to Chay's, as if they are strolling along a quiet lane for lovers. Vishnu, sharp as a sniffer hound, walks ahead of us. I bring up the rear, carrying the binder, still feeling the distrust in the pit of my stomach. What would I have told my emperor if he asked me, Chanakya, what do you advise? I would tell him, negotiate, make the enemy your friend if he's willing to surrender, and he will serve you well. Do not waste further resources on this war. But the man I am advising, the President, whom I distrust, harbours hate, and it blinds him to compromise, he only wishes to use his power as a bludgeon. He will make even more enemies. Ahead of me, Chay and Shakuntala whisper to each other.

We're nearing the edge of the jungle, the boundary line of

safety. We stop. Vishnu moves ahead to look for Vikram and the press.

He steps out into the open. A single shot, and he falls. Chay pushes Shakuntala away from his side, moving for cover towards a tree with a wide trunk. He takes two steps, and more guns open up. He stumbles, loses his balance, and slides to the ground.

Samir Bose and three heavily armed cops, emerge from where they have been hiding. He looks down at Chay, and then at Shakuntala, before looking at me. Shakuntala remains where she's fallen, looking at Chay, not moving towards him, knowing he's dead. She has no tears, just a steady stare at the man she loved. Not a sound, not a whimper.

Bose uses his cell phone. When it connects, he says: Yes, he's dead, sir. It was an encounter. No witnesses. Your wife is safe. Yes, sir. We will bring her and take care of him. He disconnects.

-How did you know where I was?

He plucks the binder from my hand. With a sharp fingernail, he digs into the spine and removes a small, silvery object. He drops it and, like a cigarette, mashes it into the ground. He signals to his men. One moves to Shakuntala to pick her up. We're ten metres apart. She remains on the ground, still watching Chay. The other cop turns and points his gun at me. In my previous life, I made the choice to end my life by abstaining from all food and liquid, now I am to leave once again, but against my wishes. I hope I don't ever return.

From inside the jungle, guns open fire. The three cops are hit, riddled by bullets and fall like rag dolls. Bose drops the phone, turns, and runs. The bullets follow him, snapping at his heels, then hit him in the back. He somersaults and falls. The two young women, guerrillas whose names I still do not know, along with three others, creep out from cover. They ignore the dead policemen and only look down at Chay. They are used to death, used to betrayal. One of the girls collects the weapons of the dead cops. The men hand their AKs to the girls, then bend and lift Chay, the third one the boy, Vishnu. They carry them carefully, as if they're only asleep, into the jungle. Shakuntala rises, and, without looking at me, follows them. They're gone, vanished, the silence claims the jungle again.

I ignore Bose, the dead cops, instead pick up the small transmitter. Spies are not always human. I should not have returned to this new age that I don't understand any more. When I return to my delegation, a hundred cops cordon off the press, bunched together.

Vikram is among them, a hopeless shrug. They have heard the gunfire and shout questions at me.

–What happened? Where is Chay? Was anyone killed?

I get into the vehicle and close the door. You must understand that power has no pity. Nor has the State. It is self preservation, self perpetuating, whether as a monarchy or a democracy, always, always, watching its subjects to control and curtail their actions and thoughts. Look at what I hold in my palm, a silver souvenir. It's the new spy in our lives, tirelessly watching, listening, seeing, encircling us in its tightening hold.

■

–Where is mother? Avanti demands when I see her a few days later. Caged in her office, she prowls around her desk, paces to the window and back.

–She returned to the jungle. I didn't stop her.

–I want her to come home, she must. She promised.

–He broke his promise. She is home now, where she wants to be.

–How can she live in the jungle with those…people. She spits the last word.

–They are family.

–He's reneged, she says bitterly. I will not be the vice president. He's going to appoint his old crony, the Home Minister, as his deputy at the next party meeting. What should I do?

–Appeal to your followers, confront him at the meeting. You have more votes than he does and you can prove your popularity. He will only take the party down. The public are tired of him.

–I'll do that. She smiles smugly…but he is distracted, you know. I've just received news that they have found the wreckage of the helicopter. They have recovered the body of the dead pilot but there's no sign of Siggy, her son, or her mother.

–So I was told. Perhaps they are still alive.

–Well my father's going crazy. He still has hundreds combing those foothills and mountains. But I feel it in my bones they will never be found. Until the day Siggy decides to challenge me with that bastard child.

My cell phone sings. I will smash it soon. I listen and disconnect. It's Shakuntala. She's returning home, and wants to meet me.

EIGHTEEN

I AM WARY of women who honour their word. Honour doesn't exist in their emotional vocabulary, unlike foolish men who impale themselves and others on that high principle. Shakuntala is waiting precisely where she said she would, by the Gandhi statue, tucked away in a bagh; her face is partially covered by her dupatta, and nobody gives her a second glance. I thought she'd be dressed in white to signify mourning. Instead, she's wearing a cheerful blue salwar kameez decorated with roses and green stems. She carries a handbag and radiates a calm grace in her patient posture. She is alone; I don't see the girls or any men hovering protectively nearby. I didn't expect her to obey her husband's commands, the agreement between them invalidated by Chay's death. No, Chay's murder. The police claimed he ambushed them and in the fire-fight, Chay, four cops, including an IG, were killed. As I approach she rises from the bench, dusk is gradually enveloping the city, and embraces me.

–I thought you'd be angry with me, I say as we sit down.

–Why? You weren't responsible. We cremated Mayur and scattered his ashes in the jungle, she says matter-of-factly. There was a huge crowd for the funeral; they'll now all join the movement. From her tone, she could well be discussing the weather. Not a note of mourning in her voice.

–Who'll lead them?

–They are all leaders.

–I didn't expect to see you here.

She smiles. A good wife is always submissive to her husband's demands, and I intend to follow that custom. See, I even brought a peace offering. From her handbag, she pulls out a cardboard box covered with gold foil and the lettering 'Lalchand Mithai'. My mouth waters, my favourite sweet-maker in the city. A good wife also feeds her husband sweets to show her affection on his special day. I want you to take this.

She passes the box over.

–Help yourself to the sweets and give me what's left when I am in the palace. I'll be searched, you won't. Has our beloved President changed his drinks ritual in any way?

-No, it's the same. It takes place around eight at night.

-I'll be there at eight-thirty.

-You know what you're doing?

-Is there another way?

-No.

She smiles. She stands up. Now, I'm going to the temple.

I remain seated, holding the box, watching her walk purposefully down the path, then she's out of the park, lost in the crowd. When she's gone, I go to my scooter, put the box in the cavity under the seat. When I get to the palace side gate, security lifts the barrier and waves me through. I park and take the box with me to my room. When I've locked the door, I open it. The jalebis are on top, temptingly golden, neatly arranged on grease-proof paper, and I don't need to remove them to see what is beneath the layer. I'm tempted to take one, but realize they could be poisoned. I put the box away, and lie down on my bed, remembering the time when Chandragupta and I stepped over the body of the king to enter the throne room.

At eight-fifteen, I slip into the reception hall through a side door, carrying the box. The President sits on his golden chair in the gloom, head sunk to his chest. The Chivas and the glass are placed on the table by his side. The chair on the other side is no longer within touching distance.

-Shakuntala will be here soon, as you had ordered her to. I've told security to bring her in.

He doesn't appear to have heard me, his thoughts are in the distant mountains. He has aged, the lines are deeper, his eyes too bright, the whites the colour of rose petals, and his hands, resting on his lap, look skeletal. His face is covered with the frost of neglect. He has lost weight too, shrinking into the kurta, now a loose shroud. He grieves for his true love.

Shakuntala is punctual. A commando opens the far door to allow her in, empty-handed, and for a long moment she is framed in the light of the corridor, her shadow stretching out towards me, before the door closes. She waits in the gloom. I move to meet her and give her the box. She hefts it and smiles.

She looks around and says, I have always thought this room reminds me of a mausoleum.

She walks calmly beside me towards the President. We stop a few feet away, waiting for him to lift his head and look at her. She stares at him. It's the same stare that she held at Chay's body.

-As we agreed, I am here, Shakuntala announces when he finally deigns to look at her.

He snaps: As we've agreed, you will now stay at home.

She laughs. Not beside you in this palace, now that you've lost your lover?

He waves her away. Go home. And don't leave it without my permission. You will not meet any other men. Your lover, Mayur, is dead. He was such a weakling anyway, the same cowardly boy you met in college. I ordered his execution, so you can see what will happen to any other man who wants to be your lover. I've agreed for the mining to resume, immediately.

-Do you ever keep your word? she asks mildly in admonishment.

He ignores her retort, and says: If I need you for any functions, you will come to them and stand beside me, until I order you to leave. Do you understand? He bares his teeth in what passes for a grin. You have your many degrees but you are a stupid woman to live in the jungle with a terrorist and bring such shame on me. Now that your lover is dead, we're even.

-No, we're not. He's not dead.

-Are you insane? The police killed him.

-It's not the same as dying, he'll live on. You can't kill men like Chay. They're an idea whose time has come.

-Go, I don't want to see you until I send for you.

-You won't have to. She holds out the box. See, I've brought you a present.

She opens the box, the jalebis spill to the floor, followed by the empty box. She holds the gun with both hands. Expertly, she flicks off the safety and points it at the President. I remember Chay taught her to shoot.

-Put away that toy, he says petulantly.

-It's an Ashani .32 calibre 7.56 millimetre semi-automatic not a toy.

He glares at her, believing he can still intimidate his wife, will her to put the gun down.

-How did you get it past security? Chanakya, call security. I'll have her shot, and she can be with her Chay forever.

His eyes slide towards me. I don't move. My arms are folded and I smile in triumph. He looks down at the fallen jalebis and the box. Then squints back at me, as if staring into the sun, unravelling a puzzle, skimming over the past, knowing now I have constantly worked against him. That it is I who has conjured up this moment, even to the gun carried by a vengeful wife.

-You won't understand.

He will not remember raping my mother all those years ago, she was just another woman he abused. For us it was shame and exile, and I led Avanti to power, as I did Chandragupta, to exact my revenge. Always keep your secrets secret. Shakuntala and Avanti need not know that I have guided them here for my own selfish reasons.

Her hands are steady as she squeezes the trigger. The bullet hits the President in the heart, and he tumbles back in his chair. She watches as he slips to the floor and lies there, curled up like a snail.

A commando runs into the hall at the sound of the gunshot, followed by others. Shakuntala lowers the gun to the floor and raises her hands. I do the same.

-I shot the President, she says quietly.

■

Love, I tell you, and I speak from experience, is fragile as rotting silks and will disintegrate when infidelities, jealousy, betrayals, impotence infect it. The heart is not to be trusted as it is brainless and mistakes lust for love while the loins mistake love for lust. Love is a watery foundation on which to build one's life. Love is violent too, be warned of its treachery. Men and women murder for love, the clash of bodies, hearts and souls only leave the ashes of defeat when one is vanquished and abandoned on the battlefield of the bed. Believe me, love has sent more men and women to the gallows of tears, despair, grief and suicide than a thousand tyrants enemies to an executioner. No, love will prove to be unfulfilling and transitory but power (and I shiver at the word) on the other hand is to be pursued. It is an aphrodisiac, it is unending hot sex of 1001 positions, it is magical, it is miraculous. Your followers will worship you like an idol that can confer riches and miracles, more than any god, on those fortunate to worship you, and you will feel their outpouring of love in gratitude. Your subjects cannot take it from you, unless you give it away through foolishness, and you can keep hold of that lightning rod until you are buried in a grand tomb, accompanied by great pomp and ceremony and outpourings of grief.

Acknowledgements

I thank Anupama Chandrasekar for her astute comments, also William, Monika, David and Simar for their wise editorial suggestions.